THUNDERHEADS

'You are now the white man's whore, Subaye, the slut of the man who murdered my brother. Temba loved you but he lost you to the white man whom I have sworn to kill. But we will leave you alive so that he can see what we have done to you. Tell him not to search for us because he will not find us, we will find him when we are ready to. The white men will not take this land as they have from our brothers by the great water, we will strike in the night and kill them all. It may take many thousands of summers, but we will do it. Our sons and their sons will succeed eventually.'

Colin Sharp is the author of:

BIRTHRIGHT
BORDERLINE

THUNDERHEADS

Colin Sharp

A STAR BOOK
published by
the Paperback Division of
W. H. Allen & Co. PLC

A Star Book
Published in 1985
by the Paperback Division of
W. H. Allen & Co. PLC
44 Hill Street, London, W1X 8LB

First published in Great Britain by
W. H. Allen & Co. PLC, 1984

Copyright © Colin Sharp, 1984

Printed and bound in Great Britain by
Anchor Brendon Ltd, Tiptree, Essex

ISBN 0 352 31513 X

*This book is dedicated to my children Amanda,
Robin and Karla*

Acknowledgements

My thanks to A1 J. Venter, whose book *Coloured -
A portrait of two million South Africans* (Human &
Rousseau, Cape Town) I once again referred to.

Special thanks to my secretary Angela du Preez who
typed and edited the manuscript and to many friends
who assisted with the research.

Colin Sharp
Johannesburg
January 1984

PROLOGUE

Undoubtedly recent progress was encouraging. His star was in the ascendant. It had started about two years ago it seemed, although he hadn't done anything in particular to make it happen. At long last, the magazine was going, taking off in fact; becoming appreciated. Above all else, it was making money.

The recovery had been gradual though and these days he often thought back to the bad times, those years between 1975 and 1978 when the oil crisis had really bitten hard and wrought havoc in sophisticated societies like his. Luxury items and 'good living' accoutrements had been cut to the bone and magazine advertising had suffered badly. His own journal was up-market and targeted at the marginal group that aspired to good living, wine, food and interior design of the very best. It had obviously suffered more than most.

Smaller had struggled. His specialised little journal had got thinner and its colour spreads much leaner. The circle had been a vicious one because it meant that both readers and advertisers got less for their money. They'd seen the writing on the wall and had lost faith in him and so the situation had gone from bad to worse.

Basically he was a small operator, a one-man band, and his journal reflected his own tastes and aspirations. But with no cash reserves to draw on he had just had to go on cutting back; trying to exist. Unfortunately this became the negative image that the magazine had highlighted, although its purpose was actually to reflect a far more exotic way of life. After all, the name of the journal was *Lifestyle* and if this was Smaller's lifestyle he had better do something about improving it. So his critics had said.

Slowly the line on the graph had changed and the trough had gradually become a gentle valley; the peaks had been later in coming. In the past eighteen months though, he had doubled his advertising revenue and circulation was climbing steadily. This pleasing increase in turnover had meant that he had to find a way of losing profits and his auditor had actually advised him to buy an expensive car on the company. 'Either you drive a fancy car, Martin, or the Receiver gets the cash,' he had said smilingly.

Smaller had not believed him but young Leon Goldberg was a rising star in small-company finance and if he couldn't lose the loot nobody could. Not wanting to rush, Smaller had waited another six months, watching the advance space bookings and pondering whether the apparent boom was a temporary one. The thought of owning an exotic sports car was very exciting and he had always wanted one since he first became interested in motor sport at the age of fifteen. But he wanted to make absolutely sure that if he went ahead and bought the car, he would be able to afford and enjoy it.

In fact, the only unhappy factor about the first six months of this year had been that Isobelle had left him. They'd met eight years back and had lived together before drifting naturally into marriage. She had stuck with him through all the bad times and her salary as a dental nurse had helped to support them more often than not. Recently, just when they had been able to realise a better existence, she'd met that bloody French bastard and left Smaller. Divorced him and pissed off to live in St Paul de Vence above the Riviera.

The divorce had been swift but basically amicable and Smaller had sold the house they had lived in for six years and spent a lot of money on in renovation. The price realised had been a good one and he'd given Isobelle half the money and let her pick which furnishings she wanted and then he'd put some money down on a smart little townhouse and begun all over again as a bachelor.

Isobelle had taken their five-year-old daughter Rebecca and left suddenly one Friday night in June on a UTA flight to Nice. She'd cried and held his hands tight and said she was sorry to have hurt him. Smaller had kissed her once and hugged his little daughter and then walked away. That evening he had got horribly drunk and slept for most of the weekend.

That was four months ago and now it was early summer in South Africa and the Bignonia creepers on his terrace were in full bloom. Still, everything was great and the magazine continued to thrive, in fact it almost ran itself. His social life was not too bad either. He had three women on a regular basis and occasionally made a new score without too much trouble, it all seemed so easy and the car would undoubtedly help further in that direction. Everybody loved him and wanted him for dinner parties and it seemed as if he'd been rediscovered with the second coming of *Lifestyle*.

It was all wonderful and he really enjoyed it for a few short weeks. But then, more often alone now in his own bed, he would wonder where he was going. What did he have to look forward to now that he could no longer see little Rebecca growing up, what was he working for except more issues of *Lifestyle* and probably more money? Occasionally he would sit alone and drink half a bottle of whisky and smoke a little pot; it was then that odd ideas began to foment in his mind. The next day they seemed like bad dreams but they re-occurred and he knew that they were real; not dreams. His life carried on and his successes increased but so did his restlessness.

CHAPTER 1

Martin Smaller loved his car. It was a white Ferrari 308 GTSi and he had owned it for just seven months, having paid R62,000 for it, around £36,000 in England which was where he had come from in 1969. It had taken Smaller fourteen years to reach the income bracket in which he could afford the Ferrari and he'd taken a great deal of pleasure in going into the showroom and buying it with a cash cheque. Even as he had done so, he'd realised that the price was ludicrously high, especially as the car was fifteen months old at the time. But things had been good these last few years and he felt he owed it to himself. Furthermore, he could afford the bloody thing.

Smaller was slightly drunk and very tired, it being well after two o'clock in the morning. He'd been awake since 6.30 a.m. the previous day and had played forty minutes of hard squash before making it to the office for an 8.30 planning meeting. That evening there had been the cocktail party in Pretoria and a drive of sixty kilometres through the inter-city rush-hour traffic. The girl had been there waiting, as he had known she would be, and they had left at around 8.00, had a quick steak and a bottle of wine and then gone back to her flat. They'd been in bed within five minutes and gone at it like lunatics for nearly five hours solid.

Jesus, he breathed to himself, she really did take the cake, old Lucy. Smaller categorised his women into three basic groups; moaners, screamers and panters. But Lucy

8

was all three rolled into one and seemed to go right off her trolley at the end. He smiled to himself in the dark cockpit of the car. You could never have Lucy in a hotel room because residents in the rooms on either side would complain to the management. Or try and get in to join in the action.

The Ferrari sped along the Ben Schoeman highway from Pretoria to Johannesburg at a speed of 160 kilometres per hour which was 60 kph over the legal limit. At this time of the night though, there was virtually no traffic except the odd long-distance truck which he passed as if they were standing still. The rev counter read 4,200 rpm in fifth gear and Smaller reckoned that he had at least another 2,500 revs in hand which would take the car up to 240 kph with ease. He'd never been faster than 220 in it though and that had been on this very road just a few weeks after he'd taken delivery. Even now, his right foot itched to press the pedal to the floor.

But Christ no. He was too tired and the radio seemed to be lulling him into semi-consciousness. He turned it down and was glad that the small canvas 'Targa' top was off. Cool night air rushing over the car created minimum draft yet began to revive him a little.

It was a fine summer night and as he cleared a long uphill stretch, Smaller thankfully saw the lights of Johannesburg ahead. The city was still twenty kilometres away but getting closer by the second with the Ferrari's speed increasing as it burbled effortlessly down the slight incline. Smaller backed off a little and it was then that he saw the parked vehicle about five hundred metres ahead. It was stopped in the emergency lane on the nearside and the hazard flashers were on. Someone was waving a torch around.

Immediately, Smaller felt wide awake and a little uneasy. He slowed the Ferrari to around seventy as he approached the other car. It was a red Mercedes 280SE and the figure waving the torch was obviously female. Momentarily in the headlights he saw a pale face, blond hair and a long coat of some sort as he passed. He pulled the Ferrari into the emergency lane and stopped about fifty metres past the Mercedes. Switching off the ignition he sat looking back in the mirror.

The woman began to walk towards him, the torch bobbing with a dim yellow light. Then she seemed to hesitate and stopped, still shining the puny beam in his direction. Smaller continued to sit, staring into the mirror, wondering what the hell was going on. Something was wrong with this whole thing; he had one of his strong hunches and they were never wrong. He decided to leave, feeling sudden irrational fear, and his hand went out to turn on the ignition key and then he sensed rather than heard something above him. A heavy weight seemed to crash into his head, knocking him forward across the steering wheel and he couldn't believe it was happening. Then the pain came in a great unorchestrated roar and he was falling down a long black tunnel and the sound was receding. And then there was nothing.

He awoke to the pain and wondered where he was, feeling the cold rough surface of the road under him. Then he remembered and raised his head agonisingly from the tarmac. He sat up feeling nauseous. The Mercedes was gone and, unbelievingly, he saw that his jacket too was missing and with it his watch and shoes. He felt the cold on his body and then, incredibly, he realised that the Ferrari was still there. He supposed that they had not taken it because it was too easily recognisable. He staggered to his feet and stumbled to the car.

His briefcase containing his wallet and credit cards had gone, and the radio/tape recorder had been crudely prised from the centre console. Wires hung everywhere and the ignition key was missing but he felt behind the front over-rider on the right side and found the spare held there with Prestik and insulation tape.

He climbed into the car and switched on the ignition and the engine fired immediately, but there were no headlights.

He supposed that they had kicked them in before they left and then frantically, he felt behind the passenger seat, groping in the battery recess under the carpet. The gun was still there.

Head throbbing and trembling slightly with shock he eased the car out into the nearside lane and changed up through the gears. The side-lights just managed to pick up the cat's eye reflectors on the edge of the emergency lane but there was no real need of them because the moon was full and bright in the clear air and he could see quite easily. He looked in the mirror and saw the dim red glow from the tail-lights, all OK there.

The bastards must have been disturbed, he thought. Another car or perhaps a truck but nobody would have stopped, never would at this time of the night, even for an accident. In South Africa it was just too bloody dangerous these days and he'd been a bloody idiot to fall for the trap. But what the hell, he was still alive and there'd only been about forty rands in the wallet.

The cheque book and credit cards could be cancelled, of course, and he would claim the radio on his insurance, together with the other damage. He looked at the digital clock which still glowed redly on the right hand side of the dashboard, 02.47. Jesus, he had only been out for a few minutes, perhaps he could catch up with them, they wouldn't be expecting him because of the stolen keys

They would stay on the motorway, circling right around Johannesburg heading for Soweto, the sprawling Black township in the south west. There they would lose the Mercedes before morning and by midday it would be well hidden. Within a week the car which was almost certainly stolen would be re-sprayed or dismantled into parts and sold to the crooked scrap dealers in the southern suburbs.

Only five kilometres ahead were the yellow sodium lights of the city. Smaller increased his speed to 150 kph, he could see clearly enough if he held the car on the yellow line between the fast lane and the outside emergency lane. In just two minutes he was under the sodium lights which seemed like daylight after the gloom of the unlit highway and he increased speed to 180. There was nobody else on the road.

He caught up with them on the M2 south. The Mercedes was travelling sedately at the prescribed 100 kph and as he came up behind them without headlights he realised that they had not seen him. They were both males alright and as black as the ace of spades, he looked again and there was the blond wig on the shelf below the rear window. Shit, but they must be confident these two, he thought.

The bastards. What a fantastically simple trick that was. All they needed was a stolen car, a bit of white make-up, a long coat and a blond wig. The trap was that easy to spring and, of course, the damsel-in-distress ruse was the most likely to work as it had with him. A bit risky perhaps, should the cops come along, but it was almost ninety per cent certain that they wouldn't be about at that time of the morning. Currently, there was a diabolical shortage of recruits in the country, so much so that the Minister of Police had been talking about a youth reservist force. Just like the Hitler Youth, Smaller thought.

He went back in his mind over the attack. The other bugger must have been lurking over the bank back there on the verge, waiting for him to get out of the car and walk back towards the Mercedes. They must have worked out the distances quite well but they were fast these sods and the other one must have crept up and belted him through the sun roof. Smaller smiled to himself. Now it was his turn to feel confident. He felt for the .357 Magnum Astra revolver with his right hand and pulled up on the outside of the Mercedes. An odd excitement filled him and he somehow felt that he was acting out a part. He placed the gun on the passenger seat and pressed the button on the tunnel between the seats so that the driver's window wound down.

The black who was driving must have got a horrible shock

but he recovered quickly and put his foot down. Smaller had expected this and the Ferrari responded instantly to his gentle pressure on the accelerator and he lifted the pistol with his left hand gesturing to the driver of the Mercedes to pull over. Because the Ferrari was left-hand drive, he was only about a metre from the big sedan and he could see the naked fear in the black's face. His eyes rolled back and the whites were clearly visible, then, with a grimace, he wrenched the big car at the Ferrari.

Again it was as if every move was pre-ordained. Smaller was in fourth gear and a dab on the throttle pushed him forward, clear of the swerving Mercedes. He eased off again and widened the gap between himself and the larger car, but again the Mercedes came swerving across the three lanes of highway at him. This time he braked sharply instead of accelerating and came in fast behind the stolen vehicle.

Jesus Christ, thought Smaller, the bastards were trying to kill him. Rage built in him and the adrenalin coursed through his bloodstream causing him to perspire profusely. He nosed in behind the big sedan and pointed the pistol out of the window at the right rear tyre. His heart was drumming hard but he felt the same strange controlled excitement and his hand did not shake. Carefully he took up the pressure and squeezed the trigger, the Astra roared and bucked in his hand causing him to brake instinctively. They were travelling at over 100 kph and the Mercedes reacted instantly. With the off-side rear tyre punctured and already shredding, the car swerved to the left and then more acutely to the right as the driver over-corrected.

Smaller watched, fascinated, as the big red car slewed back violently to the left again and then, in slow motion, began to topple over sideways. It all seemed to be happening with great deliberation and in the glare of the sodium lights he could clearly see the dark underbelly of the car, its transmission shaft still spinning. Then it seemed to gather momentum and went over with wheels in the air, tumbling and rolling like a demented beast intent on self-destruction.

Even with the wind noise from his open window, Smaller could clearly hear the screeching and grinding and the howl of the racing engine in the stricken vehicle.

What happened next was a nightmare which was to affect Smaller more than he realised. The Mercedes came to rest against the central Armco barrier and Smaller passed it slowly, very aware of the sudden hush. He pulled the Ferrari into the nearside emergency lane again and switched on the hazard warning lights. Before leaving the car, he glanced out of habit in the rear-view mirror and it was then that he saw the flash of fire which engulfed the Mercedes.

Leaving the pistol on the passenger seat, he raced across to the wreck but already the heat was frightening. He could see one lifeless body pinned between the crumpled hood of the car and the metal barrier but the other man was still inside and moving around, clearly lit by the oily flames. Smaller got to within three metres and he could hear the black screaming above the roaring of the petrol fire. Horrified, he watched the man's struggle become weaker and then his head and torso began to glow and his hair flashed suddenly with an incandescent light. Smaller turned away and walked a few paces before violently vomiting up his supper of fillet steak and the bottle of Cabernet Sauvignon.

The bizarre act continued. A small panel van pulled in behind the Ferrari and a middle-aged bespectacled white man ran across the highway towards Smaller. Instead of showing concern however, he stood a few metres away and, incredibly, began to shout and rant. 'You murderer, you evil man!' he yelled, his voice high yet powerful and obviously well-used to oratory. 'I saw you firing on that car, you killed those poor people.' He paused then continued in a voice now pious and refined, 'Oh great Lord above, have mercy. Have mercy on this sinner's soul.'

Smaller became aware of the voice and, eventually, of what the man was saying. He looked up and wiped his vomit-streaked mouth with the back of his hand, noting the van pulled in behind the Ferrari and the white dog-collar at the man's throat. 'Southern Johannesburg branch of the Black Sash,' said the legend on the side of the van. The rage returned. 'Fuck off you stupid sod, you don't know what you're talking about,' he said bitingly.

The whole thing began to seem funny to Smaller and he started to laugh inanely. The cleric stepped back a few paces, his face registering shock and horror. Then Smaller heard the sirens and within minutes the highway was full of vehicles with blue flashing lights and men in uniform. Smaller felt a hand go around his shoulder and a strong grip on his upper right arm, then he was led away. He could smell a strangely familiar odour. It was similar to the one that had filled the house when Isobelle had once forgotten a grilling pork fillet and charred it badly. He pulled away from the ambulance man and retched drily once more when he realised what had caused it here and now on this midnight highway.

They took him to John Vorster Square and gave him a blanket to put around his shoulders. Someone brought him a mug of hot sweet tea and he sat quietly in a pale green room with a dark green linoleum floor, drinking his tea and waiting. He supposed one of the policemen must have driven the Ferrari to the police station and then he remembered the Astra on the passenger seat. A small doubt floated towards the surface of his tired mind like detritus in a fishtank.

After almost half an hour a thick-set blond man in plain clothes came into the room and sat down at a battered old oak desk with pigeon holes in the top. He pulled a packet of Camels from his trouser pocket and lit one without offering the cigarettes to Smaller. The policeman carried a brown card folder which he placed on the desk in front of him, making a show of straightening it up with the front edge. Precisely in the centre of the folder he placed a yellow pencil.

'My name is Detective Sergeant Karstens, Mr Smaller,'

he said, the voice soft and clipped, unmistakably Afrikaans. 'Would you please mind telling me what happened there on the highway.' Smaller smiled tiredly and looked up into the policeman's pale blue eyes. There was absolutely no humour in them.

'It all started on the Pretoria highway, Sergeant,' said Smaller and Karstens sat without speaking whilst he outlined the happenings at the roadside. Finally Smaller finished and Karstens paused before coming out with a statement which made Smaller sit up in his blanket.

'Mr Smaller, there is no evidence to support your story at this stage but we will check the engine number of that Mercedes and find out if it was stolen. You see, the number plates were plastic so they've gone in the fire. The car is completely burned inside.' He sat up in his chair and looked hard at Smaller. 'In the meantime, I must warn you that anything you say may be taken down and used in evidence against you in a court of law.' Smaller failed to speak, so amazed was he at this apparent misdirection of justice. Karstens continued, 'You see, the Reverend Morris Smythey has made a statement which indicated that you deliberately fired on that vehicle and we have found a pistol in your car with one round fired.'

Smaller snapped out of his dreamworld and felt his temper rising as he looked at this plodding policemen who was interrogating him. 'Of course I fired at the car, man. Wouldn't you if they were trying to kill you after already assaulting you, damaging your car and robbing you of your valuables? If you take the trouble to check on the Ben Schoeman highway, about twenty-five kilometres from Johannesburg, you'll find bits of my car's headlights that they kicked in.' He thought furiously and went on. 'They pinched my car keys too. Maybe you'll find them on one of the bodies. And my briefcase. It had metal corners so you should find the frame and locks in the wreck or the whole thing somewhere on the road between the M2 south and where I stopped first.' Karstens grunted and made a short comment to the effect that he would investigate the matter.

At almost four in the morning they allowed Smaller to call Frank Liebenberg, his attorney. Bail was set at R1,000 and Frank promised to be there with the cash in an hour. He eventually arrived at 5.30 and it was getting light when Smaller and he drove away from John Vorster Square. Liebenberg chattered on encouragingly. 'Just get some rest Martin and leave everything to me. They're bound to come up with the evidence you described. Don't worry about it, I'll call you later.'

Smaller let himself in and wearily climbed the stairs to his bedroom. He pulled off his clothes and collapsed on the bed. The telephone woke him at 10.30. It was a black reporter from the *Sowetan* asking if he could come around with a photographer at eleven. He said he wanted a statement on the 'highway holocaust' as he had fancifully titled the story of the cremation of the two blacks in the Mercedes. Smaller refused to speak to him and slammed the receiver down angrily.

It was Saturday and he wondered how they had got his number, which was unlisted. Perhaps from the printers who were the only ones who had an emergency number for him, apart from his personal assistant, Natalie. She would never give it to anyone. He tried to go back to sleep but then the phone rang again, this time it was the *Sunday Times* with a similar request and he briefly went over the happenings of the early morning to the girl on the other end of the line. 'Thanks, Mr Smaller,' she said. 'We have a recent pic of you to use.' Smaller hung up and took the receiver off the hook. He dozed until 12.30.

After one, Frank Liebenberg called to say that the police had found the Ferrari keys on one of the charred bodies and added that the four brass corners of the leather briefcase had been found in the wreck. 'Naturally, they're dropping the case against you, Martin, and they'll send the car back

17

this afternoon and drop off the keys if you're not in. Of course, you'll have to wait until Monday for the bail money and very likely more than a few weeks for the gun because they need that for evidence at the inquest. Incidentally, you hit the tyre alright, they found a big dent in the offside rear wheel and tiny traces of lead oxide from the bullet. God, it must have been hot to oxidise the lead scrapings, eh.'

Smaller put down the receiver thankfully and went downstairs to the kitchen. He took a beer from the fridge and leaned there against the dishwasher drinking from the can, savouring the ice-cold golden liquid and feeling much better. He glanced up at the electric clock over the sink and saw that it was almost 2.15. Jesus, it was good to be alive, he thought and then abruptly he recalled the two Africans who had died so horribly in the Mercedes. He felt suddenly like having a drink, in fact a good session. Bob and Johan would probably be at the pub and he would walk down there in ten minutes and get a steak roll in the bar. That would do for food.

He had picked up the blonde girl during the afternoon. She was a computer operator with a Johannesburg finance company and her fiancé was in the army, on the border, in South West Africa. Her name was Carleen and she had become more attached to him as the afternoon progressed so that eventually she had asked him what he was doing that evening. Smaller said that he had no plans and then the girl took over, saying that she and her friend had planned to visit a new French restaurant. The friend was a short redhead called Jenny and she had latched onto Johan who didn't seem to be resisting. They all left the pub at eight in Johan's old Jaguar.

Later, he and the girl had been dropped back at the pub and they had collected her car and gone over to the townhouse. The police had delivered the Ferrari, locked it and put the keys through the letter box together with a short note saying that they regretted the inconvenience.

Smaller recalled Detective Sergeant Karstens' attitude of that morning and marvelled at the about-face. The girl was most impressed with the car, the townhouse and Smaller. She virtually seduced him on the corduroy couch in his sitting room and he'd had no trouble getting her up to bed. By that time she'd been pretty smashed and he was by no means sober from the wine at dinner and a couple of Kahlúas downstairs. Their coupling had been ineffectual but she had proved to be a panter of sorts.

He had not particularly enjoyed her and had fallen asleep immediately to awake sweating and writhing at four in the morning. His mind was filled with an image of the African trapped and screaming inside the blazing Mercedes. But the girl had not awoken, even with his frenetic movements in the bed. She lay as he had left her, on her back with her legs apart and her mouth open, her make-up smudged and smeared. She looks like a bedraggled clown, thought Smaller, his heart still thumping. He grinned to himself, despite his pounding headache, happy to be awake from the nightmare. She wasn't a genuine blonde either.

Feeling thirsty and overhung, he went downstairs to the kitchen and drank half a pint of orange juice and a large glass of water. For him, vitamin C always seemed to help. After a while he went back upstairs and ~t into bed without disturbing the girl. They slept untroubled until after nine that morning.

After she had awoken, the girl had gone to the bathroom immediately and Smaller heard the rushing of the shower. Then she had come out all clean and bright and smelling of his Givenchy cologne. Her hair was wet and combed straight and her face shone without make-up. He saw now that her body was lithe and firm and recognised that she was actually quite young. Peering at her through half-closed lids, he found that he couldn't recall their love-making of the night, but now she looked wonderful and girlish and he wanted her. Smiling, she slipped under the duvet beside him.

As usual when he had a hangover, Smaller felt incredibly

randy. He began to explore the girl whose breathing quickened with his persistent hands and then he took her hand and placed it on him and heard her gasp at his size. Then he was moving his face down her breasts and stomach and she was wide open like some tender little flower and he buried his face in her sweetness. When she began to moan and clasp him to her he moved his body up hers until he reached her. She felt very tight but gently he moved into her and soon she was clenching herself under him and beginning to breathe raggedly, getting into her rhythm.

Smaller felt that she had not had many men and he was excited by her inexperience. He managed to hold back and rode her, moving in deep but gentle strokes and she clung to him gasping and moaning unintelligibly and he recognised that already she had climaxed twice.

Eventually he lost himself in the firm young body and began to thrust harder so that he could feel the full length of her with himself pushing against the top. In a sort of controlled rush, he came in great boiling surges and at the end she opened her eyes wide and threw back her head, bowing her back and thrusting her hips up into him. She gave one last long shudder and then made little mewing noises and was still.

Smaller pulled himself off her and lay on his back. Almost immediately he fell into a deep dreamless sleep, exhausted and still drained from the intake of alcohol. The girl lay quietly beside him and then she propped herself up onto one elbow and studied him at her leisure.

She thought that this man was the sort women either like or dislike on sight. He was tall and undoubtedly attractive but there was a restless detachment about him that she could not really describe. For his six foot he was not heavily built. He wore his dark blond curly hair quite short. Her eyes ran down his body, noticing that the same hair matted his chest and ran in an indistinct line down the centre of his stomach until it reached the thatch in his groin. He had a deep chest and narrow waist and his legs were slim and muscular, his body a light golden colour all over except for a narrow band of white around his hips. She thought that he looked very good without clothes on.

Carleen Davis decided that she liked Smaller, especially on this peaceful Sunday morning. Last night she hadn't liked him so much but she had needed him because it had been almost three months since she'd been with Peter. Really, when she came to think of the matter, she wasn't all that sure that Pete was what she wanted for the rest of her life. He was a nice boy, but really only that, a boy who wanted to get married, for God's sake. Now that he was coming out of his two years in the army he would want to get married straight away and she wasn't sure that she needed that yet. She had seen what men could be like, what it could be like with a man like this one for instance. Now she was even more in doubt but quite sure of one thing. It was unlikely that there would be a future with Smaller, he was not the kind for that and she had recognised it immediately.

Smaller awoke when the Sunday papers landed with a solid thwack in the tiny courtyard below his bedroom window. Whilst still on his bicycle, the African delivery boy simply lobbed them over the wall. Rain or shine it didn't matter. You just had to get to them faster if it was raining. He sat up in bed and smiled at the girl. 'Coffee OK?' he said.

She smiled back. 'Point me towards the kitchen and I'll do it.'

He put a hand out and touched her still damp hair and then ran his fingers down her cheek. 'Thanks Carleen, it was a wonderful Saturday night and Sunday morning. Particularly Sunday morning.'

'Thank you Martin.' She smiled up at him. 'I feel much better about things now. It's all less complicated than I thought. Perhaps I'll get to tell you about it sometime,' she added hopefully.

He leaped from the bed and grabbed his robe from the

back of the bathroom door. 'I'll hold you to that,' he said laughingly and went downstairs for the papers.

Carrying them inside, he glanced at the front page of the *Sunday Times* and saw a photograph of himself. 'Magazine Publisher in Motorway Shootout; see p.11' read the caption. Smaller turned to the page and found another photograph of himself, one of the charred Mercedes and a third of two blanket-shrouded stunted shapes at the side of the road.

Martin Smaller, man-about-town publisher of *Lifestyle* magazine, was involved in a real-life drama early yesterday morning when he stopped his exotic sports car on the Ben Schoeman highway in answer to a cry for help from another motorist. What Smaller at first thought to be a blonde woman turned out to be a decoy in the form of an African male. The man's accomplice mugged Smaller, stole his watch, shoes, jacket, briefcase and the radio/tape from his car and the two made off in a stolen Mercedes saloon.

Smaller recovered consciousness and although his head-lights had been put out of action by the thieves, made a high-speed pursuit in the bright moonlight in his Ferrari sports car. Once on the M1 he was able to increase speed under the overhead lamps and finally caught up with the fugitives on the M2 south. 'I must have been doing around 190 kph,' said Smaller to our reporter, Lindy Fyles. 'When I caught up with them I saw the blond wig on the back shelf of the Mercedes and realised how they had duped me. Then they tried to drive me off the road but luckily they hadn't found the gun I keep hidden in my car and I managed to shoot out their rear offside tyre. The Mercedes overturned at over 100 kph and unfortunately burst into flame immediately. I couldn't do anything to get the men out.' Mr Smaller told our reporter that he had not had any formal pistol training but had acted instinctively. 'I just shoot for fun,' he said.

Police ruled out foul play after certain objects stolen

from Mr Smaller were found in the burned-out wreck. These were badly charred but were identifiable.'

Sitting at the top of the stairs Smaller grimaced at the story which, although basically correct, was written in somewhat sensationalistic style. 'Oh fuck,' he said aloud. This would only make his reputation more notorious. His so-called friends would start phoning him as soon as they read it. As he completed this thought the telephone bell shrilled loudly, shattering the tranquillity of the little house. Smaller's pleasant mood was broken and he pulled himself to his feet, dropping the newspaper on the carpet. It would probably go on all week and then there would be the battle with the insurance company for the damage to the Ferrari. What a lovely Monday morning it's going to be, he thought dejectedly.

CHAPTER 2

Subaye Matsamela had watched the sunrise on that same fine Sunday morning. Now she sat quietly, having already worked for two and a half hours doing the chores that her family demanded of her, especially her father. These included walking two kilometres to the river to get water, making the fire and then boiling up the breakfast mealie porridge. After that she had to sweep out the central living area of the house and the small yard in the front. Of course, her mother and younger sister sometimes helped a bit but it always seemed that she was left to do the major tasks. If she didn't do them they just didn't get done and it was always she who was on the receiving end of her father's wrath in the final analysis.

Her father still slept and she could hear his loud, rasping snores coming from the bedroom that they all shared. Subaye had noted the number of empty cardboard beer cartons outside in the yard that morning and had long since cleared them away. She had also brushed the hard-baked mud surface clean of corn husks, bones and all the other trash that seemed to collect there each day. There was even more on weekends.

Every Saturday her father got drunk. He sat in the yard from around two o'clock when he finished at the farm and drank mealie beer with his old cronies. Subaye shook her head in disgust as she sat on the low wall of baked mud bricks that demarcated the Matsamela house from the other eleven in the tiny village. The sun was warm and she felt a little drowsy from the generous portion of porridge and a large mug of hot sweet tea that had constituted her breakfast. Her eyes fluttered closed, and she began to dream . . .

She is a princess in the old times. Everybody lives in crude round mud huts with grass roofs. But the village, her home, is large and rich, being successful in trade and having a large regiment of guards – proud strong warriors who are loyal to her family. One of these is her father's favourite, the captain of the guard. His name is Temba and he is also her secret lover. But now, at sunset, a stranger comes galloping over the crest of hills that overlook the village. The guard sounds the alarm and Temba and an Impi of warriors go out to meet the small cavalcade. In the absence of her father on a hunting trip, the stranger is brought to her. He is one of the white men whom they have heard of but never seen. He is a big man, wide of shoulder but narrow in the waist so that he looks like the big Eland antelopes of the veld, powerful yet graceful. His hair is another matter for fascination because it is yellow like corn and long, hanging down to his shoulders and worn around his mouth in a thick moustache. He rides a mighty black horse and there are six black men following him as bearers, carrying many boxes and bulky packages. She has the stranger brought to her living hut and orders that he be given food and drink. She studies him while he eats and tries to talk to him, but he replies in such a strange tongue that it makes her laugh. She feels his eyes on her body, recognises the maleness in him and her female instincts respond involuntarily. His eyes bewitch her. Grey blue and large, they seem to smile at her with great warmth, crinkling at the corners and holding her spellbound. It is night time. She lies awake on her bed of skins, tossing and turning, feeling the accustomed warmth between her thighs and wanting the stranger with a lust that she has never felt previously. The village is silent. She whispers to her personal maid, Noni, to go and call Temba to her. He comes and she falls on him like an animal, drawing the seed from his body so quickly that it leaves him spent and gasping for breath. But now she no longer requires his presence – he irritates her. She pushes him from the bed where he lies trying to caress her still. It is daytime again. She rides out with the white man, she on her small, wiry Basuto pony and he on his great black stallion. She shows him her father's kingdom and they ride towards the boundary with the far off mountains in the north. They communicate with each other by nods and shakes of the head, using simple sign language. An instinctive understanding develops between them. At the river they stop to rest in the shade. Subaye takes off her short reed skirt. Shrieking with delight she jumps naked into the rock pool at the base of the waterfall where she has played and bathed since childhood. He strips off his shirt and breeches and leaps after her. She glimpses the whiteness of his body where it is normally covered from the sun. They splash together like children and lie on the river bank under the huge willows where the grass is long and lush and cool to the skin. He looks at her with wonder and she knows he finds her beautiful. In her dream her tribe is an offshoot of the Northern Sotho people whose ancestors inhabited the mountain kingdom of Basutoland farther to the south. Led there generations ago by King Moshoeshoe, to escape domination by marauding bands of Zulu and Matabele, some of the Sotho had declined the inhospitable mountains in favour of the lush grasslands they had always known. Splitting up, they had fled in all directions and many had been slaughtered or bred to extinction by their captors. Her family have always been strong fighters, beating off small bands. Trekking to the north, they found sanctuary in the foothills of what the invading white man are later to call the Magaliesberg Mountains. There they have remained for four generations, growing stronger and more handsome with the introduction of selected Zulu and Ndebele blood from the surrounding territories. Now nineteen years old, she is

26

indeed a princess, tall and slim yet muscular and strong; a girl who can throw an assegai almost as far as her elder brother, himself a respected warrior. Her skin is a light coffee colour and her hair black and tightly curled to her scalp but her features are almost Arabic with none of the coarseness of the bush African. She has high cheekbones, fine lips and a flawlessly sculpted nose. Her face seems to have been carved rather than moulded, so perfect are its lines. Her long legs and firm buttocks are only equalled by a slender neck, quite wide shoulders and high, beautifully formed breasts with nipples far paler than those of most Africans. Her features speak of mixed blood in her lineage, perhaps from the Arab traders who were said to have built a mighty trading partner in the lost city of Zimbabwe centuries before, though many thought it was really a ghastly slave centre. She knows the white man desires her. His large maleness is erect and strangely red and angry-looking. The sight excites her tremendously and she opens her lips and lies back on the grass. He rolls over on top of her and straddles her hips and she clasps him to her so that they seem to melt together. The afternoon sun, filtering through the old willows, dapples their bodies with light and shade. The white man loves her in a way no man has before. Temba becomes jealous, and word gets to her father that the man he has befriended, whose name is Gregory, is lying with his daughter. The King is angered but blames Subaye rather than Gregory who is a fair man and a valued trading partner. All enjoy the salt, cloth and tobacco he offers, and the knives and axes he trades for skins and ivory are of good steel and keep their sharpness. Subaye is confined to her hut and pines for Gregory. She lies on her bed without eating. Her maid, fearful for her life, goes to the white man and informs him of her mistress's state of health. Gregory comes for Subaye and the maid helps them pack a few things, even though she will be severely punished for this act of betrayal against the King's word. Gregory has bribed the guards, offering tobacco and whisky that makes them sleep as the dead. They creep from the village like thieves, leading their horses with muffled hooves. Subaye knows that she is leaving her father and brothers forever. On the crest of the hill she looks back at her home in the valley, at the single flickering light from the sleeping guards' fire. Her heart is heavy but Gregory takes her hand and she turns her back on her village and rides with him towards the north and the mountains. Out of her kingdom forever. The King sends out a pursuit party, but the white man has his long rifle and shoots three of the warriors, including Temba. Subaye feels little as she sees her former lover fall, her heart now totally bound to this man. She will go wherever he leads her. She will even kill for him, so strong are her feelings. They reach the mountains and search for a base camp to operate from. None of Gregory's porters have made the escape from the village with them but two of them arrive having followed their master's tracks. Gregory is alarmed, thinking they have been followed, but after posting each as a guard he relaxes and the four of them construct a permanent camp. Subaye is happy and satisfied to be with this white man who teaches her many things, amongst them the rudiments of his language. Soon they have the foundations of a house laid, high on the edge of a hill in a safe position from attack. She sits one morning resting from her labours of carrying logs and forming clay bricks to be baked in the sun. The valley is sunlit and beautiful and she seems to be drowsy . . .

Suddenly she awoke when her father landed a sharp blow to her head. A sense of extreme desolation mingled with her shock at coming awake because the dream was lost and her white lover with it. Tears sprang to her eyes and her father, thinking he had hit her too hard stepped back and gruffly instructed her to clean out the bedroom.

CHAPTER 3

Smaller served the ball forehand from the right hand court. He hit it well and it bounced off the front wall about two thirds of the way up, between the two red lines. It was a classical service that came looping back into the left hand rear corner of the court, an almost impossible shot for his partner's backhand. The ball seemed to scrape down the wall and drop right into the corner of the court, dying immediately so that Norman Ashley never even connected his racquet with it.

Smaller grinned wolfishly and crossed to the left-hand court preparing to serve again. The score was now 6 – 7 in this game and they were drawn at two games each. This one would be the clincher and the winner would have the set at 3 – 2. Once again he served well but the ball failed to slither down the wall as it had on his last shot. Even so, it was not easy to return and Ashley caught it awkwardly with a wild defensive cross-court volley so that it came off the front wall bouncing high onto Smaller's backhand.

In that split-second before he hit the ball, Smaller decided that his opponent would expect a backhand drive down the left-hand wall and imagined him pounding across the back of the court to retrieve it. Smaller therefore chose to backhand the ball across court, in a high lob, sending it back to where his serve had landed.

Ashley stopped in mid-flight and desperately spun on his left foot to get back into the right hand corner and take the lob off the back wall on his forehand. Grunting with exertion, he made the shot poorly, hitting a slow cross-court drive and Smaller moved in for the kill. Stepping two easy metres from the central T with elbow bent and wrist cocked in the prescribed manner, he drove the ball down the left-hand wall in a perfect-length backhand shot. As he made it he thought that this was the sort of shot that made the game worth playing; when you had the time to concentrate and do it right.

Ashley was caught flat-footed, not knowing where the ball would go, and his instinctive dive to the left was just that. He failed to get to the ball and Smaller smiled again, wiping the sweat from his face with his wrist band. They were now seven all, just two more points and the match would be his.

Norman Ashley was sales director of *Lifestyle* and he handled both circulation and advertising with deceptively casual expertise. It was Ashley's efforts that had been largely responsible for boosting revenues in the past eighteen months and with his personal control of their three sales girls, he had become almost indispensable to Smaller. For this reason Smaller had made him a director of the company with a twenty per cent share of annual profits. He had never regretted this decision.

Ashley and Smaller played squash together three times a week and were very well matched. Although Smaller was the lighter and more agile of the two, Ashley had been playing since school and had excellent ball control on his good days. Both men loved the game because of the intensive exercise it provided for never longer than fifty minutes. After a shower and sometimes a sauna if there was time Smaller found that he felt new-born and would sleep like a baby.

The last few days had not been great. In fact the whole bloody week had been one of the most frustrating he had experienced in recent months. As expected, the insurance brokers had hassled over the Ferrari claim because he had insisted on a new dashboard to replace the one damaged when the blacks had prised the radio out. This had to be imported from Italy at a cost of around R2,000 and his insurers had more than baulked, preferring obviously to repair the old one. Then there'd been calls from a few more reporters including one from the sensationalist *Man's World* magazine which was a sort of mercenary's handbook filled with trashy features and even trashier girls.

Carleen Davis had called him again and he had aquiesced and agreed to take her to dinner that evening. Why not? he thought. Her fiancé was due out of the army next week and would no doubt be at her immediately like a rampant bull. Very likely that would be the end of the story as far as he was concerned. Thank God it was Friday, anyway, thought Smaller as he served for the match.

It was Saturday afternoon and Temba Mthombeni was pleasantly drunk. He had been in Magaliesberg which was the nearest town to his village in the low hills near Swartplaas. With him, in a similar condition, was Benjamin Ndadza, his best friend since childhood and a young man of great wit and innate fun.

The two had been drinking with a group of 'town' youths on the patch of open grassland behind the bottle store at the Magaliesberg Hotel. Eventually after the store had closed they had become rowdy, singing their own tribal songs and swigging mealie beer happily in the sun. A white man from the bottle store had called out to them to *voetsak* and Benjie had made a rude sign at him. That had been that and the police had come suddenly, running straight at them with truncheons drawn. Two of the town boys had been caught to be charged with consuming liquor in a public place and disturbing the peace; they would be discharged next morning on payment of fines of thirty or forty rand. As this was often a month's salary to an urban African, Temba and Benjie had been lucky indeed, managing to escape and running off drunkenly through the veld before circling back to the road on the outskirts of town.

Benjie had received a glancing blow from one of the white policemen who had swiped at him with a riot baton and a shout of 'Come here you fokking kaffir!' A sizeable bump had soon grown above his left ear to prove the closeness of his escape. Later the two young Africans had found the whole matter highly amusing and had rolled in the dust, hands clasped to their stomachs, laughing uncontrollably. It was amazing how soon the severe fright of almost being arrested had passed.

Still giggling and laughing, they walked along the road from Boons to the Swartplaas turn-off. There was little traffic but so far they'd been lucky to get two lifts so that it had taken them just over four hours to travel fifty kilometres along the road. This straight stretch of tarmac ran parallel with the railway line at this point and they could see the long lines of goods coaches moving steadily south from the north western border of the Transvaal where it met up with Botswana and Zimbabwe.

Temba wondered what this rolling stock carried because his friends in town had told him that South Africa had virtually cut all rail links with Zimbabwe because of the ANC freedom fighters who were allowed to live there by the country's saviour, Robert Mugabe. Perhaps it was stuff from the mines in Botswana, he thought absently. He knew that they mined something there but had no idea what it might be.

Temba had been told that the freedom fighters were a real force and that some had even made it down as far as the Magaliesberg area. He had never actually met one of course, but there was a general belief amongst his friends in town that groups of these men existed in the northern and north western Transvaal. This rumour was an exciting one and Temba had often considered what it would be like to become such a guerilla soldier, like his cousins in Zimbabwe who had freed that country from the white man.

Unlike Benjie, who was squat and muscular, Temba displayed a height and grace typical of his Matabele heritage. He was slender, yet powerful and he had dark, almost plum coloured skin and fine, albeit negroid, features with perfect white teeth. He walked with the effortless lope of the bush African and had to keep slowing down to allow his shorter companion to keep up. They had walked over fifteen kilometres but the terrain was flat and the road ran parallel with the mealie fields stretching out on either side. On the western side were the distant hills looking lilac blue in the late afternoon sunlight but towards the east there was nothing except the endless fields of high maize stalks. Even Benjie's constant babble had subsided and both men were feeling the effects of the morning's drinking and would dearly have liked a drink of water. Then, miraculously, Temba heard the unmistakable rattling clatter of Moosa's bus which should have been well past the Swartplaas turn-off by now because it was long after six o'clock.

Both men stood in the road and the ancient Leyland single-decker shuddered to a halt, ticking over raggedly, panting like an old horse after a long walk. The bus was only half full and Temba and Benjie climbed the steps and began negotiations with Moosa's son, Ishrath, who was driving.

'It's fifty cents each' said the young Indian importantly. He was resplendent in immaculate white shirt and a heavy gold chain hung around his neck. The only thing that shattered the image was his pair of dusty black trousers. Temba smiled and shook his head slightly.

'No my *Baas*,' he said respectfully, although he did not consider Indians to be his superiors in any way. The young brown man looked impatient. 'Oh *Baas,* please, we have only forty cents together and it is not far to our stop.'

Ishrath nodded. 'Alright, make it thirty cents each or get off,' he said brusquely, shoving the bus into gear with a sickening crunch. The jolt almost knocked Benjie from his precarious perch at the top of the steps where he crouched behind Temba. He fished in his pocket and held a gleaming fifty cent coin in the air over his friend's head.

'That's all we have, *Baas,*' he whined deferentially.

'OK, get in,' said Ishrath crossly and the two of them scrambled inside as the old diesel chugged off into the lengthening shadows.

Temba and Benjie moved to the back and found two men that they vaguely knew from the township near Boons. 'Ho, where are you going friends?' said Benjie in his most engaging manner.

The eldest of the two, a saturnine man dressed in a red T-shirt and blue jeans spat out of the open window but his companion answered in a reasonable tone. 'There is a big beer drink at *Baas* van der Linde's farm this night. The chief's daughter is getting married and they are roasting a goat.' He paused for effect. 'That man is rich and has many wives and *Baas* van der Linde loves him like a brother because he saved the *Baas's* son's life many years ago. The *Baas* is paying for the party,' he finished breathlessly with an exclamation, as if he found this fact very difficult to believe.

Temba mused on the information. Perhaps they would go to van der Linde's, he, Benjie and Subaye. There would be food and drink for all by the sounds of it and it was only about two hours' walk through the veld from his village. About seven miles west, or so he reckoned. Undoubtedly it would be worth it. 'We may come,' he said confidently and the grim-looking man stared at him in annoyance so that he felt uncomfortable. 'I know that girl's sister, she used to go to the Sunday School with me when I was a boy. They will not mind if I come,' Temba added convincingly.

The elder man smiled revealing missing teeth. 'You are still a boy,' he said and spat again out of the window.

Subaye had enjoyed the unexpected evening out with Temba, up to a point that was. He had managed to borrow the old Ford from his friend, Tom, at a price of course, and he and Benjie had come bouncing down the track to her village, the battered car clanging and roaring so that she heard it half a mile away. Then it had been another half an hour of rough farm roads before they got to *Baas* van der Linde's place and the glow in the sky had been visible from a mile or more.

There had been at least two hundred people there to celebrate the wedding of Maureen Sulupha who had married Jo Langa, old Moosa's so-called transport manager. Langa was a fleshy forty-year-old Ndebele who had no qualms about trying to seduce every woman he met. He had tried with Subaye, more than once, but she had slapped his face hard on the last occasion and that had stopped him. The man was a born womaniser and he had a high opinion of himself, although Subaye reckoned she would not sleep with him for any money. Not even twenty rand.

She liked Temba though. He was very handsome and not at all stupid like some of the farm boys. He looked very good in his white slacks and black cotton shirt and had sat smoking in the car whilst she washed herself quickly and changed into her red dress and sandals. When they left, her father had not even noticed because he was well on the way with his friends in the yard and her mother didn't seem to care what she did in the evenings. After all, she was nineteen years old.

The beer drink was well in progress when they had arrived and old man Sulupha was getting himself nicely drunk and clapping everybody on the back. What was left of the goat was being fought over on the ground by several dogs but there was still plenty of beer and the cardboard cartons littered the grass everywhere. A huge bonfire burned in the corner of the field where the earth had been turned over and where no dry mealie stalks could catch alight. It was very well organised, Subaye thought.

She had greeted the bridal couple and Jo Langa had leered at her as usual and even had the gall to try to push himself against her thighs. Poor Maureen had noticed but

35

she had hidden her feelings well and Subaye had felt like slapping her pig husband again. She reckoned correctly that Langa had only married Maureen for her father's money. Everyone knew that 'Chief' Sulupha had plenty. He was the foreman on van der Linde's farm and earned almost as much as a white man.

Temba had quickly managed to get himself drunk and Benjie had driven home, allowing her and Temba to sit in the back. She had let Temba feel her and had put her hand on him and rubbed him a bit so that he began to breathe heavily. Then suddenly, her hand had become all sticky and his mess had shot out all over her red dress.

Subaye had pushed him away viciously, cursing him for being an idiot. 'You call yourself a man,' she had said. 'You are worse than a little boy who plays with himself.' She smiled within herself as she considered the words which were not really true because Temba had loved her before and had performed more than adequately. Although he was unaware of the fact, he had been her only lover and she had thought of lying with him for a short while when they got back to her home. It was a warm night and the grass was soft and high enough to hide them. She was already aroused to a point where he could have satisfied her very quickly. Now it was all wasted; and all over her dress at that.

Subaye mused on these thoughts as she swept out the musty smelling bedroom and tidied the soiled bed on which her parents slept. Temba had practically passed out after his sorry performance and Benjie had driven away quickly, obviously embarrassed by what had happened. He couldn't have failed to understand after what she'd said.

With sudden clarity, she recalled the dream and the handsome white man who had changed her life. She grimaced. Reality was very different she thought, as she lifted her father's reeking socks from underneath the bed. Tomorrow it was Monday and she would start her working week again on the farm. Day in and day out it was the same and often she was so tired after making the meal and helping to clear up afterwards that she just fell exhausted onto her old mattress. She looked in the cracked mirror over her mother's ancient, stained dressing table. The face that looked back was poised and beautiful, the neck slender and the breasts firm and proud beneath the thin washed-out blue T-shirt. I am beautiful, she thought and perhaps one day things will change. One day I will get away from here.

CHAPTER 4

Smaller rolled off Carleen Davis' firm buttocks and lay on his back, his heart pounding. They had smoked the joint between them and the session they'd just finished had seemed like a real marathon. That was the thing with grass. It made the whole thing last much longer; in the mind it seemed so anyway. Smaller vaguely considered that this may well be an illusion. The practical way to find out would be to make a video movie of the whole procedure and look at it objectively. Alone, when he was completely sober, of course.

The girl had been good. Better than ever in fact. Undoubtedly better than last night when they had both been a bit drunk again. Against his better judgement, he'd finished up spending the whole weekend with her and sure enough she'd started the hints about giving up her fiancé whom she now considered too young for her. Smaller had seen the writing on the wall alright and backed off, then she'd cried and he'd tried to comfort her a bit. To relax her, he'd offered the bloody joint and she'd taken it like a shot and they'd smoked the whole thing between them finishing up screwing like rabbits again.

He lay in the semi-dark, heart still pounding from the dope. Outside it was pouring with rain, one of those summer storms so typical of the Transvaal. The rain lashed at the windows and thunder rolled, after occasional flashes of lightning which lit the darkened bedroom vividly. Beside him,

Carleen lay quietly, sleeping like a baby. Well, that was the last time, thought Smaller. She was sweet, good in bed and nice to look at but he couldn't handle any more attachments. He didn't need any grasping females at this stage of his life.

His thoughts went to his ex-wife and Rebecca. It had been almost five months since they'd left. Twenty bloody weeks, one hundred and forty days or thereabouts since he'd seen them. Before the break-up, Sundays had been quite pleasant. Sometimes a couple of friends would come over for lunch and they'd have a few beers and a barbecue by the pool. He thought back to last summer. Rebecca loved to swim and he'd brought her a polystyrene canoe that had given her a lot of fun. More often than not, their friends had brought their kids along and the pool had been full of squealing children. Very domesticated. Sometimes he'd felt like a bit of peace and quiet but six months ago this very Sunday afternoon he could never have imagined himself lying in his own bed dreaming abstractedly after smoking a joint and screwing the arse off a girl he hadn't even known existed in those days.

Of course, he was now *persona non grata* with those same old friends and he never saw them these days. The married fellows seemed to regard him enviously as a sort of gay bachelor figure, hurtling around in his Ferrari with a different woman every night. He had to confess to himself that there had been weeks like that lately, although it never was intentional. He just seemed to have got caught up in a meaningless social whirl.

As for his old pals' wives, they regarded him with the utmost suspicion. He reckoned that somehow they expected him to drag off their husbands to cavort with his women, lead them astray and shatter the so-called family unit and their precious security. Silly bitches, he mused. He didn't miss their stupid invitations to boring dinner parties. Their endless prattle about kids, domestic servants, how the government was ballsing everything up in the country and how bloody expensive it was getting to live reasonably well in South Africa. How terrible their lives were with their servant and the garden boy, hubbie's Merc or BMW and their Golf or Mazda, the wine cellar full, the fridge loaded with beers and imported pâtés. The government should send the whole lot of them back to England, thought Smaller bleakly. See how they'd like it there with the pound buying only as much as the rand did here. They'd really have something to moan about then, that was for sure.

Isobelle Cordier, previously Smaller, was a deliriously happy woman. She and Henri had been married precisely six weeks to the day and it was the last Saturday in November. The Riviera was experiencing the odd cold morning and evening, especially up here in the mountains away from the coast. Otherwise, 'Vence was the most wonderful place in the world in which to live.

She loved the little ancient artists' town with its narrow streets and quaint old stone buildings. In one of these, a fairy-tale place, she, Isobelle Cordier, lived with her husband, Henri, and daughter, Rebecca. Sometimes she couldn't believe it had all happened but Rebecca would be six in February and already she was installed at the village *crèche* prior to going to junior school in January. She could understand basic French and Henri was marvellous with her and taught her patiently every night. Isobelle's own school French had helped a lot and she had picked it up again quite fast really. Rebecca would be no problem, children learned languages so fast when they played together.

Rebecca sometimes asked after Martin but she never really seemed to miss him because Henri poured so much affection on her. She adored him too and he, never having had children, idolised her as a tiny version of her mother, seeing her as the child he had never had and loving her as such. Now, they were really both a bit old to contemplate another child. He was nearly fifty and she was thirty-seven. Henri had been married before, very briefly to a French woman but he hadn't spoken much about it. Anyway it had been years back in 1959. Oh God, I'm so lucky, Isobelle thought as she looked out towards the sea and faraway Nice on the coast. It was a perfect Provence early winter morning and the sun shone brightly from a sky of palest cornflour blue. The blooms still wafted on the Bougainvillea which covered the ancient stone wall on the southern side of the house and although Isobelle knew they would drop within the month, they would be in bud again by March. There was no real winter on the Riviera.

Below in the first-floor room he used as a study, she could hear the clattering of Henri's typewriter. He was a brilliant writer, sought after by magazines all over France for his superbly satirical and lightly political pieces. Now, he was working on his second novel and already, the first one was earning well so that Henri talked of buying a flat in Paris 'as a little investment'.

Everything was wonderful. France was a beautiful, marvellously stimulating country and everything was so ethnic and village-like up here in the mountains behind the Cote d'Azur, especially now with the summer tourists gone. Only the artists of St Paul de Vence remained, they and the writers and a few old families made up the total population. The painters idled away the winter, working for galleries in Paris and Frankfurt until the summer when 'Vence would again be full of rich Germans and Japanese, Americans and a few English. Some artists had contacts down on the coast at Cannes and Nice where a few rich foreigners came for the winter months. She and Henri had talked about the way their neighbours existed only the other night, in a small restaurant in Biot. Isobelle laughed to herself: already she was thinking like a local.

Above all, Isobelle loved her husband Henri Cordier. He was a wonderful man, typically Gallic and sometimes short-tempered but with a marvellous zest for living. Henri was a Breton who ate and drank without worrying too much about the next day and who loved women. Isobelle had no doubts that he'd enjoyed his fair share in the years he'd

41

been single and she'd found a few old letters in the bureau drawer, some dramatically marked with lipstick kisses. She hadn't been jealous but had mentioned it to Henri and he had smiled ruefully and shrugged in his usual way. The matter had been forgotten and wouldn't be mentioned again by Isobelle.

She had no doubts that he loved her. She knew it by the way he would look at her across the table at home or in a restaurant and by the way he made love to her in this very room. Never had she known such passion and joy. The pleasures he gave her had almost erased the memories of Martin who had been an adequate yet unremarkable lover. For her anyway.

She'd always suspected that Martin had other women from time to time but hadn't really cared because she'd been resigned to life with him and his bloody magazine. There had been no real regrets when she left and she hadn't worried much about his sensitivity because he wasn't a sensitive person at all. Sometimes he'd hurt her with his thing, jamming it into her before she was aroused and ready. She had to admit it was bigger than Henri's but with Henri she was always ready because he was such a gentle lover and so considerate and he always started by kissing her there, something Martin had never enjoyed very much, although he had liked her doing it to him.

Her thoughts of Henri excited her as she sat dreaming by the window, and suddenly she felt hot and wet. She stood up and went down the narrow stairs and opened the door to his study. He looked up and smiled, noting her flushed face, '*Oui, ma cheri,* is anything the matter?' She looked at him, sitting there in his old Levis and the navy blue workshirt she had stitched a button on yesterday. He was unshaven and could have done with a haircut but he was like this room of his, wonderfully male.

She looked around whilst still smiling at him. The room was full of his junk. Stuff that he had collected all over the world on his journalistic forays. There was an old shotgun propped in one corner and various maps on the walls, an assortment of pipes and some little ivory figures he'd brought back from the Far East. Hats and walking canes were hanging from an old bentwood hat stand and a bottle of Martell Cognac stood half full on the desk beside a dirty glass from last night. His pipe smouldered in the ashtray and a faint blue smoke clouded the area around the desk where he sat, poised over the ancient Remington.

Smilingly he got up from his chair and walked over to her with his easy grace. The dark hair was very grey at the temples and the face was tanned and ruddy and lined deeply around the eyes but he was the most attractive man she had ever seen; and he was hers.

He took her in his arms and immediately felt the heat in her. She pulled him against her and buried her face against his neck which was prickly with a day's growth of beard. His moustache tickled her forehead and she smelled the warmth of his skin and the tobacco on his breath and a faint odour of perspiration from the shirt he had worn the night before. It was an amazingly erotic combination of odours.

'I want you, Henri,' she said softly. 'I was thinking of you and I am so happy and I started wanting you. Am I disturbing you darling?'

Henri laughed softly into her hair and she felt him hardening against her thigh. 'Oh, Isobelle, I think you are disturbing me.' He chuckled again and she laughed too, low in her throat, feeling wanton. Then she pulled him through the doorway towards the stairs and their bedroom.

Fifteen minutes later, Isobelle lay back exhausted against the big pillows in their bed. Henri had already showered and gone back downstairs to carry on with his book. 'I'll write you into my story,' he had said laughingly. It had been better than ever before – she had just kept on coming over and over again. It had happened three times for sure, and she had never experienced such ecstasy.

She'd just held him tightly to her, writhing beneath him and it had seemed as if only his thing, his wonderful maleness, had kept her pinned there under him, thrust far into her, holding her in place. Henri was amazing, she thought dreamily. He could carry on for ages without coming to climax and he would whisper in her ear and kiss her neck and move with a glorious fluid rhythm so that she would get herself excited all over again.

Her stomach muscles ached slightly and she was damp and hot between the legs where she had wadded several tissues. She rolled off the bed and made for the shower in the little bathroom. 'God, I'm so happy,' she said aloud. 'Thank you Lord for allowing me to meet him back there in Johannesburg. He's changed my life and it's all so wonderful.' Isobelle hummed as she showered quickly. She had lunch to make for both of them. They'd have a slice of cold quiche, some fresh bread from the bakery up the road and then some Brie, all washed down with a bottle of Provence rosé. That would keep them going until supper, especially Henri who had an appetite like a horse when he was writing.

This afternoon she would clean the house and dust, do the washing and then fetch Rebecca from the *crèche*. She'd never done those sort of chores for years, having always had the servants in South Africa. But now she actually found housework stimulating; it was a whole new world really.

Tomorrow was Sunday and they had a wonderful day planned down on the coast. Henri's best friend Jean-Paul had his own helicopter and they were flying down to Menton on the Italian border and would lunch at a sea-food restaurant of great fame. Jean-Paul's little boy, Christian, would be there for Rebecca to play with and Isobelle would have his wife Marie who was fast becoming a firm and dear friend. *La belle France,* Isobelle thought happily as she hurried downstairs, linen basket in hand.

Smaller's Monday had been horribly frustrating. As the afternoon lengthened into evening he felt the tension building to an unbearable pitch. It was after five when he began to work through the advertising bookings for the next issue and he knew it would take him at least forty minutes to complete the check. He saw the memo from Ashley and noted the request for a move-up of the double-page colour spread for Bang & Olufsen hi-fi. Cursing, he noticed that if they couldn't reschedule the insertion they'd lose the booking and he'd be over two thousand rands worse off. He broke the pencil he was holding in his frustration.

The November/December issue was well and truly full, he couldn't add any more pages, at least not for bloody B& O's spread. He swore loudly so that the clacking of Natalie's typewriter abruptly ceased in her next-door office. How many times, countless bloody times, had he tried to explain to Ashley and his girls that you just couldn't add pages to an issue at will. The magazine was assembled in forms of sixteen pages which was the most economical way to print the thing. Sometimes they could add an extra eight in an emergency, but already the deadline was past and he was supposed to add an eight-page section just to facilitate B& O. What in God's name was he supposed to do with the other six pages?

He decided abruptly to pack it in for the day. Perhaps he could solve the problem with a fresh look at it tomorrow but now there was squash with Ashley at 6.30. He felt somewhat better at the thought of bashing the little ball around the walls, venting his frustrations out on that piece of round green rubber and having a good sweat. He grabbed his briefcase and stopped at Ashley's open door down the passage. 'I'll see you there Norman, I'm going to stuff you up, like your little Jayney stuffed up that B&O booking for November.'

Ashley obviously sensed his aggravation because he paused before replying carefully, 'OK Martin, we'll talk about that tomorrow, I'll see you on the court in twenty-five minutes.'

The squash had done the trick. Smaller felt relaxed and pleasantly exhausted after the strenuous game in which he had again beaten Ashley. Sure enough, the problems of the day seemed more manageable now and he even grinned to himself as the perspiration dripped off his nose and fell with audible plops onto the pine planking. He was sitting in the sauna, sweating like a pig, the other chap in there with him had just sloshed another ladleful of water onto the stones so that the humidity rose even more. Smaller gasped and listened to his accelerated heart beat. Ashley had forgone the pleasure of the sauna as he usually did. He wasn't keen on the 'sweat bath' as he called it but Smaller enjoyed a sauna once a week because he felt completely cleansed afterwards. He would have one Cognac at home and go out like a light.

Lying back on the top shelf of the sauna on a wringing wet towel he felt the other man's eyes on him and sat up awkwardly. The young man was really little more than a boy, blond and slender with hardly any body hair, even around his groin. Smaller was embarrassed to see that he had a partial erection and he coughed slightly, not knowing what to do but trying to make light of the matter.

'Hot, eh,' he said quite loudly and then laughed at his own stupidity.

'Yes it is,' said the younger man softly. 'I'm David Grant by the way.'

Smaller took the limp wet hand. 'Martin Smaller,' he said quickly pulling his hand back after only the briefest of grips.

Grant plunged on unabashed. 'Do you play here often, Martin? How is your game?'

Despite himself, Smaller found that he was warming to the youth. He couldn't have been much more than seventeen and thank God he'd covered himself with a towel. They chattered on idly for five more minutes and then both made for the plunge pool, Smaller going in first. As he climbed out, Grant looked straight at him, at his crotch and Smaller felt an odd prickling sensation there. Despite his trying not to, he twitched spasmodically. 'Have you ever had a gay experience, Martin?' said David Grant directly, smiling like an innocent child.

At first Smaller had felt like hitting the boy and had not answered, not trusting himself to speak. But then he'd talked again as they dressed and Grant had explained that he was very much into girls but that occasionally he liked it with a man. Against every instinct that he had Smaller found himself responding to the quiet young student and he recalled the time that he and his cousin Simon had touched each other when they'd slept together as teenagers. I wonder? he thought. And that had been it.

He'd made pizzas from the deep freeze and they'd drunk a bottle of white wine and then Grant had come to him without warning and pushed him gently back on the sofa. The boy had gone down on him and at first Smaller had pulled back but, inevitably, he'd grown erect and then David had given him the most amazing blow-job. He hadn't even tried to get Smaller to touch him and had remained fully dressed the whole time. Grant had worked skilfully, making it last, and then Smaller had been unable to hang on any longer and the boy had taken the lot in his mouth. He'd got up, gone for a towel and then left quickly, smiling happily. 'Thank you, Martin. I don't suppose I'll see you again but it was nice to have known you.' Then he'd disappeared on his motorbike and Smaller had just lain there on the couch, not believing that it had really happened.

He'd showered and had a double whisky in a glass of warm milk, hoping that it would put him to sleep and it did. But then he awoke sweating and groaning around four in the morning, dreaming that some strange man was touching him. He felt unclean and bewildered. Oh good Christ, what is happening to me? he mouthed into the damp pillow. Why am I carrying on like this, screwing around all over the place and now letting some little queen play with me? He lay awake until dawn, then got up and shaved early. It was 6.50 when the telephone rang.

CHAPTER 5

Jean-Paul Devereaux's Bell Long Ranger was painted in French racing blue and silver. The gas turbine six/seven seater was an ideal family helicopter for medium-range flips up and down the Riviera and Jean-Paul enjoyed flying it as much as he loved driving his Porsche 928S which was painted in exactly the same colours.

Devereaux was a more than successful industrialist with homes in Paris, Nice and London. His company supplied the French government's aerospace requirements for certain highly specialised micro-computers used in the guidance systems of missiles and had grown rapidly since the mid-sixties. Now it was a multi-million franc operation and even socialist President François Mitterrand was loathe to try to nationalise it, so complex was the operation.

They had made it down to Menton in twenty-five minutes in the Bell and the flight was an absolute joy to Isobelle. Their route took them over Villefranche and the medieval village of Eze, perched high on its tiny promontory above the winding Corniche. Isobelle loved these flights along the coast and it was a wonderful sunny winter's morning with the Mediterranean a sparkling cobalt blue and empty of all but a few hardy fishing craft. They passed over Monaco harbour at three thousand feet and down below were moored dozens of big pleasure yachts at upwards of a million francs apiece. Isobelle could see canvas awnings rigged on some stern decks and brightly dressed people enjoying the midday winter sun.

Lunch on Menton's quaint promenade had been absolutely perfect and they'd enjoyed tiny fresh shrimps, fried in butter and garlic followed by grilled line fish with *salade Niçoise* on the side. The rosé had flowed, then Henri had insisted on cognacs with their coffee. Isobelle had frowned at this and Jean-Paul had noticed and laughed loudly, clapping Henri on the back. 'She is careful your Isobelle, eh, *mon ami*? Did you not tell her of the time we flew in the Congo with a bottle of whisky inside each of us. Those were the days, eh?'

Isobelle smiled. She knew Jean-Paul was an excellent pilot who had handled aircraft much larger than the little helicopter. The man was a born adventurer and he had ferried supplies into Elizabethville in an ageing Dakota. Already wealthy at that stage of his life, he had volunteered to become a mercenary pilot flying for Tshombe, and Henri had been with him, covering the uprisings in the days when he had specialised in wars and strife. Isobelle had heard the stories before and they were hair-raising to say the least. She sat in the sun with Marie drinking black coffee and half listening to the men reliving their exploits in central Africa. The children played happily together on the quay and Rebecca chattered away in a pidgin English and French which little Christian seemed to understand well enough.

Eventually, Jean-Paul decided it was time to leave and he paid the bill, tipping the waiter expansively. They all squeezed into the hired Peugeot and headed for the heliport only five minutes away, Henri telling jokes in French and then translating into English the bits Isobelle didn't understand. As they drove, Isobelle thought back to Sundays in Johannesburg and the basically boring afternoons after lunch when there had been little else to do except swim, sunbathe or take the dog for a walk at Zoo Lake in the winter. What a different world she lived in now. Here she was, flying about the Riviera with her wonderful husband

and his friend who was one of the richest men in France. It really was a little difficult to believe sometimes.

Once in the aircraft, Jean-Paul became a little more serious and went through the pre-flight checklist in his normally efficient fashion. He twisted the ignition key and the turbine whined, then fired and ran smoothly. Isobelle felt a strange sensation in her stomach, like the butterfly feelings she had had as a child whilst sitting in the dentist waiting-room. Then the children giggled and chattered behind her and she shook off the oddly disturbing thoughts, refusing to recognise them as a premonition of disaster.

Soon they were clattering and shuddering, then the engine noise rose in pitch and the little helicopter lifted slightly off the concrete. Henri smiled back happily at Isobelle as he listened to Rebecca's amusing attempts at French but then he turned back sensing something amiss. The Bell seemed to be glued just above the ground, resisting the forces of gravity; he felt that instinctively. The engine sounded strangely off revs and he glanced sideways at Jean-Paul whose eyes were barely visible behind his flying glasses.

Still they remained in a hover, the altimeter registering only 100 feet. Then the square of concrete slowly began to shrink away underneath the skids and Henri felt a slight sinking sensation, realising that they were up, thank God, clawing at the air and turning gradually to the left, towards the ocean.

Jean-Paul felt something was wrong – the motor seemed to lack power – and then he heard the dreadful sound of the rotor failure buzzer and the Bell seemed to judder slightly, lifting its nose higher and pancaking into the air losing forward momentum. Recognizing an impending loss of power, Jean-Paul put the nose down and checked that the throttle was pulled all the way out, trying to gain airspeed and keep the aircraft flying. The indicator crept upwards towards 70 mph but the Bell, falling away to the left, responded sluggishly to the controls and began spinning slowly on its axis. Then, without warning, the motor faltered, coughed and the helicopter dropped sickeningly by the nose. The control column juddered in Jean-Paul's hands.

Henri gasped and Marie screamed, suddenly aware of their imminent danger. The children began to wail and only Isobelle remained silent, mute with terror at what she had somehow known was going to happen. She watched the surface of the sea rushing up to meet them out of the left-hand window.

Watchers on the ground had heard the engine falter and saw the helicopter spin into a dive and fall away into the sea. It struck the surface and crumpled in a cloud of spray about two hundred metres offshore and disappeared immediately. A few fishermen rushed for their little boats which were pulled up on the beach and began to push them frantically into the placid Mediterranean.

Hitting the surface of the sea at 70 mph is almost like striking solid ground. Henri was killed instantly by the cabin roof's collapsing. A twenty-five centimetre length of dural-umin support rod pierced him like a spear, passing right through the left side of his chest and into the seat upright. Jean-Paul slammed forward and the dashboard rose to meet him, crashing into his head and face and concussing him badly. Marie was jolted upwards and f... ·ards in her loose lap harness and she struck her head against the cabin roof, a blow which snapped her slender neck cleanly so that she slumped back in her seat like a rag doll.

Only Isobelle and the two children were held securely in their seats by the restraining harnesses and although they were flung against the backrests in front of them, they did not lose consciousness. They were trapped in the rear of the shattered cabin and dimly Isobelle heard the cries of terror and recognised the loudest voice as her own. Franti-cally, she fumbled with the release catch of her lap strap but the weight of the turbine was already dragging the Bell under and it began to sink swiftly by the nose so that a sudden rush of cold water took her breath away. She inhaled instinctively, gulping almost half a pint of cold sea water directly into her lungs. The nightmare continued, and spluttering and choking she thrashed about in hopeless terror.

Then the sun disappeared to be replaced by a greenish glow and Isobelle found she could no longer breathe, feeling the coldness of the water numbing her body. Red lights exploded in her brain and it got darker as an onrushing blackness enveloped her. Her last desperate thought was of little Rebecca still strapped behind her.

The short fuselage, with its shattered plexiglass cabin, sank nose first and a small pocket of air remained, briefly trapped in the rear portion. Bewildered and terrified, the two small children screamed and sobbed as the pressure ruptured their ear drums and the water rose in the doomed cabin, inching steadily up over their faces. The wreck settled quickly to the smooth floor of the Mediterranean after sinking fifty metres in just over a minute. The air lasted a little less than that and both the children were dead by the time their tomb touched the bottom. The whole horrifying sequence of events had taken less than three minutes from take-off to impact with the sea-bed.

Smaller listened unbelievingly to the young constable. The accent was thick but the message was horrifically clear. 'Mr Smaller, sir. *Ag,* this is constable Smit from Sandton Police, I'm afraid I've got some bad news, sir. There has been an accident, sir, in France it was. Are you there Mr Smaller?'

He knew then. Felt it deep in his bones. They were dead, Isobelle and Rebecca, he didn't need to listen any more and the policeman's voice droned on, barely penetrating his shock. 'It was a private helicopter crash, sir, into the sea apparently in the South of France. Sir, the French consul has more details and would like you to telephone him. The number's in the book, sir. *Ag,* man – I'm sorry to tell you that your ex-wife and daughter were killed, sir. Did you get that, Mr Smaller?'

'Yes', said Smaller woodenly. 'Thank you constable.' He

put down the instrument and sank back onto the bed, the bed he had fornicated in with Carleen Davis and several others. Pictures flashed across his brain and he kept his eyes tightly closed, trying to see Isobelle and Rebecca as they had been. As he had loved them.

With amazing clarity he could see himself in the nursing home when Rebecca was born. He was dressed in a green hospital gown with cream rubber boots and had a paper mask over his mouth. He gripped Isobelle's left hand tightly as she moaned and tried to turn on the delivery table, legs apart, knees raised and head thrown back in agony. The similarly robed gynaecologist peered into the green tent formed by the scrub sheets and her raised legs, and his voice was muffled as he bent forward. 'I can see the head, Isobelle. Come on, push for me nicely. Take a deep breath and push, that's it, that's the way. There's my girl.'

It had been a long delivery and Isobelle was in labour for twenty hours but finally, miraculously, the tiny slippery body emerged, to be lifted up by the legs and pronounced a girl. He recalled the prompt action of the theatre sister who had used a plastic tube to clear mucous from the baby's trachea, and then had come the first tentative cry, followed by a fully fledged wail of determination.

Rebecca had been a perfect child. Feminine and slender from birth, she was dark and delicate like her mother. Affectionate and intelligent and quite single-minded, from an early age she seemed to want to find out exactly what life was all about. Hers had been a childhood filled with sunny days and happiness and with most of the things she wanted. Isobelle had insisted on dressing her well and the little girl had a wardrobe which was the envy of many of her friends, yet she was never precocious. But now she was gone.

Smaller put his head in his hands and wept for his little daughter and the wife he had loved so much; it seemed now so long ago. In his despair he recalled only the good times, the simple pleasures of family life and the unparalleled joys of parenthood. He curled into a ball on the mattress as visions of Rebecca and Isobelle burst through his consciousness. He would have to go to France to the funeral – he couldn't just let them be buried alone like that without anyone there who had loved them. Perhaps that bloody Frog bastard had lived. If so, he would get the swine, would personally make him pay for taking his wife and child away and killing them in a bloody foreign land. Smaller sat up, suddenly white hot with anger and rage. His sorrow was undiluted but he had a figure to channel his hate against; he would phone the consulate now and find out what had happened and whether Cordier had survived.

The French consul had been sympathetic and understanding, somehow imparting into his voice a solemnity which matched the occasion and the terrible and tragic loss Smaller had suffered. They were all the same these Frogs, thought Smaller, becoming increasingly hateful as his despair grew. Drama-mongers of the first order, switching on the agony for the record. It was almost as if the consul were taking a sort of personal responsibility because the accident had happened in France, while at the same time absolving himself with the professional 'It was God's will' attitude which was not far under the surface.

For sure it wasn't this chap's fault but at the moment Smaller detested all Frenchmen and wanted no honeyed words of sympathy. When he learned the facts, that Cordier had died too, together with another couple and their child – 'One of France's leading industrialists' the Consul had said – Smaller felt suddenly empty. He now had only himself to hate for allowing the Frenchman to take Isobelle and his daughter away in the first place.

He'd agreed to their being buried in France and the funeral was to be on Saturday in St Paul de Vence – today was Tuesday. He would fly out on UTA on Friday night but in the meantime he would get drunk, stone-blind drunk and paralytic. And fuck the bloody magazine to hell and gone. First he'd phone Isobelle's aunt in London; her parents were dead long ago, killed in a car crash when she was sixteen.

He didn't go to the office on Tuesday and by 9.15 when Natalie phoned he was already maudlin drunk. 'Sod the fucking magazine,' he said viciously when she asked what time he would be in. Startled and recognising his slurred tones, Natalie asked innocently if anything was the matter. 'Is anything the matter?' Smaller repeated. 'Yes, something is the bloody matter alright. Isobelle and Rebecca are dead, that's what's the matter.' Natalie expressed horrified regret and called Ashley immediately on the intercom. Within five minutes they were both on the way to the townhouse.

Smaller remained insensible for most of Tuesday and continued to drink into the early hours of Wednesday morning. By midnight, Ashley had given up hope of getting him out of it and went home to his wife and children, thanking God for his own good fortune. There but for the grace of God go I, he thought as he walked the short distance from his garage to the front porch. He opened the front door softly and silently climbed the stairs, pausing outside the bedroom which contained his two small children. He went in, kissed them and gently stroked their soft hair, tempted to gather them up and kiss them but making do with caressing their cheeks lightly. The little girl moved in her sleep and rolled over so that her innocent heart-shaped face looked up at his. In the half dark she opened her eyes and saw him bending over her, 'Night, Daddy,' she said reflexively and turned back into her pillow.

Ashley looked down at his sleeping daughter and thought of little Rebecca Smaller. What a ghastly, bloody tragedy it was. This would send Martin over the top, thought Ashley. He had been going gradually off the rails since Isobelle had left him. He was drinking far too much and, Ashley suspected, taking drugs as well. He sighed and tiptoed to his bedroom, silently opening the door so as not to disturb his wife. It was almost one o'clock in the morning.

Surfacing sluggishly to the worst hangover he could ever remember, Smaller was faced once again with the awful reality of the accident. He was drained of emotion, after staying awake for most of the night, but the loss was nonetheless real and remained like a great weight pressing on his chest. It left him without appetite or motivation.

He got up and made some coffee then phoned Natalie to tell her he wouldn't be coming into the office because he felt bloody terrible and hadn't been able to sleep all night. She mouthed platitudes and made sympathetic noises but he cut her short, asking her to book him on Friday evening's UTA flight returning on Monday night. He told her that he might be in briefly on Thursday to collect a few things, and would she get R2,000 worth of French franc travellers cheques organised at the bank – he'd take his passport in and collect them on Friday morning.

Natalie went through to Ashley's office as soon as Smaller broke the connection. 'He's not coming in any more this week, Norman,' she said worriedly, 'and he's going to France for the funeral so he won't be back until Tuesday.'

Ashley groaned and put his hand to his forehead in a characteristically dramatic gesture. 'Oh balls,' he said harshly. 'That's really great. We're already a week over deadline for the January/February issue and the planning meeting was for Monday morning. At the moment the issue's got fuck-all advertising in it and only about twenty per cent of the editorial is complete.' He grimaced at Natalie. 'As if that's not enough, nobody has any idea what Martin has planned for January. As usual, he's got it all in his head and he's left it to the last moment. The poor editor is going up the wall and is none the bloody wiser.'

He spun in his chair and looked at the charts on the wall which showed advance advertising bookings until the financial year end. 'January/February is the worst bloody issue of the year,' he continued moodily. 'We could do with a special décor feature, a big juicy one to sell advertising off.' He scratched his head and looked at Natalie, although

56

he wasn't seeing her. Decisively he slapped one hand on the desk top, 'I'll just have to organise it myself. We'll do kitchens again, it's about eighteen months since we last touched them and we made a fortune from that supplement. We've got stock shots in the art department and Tom can go out and shoot some more in that new kitchen boutique place in Sandown. They're bound to advertise if we give them a courtesy line.'

Happy now that he had made a decision, Ashley smiled at Natalie. 'I'll just have to organise it all myself but at least the girls will have something to sell off and we'll get some bookings, even at this time of year. To hell with Martin. If the shit hits the fan, you'll back me up won't you Natters?'

By seven o'clock on Friday evening Smaller was drunk again. He had been only partially sober all week since Tuesday morning and now he was in the taxi going to the airport. He sat hunched in the back seat sipping from a half bottle of Bell's whisky and replying monosyllabically to the friendly remarks made by the driver. This surly treatment by his passenger failed to rile Piet de Bruyn however. He had carried all types in his fifteen years driving a cab in Johannesburg and he was polite to them all because that way you were always assured of a tip. Especial'y ...ien the passenger felt a bit guilty about being incommunicative. This one was a rude bastard alright.

'International Departures, is it, sir?' he said brightly as the Toyota joined the airport approach road. From the rear, Smaller mumbled an affirmative and de Bruyn smiled to himself in the mirror. The bugger was half-pissed, he could smell it quite positively and he'd noticed him taking a nip now and again from a bottle in the inside pocket of his jacket. He pulled the cab up smoothly and ran around smartly to unlock the trunk.

Smaller got out wearily, 'How much?' he asked thickly.

De Bruyn looked at him carefully. He'd noted the pigskin briefcase and the lightweight luggage and the bugger had a lovely leather jacket on that must have cost all of three hundred rands. 'Make it twenty-five rands, sir,' he said positively.

Smaller gave him three ten rand notes from the top pocket of his jacket, peeling them carelessly from a thick roll. 'Keep the change,' he said, smiling bleakly. As the driver pocketed the bills he added a postscript. 'Oh, by the way,' he said casually. 'You're a fucking rip-off.'

De Bruyn failed to reply as Smaller turned and walked into the Departures Hall, following a black porter with his luggage. Then he shook his head and got into the Toyota, pushing the gear lever forward angrily so that it engaged with a clanging sound. He had only moved a few metres when an attractive middle-aged woman flagged him down, a practice which was not allowed by law in South Africa.

De Bruyn checked quickly to see if any of the olive-uniformed police from the Department of Railways and Harbours were about and stopped the car again smartly. He jumped out and smiled winningly at the woman who smelled like a perfume factory. Walking around behind her he graciously opened the rear door and ushered her inside. 'Where to, madam?' he said closing the door and hovering on the pavement near the luggage.

The lady looked at him questioningly, 'How much to the Carlton Hotel?' she asked, her accent unmistakably American.

Piet opened the trunk and put the two suitcases in together with the Pan Am flight bag. He noticed the First Class label tied to the strap. They're all fucking mugs, he thought as he jumped into the driver's seat. 'It will be about thirty dollars, madam,' he said smiling brightly.

Smaller sat in First Class in the DC10. As he was going for such a short time it was only a little more expensive to travel First and he wanted to try to sleep on the aircraft because he was absolutely bloody exhausted. The steward came around with a bottle of Moet et Chandon and flute glasses on a silver tray. You had to give it to the French thought Smaller, they had a lot of class. But the fact that UTA was a private airline probably had a lot to do with it.

He sat by the window and absently watched all the service vehicles trundling around on the brightly lit apron. Friday night was the busiest international night at Jan Smuts airport and he could see British Airways, Lufthansa, Swissair and KLM all preparing for departure, the huge aircraft surrounded as his was with an entourage of crab-like service vehicles from which snaked cables and thicker liquid-feed lines.

Under normal circumstances, Smaller enjoyed flying and would have looked forward to this flight, a pleasant all-night hop to Europe. But this time he would be going to see Isobelle and Rebecca for the last time and he dreaded actually looking at their faces, as he knew he would have to in identifying the bodies. A wave of great sorrow hit him again and he slumped forward in the seat, resting his head against the backrest in front of him. The steward came immediately, all Gallic concern and professional service. 'Is *monsieur* alright, can I get you anything?'

Smaller looked up and the tears had come again, they were running down his pale cheeks. 'A large Cognac, I think,' he said haltingly.

Strong gusts of wind buffeted the big DC10 as it dropped down through the murk over the Bay of Angels between Nice and Cannes. The pyramid-like towers of the Marina Baie des Anges rose stark white against the grey of the Mediterranean and Smaller remembered a holiday long ago when he and Isobelle had spent a week on the Riviera and they had been building those monstrous structures which looked like huge wedding cakes placed incongruously on the beach below the rolling hills of Provence. Vaguely he imagined them to be waiting for the monster wave which would sweep into the wide bay and break them into rubble like a child's sandcastle before the tide. This thought provoked other memories of holidays at the coast in Durban and Cape Town with little Rebecca running tanned and naked on the golden beaches, splashing with him in the sea, pleading for ice-creams, digging in the sand.

Smaller had come to terms with the loss of his daughter but he would never be able to accept the future loss; the growing of the little girl into a teenager and finally a woman. The night had been ghastly and the cognacs had not helped to dull the pain. He had slept fitfully and dreamed as he always did in an aircraft, violent dreams which he imagined were somehow linked to the precarious nature of his temporary location up there at 35,000 feet. He awoke in the morning when the stewardess pressed the intercom button which sent a dull pinging sound through the cabin. There had been orange juice, hot fragrant towels, then breakfast of coffee and croissant. Now he felt congested and uncomfortable. He always swore he wouldn't eat on airliners but inevitably he did.

The big jet shuddered in the squalls as it made its final approach for Nice, an airport built out into the sea and reached after a long approach over the ocean at seemingly wave-top height. Rain lashed the perspex porthole and Smaller could see little else but a gunmetal grey sea whipped by the wind into white tops that threw occasional spumes of spray into the air.

With a final whine and judder the DC10 thumped down onto the concrete and Smaller held his coffee cup to prevent it spilling with the reverse thrust and quite severe braking. Must have made a bit of a balls-up, he thought idly, noting the white face of the man in the seat across the aisle. I couldn't care if the bloody thing fell apart. Maybe I should tell him that. He smiled at the man who looked back at him as if he were insane.

After customs he went to the Hertz desk and rented a Peugeot 104 for two days. They had been delayed for forty minutes at Kinshasa and it was 8.15 a.m. but already everything was open and he bought a map of Provence from the book stall. The attractive French girl from Hertz spoke excellent English and apologised for the weather as she showed him to the hire car park. Smaller thanked her brusquely stowing his luggage in the hatchback trunk. He started the little car and drove carefully out of the car park turning left onto the access road for the autoroute north.

The road was quiet and little traffic passed him even though he kept well on the right, unused to driving on the continental side of the road. The signs overhead said Aix en Provence and he watched for the one which would point off right to Antibes and St Paul de Vence. After twenty minutes he took the exit and was soon winding up into the hills, the windscreen wipers whipping back and forth, the car steaming up inside from the heat of his body.

He arrived in the picturesque little village at 9.15 and parked the Peugeot in the square. Conveniently enough the police station was right there so he went in and asked the gendarme on duty in halting French to tell him the way to the cemetery. The funeral was scheduled for ten o'clock but Smaller had nothing else to do and he planned to sit in the car and drink some whisky from the bottle in his briefcase. Vaguely he wondered if he were becoming an alcoholic.

The gendarme's attitude changed when he heard Smaller's name. He sat up suddenly in his chair and came out from around his desk. He looked to Smaller strangely like the consul in Johannesburg. He led Smaller through the back of the police station and across a narrow cobbled yard to the rear of the small village hospital. They walked silently down a narrow corridor and approached a large cream-painted door, '*Monsieur,*' said the gendarme gravely, gesturing Smaller forward as he opened the huge sprung latch.

Inside it was cold and damp and the smell was unmistakably unpleasant; almost the direct opposite of fetid, a sort of clinical odour which brought memories of his biology laboratory at school. He recalled small reptilian bodies floating in jars of alcohol and the omnipresent odour of formaldehide, which they had all referred to as pickling

61

juice. He knew that this was the morgue, although he had never entered one before in his life. He realised too that, within seconds, he would see his ex-wife and little daughter again for the last time and that their bodies may be horribly disfigured. Oh God, please let it be quick, he thought.

A white-coated, grey-haired figure approached and Smaller automatically held out his hand. 'This way, *Monsieur*,' said the older man in very acceptable English. They walked slowly to the two tiers of drawers set into the wall. Smaller swallowed and tried to turn away, but the policeman was right at his shoulder and the pathologist had pulled out the lower drawer, right there at his feet. Without warning he was looking down on Isobelle.

Her skin was waxy-white and as the sheet was drawn away he saw that there were absolutely no marks on her body. She seemed to be sleeping as he looked incredulously at her flawless skin and firm breasts, the long slender legs and dark-haired mound that he had known so well. They had brushed out her fine black hair, her lips were slightly parted, her cheeks lightly rouged. He looked away sickened.

Then came Rebecca. She lay doll-like and pale, like her mother in her now eternal sleep, resting on her back just as she had in her little bed in Johannesburg. Her eyes were closed but he could imagine them opening suddenly as they had done sometimes when he had gone into her room to kiss her goodnight. The light brown curls were teased around her delicate little face and again, there was not a mark on her body. It was all he could do to prevent himself from picking her up and clutching her to him as he had so many times and squeezing her until she had cried in her breathless child's voice, 'Oh Daddy, stop, you'll squeeze me to death.'

Instead, he bent and kissed the ice-cold lips of his daughter and brushed the cheek of the woman who had been his wife. There were no tears now, just the rage building up again inside him together with the self-retribution, a terrible loathing of himself as a failed father and husband. If only, he thought in hopeless ice-cold anger.

'Where are the others,' he asked the gendarme who looked questioningly at the doctor.

'Ah, they have gone to Paris three days ago, Mr Smaller. The family came and took them away.' He looked sadly down at the two bodies in the trays beneath them and gently closed the drawers. 'A great tragedy,' he muttered as Smaller turned away in despair.

He had almost two hours to kill before the funeral and the policeman directed him to a small café across the square where he ordered a pot of coffee and a croissant. He opened his briefcase and took out the flat bottle of whisky whilst the old proprietor looked on with interest. He poured a generous measure of the amber-coloured Bell's into the coffee cup and added black coffee with two spoons of sugar. The mixture seemed to warm the chill from his bones but not the numbness from his brain.

Outside it continued to rain and there was little activity in the square. The small town seemed grey and sodden like the skies which emptied the steady deluge upon it. The weather suited Smaller's mood perfectly. It was almost custom-ordered he thought morosely, like an Italian or possibly Greek movie-set; tragedy by the gallon. He'd stay here in a hotel tonight though and be near them for one last night after he'd seen them into the ground forever.

As he sat numbly sipping the fortified coffee, Smaller's tortured brain conjured visions of the two bodies decomposing; becoming worm-infested as the wooden coffins rotted away to allow water and insects in. But he couldn't bear the thought of cremating them, burning them to ashes in a few short seconds. Gulping down the remains of the coffee, he left ten francs on the table and shuffled out into the rain, heading for the little Peugeot and the journey he dreaded so much. The policeman had offered to ride with him to the cemetery and Smaller had agreed, not really caring.

Now he climbed into the steamy interior of the car and sat staring out at the rain and the drab greyness of the old stone buildings. Between his identification and the burial they would dress the bodies and put them into the coffins. His mind fantasised as to how the undertakers would pull the clothes over those cold waxen limbs, what the men must talk of as they worked, whether they would lust over Isobelle's slim figure.

The police had kept the bodies in their own morgue in the adjoining hospital but the undertakers had obviously worked on them to alter the expressions to the present acceptable repose. After the crash, Smaller suspected that they would have been frozen in grimaces of horror; nobody died without fear and some sort of pain, unless they passed away in their sleep.

He pulled the bottle of Bell's out again and took another generous swig. Although the amber liquid burned down into his stomach, the warmth was only momentary and his despair continued to increase as he sat slumped in the car in the waterlogged, silvery light of the square. He smiled slightly in a twisted grimace. Somehow it wouldn't have been right if the weather was bright and sunny – better this gloom and dripping greyness. One thing was for sure, he wouldn't forget fucking St Paul de Vence. Not ever, for all the rest of his worthless bloody life.

They had driven out into the countryside slowly, following the big black Citroën with the two coffins, one of normal size and the other so very, very small. The funeral was swift and efficient and the soft slanting rain seemed to deaden all sound creating thick mud from the first shovelful of soil that Smaller tossed into the double grave.

The undertaker's assistants had been properly mournful and had not spoken as they added more soil, so that within a minute the polished oak caskets had disappeared under the rich clay. Now that they were gone Smaller found it strangely final, almost a relief. The rain trickled through his hair and ran down over his face and neck but he was thankful because it meant that the few onlookers could not witness his tears. They left him there for a few more minutes

64

alone while he stared down at the neatly flattened earth and the pristine white marble headstone. He memorised the scene and noted such details as the incorrect spacing of the letters forming the word Isobelle which had finished up a bit left of centre. Bitterly he saw that the surname, Cordier, was used. There was no mention of Smaller in either inscription.

Later at the little hotel he tried to eat some lunch and stared out through the rain-slick window to the far-off coast and Nice. The food was superb, rich oxtail ragout and croquette potatoes but he merely picked at it and instead drank steadily from a bottle of Burgundy. In the afternoon he slept in his room, fully dressed on the bed, dozing in a shallow sleep brought on by total mental exhaustion.

He left St Paul de Vence the next day and drove the Peugeot back to Nice. He caught an Air Inter flight to Charles de Gaulle, Paris, connecting on the SAA flight back to Johannesburg. It was Sunday night and the flight was full, even in First Class. Smaller needed five double cognacs to anaesthetise himself. They were late at Jan Smuts but Ashley was there to collect him and take him back to the townhouse. He chattered on gaily about the magazine and how the bookings for the issue had gone up remarkably with the inclusion of the kitchen feature. Smaller passed no comment and merely mumbled a short thank you when they reached Sandton. 'I may be in tomorrow, Norman,' he said and turned towards the front door.

Ashley watched him go worriedly. Martin was heading for a complete breakdown and despite his own position at *Lifestyle* he felt a great deal for his employer. I'll have to try to get him away to a health farm or something, he thought as he drove the Audi through the crystal-clear high-veld morning towards Johannesburg. Jesus, if I can't get him right we can say goodbye to any growth this year.

His thoughts developed and he felt the butterflies of alarm in his stomach. The magazine needed Martin, it was not much more than a shell without his personality and guidance even as far as basic content. Ashley pulled at his lower lip with his large front teeth as he drove. Things didn't look as if they were likely to get better very rapidly.

They had repaired the Ferrari very well, Smaller thought, and it had been brought back only two days before he had left for France so that he hadn't had a chance to drive it, hadn't wanted to anyway. He opened the garage door and stared moodily at the glistening machine sitting there, poised and elegant yet somehow crouched for action, threatening in its aerodynamic perfection.

He had slept for most of Monday and had made no effort to go to the office on this Tuesday morning. Now it was three in the afternoon, he had drunk a full bottle of sparkling wine for lunch and had tried heating up a frozen pizza from the deep freeze. But he hadn't managed to eat more than a few mouthfuls and still hadn't any sort of an appetite although the alcohol had numbed his brain nicely. It had given him the sort of lift that champagne sometimes did so that now he felt better, almost normal, if a little lightheaded.

He went back to the townhouse and collected the keys and his sunglasses. A bit of a thrash down the motorway was what he needed – it would blow the cobwebs out of his brain and it was a beautiful afternoon. He closed and locked the door and walked back to the Ferrari half-hidden in the gloom of the garage. 'You beautiful beast,' he said aloud and ran his hand over the glowing, mirror-like front wings.

Climbing into the cockpit, he savoured the smell of the car, a distinctly male odour that only highly bred cars seemed to have. It was a subtle mix of leather, oil, car polish and petrol and it was almost tangible; a sort of character-giving accent to the car itself. Smaller knew that he could smell his car blindfold. It was an evocatively masculine smell and very much personal to the Ferrari. He knew that women loved it.

The engine started at the first turn of the key and roared

briefly before settling to a soft burble. The tachometer read 800 rpm, and Smaller blipped the throttle a couple of times, waiting until the temperature gauge crept up a few notches before putting the car into gear. He eased the Ferrari out of the garage and pulled the seat belt down from above his left shoulder, slithering and shrugging himself deeper into the seat as the car rolled down the short brick driveway to the street.

Three minutes later he joined the motorway at the Sandton access ramp, turning north towards Pretoria and slipping immediately across onto the right-hand side of the road into the fast lane. The traffic was light at this time of the afternoon and Smaller eased his foot down on the accelerator so that the Ferrari responded within seconds with a speed of 130 kilometres per hour in fourth gear. Feeling at home in the machine and buoyed up by the alcohol, Smaller changed up into fifth at 145 kph, keeping the pressure on the pedal and passing slower vehicles in the centre lane with deceptive ease.

At 4,500 revs in fifth gear the 308 GTSi was doing almost 200 kph and Smaller sat relaxed and confident, revelling in the feeling of power that the car gave him. He lay well back in the seat, both hands on the wheel, watching other vehicles flick past to the left of him as he listened to the wonderful trombone bellow of the engine.

Very much at one with himself and the car, Smaller glanced up into the rearview mirror and saw a silver-coloured blotch there and the single flash of headlights. His eyes jerked back to the instruments and he breathed in sharply. Christ, he was doing 200 kph and some fucker was trying to pass him. An air-horn blasted briefly behind him and he saw the squat shape of the Porsche filling his mirror. He smiled to himself and seeing that the road was clear ahead, eased into the centre lane to allow the silver car to pull alongside. Instead, it blasted past in a high banshee wail of sound and he caught a glimpse of two passengers, one a woman with long dark hair. A small black legend was written on the bodywork below the rear spoiler. It said 'Turbo'.

Despite himself, Smaller felt the adrenalin pump through his system as, without consciously realising it, he pressed down on the accelerator chasing the 930 Turbo which stuck to the outside lane like a leech. Unlike the Ferrari, the Porsche was bulbous, brutal and yet beautiful. It forged ahead of him accelerating away through 230 kph as he pushed the Ferrari to keep up.

The speedometer read 250 kph, almost 150mph, and this registered on Smaller's mind as he hurtled after the Porsche, the Ferrari singing along with still some 1,000 revs to spare. He felt absolutely no fear but instead a heart-pounding excitement born of the chase and further stimulated by his lightheadedness. This in turn was due to his lack of food and the almost continual drinking of the last week. The general low ebb of his body systems resulted in a sudden burst of perspiration which ran down from his armpits and beaded his brow but he still felt marvellously high and very much in control.

He closed on the Porsche and was aware of the dark head turning to look at him through the rear window. He saw the flash of white teeth and a tanned face and he felt an immediate identity with this woman who shared a steel capsule hurtling along like his at close on two and a half times the legal speed limit. Other vehicles hooted and flashed their lights as the two sports cars screamed past but Smaller grinned at them, exulting in the pursuit and the magnificent feel of the thoroughbred machine under him. This was what it was all about, he thought, as the sweat poured down his chest and his groin twitched involuntarily.

As they breasted a slight rise, the Porsche's tail lights lit up quite suddenly shattering the lulling, aircraft smoothness of their travel. The silver car fishtailed to the left, cramming itself into the centre lane to reveal a BMW 733i burbling sedately along at around 110 kph. Smaller tapped his brakes smoothly and the Ferrari shed some 50 kph but he realised sickeningly that he was still closing fast on the big saloon, in fact at almost 190 kph. He decided in desperation to try for the centre lane as the Porsche had done but he was past it now and had fleetingly seen the white face of the driver and the girl with her hands to her mouth. Then the road was full of other vehicles. Behind him he heard a shriek of brakes and realised that it must be the Porsche still trying to lose speed and then they were all topping a rise and there was the long line of traffic backed up behind a slow-moving convoy of army trucks and some monstrous transporter that overlapped into the centre lane from the nearside.

The driver of the BMW had seen the fast-moving Ferrari coming up in his mirror and both cars were now well past the Porsche. But the congested middle lane meant that the BMW driver was unable to take evasive action either and Smaller gripped the leather-covered steering wheel tightly, not believing that this was actually happening; happening in a matter of frantically terrifying half seconds.

Years of habit made him glance in the mirror where he saw the silver car glance off the back of another vehicle and go flicking and jinking through the traffic, miraculously seeming to ricochet off two or three cars before disappearing through the cattle fence at the side of the motorway to become lost under a high cloud of dust in the scrubby *veld*. Then he was clenching his whole body as he slid into the back of the BMW and now, it all seemed to happen in slow motion and then the noise came, an awful crashing, tearing sound as the Ferrari wedged under the high boot of the 733i which slewed to the left in futile evasive action. The gap left was not wide enough and the Ferrari tore itself to pieces between the big solid saloon and the central Armco barrier.

Smaller screamed inside himself, not making any sound, his eyes wide and staring behind the Polaroids. The Ferrari seemed to reduce in size as it squeezed itself tight into the Armco, dragged along in its death throes by the heavy mass of the BMW still travelling at around 60 kph. A great weight pressed into Smaller's shoulder and something gave in his

69

chest as the steering wheel was forced backwards and into him. The noise went on and on, even after the lights had gone out. Finally it was quiet and he heard the voices calling as if from very far away. They seemed to echo down some long dark tunnel to reach him and he felt very aware, yet there was no pain. He knew that he must be dead but found it curious that he was still able to think clearly. Then the tiredness came and he seemed to close his eyes and sleep.

It took forty-three minutes to get Smaller out of the mangled Ferrari and the firemen who performed the extrication thought there was little chance of his being alive. Had the car been of right-hand-drive configuration, he would have undoubtedly been killed, 'smeared along the Armco' was the way one ambulance man phrased it. As it was, he had suffered a dislocated right shoulder when the door pillar and roof on that side had partially collapsed as the Ferrari's nose had buried itself under the BMW. This had also caused the steering box and wheel to be forced back into the cockpit and the small steering wheel had cracked two of Smaller's ribs.

But the monocoque construction of the 308 GTSi had stood up comparatively well to the battering and the cockpit shell was intact apart from the right door pillar. The Ferrari would never take to the road again however. It was a total loss, but Smaller had no knowledge of this until Wednesday afternoon because he remained unconscious for twenty-four hours.

Skittering across three lanes and smashing through a sturdy wire fence, the 930 Turbo had survived with basically only cosmetic damage. The driver and passenger were treated for shock before the former was placed in a cell in Lyttelton police station pending charges for attempted manslaughter and reckless driving. Such was the severity of the police case against the Porsche driver that he was not even allowed to contact his attorney until after the initial hearing.

Even more serious charges awaited Smaller who was found to have an alcohol count of 1,12; some forty per cent above the legal blood content level. Doctors observed that his poor state of health, due to excessive alcohol intake and little food over an extended period would make a quick recovery unlikely. He was fed intravenously with a glucose drip and other energising liquids so that by Thursday morning he had awoken properly to find himself swathed in plaster and bandages.

After the initial shock of being alive and the realisation that he was in a hospital and presumably only damaged, Smaller recovered sufficiently enough for the doctors to allow him visitors. On Thursday evening they had him propped up against the pillows and the door opened to admit Ashley, Liebenberg and the police. The attorney looked grave and brushed one finger casually across his lips in an obvious signal; Smaller nodded very slightly but did not speak.

Lieutenant van Staden of the Lyttelton SAP informed Smaller that anything he said would be recorded and used in evidence whereupon he produced a small Sony tape recorder which he placed on the bedside table and then began talking in excellent English yet with a heavy Afrikaans accent.

'You are aware, *Meneer*,' he said gravely, 'that your irresponsible driving resulted in a major pile-up on the Pretoria highway which blocked two lanes of northbound traffic for three hours and cost the State a great amount of time and money.'

Smaller failed to respond and Liebenberg's facial expression relaxed somewhat. The big policeman continued, his broad swarthy face serious and his lips seeming to move very slightly even though his enunciation was perfect. 'We have a statement from the driver of the Porsche who was involved in the chase. Is he known to you, Mr Smaller?'

Again Smaller did not comment but he did shake his head. Van Staden moved closer. 'Then I must assume that this affair was merely a matter of criminal disregard for other road users coupled with a wilful breaking of the speed limit. We have several statements from other drivers who confirmed that you passed them at speeds far in excess of the legal limit.' Liebenberg shook his head slightly, willing Smaller not to comment, knowing that any untimed speed was not usable as evidence in court unless admitted to by the accused.

Van Staden went on, 'Furthermore, you were found to be under the influence of alcohol, *Meneer,* you will therefore be charged on that count as well as one of attempted manslaughter as soon as you are able to stand trial.' He stood, glowering down on Smaller's white-shrouded torso. 'You are lucky to be alive, Mr Smaller, and further, you are extremely lucky that no other innocent persons died or were maimed as a result of your actions.'

He turned ponderously to leave. 'It is this sort of behaviour from such persons as yourself and that other maniac, de Villiers, who should not be allowed to even hold a driving licence, that makes our roads unsafe places for the innocent bystander.' There was something close to hate in his eyes as his voice became softer. 'I believe you lost two loved ones recently in an air crash, Mr Smaller, and as regards that, I am truly sorry. But imagine if your wife and daughter had been on that highway yesterday afternoon when you and de Villiers were playing your games in those lethal machines you drive. Imagine how you would have felt if your wife and baby had been killed or mutilated.' He opened the door and made one final statement. 'I have little time for your type, sir, and I intend to see you pay for your actions because, whatever you may think, our laws are there for good reasons. They are not made to be broken.'

There was utter silence after the big policeman left. His words had left an impression, not least on Smaller who felt battered by them and drained of coherent thought. Liebenberg smiled hesitantly. 'We'll sort it out, Martin, he'll never make an attempted manslaughter rap stick. It is serious of course, make no mistake, but we'll plead mitigating circumstances and I think I can influence the magistrate, after all they're human too, eh? This is your first offence and you've not been yourself since Isobelle and Rebecca died . . .' He trailed off into silence and Ashley said nothing but just stood there like a big puppet, nodding occasionally.

Smaller looked up bleakly as Liebenberg's cloying tones penetrated his thinking. 'The trouble is, Frank, that policeman was right. I could have killed a lot of people. I am guilty just as he says and I should be punished.' He closed his eyes and turned his head into the pillows. Ashley could see tears in Martin's eyes and he turned away and walked to the door. This bloody nightmare series of events had to end sometime, he thought, otherwise he might as well give up and find another job.

Liebenberg established quickly that the Porsche driver, de Villiers, had four previous offences for reckless driving and he intended to use this fact as a basis for his client's defence. He would reinforce his delivery with the important mitigating circumstances of Smaller's mental health due to his recent bereavement. The attorney hoped for a 'soft' magistrate and was confident that he could get his client off with a sizeable fine but no jail sentence. The drunk driving charge was a worrying factor but Liebenberg hoped to get around even this, on compassionate grounds.

The trial was set for the following Wednesday which was the last day in February and would be held in Lyttelton, near Pretoria. Liebenberg and Ashley had almost a week in which to get Smaller into shape and this promised to be no easy job despite the fact that the shock of what could have happened had sobered Smaller considerably. He had become withdrawn and distant and had not been able to drink alcohol for over two days. On Friday lunchtime Ashley collected him from the Sandton Clinic and they drove the short distance to the townhouse. Smaller was still pensive and seemed totally disinterested in matters relating to the magazine. Ashley's gloom deepened as he considered the immediate future; which meant the April issue.

73

CHAPTER 6

It was mid-March in the Magaliesberg mountains and already there was a slight chill in the air just before dawn. This heralded the often severe Highveld winters when the frost would be thick on the tough veld grass and withered maize stalks in July and August. Temba shivered a little as he rinsed his upper body in cold water from the old zinc tub prior to making his way to Swanepoel's farm and his working day in the fields.

Work actually began at 7.30 but the farm was a good hour's walk from Temba's village and if he got there by seven o'clock there was always hot tea and thick slices of bread and margarine for all the labourers. Old *Baas* Swanepoel was good to his men and Temba had worked for him for almost two years receiving R85 per month for his eight-hour day when he first started and R33 in his last weekly pay packet; which added up to more than R130 per month.

Temba enjoyed this crude but satisfying breakfast and always managed to arrive early enough. On old Swanepoel's part it was an inexpensive way of ensuring that his workers arrived on time and remained faithful to him. He always fed them well and provided a thick stew and mealie porridge at lunchtime which they ate like starving beasts. There was more tea then and he gave them a forty-five minute break with as much water as they could drink. In the summer a good worker would sweat out at least four or five pints in a morning and it had to be put back to keep them going.

For this reason he put plenty of salt in the stew to retain as much water as possible.

As Temba set off, he was already thinking of his second breakfast cup of tea and the hand-rolled cigarette he would enjoy with it. Old Sam rolled them like nobody else, out of brown paper and Boxer tobacco a thick, black twist that smelled wonderful and smoked smooth and strong.

After half an hour the sun was just rising behind the hills near Swartplaas and the guinea fowl were clucking and croaking in the mealie fields. Temba was walking fast along a narrow dirt track of which there were many snaking across the *veld*. He enjoyed this walk, except in the season of heavy rains between October and January.

A francolin exploded suddenly from the coarse *veld* grass at the side of the track and went gliding away over the fields after its fast jerking flight. Already it was warmer and Temba sweated slightly as he walked. He felt ready for the day, rested and happy to be alive. There were really no problems in his simple life and his thoughts were of Subaye and breakfast, in that order, but as his stomach rumbled emptily the order of priority began to change. Thinking of the strong sweet tea and thick soft slices of bread, he quickened his stride and broke into the easy lope of the bush African, a pace which he could maintain all day.

Smaller had been sober since the trial and slowly he was getting over the terrible happenings of February. Ashley had taken over much of the day-to-day responsibilities at *Lifestyle* and Smaller had drafted out the content of the next two issues so that Ashley now had a broad base from which to work. Frank Liebenberg had got him off with a fine of R1,500, one of the highest in Transvaal Traffic Department history. Frank's own fees had been a further thousand which meant that the joy-ride down the motorway that afternoon had totalled R2,500 in legal costs alone.

The Ferrari was a complete write-off and the insurance company had agreed on a settlement of R60,000 which meant a further loss of a couple of thousand on the purchase price. But Smaller was tired of arguing and had aquiesced quite readily; he felt that the Ferrari episode was a part of his life best forgotten. He rejected the thought of another expensive car and had bought a Ford Escort XR3 for R7,500 cash. He liked the agile little car and invested a further R500 on a sunroof and radio/tape. The balance of the money from the Ferrari he placed on call at 13 per cent and felt oddly satisfied with the R500 per month interest it was earning.

Carleen Davis had called him three times but Smaller had no need of her in his life at present, having told her so as gently as possible. He remained in the townhouse for much of his leisure time, reading and drinking little, other than the odd beer or glass of wine with dinner. Food was bought from the local take-away but occasionally he would experiment with a recipe from one of Isobelle's old books he had found. It seemed that he had reached a crossroads in his life and could not decide which way to turn. Although the grief had diminished, the pain was still there and there was little direction in anything he did.

Ashley had watched Smaller over the past weeks and had recognised that he was still far from right. He had come back to the office but seemed to have little of his old sparkle. On the two occasions they had played squash, Ashley had won with ease and Smaller seemed to have none of his usual killer instinct. What Martin needed was to get away completely, change his scene and remove himself from surburbia. Ashley had an idea. All he needed to do was convince Smaller and get him away, out of Johannesburg and divorced from his morbid memories.

CHAPTER 7

Temba was walking back from work tired but contented. It was month's end and he had his weekly wage packet with almost R40 in it; more than he had ever earned in a single week before. Baas Swanepoel had been generous because his boys had worked well, weeding the acres of mealies as well as planting the sugar beet for next season. Tonight it was Friday and Temba would see Subaye, then tomorrow he would go to Magaliesberg and have a beer drink with Benjie at lunchtime. The weekend stretched ahead, full of promise and pleasure. Temba felt that he was going to enjoy himself and he had money in his pocket. He sang softly as he walked.

It was 6.30 and almost dark. He was still a mile and a half from home when the two men materialised from the bush at the side of the track. Temba stopped instinctively and stood wide of them, feeling a prickle of alarm because he had nothing with which to defend himself. Involuntarily his hand strayed to the back pocket of his jeans where the wage packet rested.

A match flared in the dusk and he saw that the man who held it to his cigarette was the big toothless one he had seen on the bus last month. He had never seen the man with him though; he was shorter, squat and more threatening looking. Temba moved casually forward, trying to walk past the pair who blocked his path but they moved too and confronted him in the half light. The big man looked closely at Temba and smiled his toothless grin. 'Ho, it is the young man who is friendly with Jo Langa's bride, fair Maureen.' Temba grinned hesitantly as the man went on. 'I did not see you at that beer drink, boy. Were you there as you said you would be?'

Temba's grin widened. 'Oh yes,' he said remembering. 'Yey, but I was drunk that night.'

Both men smiled back, yet without humour and Temba again felt the threat of their presence. 'I must go, my friends,' he said winningly and moved smartly forwards. The big man stepped aside as if to let him past and then quite suddenly he struck with a short flicking backhand blow of the forearm. The karate strike caught Temba on the left temple without warning and felled him instantly. He rolled in the dust, seeing lights explode in front of his eyes.

Temba sat up with eyes watering and head spinning from the vicious blow. The big man looked down at him. 'We are not your friends,' he said quietly and then smiled grimly. 'But we would like to be, wouldn't we Ruby? Get up boy, we wish to talk with you.'

Temba got to his feet still dazed and frightened yet with a rage building inside him. Somehow he knew that it would be unwise, if not suicidal to retaliate, so he stood sullenly, hating and fearing his attackers. They led him to a little hillock some metres from the track. All three sat and the toothless man offered Temba a cigarette. 'My name is Zak,' he said, 'and this is Ruby,' he added, gesturing to the shorter man who nodded briefly. 'We want a contribution from you boy, for the party; for our struggle,' Zak said softly.

'Now, we can take it off you, or you can give it to us freely, it's up to you, boy,' he said in the same soft voice. Temba's eyes rolled and his hand strayed again to his back pocket.

'How much?' he said in a whisper.

'Five rand will do,' said Zak. 'We don't want to take all your wages, do we Rube?' The two men smiled at each other and Temba felt a chill run through him even though the evening was still mild. He pulled out his wage packet and fished inside for a R5 note, trying not to let the two men see how much it contained.

Zak smiled again at Ruby. Now this strong and seemingly intelligent boy was committed. It had been easy.

It was 7.15 and Subaye cursed Temba for being late. She had been ready for almost forty minutes and she sat silently on the low wall outside her father's house fuming inwardly and railing against all men and particularly Temba.

It was almost totally dark and the indigo vastness of the sky showed the bright pin-pricks of myriad stars whilst to the west was a faint yellowing glow which marked the passage of day into night. As Subaye waited unmoving, bats fluttered by in the dusk, jinking around the small red earth square of the village, hunting for any flies which might still remain from the waning heat of the afternoon. Against the slight chill of early evening Subaye wore a brown knitted dress over pantihose and knee-length PVC boots. Her hair was freshly washed and teased out into a semi-Afro style and her lips were painted red and inviting. She smelled of 4711 cologne. Her plastic handbag and canvas zipper jacket lay on the wall beside her. They were supposed to be going to a dance in the township between Boons and Magaliesberg, if Temba ever arrived, of course.

Subaye sensed movement in the gloom and then saw Temba walking slowly towards her. She noted that his new jeans were dusty and that the clean white shirt she had washed for him was torn on the right sleeve. But more than that, his expression was strange. He seemed angry at something while at the same time thoughtful and pensive.

The girl forgot her own anger. 'What is it, Temba? What has happened to you?'

The tall handsome black looked down at the slender girl, noting her clothes and the clean woman smell of her. Yey, but she was a woman, his Subaye. He wanted her with a sudden longing which was more loving desire than lust and he pulled her to him roughly. 'I met some boys from the bush,' he muttered cryptically into the dark mass of Subaye's springy hair. He felt her stiffen against him but she did not speak. 'They took five rands from me, for the cause, they said. They want me to join the ANC and be like them.' He paused for effect. 'They say they have guns and bombs.'

Subaye had heard of the boys in the bush. They were the freedom fighters, rough, hard men who allegedly were fighting for the independence of South Africa from the white men. They boasted that they would take the country through the barrel of a gun like Robert Mugabe had done in Zimbabwe. She understood little of this though, because as far back as she could remember in local history, the white man had always ruled. He had always had the money and power, the police and army behind him and, of course, the guns to control everybody with.

'How did you get all dirty, Temba?' she asked quickly.

Temba looked into her upturned face and brought his lips down tenderly on her soft full mouth. 'I had a bit of a fight first of all, but then we talked. There were many things they said that made sense to me.'

Subaye pulled at his arm worriedly. 'Don't even think about it, Temba, you'll just finish up dead or in jail if you run with that crowd.' She looked at him closely but he appeared to be far away. 'Come on,' she said sharply, 'we'll never get there if you stand around like a stupid baboon. If Benjie's still waiting for us at the crossroads, he's more of a fool than you are!'

In the *shebeen* at Boons Waltersville township Temba used another seven rands of his pay packet to buy brandies and Coca Colas for himself and Benjie. Subaye sipped slowly from a tall glass of beer and lemonade shandy watching Temba becoming steadily more aggressive as the brandy took effect. Before he could pick a fight with anyone she was determined to leave and knew that she would perhaps have to threaten him with a denial of her body to get him to move. 'If you think that I'm going to let you paw me like a drunken animal, you can forget it,' she whispered loudly in his ear.

This information seemed to register on Temba's consciousness as he was embroiled in staring down a burly young man who had danced with Subaye earlier in the evening. He turned to Benjie theatrically. 'It seems I have to leave,' he said loudly.

Benjie smiled knowingly. 'I would if I was sitting in your shorts my friend. Take the car. Tom is away until tomorrow morning and I'll get a lift back with Wilson. I'll see you in the morning and we'll all go into town to do some serious drinking, eh.' Temba and Subaye stood up and Benjie threw the keys for the Ford across the table. He winked at Subaye. 'Hey man, drive slowly, eh.'

Temba recovered fast once they were outside in the fresh air. They got into the old Fairlane and the V8 started at the first turn of the key as it always did, despite the fact that it had well over two hundred thousand kilometres on the clock. It was a wonderful old car, even though the shock absorbers were finished and the body badly dented in parts. There was little rust though because of the clean dry Highveld air; Temba loved to drive the car and it had been a part of his life for over two years.

They set off carefully down the dirt road to the tarmac, turning left towards Derby and Swartplaas. Subaye was snuggled beside him on the big bench seat and Elton John sang softly on the radio. Temba pulled Subaye closer, driving at only fifty kilometres per hour with one hand on the wheel. His left hand moved up over her hip and brushed the side of her left breast. She felt warm and soft and he heard her murmur contentedly like a cat. In the dark of the car Temba smiled to himself, it was only about twenty minutes to the Swartplaas turn-off, then they could do it. He began to harden.

Suddenly, the car was lit from behind by bright headlights and Temba swerved left onto the dirt to allow the fast moving vehicle to pass. He watched a large white Chevrolet pull in front and then he saw the red brake lights and the reflective green police sign on the boot. 'Oh, no,' he said to Subaye in resignation and he saw the fear in her face.

Two white men in the blue and navy uniform of the South African Police got out of the Chevrolet and approached the parked Ford. Temba sat tight and wound down the window. He saw sergeant's stripes on the sleeve of the first policeman's jacket and noted that the other one stood back, his right hand resting casually on his holstered pistol. Temba felt a prickle of fear in his stomach – he had done nothing wrong but with men like this there was no telling what could happen. The sergeant was big and redfaced with fair hair shaved high above his ears and up the back of his neck. He put out his hand. 'Licence and pass book,' he said importantly and then changed his mind and added, 'Out of the car slowly, both of you.'

Temba and Subaye were made to stand with their hands on the roof of the Fairlane. Both had produced their passbooks and Temba had shown his driving licence which *Baas* Swanepoel had helped him to get so that he could drive the tractor and the farm trucks. The two policemen had opened the trunk and searched inside the car for weapons. The sergeant spoke harshly. 'This your car, *Kaffir*?'

'No, sir,' said Temba deferentially. 'It belongs to my friend, Tom Ndhlovu, but we all pay towards it, sir, for petrol and oil and things like that. Tom allows me to drive it, sir,' he added lamely.

The sergeant grinned at his constable. 'It's a fucking old heap anyway, *Kaffir*, don't let the traffic police find you with it in Magaliesberg or they'll have you off the road before you can say two twos, my mate.' He looked closely at Subaye. 'You got yourself a nice little black cherry there, eh, smells good too. Bet you only fuck the arse of her eh, boy?' The younger policeman moved closer but Subaye did not flinch as he felt inside her jacket and down her thighs;

the sergeant did likewise and then searched Temba perfunctorily.

The younger constable was looking thoughtfully at Subaye when the sergeant became tired of the charade. 'Go on, fuck off quickly both of you,' he rasped, 'before I change my mind and find some reason to book you, you'd like a night in the cells in Magaliesberg, heh, my girl. Koos here would like that, wouldn't you, constable; randy little bastard you are, that's for sure!'

Temba was unsure whether the sergeant was talking about his constable or Subaye but they both got back into the car hurriedly. Temba started the engine, his hand shaking whilst the two policemen looked on. He moved off carefully not looking at Subaye who stared ahead through the windscreen, not daring to speak until they were out of earshot of the policemen.

By the time they reached the turn-off from the tarmac Temba's anger had all but subsided and Subaye was once more enclosed within the circle of his left arm. Again he noticed her fresh perfumed smell accentuated by the warm interior of the car. He felt his heart quicken in anticipation. About two kilometres down the dirt road towards Swartplaas, Temba parked the Ford under some tall old willows, driving in under their curtainlike fronds so that the car was almost invisible from the road. He switched off the lights and they sat listening to the soft night sounds of the veld. Then he pulled her towards him. Within a minute her hand moved over the zipper of his jeans.

Subaye rolled down her pantihose and Temba pushed up her dress. They were on the back seat where Tom thoughtfully kept an old threadbare blanket. Temba struggled out of his jeans and boxer shorts and then he was kneeling between Subaye's thighs savouring this moment of surrender. He knew she wanted him, needed him, and she writhed and twisted and then her hands went to him and pulled him down. He sank onto her, his maleness hard and heavy. She twisted slightly to find him and then they were together as he moved smoothly into her. Slowly, tenderly he built up rhythm, his mind filled with conflicting thoughts. He realised that he loved Subaye and that it was very likely that they would marry in the not too distant future. If he could ever afford to pay *lobola* to her conniving old father.

Temba considered where they might live. In her village very likely, or in the married quarters at *Baas* Swanepoel's. If they married he could not really consider any further contact with Zak and Ruby and the ANC, because that would not be fair to Subaye or the family they were sure to raise. These thoughts brought him back to the present and Subaye's panted instructions. 'Not inside, Temba, it's right in the middle of my month, you must take it out,' but she writhed and gasped as her climax was reached and Temba froze, desperately struggling to hold back and finally feeling unusually masterful as Subaye squirmed beneath him and grasped him, pulling him into her.

Finally he pulled back and sat back on his calves. She moved aside allowing him to stretch his legs out straight on the wide seat. Smiling, catlike, she took him in her hand and brought her mouth down close so that he felt the warmth of her breath on his nudity. In the half-light from the full moon he could see her dark lips and the glistening whiteness of her teeth and her hand moving on him. Then he gasped as her mouth enclosed him. A great surging warmth began in the very root of his manhood as Subaye's tongue continued to move on him, her lips still enclosing him firmly. He exploded into her mouth and she held him, swallowing fast, draining him. Never had she done this to him before and Temba looked down at her with wonder and gratitude in his eyes. 'You are some woman, Subaye,' he said softly. She smiled and looked up at him, her big brown eyes half-closed and feline.

The next day Subaye awoke early feeling vigorous and refreshed. She was to see Temba in town at midday but, in the meantime, she had the cleaning to do and the breakfast porridge to make. By the time she was finished and had set out to walk the five or six kilometres across the veld to the bus stop, it was after ten. Moosa's bus would leave from the crossroads near Temba's village at 11.15.

Temba had also slept well and Benjie had awoken him to some good-hearted ribbing from both him and Tom. 'You look tired, boy,' said the small chubby man, his eyes crinkling knowingly.

Temba took a half-hearted swipe at him but then both his friends listened attentively as he recounted the episode with the police. Remembering his loving with Subaye, Temba still felt masterful and confident. 'Those white bastards didn't bother me too much,' he said. 'Come on, let's go to town and do some drinking, I still have some money to spend.'

By the time Subaye boarded Moosa's bus at 11.15, Temba, Tom and Benjie were already quite drunk on Carling Black Label beer which they swigged openly in the bright morning sunlight at the back of the Magaliesberg Hotel off-sales. Just over one hour later they were in jail for disturbing the peace and consuming liquor in a public place.

Subaye waited until 1.30 for Temba outside the Greek café in Main Street. Then she walked across to the hotel once again fuming with anger. There were two old black men sitting outside and she asked whether they had perhaps seen Temba Mthombeni or Benjamin Ndadza from *Ou-Baas* Swanepoel's farm. They shook their heads. 'Don't know those names, girl,' said one, leering appreciatively at Subaye. 'But the police took away some young fellahs who were drinking and shouting round the back of the off-sales.'

Subaye felt her stomach sink. That fool Temba, she thought angrily. He never knows when to stop. Despite herself she felt fear for her lover but this soon dissipated when the anger built inside her at the realisation that the regular buses had finished running and Moosa's would not leave town again until around six that evening. She would have to try to get a lift. Walking briskly, she set off down

Main Street heading for the junction at the end of town and the left fork to the Boons road and Swartplaas.

Smaller had eventually succumbed to Ashley's suggestions and innuendos. The April issue had gone to press with almost R40,000 in advertising revenue and June was looking good so far. Everything was now very much under control, Ashley said. He, Smaller, should get away, go off for a break and relax. Ashley had just the right idea and discussed it at length. Smaller had to admit it did sound pretty good.

Ashley had borrowed a late model VW microbus camper from a friend. It had a double bunk, bottle gas stove, small sink and several cupboards for provisions. It even had a compact but defunct refrigerator in which to keep beer and wine cool. Smaller had phoned Danie Bester who owned the farm out past Magaliesberg where he shot francolin and guinea fowl in the winter and occasionally rock pigeons during the summer months. Of course, he was more than welcome, Danie had said. He should take the VW through the mealie fields and camp out at the bottom of the hill where the old tin mine was. It would be nicely sheltered there; it was by far the best place.

'Bring your shotgun with you, man,' Bester had said in his rapid Afrikaans-accented English. 'You can get some of those *bliksemse* pigeons for me. The bastards, they are eating all my sunflowers. Later on you'll be up for the fowl, eh. The season starts on June the first man, you can stay until then as far as I'm concerned – as long as you come by and have a *dop* with me some evening, man.'

The Bester farm was some ten kilometres from Swartplaas, about fifty kilometres by dirt and tarred road from Magaliesberg, the nearest town. Smaller knew this territory fairly well, having shot there for the past four years. It was typical, rolling Transvaal bushveld, fairly rocky and with little real cover except for a few low thorn trees and the inevitable man-made acres of mealie – or maize, as it was called in the USA.

Smaller loaded the Volkswagen with tinned food, dry biscuits, margarine, three dozen beers, a few bottles of wine and six bottles of Scotch. He packed two sets of khakis, T-shirts, jeans, tennis shoes and shorts marvelling at the cleverly planned spaces which were still half-empty after he had finished. Finally, he slotted in the guns with their cases; the Luigi Franchi twelve bore and his Anschutz .22 auto rifle with its Tasco telescopic sight.

There would be little likelihood of rain at this time of the year so Smaller included a 25 gallon jerry can of fresh water and on the last Saturday in March he pulled out his old hunting boots, soft and pliable with many applications of dubbin. He left Johannesburg after midday feeling much more excited than when he was taking a plane somewhere. It really seemed as if he were going on an adventure.

The VW hummed along steadily at 90 kph and he passed through Magaliesberg at 1.45 pm. The village was almost deserted, as are most South African towns and cities from closing time on Saturday until Monday morning. Smaller followed the left fork to Boons and the straight and narrow ribbon of black tarmac stretched ahead of him, shimmering in the late autumn sun. On the left, the maize fields undulated away to a line of low hills on the horizon. Some forty kilometres further on he would take the left turn onto the dirt road and head towards Swartplaas and the hills on Bester's farm.

There was little traffic and even fewer pedestrians. Then Smaller noticed the slight figure walking up ahead. As he approached he saw that it was a woman, a black girl in fact, and she was dressed attractively in blue jeans and a white T-shirt. Seeing that she was hitchhiking he slowed the microbus involuntarily and rolled up behind her.

Subaye walked on the left hand side of the road with her right arm swinging, the thumb stuck out in the age-old hitchhiker's sign. She heard the sound of an engine approaching and noted that the vehicle seemed to be slowing. Her heart leapt at the prospect of a lift because this was only the third car to pass her in over an hour, although she had refused one lift in a truck which appeared to be filled with drunken farm labourers. She turned and saw that this was a little bus driven by a white man. Shyly she stood by the roadside as Smaller drew up beside her.

Smaller appraised the girl. He guessed that she was around twenty although she could have been younger – it was often hard to tell with Africans. Her skin was a light coffee colour and her cheek bones were high, the nose proud and aquiline over full sensual lips. She was slim and straight-backed and undoubtedly had natural poise and elegance. Her neck was slender and her breasts full and firm under the clean white T-shirt; Smaller felt odd butterflies in his stomach because she was one of the most captivating women he had ever seen.

He leaned over and pushed open the passenger door, feeling the sense of adventure even more and a secondary sensation of involving himself with forbidden fruit. In South Africa one could, in theory, be stopped by the police for carrying blacks of the opposite sex in a vehicle, although these days such practices were not unusual in some of the bigger cities like Johannesburg.

'Jump in,' he said brightly and smiled at the girl; then, as an afterthought, he felt he should have asked where she was going.

She climbed into the passenger seat and looked at him sideways. 'Should I sit in the back, master?' she asked in a soft mellifluous voice, the English well-pronounced and the eyes downcast in respect to him, a white man.

'No need to call me master,' said Smaller quickly. 'My name's Martin and I come from England. What's your name?'

The girl smiled showing impossibly white teeth that were so even that they seemed false. 'I am called Subaye,' she said quietly pronouncing the name *Zu-bay-a* which to Smaller had a wonderful sing-song beauty about it. 'I am going to my village which is near Swartplaas. Perhaps you could drop me by the turn-off from this road, mas . . ., er Martin, sir,' she said politely.

Smaller smiled. 'I can do better, I am turning off there too because I am going to camp at *Baas* Bester's farm, do you know it?'

They talked quietly as Smaller drove on slowly at seventy, wanting to make the time with her last. He stopped the VW and rummaged in the back for the beers, then offered her a cigarette. She took neither but watched him while he sipped the beer and then lit a small Villiger cigar. He rarely smoked but always carried a pack of cigarettes and the Villigers. At this moment the cold malty liquid and the mild aromatic taste of the cigar combined to produce one of the most enjoyable sensations he could recall. Christ, she's beautiful he thought as he glanced sideways at her. The road unwound ahead, empty and still warm in the golden glow of mid-afternoon.

To Subaye it was like a dream that had become reality. This man, Martin, must be her man from the dream. The dream she had kept on having these last few months. He was Gregory, the white man who had come and taken her from her father's village, from a life of sameness and drudgery and from Temba who loved her yet was not everything she wanted. His hair was shorter and he was not as blond as Gregory from the dream and he had no moustache. But the eyes were the same, blue grey and penetrating and beautiful and her heart beat strongly in her chest because she had felt them looking at her. His gaze had run swiftly over her face and body like a touch and she felt her face burn as though he had actually put his hands on her.

It was madness, she thought. In her dream it was all very well, but in reality the white men did not take black women. She had once read in the white newspapers of some white men who had been found with black women and the shame that had come to them and their families. One had even killed himself and others had left South Africa forever; cast out by their race for committing the unforgivable sin.

89

Subaye understood little about politics and had never been to Johannesburg. She had learned her English in the village school at Boons and had taken to it well, recognising it as the language of the future after the terrible riots in Soweto which were said to have started because the schoolchildren were being forced to learn Afrikaans. She spoke Afrikaans as well as English because it was the language of the white people she had grown up with here in the Magaliesberg. The village of Magaliesberg was 'Town' to her, the centre of her world, the place where she bought clothes and special foodstuffs when she had enough money saved.

She worked at *Baas* Hofmeyer's farm; in the big sorting sheds where the roar of the machinery made it almost impossible to speak. But he paid her R25 per week which was quite good for the Transvaal platteland and the bushveld villages.

Subaye had also read in the white papers of some white men from other countries, like Martin, who lived with coloured women in Cape Town. She had heard that the police there accepted this behaviour and that things were changing with the coloureds and the whites. But Cape Town was so far away from her life and the narrow sphere of activity in which she lived that she could not actually visualise such a permissive set of circumstances.

Blacks were different to coloureds, of course. Her people were not accepted in the same way as the brown people. The coloureds were an embarrassing part of Afrikaner history, a race created by the cohabitation of blacks and whites in the days prior to 1948 when the Afrikaners took over the governing of the country. Subaye's mother had told her once, when she was drunk, that she had lain with white men as a young girl. Men from the farms around here in the Magaliesberg. It was not against the law in those days, before the coming of the Afrikaners to power. Her mother had told her that shortly afterwards a new word, *apartheid,* had first been heard and that then everything had changed.

Despite herself and these forbidding thoughts, Subaye could not help but look approvingly at this white man who sat beside her, as he in turn had looked at her. He seemed like one of the film stars she had seen in the TV magazine which was sold at the Greek café in town, although she had never seen TV herself properly. Once when she had been working overtime during the harvest she had left late and walked past Mr Hofmeyer's house and had looked in through the sitting-room window and seen the blue flickering light on the little screen. She had wanted to stay and watch but Mrs Hofmeyer had seen her and shooed her away, telling her to get off home and not hang around outside her windows or else she'd let the dogs out to shift her.

Martin wore blue jeans like hers, only they seemed newer and more like real trousers and they had leather stitched around the pockets. His shirt was corduroy, a warm beige colour like a dry mealie husk and it looked soft and velvety. He had brown suede boots on and a thick leather belt with a brass buckle and his sunglasses were pushed up into his curly dark blond hair. His eyes watched the road, but occasionally they would flick to her as he chatted and crinkle at the edges when he smiled quickly. He talked on and on about his house in Johannesburg and the magazine which he owned that she had never heard of.

Then suddenly they were off the tar, turning onto the red dirt road that led towards the hills, watching it open up in front of them like a clean scarlet wound between the mealie fields. The sun was lower in the sky and a dust cloud whirled and rolled behind from their passage over the powder-dry clay. Subaye felt strangely elated; even though she had seen all this before she noticed its beauty as if for the first time.

En route to Bester's farm, Smaller stopped the microbus only a few kilometres from where Subaye's village was located. Both seemed loathe to part with the other's company and when Smaller finally put the VW into gear he looked in the rear mirror to see the young black girl still standing on the dusty road looking after him as he pulled away. 'Perhaps we'll run into each other again, Subaye,' he had said almost regretfully. 'It's been great talking to you and I'll be here for a few weeks.'

Subaye had smiled back at him, her huge black eyes wide and her full lower lip slightly tremulous. 'I'd like that Martin,' she'd murmured.

Smaller had stopped off and had a beer with Danie Bester and then pressed on for the last half an hour's drive at very low speed through the maize fields to the old mine on the side of the low hill. By the time he arrived the light was beginning to dim and the pigeons were wheeling in the thorn trees on the slopes of the hill prior to finding their way into the old mine workings where they would roost for the night. It was absolutely silent in the late afternoon *veld* and Smaller felt a strangely pleasing sense of solitude made more apparent by the purity of the air and the lack of wind. It was so still that he could hear the odd warble from the pigeons up on the hill and they were easily half a kilometre away.

He pulled out a folding chair and sat with his back to the Volkswagen sipping another beer. It was ages since he had felt so completely alone because back in Johannesburg there was always the noise of traffic and the television or radio. And the bloody telephone, of course, which intruded on anybody's privacy. As the light fell, Smaller thought of the girl Subaye, comparing her with the other women that he had known in recent years. It was a difficult comparison because, first off, he didn't really know anything about the black girl and her lifestyle, and her values would be totally different from those of any other woman he had known. Carleen Davis was almost the same age and also unmarried, but that was all the two women could possibly ever have in common. He hadn't seen Carleen since coming back from France, hadn't even been tempted when she had told him how sorry she was about his wife and child or how worried she was after reading about the crash in the newspapers.

She'd offered solace and comfort, saying she just wanted to be with him. 'To look after him', she'd said. Smaller had finally told her that he didn't need her or anyone else. She'd cried of course but they all did when they couldn't get what they wanted.

Funnily enough, he hadn't thought much about Isobelle since the funeral but the pain of Rebecca was still there inside him and if he closed his eyes when he was alone, like now without any interruptions or distractions, he could see her little face quite clearly. Sitting there in the beautiful clarity of the silent bushveld evening he cursed once more at the loss of his perfect child and blamed himself yet again.

Morosely Smaller continued to ponder on his life and pronounced it fairly pointless in the main. He didn't really care about material things but admitted to himself that he had coveted the Ferrari as a machine of flawless performance rather than a possession worth R60,000 plus. Since he'd come back from France he'd begun to question both his lifestyle and his social sphere, limited though it was. Most invitations that he did receive were for 'The publisher of *Lifestyle* magazine' rather than for Martin Smaller the person. Realising this, he was often abrasive or incommunicative at dinners and cocktail parties with the result that his hosts judged him to be an arrogant and boorish guest. Smaller thought of several recent reactions when he had attempted to get back into some sort of social circle just for the hell of it. The cocktail party glitterati crowd had stupid questions to ask about the Ferrari debacle and the slight lull in *Lifestyle*'s advertising content and frequency, seeing the latter as a sign of impending disaster. Johannesburg was such a God-awful reactionary place, thought Smaller as he sat in the dusk smoking his second Villiger. He'd ended one recent conversation with a hostess by telling her to mind her own stupid business and he smiled wryly again, recalling the expression on her face. He took another long swig from the can of Castle lager; they could all go and pole vault for all he cared.

Later that night he awoke in the comfortable double bunk feeling slightly constricted by the proximity of the VW's roof. The silence was absolute and he wondered why he had awoken. His stomach rumbled and he remembered that he hadn't eaten since breakfast back in Johannesburg. Although he was only a matter of two hours away, it seemed like another country. Smaller rolled over, snuggling down into his quilt thinking of the black girl, Subaye. He started awake once more when an owl called close by in the fields, then, remembering where he was, he relaxed and fell back into sleep within a matter of seconds.

Six and a half kilometres across the quiet of the moonlit veld Subaye tossed and turned in a fitful doze. She had thought of little other than the white man since he had dropped her at the crossroads, and her stomach had retained an odd empty feeling since she had watched the little bus disappear down the dirt road, its following dust cloud gilded by the low sun of the autumn afternoon.

After ten she had slept shallowly but the dream had not come to her in the clarity she had become accustomed to. Half-awake for hours she had begun to fantasise about Martin Smaller, seeing his face quite clearly and the way his mouth broke easily into a wide smile, accentuated by the little lines at the sides of his blue-grey eyes. Her hands had moved over her body involuntarily and she had become aroused. Feeling herself moist, warm and wanting, she had counterfeited the presence of a man's body and brought herself to a silent yet shuddering climax. But still she could not sleep and, if anything, she felt more empty, somehow knowing how it would be with the white man. She yearned for him like forbidden fruit, lying quietly in the musty darkness of the tiny alcove off her parent's bedroom.

As the first light brought dim grey outlines to the window, she eventually fell into real sleep and sank into the deep dreamless depths of emotional exhaustion. It seemed only minutes before her father shook her awake, dragging her back from the woolly warmth that had cocooned her in an oblivion close to death; the time in most people's sleep cycle which is experienced usually between three and four in the morning. She became aware of the slightly rancid smell of her father's body and then the stronger odour of his stale, sour breath, heavy with Saturday afternoon's beer drink.

'Get up, girl. Do you think it is a bloody hotel here? By now you should have swept the yard and made the porridge.' He hawked and spat out of the open window where only three panes remained unbroken. 'Yey, but you young ones these days, probably dreaming of that idiot Temba, eh? Well, I hope they keep him in the jail so that I don't have to see his stupid face around here. Following you about like a randy goat, good for nothing bastard, that he is.'

He turned and left the room through the open door frame and Subaye listened to the creak of the old springs as he lowered himself back into the bed he shared with her mother who had no doubt slept on through the brief noisy harangue. Her head still clogged with the aftermath of a broken sleep, Subaye rolled out of bed and stared outside at the bright morning; the first thing she recalled was the meeting with Martin Smaller.

Smaller opened his eyes at around eight, feeling rested and content to be back in the bush. The unaccustomed silence was the main reason for awakening and he lay in the light-weight Dacron sleeping bag staring at the cream-painted ceiling of the Volkswagen only a metre or so above his head. On the other side of the hill was the corrugated-iron water-storage tank where they often took a shower on summer evenings after the pigeon shooting. At this time of the year, the water would be freezing but it would wake him up alright and then he'd cook a bit of breakfast. He slithered off the bunk and took a towel from the cupboard and the plastic bottle of Pino Silvestre shower and shampoo. Might as well smell sweetly, even here in the veld, he thought, and grinned to himself. Then he remembered the black girl he had given the lift to and his groin stiffened slightly. God, but she was beautiful.

Naked, Smaller stood in the cool morning air and draped the towel around his waist. He didn't intend to shave whilst he was here in the bush and so he set off clutching the bottle of liquid soap and whistling tunelessly to himself. He wore tennis shoes because the ground was dry and hard and there were many flints and sharp stones in the tough veld grass.

Skirting the base of the hill, Smaller wandered slowly through the grass and low bushes listening to the sounds of the veld and the cooing of the pigeons up on the hill. A small hare broke cover in front of him and zigzagged away, a reddish-brown flash of movement, its white tail, like a bull's-eye, visible for fleeting seconds before it went to earth. The raucous clucking of guinea fowl sounded from the mealie fields and Smaller thought of the shooting he would do after the first of June when the mornings were often so cold that the veld was frosted with white crystals and the mist rose from the fields as the sun's great orange orb lifted over the hills.

He reached the storage tank and draped the towel over one of the angle iron girders that supported the huge round drum above. He could have climbed up the twelve foot tower and clambered over the side into the water but it was much easier to stand down below under the big bore tap and have a shower. Bracing himself, Smaller reached up and turned the wheel but, even though he was expecting it, the deluge of cold water took his breath away. He shampooed and showered briskly and rinsed his mouth momentarily cursing himself for forgetting his toothbrush. He stood finally, heart pounding from the coldness of the water, naked there in the veld yet feeling completely natural and more at peace with himself than he had been since returning from Nice. Jogging back to the VW, he thought again of the girl. Perhaps she would come. It seemed ridiculous even to consider it but somehow he felt that it was possible, even likely.

Temba awoke on Sunday morning with what he could only imagine was severe damage to his head. In fact it was a monstrous hangover, augmented by the blow from a sapele mahogany police baton with which Sergeant Hendriks had hit him. It was indeed unfortunate for Temba that the big blond sergeant had happened to be in the catcher van that had answered the call from the manager of the Magaliesberg Hotel off-sales. First, he and Benjie had been forced to lay face down in the dust and searched before being bundled into the big Ford truck, the windows of which were covered from the outside with stout wire mesh.

Once back at the police station, only minutes from the hotel, Hendriks had singled out Temba and pushed him around the corner close to the small cell block. Somewhat sobered and more afraid than he ever remembered, Temba had cowered in the dirt and put his hands over his head. The sergeant had laughed and shouted at him crudely. 'Oh yes, here he is, the lover boy, the one with the nice black *meisie,* eh. Did you fok her well last night boy? Did she like it when you gave it to her, eh. You fokking *kaffir,* you. Disturbing the peace of our town here and getting pissed on that fokking filth you drink.' Hendriks was obviously unaware that Temba and his friends had in fact been drinking Carling Black Label, not the sour maize beer that many Africans consumed in large quantities.

Hendriks had seemed to stir himself up into a frenzy but still Temba had not moved. He had remained crouching, not even daring to look up. Then the great blinding light had flashed across his consciousness and the pain had come and developed into massive throbbing waves which kept time with the beat of his heart. Hendriks had pulled him to his feet and hustled him into the cell with the others. Then the barred door had slammed and they had been left there in the semi-darkness on the cement floor which grew gradually colder as the afternoon faded into evening.

Benjie had tried to joke and make light of their plight but Tom and Temba had sat silent and dismal; they had all felt the lump on Temba's head and then as night came they had curled up together for warmth. In the morning there had been a plate of mealie porridge and some watery gravy with a few lumps of gristly meat. Battered aluminium cups of sweet tea had followed but Temba had still sat in the corner, his head pounding. Further misery would come when they were told what their fines would be; there was only R28 left between the three of them.

That afternoon Zak and Ruby had gone looking for Temba. Word had got back to his village to say that he and two friends were in jail in Magaliesberg, and Zak had grinned to his companion. This was just what they needed to bring the young men into the ANC fold. Both he and Ruby had experienced similar short terms of imprisonment and they knew that, for such petty crimes as disturbing the peace, the South African police wanted the payment of a fine and nothing else. These fines were high, in black terms, often representing more than a week's wage and were thus a forceful deterrent to the offender. The South African government had no wish to incur the expense of unnecessary non-paying guests. Minor offenders such as Temba, Tom and Benjie were usually let out the day after being arrested on settlement of any amount between R25 and R35, the scale of charges being somewhat vague.

Zak had a cash reserve for such matters and he and Ruby would drive into Magaliesberg and get a local boy from the town to go to the police station and pay the fine. Zak had over R1,800 safely secreted away in Waltersville township; perhaps some knew of the existence of this money but none would dare to tell of it.

These days the African Nationalist Congress was making headlines all over South Africa. There had been attacks on fuel depots in the Northern Transvaal and bombings right across the south of the country from Natal to the Cape. Zak believed that the day of reckoning was coming before too long but they needed more members, intelligent thinking men who would believe in and fight for the ANC when the time was right. Unfortunately, here in the Magaliesberg the average African was not much more than a *bush kaffir*; Zak had little compunction in using the white term of derision. But this Temba was a likely candidate because he was bright and quite cunning yet still young enough to rise up through the ranks if he could be trained properly.

Zak was the cadre leader for the Magaliesberg area and there were some two hundred party members under his direction. About fifty of these men and women lived in the Waltersville township near Boons, a sprawling shanty town of some five thousand souls who worked in Magaliesberg and on the surrounding farms. Within the township were several small arms caches, the locations of which were known only to Zak and four other men.

The caches had been built up painstakingly over five years and Zak was glad that they were now quite reasonable little arsenals because lately the SAP had become much more conscious of the ANC presence within South Africa's borders. There were often surprise roadblocks on both sides of Magaliesberg and around Waltersville, and a squad of the hated Riot Police, in their distinctive leaf camouflage, had arrived at Magaliesberg SAP station about a month back. As far as Zak knew, they were still there. He wondered for the hundredth time whether someone might have talked but discounted the idea as he had before. If there had been any whisper about arms caches inside Waltersville the police would have turned the whole place over, probably with the help of the army. There had been occasional raids and searches in the early hours of the morning and once the police had found a stolen handgun, but that was all. So far so good, Zak thought.

Another fortunate factor was the location of Waltersville close to the railway line which came from Zeerust. This town was virtually on the border with Bophuthatswana, the so-called black homeland which at its westernmost point was only about fifty kilometres from the neighbouring black state of Botswana. ANC friends in Botswana would cross the makeshift border into Bophuthatswana with weapons, and other sympathisers would smuggle them onto the trains bound for Johannesburg. The Railway Police were thankfully not in the same class as the regular SAP and it had been quite easy in the past just to shove off the odd package as the train trundled towards Boons where it often stopped.

Just the other day, they'd got a case of six Kalashnikovs, all nicely crated and labelled 'Industrial Abrasives'. They even had a 'Carborundum Universal' stamp on the wood and had been so well packed and strengthened with steel bands that the case had remained intact after falling off the flat-bed bogey at around forty kilometres an hour. Zak had supervised the unpacking and he, Ruby and two others had marvelled at the styrofoam and polythene wadding inside the crate. Then had come the oiled brown paper and finally the brand new assault rifles, gleaming a dull black in the light from the oil lamp. These had been the latest short carbine version of the AK 47 with the folding alloy stock and plastic forepiece, a wonderful weapon for the freedom fighter which could be secreted away inside a jacket or coat. Zak resisted keeping one for himself but what Temba didn't know was that one had very recently been earmarked for him.

Subaye knew that it was unlikely that the white man would come to her. All Monday, in the noise and controlled chaos of the sorting shed, she had thought of Martin Smaller. Her friend, Elsie, had chattered on as usual, talking about her boyfriend and what she'd done with him that weekend, but Subaye had hardly heard her. She had decided that the only way she would get to see Smaller again would be to go and visit him on Bester's farm.

That evening she ate her usual plate of porridge and meat with her mother, father and younger sister as she did every day of her life. Temba was still in jail as far as she knew but in any event his importance had faded markedly since her meeting with Smaller. She washed the battered metal plates and mugs in the water bucket in the yard, returning them to the shelf in her mother's cupboard. Then she took soap, a threadbare towel and clean underclothes before setting off through the dusk towards the river. At a good pace it would take her about twenty minutes to get there.

It was quite cool in the veld as she hurried along, listening to the sounds of the small animals and birds as they prepared themselves for their rest. She had no fear of the dark and could see quite easily in the light from a three-quarter moon which had risen early and now hung large and yellow over the horizon. She reached the river and scrambled down the bank to her favourite spot where the current had polished the stones to a shiny smoothness. The water rippled and gurgled and glinted silver in the moonlight. Subaye stripped off her denim shirt and corduroy trousers and stood in her cotton vest and panties, then she removed these too and stepped into the water with her small bar of Lux toilet soap.

The river was shallow at this point and the bottom sandy and smooth. She sluiced herself all over and then lathered up with the creamy soap. The water was soft and not very cold and she washed herself swiftly yet efficiently, then dried off with the towel. She had used the soap on her springy black hair and she finally dipped her head under the water, leaning forward from the rocks and letting the current rinse the soap away. Walking back from the bank she secreted the towel under a low thorn tree and put on her clean pants and vest. Then she soaked her soiled underclothes and rubbed them briskly with the soap before rinsing them and hanging them in the lower branches of the thorn bush. She would return for them in the morning.

Distance means little to the bush African whose measurements are calculated in time rather than kilometres or miles. Subaye set off at a forty-five degree angle to the normal route back to her village. She was heading almost directly west, cutting across the veld, and would pass south of the tiny *dorp* of Swartplaas by some five kilometres. She reckoned that it would take her about an hour and a half to reach Bester's farm. Once there she would have to find out where Smaller was camped.

Subaye's heart pounded as she walked. She had little idea of what she would do when she found Smaller, and her head was filled with doubts as to his reaction. The worst that would happen would be that he could reject her outright and ask her to leave him alone; by her scale of experience with white people, this was a distinct possibility.

With the ease of the bush African she walked overland negotiating rocks, heavy undergrowth and the metre-deep crevices caused by soil erosion. All the time she maintained a westerly direction which was both instinctive and accurate and after almost two hours she topped a low rise and saw the lights of Bester's smallholding and the cooking fires of his African workers whose *kraal* was some two hundred metres beyond the farm buildings. She trotted down the slope soundlessly and reached the small collection of huts without causing any of the mangy *kraal* dogs to bark. She had chosen the end hut and knocked lightly on the door, wishing that she didn't have to ask where the white man was camped.

An old woman answered and listened to Subaye's statement that she had a message from *Baas* Hofmeyer for the white man who was living in the little bus on *Baas* Bester's farm. If the old crone had any suspicions about this odd nocturnal messenger she did not comment and told Subaye that the white man was over in the mealie fields on the edge of the little hill with the big hole inside it. He had been here earlier at the farm, drinking with *Baas* Bester; they had sat out on the back stoep and finished many beers. The old woman shook her head marvelling that two men could be able to afford to drink so much.

Smaller enjoyed the drink with Danie Bester. He had had a wonderful Monday doing absolutely nothing as he had on Sunday. At noon the sun was very warm so he had pulled one of the mattresses off the bunk and lain out in the sun naked, soaking up the rays and getting a light tan on his chest and legs. He had walked all around the area, taking a rubber torch from the Volkswagen to explore the old mine workings which honeycombed the hill. The torch battery had been almost flat so that he had seen little and had not ventured much further than fifty metres from the entrance but he'd vowed to get new batteries in Magaliesberg and have another look later in the week.

He ate a late breakfast of egg, bacon and sausage. Then he'd taken his plate and utensils with the dishwashing liquid to clean them under the tap from the water tower. Feeling wonderfully self-sufficient he'd washed out his underwear, two T-shirts and a pair of jeans and draped them over the girders in the morning sun; by mid-afternoon they were completely dry.

There was plenty of game about and he'd considered taking the .22 and trying for a hare but had finished up lying in the sun reading a paperback and drinking beer. By five he was feeling like company so he'd stowed everything away and driven through the mealies to Bester's place. The Afrikaner had been pleased to see him and had ushered him onto the back stoep where they could watch the sun go down.

'*Ja,* man. But it's only good to have a sundowner, eh. *Here,* but I like my beer of an evening and I bloody felt like one at midday man, hell but it was only hot then, eh.' He rambled on happily while Smaller sat contentedly, listening to the talk of the land and last year's harvest, of the seven lambs that had been taken by jackal and how the fokking *tarantaal* were eating all the mealies.

Their sundowners lasted longer than usual and Bester called for bread and cheese. His servant girl brought the crusty loaf hot and yeasty straight from the big coal stove that is a part of most Afrikaner country kitchens. The cheese was from a neighbour's farm and the butter from Bester's own cows. Smaller couldn't remember when he had enjoyed such simple food more. Six beers later he stood up refusing

Bester's invitation to supper with his wife and two small sons but promising to come later in the week for a *braaivleis*. He staggered off to the VW and headed back through the mealie fields. Guinea fowl ran across the track in front of him and a hare zigzagged, trapped in the beams of his headlights. As he neared the hill, Smaller thought of bed and a last whisky. It must be the fresh air, he thought, blinking tiredly.

Subaye followed the same track through the mealie fields as Smaller, but the journey that had taken him less than twenty minutes in the VW would take her more than twice that long even though she ran now, lightly and gracefully, feet skipping over the rough terrain. Occasionally she would hear the swift scamper and rustle of a small body disturbed by her almost noiseless passage. But she felt no fear because she had been moving around in this territory since she was old enough to walk and, unlike some rural Africans, had little regard for the powers of darkness and the spirits that the old ones really seem to believe in.

Some fifteen minutes out from Bester's farm Subaye passed through the edge of a copse that bordered the maize fields. Here she felt a little apprehensive because of the darkness, due to the oppressive proximity of the thorn trees hanging low over the track. She increased her speed and her heart pounded rythmically in her chest when she heard a larger animal moving in the undergrowth. But it could only be a jackal of which there were many in these parts. Wherever there were *tarantaal* or guinea fowl, as the white English-speaking people called them, the jackals would be in evidence.

To occupy her mind Subaye thought of the animals and birds of the veld as she ran on into the moonlight which made the veld almost as bright as day to her keen eyes. The farmers hated the *tarantaal* because they would do great damage in the mealie fields knocking down the tall plants to get at the corn in the husks which grew near the top. The clever *tarantaal* would peck away at the thick woody stem of the mealie plant like a tree-cutter with his axe and eventually the plant would fall to enable the *tarantaal* to have his prize. Some of the mealies in the good ground grew a head higher than a man and of course a big heavy bird like a *tarantaal* could not land on them or hover in the air whilst he ate from the husks. The smaller francolin used the same technique but he didn't do anything like as much damage as the huge flocks of *tarantaal*; some of them up to one thousand strong.

Of course, the sly old jackal fed well from the younger *tarantaal* which couldn't fly. The mother bird just laid her eggs in the mealie fields and they too were easy prey for the little *meerkats* and the black children who went looking for them in the spring. But despite all his enemies the *tarantaal* was a hardy bird and seemed to thrive mightily in the Magaliesberg. Subaye wondered where the *tarantaal* lived and what he fed on before the coming of the white man and his mealies but soon discounted the imponderable question. That was so long ago that perhaps then there were no *tarantaal*. Perhaps the white men brought them with them from their countries across the sea, although why they should want to bring such a greedy bird, she could not imagine.

Rounding a long bend in the track Subaye looked down from a slight gradient towards the base of a low hill across the short valley-floor of mealies. A light glimmered in the darkness and she could make out a faint white shape which could only be the little bus that Martin Smaller lived in. She had covered almost seven kilometres in just over fifty minutes; running with utmost concentration over rocky furrowed tracks and she stopped now on the the small crest to regain her wind. Breathing deeply and easily she walked carefully down the slope following the narrow path through the high brown stalks of maize. Above her the darkness was a deep velvet black with the moon soaring high over wraithlike ribbons of cumulus so that it seemed to be moving steadily across the huge expanse of night sky. Subaye smiled up at the moon because she had always loved its silvery gentle light and the twinkle of its little children scattered all around like corn spilled from a large bowl.

As she neared the VW Subaye heard music playing and saw that the little window in the roof of the bus was open. The light from inside was dim so she couldn't see any sign of Smaller although she knew he must be in there. Perhaps he would be sleeping although it must still be three hours before the moon would begin to sink. She walked closer, wondering what she should do if he was in bed, her resolve faltering at this imminent point of renewed contact with the fascinating white man from her dream.

Monday had been one of the best days Temba had ever had. The young boy had appeared magically late on Sunday evening and paid their fines. The desk sergeant had grimaced at them, seeming to resent the fact that they were being released. 'Just you watch yourselves in future *jou skellems*. If we pick you up next Saturday you'll sit for a week, no mistake, eh.' Temba and Tom had bent their heads respectfully but Benjie had wanted the last word as usual and had talked back to the sergeant so that the man had come out from behind his desk and chased them out with his baton. 'Bloody *kaffirs*,' he had shouted into the dusk as they ran, following the teenage boy towards town. 'We'll see to you lot one of these fine days, don't worry about that. We'll sort you fokkers out once and for all – that I promise you.' They ran like children with Benjie giggling uncontrollably.

The Toyota panel van had been waiting and the door slid back as they approached. Zak's voice boomed from the dark interior 'In the back boys, I've got a drink for you too so just sit down and we'll drive out to Swartplaas. I need to talk to all three of you.'

They had talked for two hours, finishing off a bottle of Bols brandy and a couple of litres of Coca Cola. Then Ruby and Zak had left them saying that they would return in the morning. 'Don't any of you go to work tomorrow boys, I want to take you into Waltersville to show you something.' In the alcoholic bravado of Sunday evening Benjie and Tom had agreed to stay away from work and accompany Temba to the township but in the morning they had not arrived and Temba sat with a headache waiting for Zak, wondering whether *Baas* Swanepoel would find out that he was out of jail and give him the sack.

But Zak and Ruby had arrived as promised and they'd gone to Waltersville where there had been more brandy and beer with a fine lunch of real stewed steak and piping hot porridge. Zak had finally taken Temba to the ruins of the old single-roomed schoolhouse which stood beside the shiny new brick and corrugated iron structure built by the West Rand Administration Board. It had been opened recently by the mayor of Krugersdorp, the nearest town of any size.

The children had finished school for the day and it was past four o'clock when the three men entered the derelict building. Zak walked quickly to the raised stage at the far end and beckoned Temba closer. Then he bent down to unlock a trap door in the wooden floor. 'This is just a sample of what we've got Temba my boy,' he said and magically produced the short black-coloured gun. Temba looked at it in awe and finally took it in his hands. It seemed to belong there and he lifted it, pointing it towards the soft light from the window. Zak watched him carefully. 'You like it, eh boy,' he said quietly and Temba nodded, his head filled with the feel of the wonderful rifle. He didn't want to let it go.

Smaller had drunk two whiskies and now he lay in the cocoon-like darkness of the microbus in half-sleep, his mind rambling a little with the intake of alcohol. Outside the wind sighed gently through the maize stalks and occasionally an owl would hoot eerily from the valley, hunting successfully in the full moon. It was cool without being cold and Smaller was fully covered by the Dacron sleeping bag, the zipper pulled right up to his chin, his head supported by two down cushions he had brought from the townhouse.

He slept easily despite his shallow level of consciousness and then quite suddenly he came awake, all senses tingling with the surge of adrenalin into his bloodstream. Someone was outside. In the dim interior of the VW, Smaller's heart pounded and he groped cursing under his breath for the shotgun stashed under the bunk, he couldn't see anything and there was no room to pull out the long gun without first rolling off the bunk and going forward into the cab. Then the door handle turned and his senses screamed so that he shouted hoarsely, 'Who's there? Stay where you are or I'll shoot.'

The soft voice that answered was like a breath of warm *veld* breeze and his mind registered that there was no danger, that it was the girl, Subaye. Good Christ, what was she doing here at this time of the night? His mind raced and then his groin tightened. There could only be one reason, surely. Subaye called again softly although she had stepped back five paces from the door at the mention of a gun. 'It's me Martin, Subaye. I know it's late but I have to see you.'

Smaller was dressed only in underpants and he pulled the sleeping bag around him as he scrambled over the passenger seat to open the door. The girl stood there backlit by a silver wash of moonlight so that he could only see her silhouette, slim in slacks and a shirt, poised like a springbok ready to run. 'It's alright, Subaye, I was sleeping and you startled me, but now I'm OK,' said Smaller easily. 'Would you like a drink? We can sit inside upfront, I've got whisky and beer.'

The girl came forward shyly and Smaller caught the faint perfumed smell of her, a long-ago smell which brought back memories of his childhood holidays. Then he knew it, it was the perfume his old aunt had used, there had always been a bottle on her dressing table in the little cottage near Penzance in Cornwall. She had always smelled of it and

108

even the dainty lace cushions on her bed had been impregnated with the sweet, flowery scent. It was cheap enough and that's why the girl wore it. But she had put it on for him.

They sat together in the dim light of the cab both very conscious of the unmade bed behind them. Smaller was still groggy from sleep, his mouth dry and foul from the intake of alcohol. By contrast Subaye seemed warm and alive. Mingled with her perfume was a pleasing peppery smell which attracted Smaller immensely. He made excuses and left her sitting in the passenger seat while he trotted around the base of the hill to relieve himself. The moonlight was bright enough to bathe the *veld* in a soft watery light which was sufficient to read a watch dial by. Smaller noted that it was almost nine o'clock.

After the welcome emptying of his bladder, Smaller ran on a little further to the water tower and stripping off his underpants doused himself under the torrent of icy water. He shook himself like a dog and then thrust his face under the heavy stream, drinking in great draughts of soft pure rainwater, his hair plastered to his forehead and the water hammering onto the hard-baked earth, splattering red mud over his legs.

He jogged back worried now that the girl might have left but relieved to see that she was still there, just visible in the darkness of the cab as an indefinite form. Smaller's heart quickened as he ran up on the opposite side of the Kombi and tapped on the window so that the black girl started, her eyes showing whitely in the darkness of her perfect face. 'Hand me a towel, Subaye, you'll find one on the cupboard just behind your seat.' He waited whilst she rummaged about and then the towel was draped over the driver's window. Smaller took it and knotted it around his waist.

He was chilled now as he clambered into the back of the VW to pull on jeans and a shirt. All the time the girl sat quietly staring out at the tranquil night, waiting patiently for the beer she had asked for. Finally Smaller sat beside her, two cans of Lion lager in his hand. He gave one to her and opened his own with a pop. 'I'm sorry that they are not really cold, Subaye, but the fridge is broken and I didn't have time to get it fixed before I left Johannesburg.'

The girl smiled back, her teeth white and so regular that he marvelled again at their perfection. She opened her own beer and took a long pull. 'It tastes wonderful, Martin.' They sat silently in the pale light and then she leaned suddenly against him as a jackal barked on the nearby hill. He put his beer on the defunct fridge behind him and pulled her towards him. Immediately she twisted so that he could bring her body close to his. From only inches away he stared into the darkness of her eyes and then her lips opened and he pressed his onto them, his tongue probing into her warm clean mouth. She murmured a name and he thought it had been meant for him except that it sounded like Gregory. Then he forgot everything as her fingers ran up under his shirt and fluttered over his chest.

Subaye came three nights more in that first week and Smaller spent his lazy days aching for her, dreaming of her so that when she came he couldn't wait to hold her, kiss her and finally possess her. The depth of his need amazed him and he thought that it was perhaps the novelty of her colour and the racial prejudice that had been a part of his life since he had come to South Africa in the late sixties. But he rejected this because she was a woman like any other, indeed black but nonetheless beautiful, wanton and desirable. She seemed to take as much from him as he received from her. They had talked together until quite late into the night on two occasions and he had been surprised at the depth of her knowledge and use of English. But always she would leave before midnight to run home across the *veld*, never saying when she would return. She would just look at him with her huge brown eyes, moist and unblinking and say, 'I'll come when I can Martin. Maybe

110

tomorrow.' Then she would be gone, flitting off into the darkness like a night animal, sure-footed and free.

Loving her had been another experience for Smaller because of her almost animal intensity and virtually insatiable lust. She gave herself to him with a sensuality that both excited and frightened him. There was more to this girl than any man could read, thought Smaller as he lay in the bunk, his body still damp from their lovemaking. It was as if she saw in him something more than just a man, even a white man. She had a mystical quality that was oddly disturbing whilst being wildly appealing. At that precise moment he wondered how he was going to live without her.

In the lazy days that followed, Smaller took the .22 Anschutz rifle and wandered the hill and surrounding mealie fields. He saw guinea fowl in plenty which promised a good season's shooting in a few months time. There were francolin too, the smaller pheasant-like bird whose russet-brown plumage made it almost indistinguishable from the rich clay soil of the region. One early morning Smaller took the .22 and walked halfway up the hill and then sat down on his haunches to wait. He knew that a colony of hares lived in the low bush-covered mound which encircled almost half of the hill like a ridge of scar tissue. The range was around fifty metres and Smaller was dressed in olive drab slacks and blotched camouflage bush shirt. The barrel of the Anschutz rested in the fork of two branches of a low thorn bush behind which he was partially concealed. It had been fully light for only a few minutes; Smaller knew the hares would soon come out to feed.

He had not washed and was still half asleep. It was very silent and peaceful in this early light. Smaller's back rested against a smooth grass-covered hillock and he felt totally relaxed and comfortable here in the silent *veld*. Johannesburg seemed aeons away and he was at one with himself and the bush. His eyelids drooped.

He was back in his childhood in England, in the back

garden of the semi-detached house in Bristol. In his hand was the BSA Meteor, a .177 calibre air-rifle that his father had given him for his birthday. It was young Martin's most prized possession and every evening after school he would sit in the garden with a pocket full of lead pellets, plinking away at cans and targets and, occasionally, at birds. His father had told him that if he ever caught him shooting at birds the gun would go and he, Martin, would get a severe thrashing. But still he shot at the odd bird when he was sure that nobody could see him. He'd hit one or two and had carved little notches on the butt of the BSA. Even though he sometimes felt sorry for the birds once he had downed them, he still went after them from time to time and admitted to occasional feelings of incredible power when he stood over a fluttering sparrow or thrush and put the barrel to its tiny head, blowing out its brains with the lead slug. In the heat of the West Country summer he would shoot at flies which landed on the garden wall and they would disappear in a whitish pink mash, streaked in the centre with the fresh silver smears of the pellet.

Then one day he had taken the gun out into the garden after supper and hunted about in the overgrown bottom end which he called 'the copse'. There had been no birds around but he had stayed hidden, being filled with a burning desire to kill something. The feeling was a pleasing, if not delicious, one and his adolescent body had erected so that he felt hot and masterful. It was then that the seagull had flown overhead. Martin had shot at circling gulls before and always led them well, being aware of the puny velocity of his tiny lead pellet. Once or twice he had actually hit them and the faint plop of the slug striking would cause the gull to wheel casually away with an almost patronising disregard. He knew there was absolutely no chance of doing them much harm.

It was an early summer evening. This time the gull was lower and it turned slowly overhead on a thermal a little to the right of Martin's concealed position amongst the bramble bushes of the copse. He aimed about a yard in front of it and pulled the trigger, the BSA coughed out the slug at a range of around eighty feet and nothing happened. Martin thought he had missed and then there was the thwack of the tiny rounded piece of lead hitting the body of the bird. The gull gave a surprised squawk.

The impossible occurred. The gull continued its wheel to the right and then its left wing folded suddenly and it began to shriek horribly as it spun into a tight spiral and plunged earthwards. Martin watched, mesmerised, as the large bird crashed through the roof of Mr Wallace's greenhouse next door, shattering the glass panes and falling into his precious tomatoes where it fluttered and lurched about, desperately trying to flap into the air, upsetting plant pots and containers of fertiliser. The noise was awful and Martin crouched terrified in the copse knowing there would be severe retribution for this, the best shot he had ever made. The tiny .177 pellet had shattered the thin elbow joint of the gull's wing, but otherwise the big bird was very much alive and the squawking and shrieking continued. Added to it were the shouts of Mr Wallace, the screams of his wife and the yapping of her Scottish terrier. To Martin it seemed that the nightmare would never end.

It did, however. The RSPCA came and took the lame bird away to be destroyed. Martin had crouched in the garden until his father had come for him and had been dragged into the kitchen where two large men waited for him. Both were policemen. The BSA had been confiscated and there was talk of a juvenile court and hundreds of pounds in damages to Mr Wallace's greenhouse, let alone the loss of the prize tomato plants, their delicate stems broken by the flapping of the demented gull.

Martin had been thrashed with a thin Malacca cane that his father had brought back from the war; he had called it his swagger stick. He had been locked in his bedroom every night for a week after supper while his mother continued to rant and rave at him. Eventually her husband had tired of the continuing tirade, which centred mainly around 'what the neighbours would think' and 'the terrible disgrace of having a son going to a juvenile court, let alone the shame of having the police knocking at one's door'. He had told her to shut up and leave the matter alone, saying that boys will be boys. 'Who would have thought that an air-rifle would bring down a seagull anyway?' he'd said with a half smile.

The juvenile court had never materialised although Martin had lived in dread for several weeks. The police had dropped the matter after Mr Smaller had settled Mr Wallace with a cheque for eighty-seven pounds. Martin's pocket money had been stopped indefinitely and the BSA Meteor was sold via the smalls in the evening newspaper. It was to be five years before Martin was to own another gun and this one he bought himself when he was old enough to do so by British law. It was a second-hand single-barrel Webley 12 bore shotgun and it was to start him on his hunting career; a pastime which he loved dearly and would never tire of.

He awoke without any surge of adrenalin into his bloodstream, but something had brought him back from the daydream. There on the bank, a little over forty metres in front of him and slightly to the left, were two big hares nibbling contentedly at the dew-fresh *veld* grasses. Smaller felt the usual butterflies in his stomach in anticipation of the kill and manoeuvred slightly to the right in order to swing the barrel of the Anschutz onto his target. He squinted through the Tasco telescopic sight, very much awake now and trying to breathe slowly, bringing the crosshairs round smoothly onto the nearest hare.

The .22 had a ten-shot magazine and this was loaded with hollow-point 'Blitzer' high-velocity ammunition. Smaller's finger clicked off the safety catch at the base of the trigger guard and centred the hare in his sight. Through the bright viewfinder he could see every detail, this was a mature animal its fur a rusty beige colour. The crosshairs centred below the left ear and Smaller exhaled slowly and squeezed the trigger. The Anschutz cracked sharply and the tiny bullet travelled the distance to the hare's head in under a tenth of a second, Smaller saw the slight puff of dust from the strike.

The hare just fell over onto its side without moving from its head-down feeding position but its mate quivered into a haunches-up stance poised for flight. It took Smaller one and a half seconds to bring the rifle to bear but just as he did so the hare took off with an enormous bound so that, as he fired, the bullet struck low crashing through the base of the rib cage, penetrating both lungs before passing out the other side.

Adrenalin and the strength of its huge back legs thrust the hare down the hill in four great bounds but within thirty seconds it was virtually dead on its feet and Smaller trotted down to it to fire his third shot into its head so that it shuddered for a final instance and then lay still. He gathered up the first hare and, carrying both by the legs, walked contentedly down to the VW. He would drive through to Bester's farmstead to give the animals to him. Perhaps the farmer's wife would invite him to share one with them later in the week.

Temba had heard the rumour from one of the girls working at *Baas* Hofmeyer's. Scandal spreads faster amongst Africans than in comparable white circles, even with the help of a far more sophisticated media. It was unthinkable. His Subaye with a white man! He still refused to believe it, but in his heart he knew that it could be true. She had always been flighty, fickle even, and a dreamer ever since he'd known her. His friends had always said that she was one of those women who would never know her place, would never serve him without question as a good wife should. Benjie had often laughed at the way she treated him.

But Temba loved her. He had tried to see her but for the past twelve days she had been unapproachable to the point of rudeness and towards the end of the week he had begun to think about the possibility of another man. It seemed that she had finally found something better for herself but he could not just accept it and let her go. Vague tales of the way the white men had behaved before the Boers got into government in 1948 filtered into his mind. His mother had told him stories and there were more than a few colour-eds in Magaliesberg; they had to have originated from somewhere.

He had to find out for sure, confirm the terrible suspicions that haunted his sleep but in the meantime, tonight, he had to see Zak and Ruby. The following day would be Wednesday and it was Benjie's birthday party which he just couldn't miss. But on Thursday he would go to see what that bitch, Subaye, was up to and wait for her to come from the white man's bed. Then he would beat her like the slut she was. Temba could visualise it clearly; he would hammer her into submission and then she would scream for him to stop. Eventually he would have her at his mercy and she would let him do anything to her and beg forgiveness. Perhaps he would take her back even though the loss of face would be great; at least he had a plan of action. He would take the Ford and park it near the crossroads then walk the last two or three kilometres to *Baas* Bester's farm. That loudmouth, Annie, had said that the white man was camped by the old mine workings where, it was said, the spirits of the dead lived. There had been a rock fall which had killed over fifty back in the twenties and it was said that their spirits still lived in the pigeons which had made a home there on the hill. Temba shuddered, it was an evil place and he would be afraid to go there. He marvelled at Subaye's lack of fear, but she had always been like that, ridiculing the talk of spirits, having no time for the old ways.

Temba walked lightly along the road towards Boons and the township. He felt better now that he had worked out the way to deal with Subaye. He could relax and bring his mind back to other matters like the ANC and his member-ship within its growing ranks. They had given him the AK

47 and he had been terrified, carrying it under his coat back to his village. Every moment that he was within sight of the tarmac where Zak had dropped him, saying that he had to get used to carrying the gun, he'd been expecting police vehicles to appear out of nowhere. He had visualised armed riot police pouring out of jeeps, mowing him down before he could move. But there had been no problems and he had walked the few kilometres to his village and buried the rifle in a black plastic refuse sack which Zak had given him. It was well away from the village in a bunch of blue-gum saplings and he was quite sure that nobody except him could ever find it under the carpet of dead leaves he'd brushed over the spot. Just this weekend he'd gone to look at the hiding place and had resisted digging to see if the gun was still there, knowing that he wanted to hold it again, heft it and point it, sighting on imaginary enemies. He had taken one of the shiny copper and steel bullets from the magazine to show it to Subaye, but now she wouldn't be seeing it; certainly not after becoming tainted with the white man. He now accepted the situation and felt that he might eventually settle the problem of Subaye by being an ANC member, he would find a way to deal with her; now there were more important matters at hand.

Zak sat in the hot smoky interior of the mud brick house which was typical of those in Waltersville. The shanty had a corrugated iron roof and there was an open grate at one end which had no chimney. The smoke was left to exit through a covered hole in the flat roof which was constructed from four bricks over which was placed a piece of tin; another two bricks kept this in place. Once the fire was well established the atmosphere was bearable, but when it had just been lit it was best to stay outside to avoid asphyxiation.

He and Ruby were pleased with the recruiting lately. There had been more than a few young men who had joined the cause. He drank deeply from his water glass of Coca Cola, laced with cane spirits, thinking of the boy Temba.

He would be a good one to train further because he was bright and eager to learn. Zak thought that the future looked good. Perhaps soon they could begin operations here in the Magaliesberg and knock some of those racist white farmers off their perches like the comrades had in Natal quite recently. Of course, the best target would be the police station, but he wasn't ready for that, especially with the bastard riot police around. They were bloody killers that crowd, he knew about them alright and the young psychopaths that made up their ranks. The thoughts sobered him but then there was a knock on the door and he heard Temba call softly from outside. He smiled to Ruby. The boy was keen alright. 'Come in little brother,' he said warmly.

For Subaye the days that had passed with Smaller were like a fairy tale come true. In actual fact, it was just that. Her dream of Gregory had turned into a reality and in the hot, noisy sheds at Hofmeyer's farm she worked automatically, her mind filled with thoughts of the white man. As always, her hands moved almost involuntarily, sorting and sifting, but her eyes had a faraway look and her friends noted her dreamy expression. It was fat little Annie who had asked her and she had told her, feeling a compulsion to share her burgeoning emotions with someone, even if Annie wasn't really a close friend.

Now everyone knew and the word spread throughout the farms and African *kraals* in the Swartplaas area. Subaye was regarded with differing reactions which ranged from hate through envy to jealous bantering and even open admiration. Annie and Beatrice the tall Zulu girl who was a friend from childhood, wanted to know the intimate details of Subaye's relationship with Martin. But she could not tell them, would not reveal the feelings he brought out in her, the heights to which he took her. Subaye just smiled when they whispered and giggled and asked about his maleness and how big it was and what colour. But her air of confident satisfaction told its own tale and Beatrice knew her friend well enough to realise that something very important had happened in Subaye's life.

Although she regarded Martin Smaller with almost godlike admiration and affection, Subaye was sensible enough to know that theirs was a dangerously unique situation, a relationship which was doomed from the outset. Whilst her mind accepted this, she dreamed of somehow moving with Martin to another place, a country far from South Africa where they could live together in peace and make a home for themselves. She had even considered the unthinkable; perhaps, one day, they might even have children.

To Smaller, Subaye was just what he needed, something completely different to what he had experienced in the past. She was almost a part of this rugged Magaliesberg country, a girl of the earth. Of Africa. She excited him beyond belief and he had admitted to himself that no other woman had ever taken him to those levels sexually. She seemed to burn with a passion of such depths that having her was like sinking into a bottomless pool of warmth and sensuality. He wondered what he would do back in Johannesburg. All women would pale, literally and figuratively, into insignificance when compared to Subaye.

Dozing in the pleasant warmth of a late afternoon autumn sun Smaller considered the problem at length and rashly came up with an answer. He would take her back with him to Johannesburg. She could be his maid in the townhouse, just like an *au pair* girl in England. He remembered Uncle Cyril and his Dutch *au pair,* Machteld, she'd been big and flaxen-haired, then one day she had left very suddenly. He remembered asking his mother about all the family mutterings and she'd told him to mind his own business. 'You'll understand when you're older,' she'd said.

Smaller was looking forward to the dinner at Bester's. Luna Bester had thanked him for the hares and asked him to come on Thursday for supper. Bester had been away in Magaliesberg so Smaller had not seen him when he dropped off the game. Now, in the deep russet glow of dusk, he drove slowly towards the yellow lights of the farmhouse which could be seen in a low fold of the hills, even though he was some four kilometres away. It was a wonderfully still evening as the VW chugged along the narrow track through the mealie fields in third gear. Smaller was in no hurry. He wanted to savour the magic of the twilight; the sights and sounds of the darkening *veld*.

Dark blobs stood out like small drops of ink on the graph-paper-like trellis silhouette of the electricity pylons along the track. Smaller knew these to be guinea fowl sitting to roost and the hunter in him longed for the .22 rifle with its telescopic sight. He had shot the birds like this before, from a vehicle, crawling quietly to a halt and then poking the barrel out of the window, centring the cross hairs on the dark rounded blob, made much sharper by the light-gathering lenses. The crack of the rifle would be followed by a slight movement in the target, then the guinea fowl would totter backwards off its man-made perch fifty feet above the earth. Seen briefly in the telescopic sight, its wings would open involuntarily as it plummeted to earth.

Finding them was more difficult than shooting them because the blackness of the *veld* was absolute after the lighter glow of the evening sky. Sometimes he had lost one or two but, more often than not, he would find the big warm bird stone dead, its neck broken from the fall even should it have survived the tiny high-velocity bullet.

A hare scampered ahead in the headlights and Smaller accelerated slightly, up to forty kilometres an hour, chasing the terrified animal which seemed pinned within the cone of light. Then, as the track twisted, the hare escaped the beams and was gone, disappearing between the high maize stalks. Smaller drove on slowly, smiling into the night, revelling in the twilight bushveld with its birds and animals and the sounds they made in preparation for sleep. The VW puttered quietly as Smaller drove with one hand, his other resting on the window ledge. He felt at peace with himself, more so than at any other time since the loss of his family. Pleasing hunger pangs gnawed at his stomach and his mouth salivated in anticipation of the coming meal. Later there would be Subaye but first solid, tasty food and the two bottles of good Cape wine which lay behind him in the tiny larder. Ahead in the headlights was the hard-packed red clay driveway of the farmhouse and Bester's dogs bounding out to meet him. It seemed that life was really worth living again.

Bester had heard the rumours but found it difficult to accept them. Of course, young Smaller was an Englishman, a *rooinek,* not one of the *volk* like himself. Bester knew that in England and America whites and blacks co-habited quite openly and even married. He found it hard to imagine such goings on and had never been able to touch a black woman since that time he'd tried in Lourenço Marques, back in the old days when the Portuguese still had control. She'd been a coloured really, not very black and young enough; slim, quite pretty with bright red lipstick.

Bester had been in Moçambique on a fishing trip with old Loots Smit and Hennie Oosthuizen. They'd had a skinful of the weak LM beer which you thought you could drink by the gallon without it affecting you. Pissed as tarts they were that night, that was for sure. The girls had approached them in a bar and Hennie, who spoke a bit of Portuguese, had said why not, so they had all gone off down countless back streets to creep up slippery stairs that stank of stale urine. Finally, they'd been led into a filthy flat which had two bedrooms. Hennie had disappeared with one girl and Loots with another. Bester had been left alone with the third in the seedy, brightly lit lounge.

The girl had pulled him down onto the threadbare sofa and unzipped the fly of his shorts. Then she'd started on him very skilfully and he'd begun to react despite the alcohol in his blood. She'd sat back, pulled up her dress and taken off her panties and he'd suddenly caught the rank fishy odour of her and had to swallow over and over again to prevent himself from throwing up. That had been that, he'd collapsed like a limp little boy whilst the girl sucked and pulled at him to no avail. Sickened, he'd stumbled up, shouted for the others and dropped a bundle of escuedos on the floor. Loots had said he'd made it and by the smell on him Bester thought it quite possible, but Hennie had also failed – 'overcome by fumes' as he put it.

Danie Bester smiled into the waning twilight remembering. Those had been the days alright. The three of them had had plenty of fun in Cape Town and Durban, especially at Umhlanga Rocks where Hennie's father kept a holiday cottage. There had been the three Free State schoolteachers and the two Jewish girls whose husbands were doctors in Jo'burg. Bester sipped his cold Castle lager, reminiscing on his formative years. Now all three of them were married and Hennie lived down in the Karoo, farming ostriches on a huge homestead left to him by his father's childless brother, the legendary *Oom* Piet Oosthuizen. *Oom* Piet was said to have been the richest man in Oudtshoorn and his father before him had been a millionaire at twenty-one, from ostrich feathers in the boom years of the twenties.

Old Loots lived over in Klerksdorp and occasionally came to Swartplaas for a *braaivleis* on Sundays. He had his own panel-beating and spray-painting shop and seemed to be doing alright although he always pleaded poverty. Bester's memory returned to his youth and the dreams he had of being an airline pilot, a doctor and finally a lawyer in that order. He smiled ruefully; here he was farming mealies in the Magaliesberg, like his father and grandfather before him. A faint glow of light caught his attention and he knew it to be headlights coming through the mealies from the direction of the hills. The Englishman was on his way to supper. Bester smiled again into the darkness, tonight could be an interesting evening, he thought.

Smaller parked the Kombi and jumped out to be engulfed by the bounding hounds. Bester was silhouetted on the *stoep* of his low rambling farmhouse and he called out softly to Smaller, 'Come on Martin, man. The beers are getting warm and just now Luna will call us in to table.' Smaller walked swiftly over to the long wooden verandah as Bester bent to the door of the ancient General Electric refrigerator in the corner. 'Nice and cold, eh. Just as a man should drink it after a long day.'

They sat in the rustic comfort of the *stoep,* in massive chairs made long ago in solid teak and upholstered with the tough rawhide strips that the Afrikaners called *riempie.* Bester began to talk, rambling on about his farm and the worryingly poor harvest this year which was due to a lack of steady rains early in the growing season. 'I tell you, Martin, if we don't get good rains in the spring this year it could well wipe some of us farmers out. The bloody weather has gone *bedonnered* man. *Ag,* but what a bloody way to earn your living, eh.'

Smiling into his beer glass, Smaller considered Bester's words. The *platteland* farmers were well known for the simplicity of their lifestyle but Smaller suspected that there were many of them who were incredibly rich, far wealthier than the so-called mink and manure set of Johannesburg's northern suburbs. It was true to say however, that one wouldn't think so to look at them. Bester was a good case in point, thought Smaller. He drove a Datsun truck most of the time, although there was an ageing BMW 2000 in the garage. It had belonged to Bester's father and was still used to take the family to church in Magalicsberg on Sundays.

The farmstead's furniture was even older, although it was solid and simply designed. Luna Bester cooked on a coal stove, a huge one, which was never allowed to go out, winter or summer. As a farmer's wife, she prepared three meals a day for her husband who rose at 5.30 a.m., ate breakfast and returned from his fields at 12.30 for lunch. Supper was the most important meal of the day however and each evening there would be two roast meats followed by heavy puddings and coffee. Tonight, Luna had prepared a topside roast in addition to the casseroled hare. There was enough food for twelve, although there would only be five of them, including the two boys.

They sat at the massive yellowwood table in the brightly lit dining room and two black servant girls brought in a vast tureen filled with soup. Smaller's taste buds discharged saliva into his mouth at the smell and he licked his lips in anticipation, only now realising how hungry he was. It had been almost ten days since he had eaten hot food and weeks since he'd had a home-cooked dinner.

Luna Bester watched the *Engelsman* and smiled to herself as her oldest boy clasped his hands and began to say grace rapidly in Afrikaans. She noted that Martin Smaller bowed his head and put his hands together in his lap and that he muttered 'Amen' at the end. Good, she thought, he's a Godfearing man even though he is English. He was a nice-looking man too, this Martin, and she wouldn't have minded meeting up with him in Jo'burg twelve years ago before she met Danie. She'd had all sorts of plans to travel overseas to England and the Netherlands and perhaps even America one day.

And what happened? She'd met Danie and he'd swept her right off her feet. And right into his bed too, although her father would have killed her if he'd known it then. That had been it, a *fait accompli,* as she knew the Frenchies called it. She'd wanted to go to France too. Still they'd made money out of the farm these past ten years and Danie had plenty now so perhaps one day they'd go on a world tour. He promised her every year and she had shelves full of brochures on all sorts of tours, but every time it was 'maybe next year'. There was always some problem, some crisis with the land or the *donderse* crops.

Luna smiled at Martin Smaller, proud of her cooking. 'This is a real Boere soup Martin – *boontjie sop* we call it, but it has in it *skaap,* I mean sheep.' She hesitated. 'No, it's lamb that you call it, eh. I make it with the neck of the *skaap* and thicken it up with butter beans that we soak overnight. They come from *Meneer* Swanepoel's. He grows a few, just for us farmers in the Magaliesberg.'

Smaller smiled back at Luna Bester and not just because of her quaint use of English. She was an attractive blonde Afrikaans woman in the classic blue-eyed Dutch tradition. No coloured blood there, he thought quickly. 'This is really wonderful, Luna,' he said and sipped again at the soup. It was thick and tasty with bite-sized chunks of tender lamb and the soft but crunchy beans.

Bending to his bowl, Danie Bester watched the exchange of comments and the light that shone in his wife's eyes. She was a beauty, his Luna, and he could see that she liked this *rooinek*. It was quite natural though, he was a good-looking bugger alright and Luna had always liked foreigners, wasn't she always going on about travel and foreign countries like Hong Kong and Bangkok. But they were different the English. Cold, austere people as a race and so into themselves and their bloody little island that they thought was the centre of the world. Strange that this *rooinek* should want to go and lie with a *kaffir* girl, that was usually something that only the Germans did. They were crazy for the blacks. He remembered them in Lourenço Marques and Beira, like dogs on heat, chasing the *kaffir* women.

Bester considered himself a liberal, a *verligte,* an enlightened man. Yet he could not condone what Martin Smaller was supposed to have done with this black girl. Smaller was wealthy enough, Bester knew that. He had lost his wife and child, the papers had been full of it, but they had not discussed it since Martin had arrived. Still, Smaller had money from that magazine that he sent to Luna free of charge and which she would pore over, looking at all those fancy houses in Durban and Johannesburg.

Luna looked up at him reproachfully as he sucked noisily at his soup. She spoke quietly in Afrikaans. 'You eat just like the children Daniel, in fact you're worse, man. For the Lord's sake have some manners in front of our guest.' Bester grunted and smiled back at her and then at Smaller who

125

had noticed the aside. I wonder what Luna would think if she knew that this *rooinek* friend of ours was rutting with a *kaffir* girl. He smiled knowingly at his wife and tore a huge piece of bread from the fresh loaf; he began to wipe out his soup bowl.

Smaller's bottles of riesling and cabernet went fast and Bester opened two more bottles of red. The hare was delicious and Smaller gorged himself on two portions of the rich gamey stew. Then he went on to thick slices of rare topside beef with roast potatoes, green beans and roast pumpkin. He sat back and drank deeply from the glass of water he had asked for. 'That was one of the best dinners I've had for many a year Luna,' he said and meant it.

Later, after a piece of syrup pudding that he only just managed to finish, Smaller sat with Bester on the *stoep*. Luna had gone off to bed. The two men relaxed in silence, staring out into the blackness of the nightime *veld*, replete with food and drink, alone with their thoughts. On the old pine table were two rough earthenware mugs, a battered copper coffee pot and a bottle of Oude Meester brandy with a couple of water glasses. Smaller sighed contentedly and offered his pack of Villigers to Bester.

Now's the time to ask him, thought the Afrikaner, as he lit the square cut mild cigar. I must discuss this matter with him now, whilst his defences are down and he's relaxed. But how can I? I like this man, how could I ruin what has been a perfect evening? 'When will you be going back to Jo'burg Martin?' he asked innocently. 'Not that I mind, man. You can stay as long as you like for all I care on the matter. It's been a pleasure having you here with us,' he added, almost as an afterthought.

Through the cushioning clouds of good fellowship, brought on by the vast meal and the quantity of beer, wine and brandy he had drunk, a bright light of warning shone briefly. He's heard, thought Smaller as he stared out into the limitless blackness of the night sky. He knows about Subaye. He turned to look at his sometime friend, Danie

Bester, a man he had shot with over the last four seasons, a good man with a wonderful wife and children. He'd invited them out to dinner once when they had been up in Johannesburg. This man didn't need his problems, didn't need any scandal in his small close-knit society.

'It's been wonderful Danie, but I'll have to go back. In fact, I think I'd better make a start tomorrow, otherwise Luna won't be getting any more *Lifestyles*!'

Bester smiled sadly into the darkness of the *stoep*. He knew Smaller couldn't see him but he felt an infinite regret, a sense of loss. He stood up and thrust out his hand, 'I'll see you out to the Kombi, man. Drive carefully now through the mealie fields, eh.'

Subaye ran carefully through the veld. The moon was now on the wane and she could not see as well as earlier in the week when she had last visited Martin. Her heart pounded lightly in her chest but she breathed easily, her eyes locked on the undefined track through the rough *veld* grass. She knew that an unseen rock or jackal hole could mean a turned ankle or even a broken leg.

She reached the top of the ridge which sloped down to the shallow valley where Martin camped. Here the mealie fields petered out into thorn bushes against the side of the hill where the pigeons lived. The old ones said it was a place of spirits but Subaye cared little for that superstitious claptrap – had she not spent four nights there with Martin and never seen or heard a thing which was not normal?

Jogging lightly over the rise she looked for the little bus. There was no sign of it, no lights, nothing. Now her heart beat increased and an odd fearfulness gripped her. He had gone, Martin had gone. Back to Johannesburg and his magazine, back to his white world where she could never find him, could never be with him. Then she remembered. He had said that he was going to visit *Baas* Bester. Perhaps he was still there, her eyes turned to the east, towards Bester's farm, searching in the darkness. But there were no yellow lights penetrating the blackness of the chest-high sea of mealie plants. She squatted on her haunches and looked up at the moon. It was only about ten o'clock. She would wait for him.

Temba had arrived earlier and he too had been disconcerted by the absence of the VW Kombi, a vehicle that he would dearly love to own. He had sat down to wait, on the ridge overlooking the little dip in the hills, ranging down towards the place where the spirits were supposed to live. Temba admitted to a certain fear. This was the place where the white man camped, right here where the spirits walked; it just proved the madness of the white people. But he knew they did not believe in the nightwalkers, the beings that his people knew existed.

As the minutes and eventually the hours passed, his fear gave way to a mounting rage. It seemed inconceivable that the white man had just gone, disappeared without trace. Now there would be no way in which he could prove that Subaye had lain with him. Temba's fists clenched in futility as he realised that there was now no chance of catching her as he had planned. He stretched his legs and prepared to rise when there was a movement over to the left of his position, and the rattle of small stones. He peered intently into the blackness and made out a slight, dark, figure. It must be Subaye – she had come to see the white man and was waiting just like he was. Temba smiled mirthlessly into the night and rose silently stretching stiff leg muscles.

Subaye had her back to him peering into the east, willing the lights of the Kombi to appear. She had almost given up hope when she caught a glimmer of yellow light in the distance and her heart seemed to rise in her breast. It disappeared and then was there again and then she saw two definite lights. She leaped to her feet and drew a huge breath of happiness. She would run down the ridge to meet Martin.

Temba moved quickly. He too had seen the headlights

128

and he knew that he had to close swiftly with the girl before she could make a move down the ridge. He angled in, cutting her off and grabbed her from behind as she took her first step down the slight incline.

She squealed in alarm and they fell together into the grass, his body on top, knocking all the breath out of her lungs. Then he was up and dragging her back by the waist, over the lip of the ridge, his hand covering her mouth. His nostrils caught the clean perfumed smell of her and this seemed to enrage him even more. He felt his groin begin to stiffen. When they were a good twenty paces from the crest, he threw her to the ground and stood over her panting.

Subaye's shock and terror decreased when she recognised Temba. She had always been able to handle him and now, as she looked up at him, her mouth curled in derision. Her words were calculated to sting, to shatter his already bruised ego. 'Oh, it is the strong Temba who can only fight with women. Isn't Benjie here to help you or your brave friends from the bush?' She sneered at him and made to rise and Temba's reason broke. He kicked out, catching her on the shoulder, knocking her flat on her back. Her short denim skirt had ridden up exposing the long slender legs that he had known so well. In the half-light of the moon he could dimly see her brief white panties and he bellowed like an animal, crazed with jealousy. He fell on top of her and tore at her clothes mouthing obscenities in her ear.

'You filthy slut, lying with a white man. I loved you, Subaye, I wanted to marry you and you betrayed me.'

Subaye felt his knee forcing her legs apart. She was strangely calm, knowing he was going to rape her, accepting and not caring, not allowing him any satisfaction from her struggles. But then without warning he sat back and struck her back-handed across the face and she felt her lip burst, tasting warm saline blood on her tongue. Her head spun as the blood roared in her ears. Then he hit her again, cracking her head back onto hard ground. She tried to scream but only a strangled moan escaped her lips because his forearm pressed across her throat. Subaye looked up terrified into Temba's eyes and saw the momentary insanity there. She tried to roll from under him but the pressure on her throat increased and she couldn't draw breath. The noise inside her head got louder and then the sky seemed to blacken and red lights exploded in her brain. Finally, mercifully, there was nothing.

Temba looked down abstractedly at the unconscious girl underneath him and then fear hit him. He pressed his ear to her breast and listened frantically. Her heart still thudded there, the bitch was still alive. His rage returned in seconds and he rolled her over onto her stomach and with one savage pull, ripped the flimsy cotton panties from between her legs. Unzipping his jeans, he poised himself over her and then pushed her legs apart sinking into her. Such was his madness that it was over in seconds and he collapsed on top of her his great throbbing strength gone. She had not moved a muscle and he hated her for it.

He stood up panting, heart pounding, his mouth dry with tension and excitement. Subaye lay face downwards in the grass as though dead and again he bent to her back, placing his ear between her slender shoulder blades, checking for the heartbeat. It was there and her breathing was strong though ragged. Temba turned his back on her and strode off into the night. That was the end of it. She would remember him always for what he had done to her but he, he would forget her.

But strangely his eyes misted with tears as he stumbled off through the darkness and a pain began deep within his chest. He knew he wouldn't forget her, realised that the pain was only now starting. Perhaps the white man really had gone away and it could all be the same again, perhaps they could forgive each other. On impulse he turned to go back to her, to take her in his arms, but some hopelessness within him made him walk on. The anger had gone for the moment yet the pain would always remain. It seemed

130

somehow that this had all happened before, was almost predestined. As he walked on dejectedly, Temba wondered how it would end.

Smaller realised that he was more than a little drunk. He drove faster than he should have, bouncing the Kombi around on the narrow track, everything banging and crashing about in the lockers behind him. Something seemed to be hurrying him on, drawing him to the hill and he realised suddenly how late it was, well past ten, and Subaye would be waiting. Perhaps she might have given up, thinking that he had gone back to Johannesburg. His foot thrust the right pedal to the floor.

It had been three days since he had seen her and now he ached for her body. With the alcohol inside him he felt confident, even masterful, and he threw the VW around the blind bends with abandon. On his right side was a wire cattle fence and an extended copse of thorn bushes. On the left the endless oceans of maize stalks, silver-black in the light of the half moon.

The radio blasted out pop music from nearby Bophuthatswana and Smaller sat cocooned in the jouncing cab, wrestling with the flat steering wheel as he hurtled along the uneven surface. Although his mind was on the girl, his driving was automatic, but still the cumbersome vehicle bounced and shuddered as he barely missed potholes and cairns of rocks which the black labourers cleared from the fields and often left dangerously close to the narrow track.

Then he was over the last rise and out of the shroud-like embrace of the mealies. The hill was there ahead, like a dark crouching animal, just visible as an even blacker shape against the dark night sky. Smaller slewed the Kombi to a halt and switched off the power. The radio died with it and then in the dead silence small clinking sounds came from the rear as the hot engine cooled. He peered out through the big windscreen, the blood pounding in his temples after the crazy drive, but there was nothing. He had half expected

Subaye to come running into the headlight beams, racing down from the ridge, her feet flying over the thin *veld* grass.

Heart thumping with disappointment, he doused the lights flinching at the alien blackness. He forced himself to close his eyes and opened them after a minute when his retinas had adjusted to the dark. He could see dimly now, but there was no movement out there. He scrambled out of the driver's seat and lurched backwards towards the bed, feeling the drink, yet too lazy to get out and urinate. As he sank into sleep he felt an odd sense of foreboding and admitted to himself that he didn't want to go outside anyway, not until morning.

She dreams that Gregory goes away and leaves her in the settlement alone. He says that he must go because their fresh meat supplies are almost exhausted and, even more important, his tracker reports fresh elephant spoor only half a day's ride away in the Mopani forests to the north. He will be back in two days and promises her fresh impala steaks and as much ivory as she can lift. They will have money, he says. Money to build a real house, money to buy chairs and tables from the traders at the coast. Perhaps there will even be dresses for Subaye and whisky and tobacco for him. She wants to go with him but he refuses, saying that she must stay here in the settlement. 'A woman's place is in the home,' he says smilingly at her pouting face. She throws a pot of water at him and he laughs at her, then grabs her, kissing her long and hard. 'There is no danger now, my sweet, it is almost a year since we saw anyone. And there is Ndola who would guard you with his life, and our two fine hounds.' Still smiling, he mounts his horse and waves down at her. 'Goodbye, little one. I'll be back before sunset on Friday.' They come at night, poisoning the dogs and driving an assegai through old Ndola as he lies sleeping by the fire after his evening beer drink. She fights like a wildcat but the three of them easily overpower her and throw her to the ground. They mount her brutally one after

132

the other and then beat her with their fists and leave her insensible, spitting on her unconscious body. Subaye does not hear them laugh as they leave but she recognises the tall one. He is Vusi, Temba's brother, and he hurts her the most, violating her from behind so that she screams for him to stop. When he finishes he presses his lips to her ear speaking softly, his voice filled with menace. 'You are now the white man's whore, Subaye, the slut of the man who murdered my brother. Temba loved you but he lost you to the white man whom I have sworn to kill. But we will leave you alive so that he can see what we have done to you. Tell him not to search for us because he will not find us, we will find him when we are ready to. The white men will not take this land as they have from our brothers by the great water, we will strike in the night and kill them all. It may take many thousands of summers, but we will do it. Our sons and their sons will succeed eventually.' He turns her over and smashes a fist into her face. As she loses consciousness the words remain with her and the fear only fades as merciful blackness enfolds her.

There was dirt and gravel stuck to her torn lip and grass was matted into the dried blood on her face, but it was the biting of the ants that woke her. They milled around her open mouth, feasting on the fresh blood and saliva, ripping off miniscule pieces of flesh with their tiny, yet powerful jaws. Subaye's eyes flickered open but she was only able to see out of one eye because the other was pressed into the rough grass underneath her face. There was steady movement right in front of her line of vision but the distance was too close for sharp focusing. She imagined that she was still asleep and dimly recognised that she must have experienced a bad dream but the sharp little pains continued without her even moving a muscle.

Her brain began to awaken as she swam closer towards the surface of reality. There were ants eating her, vicious

133

centimetre-long carnivorous insects that could strip a sheep's carcass to the bone in a matter of days.

Subaye tried to rise, brushing the voracious insects from her raw lips with feeble pawing movements. Her jaw ached and her face felt puffy and stiff with pain. There was a strange soreness deep within her. She saw a pale light in the sky and rolled onto her back fighting upwards into a sitting position feeling the chill of dawn on her bare legs. Awareness came faster now and with it more pain but, with the age-old resilience of the African, she shook off the mutilations to her body and her brain refused to recall the happenings of the night. Unsure of what was fact or fantasy, yet recognising her location, she staggered up the ridge praying that Martin would be there. She reached the crest and looked down. There in the grey light of dawn she saw the little white bus. Her heart leapt and she staggered down the hill, moaning with relief.

Bester awoke with a dry mouth and groped in the dim light of his room for the pint mug of water that stood on his bedside table. He drained it greedily and rose from the bed carefully feeling his way down the short passage to the bathroom. He never used the lights because Luna was a restless sleeper and she didn't need to get up until seven when the children were made ready for school. His day began over two hours earlier but everything was organised, like the workings of a well-oiled machine, and he knew that his breakfast would be waiting for him on the stove. It was made by Ethel, the kitchen girl, who rose at 4.30 every morning, winter or summer.

As he shaved, Bester thought about last night's dinner and Martin Smaller. He felt better now, after his shower and the last few seconds of cold water battering onto the top of his head. He still had a headache but he knew from experience that once he had eaten his usual porridge and eggs he would be fit for the day. He sat in the warm kitchen sipping from his second mug of coffee thinking about his life and the endless days of toil on the farm. It was a good life though and he had nearly R150,000 on fixed deposit in the Standard Bank, Magaliesberg. Then there was the farm and the machinery, all paid off during the last five years. Bester's auditor reckoned that he must be worth at least three quarters of a million, conservatively speaking that was.

Bester shouted for Ethel and asked her to call Joseph the boss boy. He sat in the silent, comfortable kitchen listening to the faint shouts of his labourers coming from the small tractor shed that they used as a canteen. They would be swigging their tea from tin mugs and eating the huge chunks of bread and jam that Ethel prepared for them each morning. He looked at his watch, it was almost 5.30, time for the working day to start. As he finished his coffee he thought again of Martin Smaller. He would drive down to the bottom pasture and say goodbye. He had no hard feelings against the Englishman and the shooting season was coming up soon. He was a bloody fine shot that *rooinek*.

The sense of *déjà vu* was all pervading. Smaller's brain resisted waking as he twisted in his sleeping bag, scrambling towards consciousness unwillingly, his head heavy with last night's alcohol. Again he heard the sounds, small scraping noises coming from just outside in the grey dawn. He recalled the words of Bester as they sat out on the stoep before dinner on the first night they had met three years earlier. 'You know the old mine down there over the hill, Martin. There're a *moer* of a lot of pigeons living there, man. Nobody shoots the bastards either and they really stuffed up my sunflower crop last year. The *kaffirs* never go anywhere near the place because they reckon that those rock pigeons are the spirits of some ancestors or other killed in the mines years back. Silly buggers they are.'

It didn't seem quite so silly now in the chill silence of dawn when the sounds came again. Smaller stiffened, willing himself to do something. He couldn't just lie there terrified, like a child, ready to shove his head under the blankets.

135

Then he heard her soft voice, 'Martin, Martin, please help
– it's me, Subaye.'

Head pounding and his throat hot with bile, Smaller
rolled off the bed and opened the door. She lay in the dirt,
face upturned towards him and the vomit rose in his throat
at the sight of her. One eye was completely closed, her lips
were swollen and encrusted with dried blood. Her T-shirt
was filthy and there seemed to be blood on the washed
out denim skirt. He knew instinctively that she had been
assaulted, probably raped. The thought revolted and yet
angered him deeply so that he felt both sympathy and revul-
sion for the tattered, soiled, black girl at his feet. He thought
that perhaps it could never be the same for them again.

'Subaye', he shouted, 'what in God's name has happened
to you, what have they done to you?' His rage made the
words echo back from the nearby hill. He dropped beside
her and immediately recognised the rank odour that emanated from her body. 'Oh the bastards, the bloody swine,'
he moaned taking her in his arms and feeling the warm
wetness of her tears on his cheek. They lay there in the cold
veld for some minutes then Smaller dragged her to her feet
and propped her against the side of the Kombi. 'Stay here
quietly, don't move Subaye. I'm going quickly to get some
water to clean you off so that I can see if you're hurt. Just
stay here, I'll be back in a few minutes.'

Smaller darted around to the driver's door and grabbed
the plastic bucket from the floor behind his seat. Luckily he
was still dressed, having fallen asleep with his jeans and
shirt on. He ran over the silent morning *veld,* his brain
flashing unbelievable images of Subaye being raped. He
didn't want to acknowledge the thoughts but they could not
be suppressed and he accepted them with an odd, fascinating
horror which seemed to make them continue.

On reaching the water tower he pulled the handle to fill
the four litre bucket. He would perhaps bring her here later
if she was alright and wash her down when it was warmer.
In the meantime, the water would get rid of some of the

filth. He jogged back trying not to spill the pail. Subaye stood where he had left her, her one big brown eye open and staring fixedly out across the valley.

Smaller brought a plastic groundsheet and a towel. Guiding her down onto it he took a bar of perfumed toilet soap and crouched close to her head, looking down into the bloody face. 'I'm going to take your clothes off Subaye and clean you, but first let's wash your face to see what the damage is.' Tenderly he sponged away the blood and grime with the ice-cold water and the girl never murmured or flinched. Her bottom lip was torn but not too badly and the eye, although puffy, was not bleeding. Smaller cursed the fact that he had not brought a first-aid kit and then he remembered the Scotch. He tore a piece off the towel, making a pad which he soaked with Bell's before pressing it to her lip, then he made another and soaked this with a watered-down solution of whisky and pressed it to her eye. 'Just hold that in place for a minute or two Subaye, I'm going to find you some clothes to change into.'

He rummaged through his lockers and found a pair of pants with a tracksuit top of fleecy-lined cotton. Grabbing a second towel he returned to Subaye. He lifted the soiled skirt and saw the torn panties which he slid down her legs. She was unresisting, not saying a word when he slipped the T-shirt over her head and rolled her onto her side. Smaller took the new towel tearing it in half and then in half again. He soaked one small piece in water and then began to sponge the girl down, rolling her onto her stomach, then back onto her other side and finally onto her back. He prised her legs apart gently and she looked up into his eyes like a wounded animal and winced a little when he washed her between the thighs. Next he soaped her all over, then rinsed her again and finally dried her off as best he could with the other piece of towel. He managed to get her into a sitting position in order to pull the soft cotton top over her head and then manhandled the pants up her thighs.

She was now lying in the spiky grass to the side of the

wet groundsheet and he put one of her arms around his neck pulling her to her feet. He lifted her gently into his arms and laid her on the bed, covering her with the sleeping bag. She looked at him in the dim light of the interior and her torn mouth trembled. 'Thank you Martin, nobody has ever done anything like that for me in my life.' Her eyes closed and she fell asleep. Smaller looked down at her and his resolve hardened. Now he would have to take her back to Johannesburg. He began to pack up his few things and secure the VW for the journey. The remains of her clothes, the soiled groundsheet and the torn towels were left outside in the *veld*.

Bester felt much better. The sun was high and it was quite warm on the tractor as he pulled into the semi-circular dirt forecourt of the farmhouse. A quick cup of coffee, a couple of Luna's homemade rusks and he'd be off in the pick-up down to the bottom fields to see old *rooinek,* Martin, and say goodbye. He was a good bloke, that Smaller, and in the warm light of day Bester thought that all the talk about him and the *kaffir* girl was probably just a load of crap. The *kaffirs* loved to chatter about everything and he'd overheard them in the kitchen two days back gabbling on in Ndebele about some girl called Subaye and the young white man with the golden hair who was camped by the spirits' hill; there by the old mine.

Bester wound the little Datsun truck through the mealie fields. On the dashboard ledge in front of him was a packet of Lexington filters and he shook one out and lit it, driving with one hand, the unloaded *bakkie* bouncing over the corrugations made by the lack of rain. Bester sucked hard on the toasted cigarette idly thinking that he must grade the road again and get some of his boys to clear out some of the bigger rocks. Joseph would handle that, he always knew boys who would work on Sundays for a few extra rands.

Daydreaming and rattling along at forty kilometres an hour Bester almost collided with Smaller's VW which was coming fast in the opposite direction. Smaller pulled to the side of the track and Bester lurched into the mealies, knocking down at least twenty of his precious plants before he got back onto the dirt road. Both vehicles reversed back towards each other and both men jumped out. Bester noted that Smaller seemed strained. The poor bugger must have reckoned his last moment had come, he thought grinning openly. Hell, but it was close and his own heart was pounding loud enough no mistake.

'*Here* man, but that was close, eh?' Bester walked up to the Kombi and examined the high side of the vehicle. '*Hell*, man but I thought we had touched each other.' He slapped his thigh laughing. 'You look as if you had a bad fright Martin, man. Maybe you need a drop of something, what have you got to drink in there?'

Bester moved towards the cab and Smaller lurched sideways to intercept him. He grinned awkwardly. 'God, Danie, I reckon I did get a fright and what with my head from last night. I feel bloody awful!' With abrupt decisiveness he stuck out his right hand. 'Thank you for the hospitality my friend, it was wonderful to be out here away from the bloody city. But now I must get going, I've been absent from that magazine of mine for too long.'

Bester took his hand and Smaller grasped it once and then turned on his heel and climbed into the cab. He put his head out of the side window turning to wave. 'I'll see you in a month or so for the season, Danie. Cheers now.'

Bester watched as the Kombi lurched off up the track. A bloody funny lot the English, he thought as he dropped the cigarette into the dirt and ground it out with his heel.

CHAPTER 8

It was colder now and not quite light as Temba walked to work at *Baas* Swanepoel's. Four days had passed since the incident at the spirits' hill when he had taken his revenge on the white man by beating and raping Subaye. Somehow, he still couldn't believe that he had done it, beaten her insensible like that and then taken her like an animal. After he'd finished and run off into the night he'd tried to hate her but now he wanted her again and his feelings for her burned inside him like an incurable growth deep in his vitals.

As far as Zak and Ruby and the ANC were concerned, nothing had happened for some weeks. They had had a few beers and there had been brave talk about attacking a white farm, killing the oppressors of their country. Temba had become drunk like the rest of them and the excitement had gripped him, the blood lust that was a part of his heritage as a son of Africa. But on the mornings after, waking with a dry mouth and pounding head, it had all seemed so stupid and pointless so that he had begun to question the motives of the ANC and his own part in the organisation that seemed to wage its war with words alone.

Zak tried to keep Temba's interest alive. He would be waiting occasionally on the path from Swanepoel's farm, appearing out of the dusk as he had on that first night just a few short months ago. So much seemed to have happened since then and Temba accepted that the root of his disorientation and depression was Subaye. He admitted to himself that he loved her, loved her in the way that the American movies told it; like the silly stories in *Drum* and *Bona* magazines. He thought of a solution and remembered the rifle buried outside his village. Perhaps he should kill himself to end the torment.

Then as he jogged along, his heart beating hard yet easily and his breath puffing white into the chill highveld dawn, the germ of an idea began in his brain. He could take the rifle and kill them both. If he couldn't have Subaye then nobody else would. As quickly as the idea came he discounted it as ridiculous. One did not die on account of a woman. It would have been inconceivable to his fore-fathers to even consider such a thing. He had learned that they treated their women as chattels, mere vessels for their seed and for the making of food and the bearing of children. He tried to picture Subaye in such a role but the image would not form. It was true that she was different, very much so for a simple farm girl. That was Subaye's trouble, he thought angrily. She was too bloody smart, always trying to put him down. Even when they had made it together he always felt as if she were laughing at him. The thought made him erect, which was uncomfortable as he jogged along the ill-defined track. He swore loudly, he would have to see her again, perhaps even apologise. There was no way he could get her out of his mind.

Smaller's heart beat slowed as Bester's Datsun disappeared round a bend in the track in his rearview mirror. What a way to start the bloody day off, he thought. Thank the Lord that Bester hadn't managed to look inside the Kombi. Behind him the girl still slept. Probably exhausted from shock and exposure, thought Smaller. He began to plot his moves when they arrived in Johannesburg. He was playing a very dangerous game, that he realised without doubt, but there were ways of evading contact with the authorities and he knew that quite a few black whores operated in

Johannesburg, especially in Hillbrow. Not that Subaye was going to live there, of course. He wondered what she would say when she realised that he had spirited her off like this. Better that she sleep and he present the whole thing as a *fait accompli*. He could always run her back to Swartplaas if she created any drama.

Her injuries were not too bad. That was just as well because he couldn't take her to a black hospital in Johannesburg because then they'd want her passbook and registration details in his name. Smaller thought quickly. Various possibilities flashed across his consciousness as he drove out of the farm and onto the wider dirt road which led to the main highway and Magaliesberg. Such was his preoccupation that he failed to see Luna Bester waving goodbye from the farmyard.

He had a fairly comprehensive first-aid kit in the townhouse and he knew that Africans healed fast from rudimentary wounds. He recalled the time that he and Ashley had returned from a trout fishing trip to the Eastern Transvaal some years back. As they'd driven up the road in Ashley's car, Smaller had seen an African sitting at the side of the road and the headlights had picked up a blackish stain on the man's white shirt. He had been sitting on the pavement, head in hands, and there was something about him that looked odd to Smaller.

Ashley had ridiculed him, saying that the vagrant was just another drunken *kaffir*. But Smaller had insisted that he reverse. Having done so, they had shone the brights full on him and Smaller had climbed out. The African was quite young, in his mid-twenties or thereabouts. He had been struck several times across the front of the head with a cane knife or panga and, in the bright quartz iodine glare of the headlights, Smaller could clearly see the white bone of his skull from the terrible slashes. The man was quite lucid and asked for a cigarette which Smaller fetched for him whilst Ashley ran to his house to call an ambulance.

Smaller had grabbed Ashley's Rothmans from the car and

carefully lit one for the injured man. A slick curtain of blood ran down the African's face and he only managed a couple of puffs before the cigarette was extinguished and sodden red. The man had talked, seemingly without effort, telling how he had been in the basement of a nearby block of flats chatting to a servant girl when her alleged husband had struck him from behind with the panga. That first blow had not been so severe but he had fallen to the ground whereupon the enraged husband had continued to strike him across the head. He had tried to protect himself with his hands but the razor-sharp cane knife had cut through them so that the two fingers were missing from the right hand, together with the top joint of the left thumb.

The man had quite calmly related this tale to an appalled Smaller who kept giving him puffs from new cigarettes before removing them from his lips so that the blood flow would not put them out. The time dragged on and eventually Ashley and Smaller began to despair that the African could possibly survive, such was the loss of blood from his wounds. After some thirty minutes, the ambulance arrived and the young man was placed gently onto a stretcher and wheeled inside. The last thing he said was, 'Thanks for the cigarettes *baas*.' Smaller never discovered whether he lived or died but neither he nor Ashley had eaten dinner that night.

The average African's tolerance for grievous injury and mutilation was legendary. Tales were rife about victims of knifings and gang fights walking into local hospitals with sharpened screwdrivers, and even hatchets, embedded in various parts of their bodies. Smaller believed that it was the lack of imagination, of the largely uneducated African masses, that prevented them from realising the damage that had been done to them. A white man with comparable wounds would often pass out with shock due to his failure to accept the horror of his injuries. But the African had no such problems, having been used to blood and gore for generations.

As he drove into the outskirts of the tiny Magaliesberg village, Smaller passed the little bungalow which housed the local South African police station. Outside was a strangely high-sided personnel carrier painted in striated camouflage colours. The number plate read SAP but Smaller knew that this was a mine-proofed Riot Police vehicle, the paramilitary unit of the SAP. He thought of Subaye still sleeping in the back and what the police reaction would be to her presence should they decide to search the Kombi in one of their occasional roadblocks. The thought made him realise the rashness of his action. If they found out anything, he could be out of the country, deported virtually overnight. He drove carefully through Magaliesberg his mind full of conflicting thoughts.

Subaye dreams that Gregory returns to find her where she lies, abandoned by the men who have used her for their violent pleasure. His rage is such that he immediately rides off again to hunt for the men who have abused his woman. He leaves two of his men and a young Zulu girl with her. As the servant girl bathes her mistress's body with cool river water, Subaye closes her eyes, recalling the disgust in his face. It is as if he almost hates her, sees her as unclean because Vusi and his gang have defiled her. Perhaps he will one day tire of hunting and take her closer to civilisation, where there are other women of her age, and where she may have the children she longs for. She sees a little village by a wide blue river. There are forests close by for wood and building timber and quiet valleys rich in game. Gregory and his men build her a big house with two rooms, or perhaps even three and when the children come they have a new hut built for them and a servant to care for them every hour of the day. She knows that Gregory is a rich man now, that he has great hordes of ivory, some of which are periodically sent off with porters to the faraway coast. He can afford to live wherever he wants in this vast land of Southern Africa and she dreads that he may one day decide

144

to leave and go back to his own people. Now that she has been used by those terrible men, Gregory may not want her again. And she looks so awful, her lips split and her face bruised and puffed. To Africans, rape and violence are almost commonplace but she knows that to the white people rape holds a social stigma which is hard to overcome. Gregory tells her a story about his young sister in the land that he came from, far across the great waters. She was raped by an older man, a farmhand or labourer, and Gregory's father caught him and beat him to within an inch of his life. Then he was taken to a sort of tree and hanged by the neck until dead. Gregory's eyes mist with the telling of the tale; his sister has never married, has never wanted a man to touch her again.

Zak was making serious plans. He had received several donations lately from various sources in Zambia, Botswana and Moçambique. They had each emanated originally from ANC headquarters in the neighbouring states but had been laundered and passed onto him via local traders and agents in the *shebeen* at Waltersville. It was fortuitous that they had all arrived together but Zak knew the reason. He realised that the R5,000 plus that he now had cached in the township was meant to be used, not to be buried in the ground for a rainy day.

The South Africans had been busy lately with a series of lightning cross-border raids and troops of their elite 41 Battalion had taken out bases in Moçambique and lately, Lesotho, the tiny mountain kingdom which had formerly been the British Protectorate of Basutoland. Although Lesotho was totally enclosed by South Africa, the white troops and their black lackeys had gone into the capital Maseru and created havoc, killing ANC personnel and blowing up arms and ammunition.

Zak knew that his masters in Moçambique would want revenge. Recently the comrades in Natal had been quite successful with urban bombings and a few attacks on outlying police stations. Last year there had been attacks in the Cape, the most impressive of which had been the bomb in the liftshaft of a high-rise office block on the Foreshore in Cape Town itself. This attack, on what was the seat of government in South Africa for half the year, had made world headlines and Zak had read of it with admiration. What could he do in the Magaliesberg that could compare? Ruby had suggested an attack on the local police station but Zak was pragmatic enough to know that such an act would be tantamount to suicide, with the Riot Police actually in residence at present.

After a great deal of thought, Zak had decided that they could risk an attack on a soft target, a local farm would probably be the easiest answer. He could count on four men to go with him. Ruby was, of course, first choice; then would come William and Smart and lastly young Temba who seemed to burn with frustration lately.

Between them they would have five AKs and about half a dozen fragmentation grenades, quite sufficient for the proposed target. If they struck at night, there would be little chance of any resistance. Zak knew that most white farmers drank plenty and ate huge meals before going to bed, usually not later than ten o'clock.

The decision had been made and preliminary discussions with Ruby had ironed out most of the problems such as transport and logistics. The most important factor was the escape route, but that too had been sorted out eventually and now Zak was ninety per cent sure that the operation would be risk free. It only remained to set a date and they would do that tonight, meeting in the *shebeen* to make sure that everybody would be available two weeks hence. The target had been decided upon. It was to be the small farmhouse of Danie Bester some five kilometres off the Swartplaas road. It was a good target, being close enough to the road for swift escape, yet far enough away from any built-up area or any other farm. Most importantly it was about forty minutes' drive from the SAP in Magaliesberg.

146

Temba caught Moosa's last bus from the Swartplaas turn-off. It cost him thirty-five cents to Boons where he walked from the main road to Waltersville. He felt a little more relaxed having made the decision to see Subaye next week. Word had spread that the white man had left Bester's farm but there was no news of Subaye. Temba tried to push her to the back of his mind because tonight it was Friday and he had money in his pocket. There was the added prospect of quite a few free drinks with Zak who spent the movement's money with abandon on such occasions. Tonight would be good, they were to decide on the date to hit *Baas* Bester's farm.

Temba knew that Bester was a friend of the white man who had stolen Subaye from him. The thought that they were to attack this man's home and family filled him with an unfamiliar joy, a lust for blood that he had not known he possessed. He had never killed, or even beaten anyone, in his life apart from Subaye who had deserved far worse than he had given her. Temba tried to imagine what it would be like to kill someone. He had obviously never fired the AK 47; could not picture the results of bullets striking flesh. He knew nothing of muzzle velocities, or trajectories, only that this gun was the rifle that all the freedom fighters carried, the ultimate guerilla weapon. There were said to be many millions in Africa alone.

In the crowded, noisy *shebeen* Temba searched for Zak and Ruby. The air was blue with cigarette smoke and Diana Ross's voice whispered squeakily from the speakers over the table that served as a bar. The beers and cheap spirits were flowing and everyone seemed to have that end-of-the-week euphoria, a feeling which lasted until Saturday lunchtime before waning during Sunday into total dissipation and finally, on Monday morning, aching disappointment when one awoke to discover that the weekend was over.

Three hours later, Temba was totally drunk. Zak had been generous as usual and they had sat apart from the rest of the drunken crowd seeming to develop a fellowship between the five of them. It was almost an *esprit de corps*. Although Temba did not know how to express it, it set them apart as an elite, a special group who were prepared to act in order to improve the lot of the black man in South Africa.

They had all drunk whisky and to begin with it seemed to have little effect. Zak had talked quietly and the date was set for Saturday night two weeks hence. 'Two weeks tomorrow and we'll be in action,' Zak had whispered conspiratorially and Temba had felt the butterflies of fear in his stomach. To quell this he had drained his Scotch in one gulp. 'A man can get thirsty around here,' he had said loudly.

Smilingly Zak had ordered a second round and then it had just gone on and on so that eventually the noise seemed to become less whilst the room faded in and out of focus periodically. It was almost twelve when they left the *shebeen* and Temba had no idea how he would get home; it was something he had not really considered earlier.

He spent the night on the floor of the tiny living room in Zak's house. Covered with a thin grey blanket, he fell into a drunken sleep to awaken cold and stiff an hour after dawn, his mouth dry and his head pounding wretchedly. Silently he crept from the house and caught the first bus from town back to the Swartplaas turn-off. All he wanted was his own bed where he could sleep away the day and rid himself of the dreadful feelings of weakness and nausea. First there was the long walk through the fields and the rising sun was warm on his shoulders so that he felt faint and the sweat sprang out greasy on his face.

He passed close to the place where the rifle was buried but didn't give it a second glance. Next week could not even be considered at this point in time and the week after that seemed aeons away. Even Subaye was far from his thoughts as he staggered along, the blood pounding in his temples, thinking only of his bed and a long cold drink of water from the big five gallon can that his mother always kept full in the yard. After what seemed like a never-ending ordeal, he eventually reached his village. His mother was up and about, sweeping the red earth of the yard with a broom made of river reeds.

'Ho, it is the young adventurer,' she said loudly, making his head pound even more.

Now that he was standing still Temba felt as if he were going to pass out and the sweat sprang out anew all over his body. He could smell himself quite clearly, the rank ammoniacal odour of unhealthy perspiration coupled with the stale whisky smell of his breath.

His mother cuffed him fondly as he staggered into the hut. 'Get to bed, stupid boy,' she said laughingly. 'I'll get you some water before you leave this world altogether.'

Some fifteen kilometres out of Magaliesberg, Subaye awoke. At first she had no idea where she was. The whine of the VW engine, combined with the road noise from the tyres, only served to heighten her confusion. She had been sleeping on her stomach, her head buried in the pile of old cushions which Smaller used as a pillow. Slowly, she turned onto her back and opened her eyes feeling the faint pain still there, deep inside her body. Her tongue probed the puffiness of swollen lips and only one eye would open but she saw the familiar cream roof of the Kombi just above her head.

Subaye's heart quickened as realisation returned with sudden clarity. She was in the little bus and it was moving, not on a dirt track but on a proper road. Martin was taking her away, away from Swartplaas, away from her village and her family. And away from that bastard Temba who had done this to her.

Actually she didn't feel too bad. The bruised eye ached dully and her mouth was still raw from where the bottom lip had split against her teeth, but she had slept for a long time and the rest had been wonderful. She moved experimentally under the sleeping bag feeling the soft fleece of the

149

tracksuit warm against her bare skin. It smelled of Martin, a faint perfumed tobacco smell that she recognised easily. Subaye pressed herself up on one elbow and saw the back of his head outlined against the straight, wide road that stretched ahead through the big windscreen.

He caught the movement and she vaguely saw his eyes, shielded by sunglasses, move in the rearview mirror. He smiled at her briefly over his shoulder. 'How is the patient?' he said softly. 'How is Subaye?' She smiled back at him feeling warm from the kindness in his voice.

The drive to Johannesburg was uneventful for Smaller but almost magical for Subaye. She had never been further west than Magaliesberg which was the largest town she had ever seen. The Volkswagen soon left the single carriage country roads and joined up eventually with the fast Western Bypass. This three-lane highway was something of a marvel to Subaye who watched the big cars flashing past on the outside lane with wide-eyed interest. Smaller smiled at her reactions and talked to her about Johannesburg and the buildings with twenty floors and more. She could not comprehend such things and when the skyline appeared, shimmering in the dry heat of midday, she gasped with disbelief even though she had seen pictures of the city in magazines.

They arrived at the townhouse just after lunch and Subaye remained out of sight, lying back on the bunk whilst Smaller parked the Kombi in his double garage. During the last half hour of the journey he had said little to her, leaving her to stare out at the so-called sophistication that she had only read of in newspapers and heard about on the radio. He was filled with contradictory thoughts and more than a few doubts about the radical step he was taking. Once away from Swartplaas, and the farm, Subaye seemed to have become just what she was – a pretty bush African. A good-looking black girl indeed, charming and very sexy, but could he justify making her a part of his household, could he really get away with what he was planning? In basic terms she was more than a potential embarrassment, more than a risky whim. She was a danger, an enormous threat to his own status and permanent residence in South Africa.

Each of the townhouses had its own maid's room but so far Smaller's had been used only for the storage of such items as water skis and his seldom-used windsurfer. Once they were into the garage, he asked Subaye to remain quietly inside the VW while he went to sort out her room. Sweating in the lunchtime heat he lugged out the big fibre-glass board and skis and slotted them in against the wall, alongside the Escort.

Breathing deeply, he examined the small cell-like servant's room. It was painted white and reasonably clean. The floor was smooth bare cement. Smaller noted the electric wall socket in one corner and the little sink with draining board and a cupboard underneath. This may not be luxury but it was far better than anything Subaye had been used to at the farm, he was pretty sure about that. At the back of the garage was a toilet adjoining the laundry room which each pair of townhouse units had use of as part of their basic services. In an angle off the toilet/laundry area was a shower cubicle with hot and cold water; the whole place was tiled in white and was clean and tidy. Smaller reckoned it could be a lot worse indeed, such was the case in most of Johannesburg's older properties.

He would have to get her a bed and some sort of a wardrobe or cupboard for her clothes. Smiling to himself, he realised that Subaye didn't have anything to wear, he'd have to buy some stuff for her, including servant's uniforms. Smaller grinned even wider, he was beginning to find the whole thing quite stimulating. In the meantime, he would take her into the kitchen and she could have a look around the townhouse, then she could make them coffee.

Smaller felt strangely satisfied with the rather silly and dangerous game he was playing. He told Subaye to get out of the Kombi and she followed him meekly into the kitchen. As she did so, the fat old maid from next door leaned out of the rear bedroom window and called down to him. 'Hello, *Baas* Martin, how is the *Baas*? Did you have a good holiday, *Baas*?'

Suddenly she seemed to notice that the young woman in the *Baas*'s tracksuit was black, not a pretty white girl as was normally the case with *Baas* Martin. Her eyes widened so that the whites showed clearly at the corners.

Smaller smiled up at her. 'Hello, Sally,' he said winningly. 'Thank you. Yes, I had a wonderful rest.' Casually he followed her gaze and looked over his shoulder at Subaye. His smile widened. 'Ah, Sally, this is Subaye, my new maid. She is from a farm in Magaliesberg, I hope she'll be your friend.'

Subaye looked up shyly at fat Sally whose face had now broken into a wide grin. The older woman spoke admiringly to Smaller. 'Yey, but she's a pretty one, eh, *Baas* Martin.'

Smaller smiled in return and then Sally began to speak rapidly in Tswana to Subaye. 'Hello and welcome to you little sister, so you are really going to work for this *Baas* Martin. He's a good man, but what a man with the young girls. Yey, but he likes them, eh. He has them to stay on the weekends and I see them crawling out in the morning looking like a mad bull has been at them. Sometimes we can hear them from the quarters at the back, there.' She gestured behind the garages. 'They scream and moan like you can't believe. I don't know what manner of things he does with them but you should hear it. This *Baas* Martin, he's a man alright, little sister.' She paused. 'I must look at your eye for you.'

If Subaye had been able to blush, she would have done so. As it was, she merely nodded at the old fat maid and answered in the same language, her voice steady. 'I'll talk with you later, Mother, but first I have to unpack the little bus and wash the *Baas*'s clothes but I will come and see you soon.'

Sally nodded and her head disappeared back inside the window which she closed with a bang.

Smaller led the way into the compact kitchen. 'Let's have some coffee Subaye, I'll show you where everything is and how to operate the stove, that sort of thing.' He stopped, noting that she was looking at him oddly, almost a feral gleam in her huge black eyes. 'What's wrong Subaye?' He asked quickly before the realisation came, the conversation with fat Sally. She must have given Subaye the word in those few short sentences. Smaller nodded to himself and chuckled disarmingly. 'Ah, I see. It must have been old Sally, eh. Don't pay any attention to her Subaye, she's full of shit, I mean, she talks a lot of rubbish. Just an old busybody, that's all she is.'

He looked at the young black girl. She stared back at him, her chin held high, her proud heritage suddenly very obvious in her bearing. But he knew she was frightened and he realised that it was because she was totally alone, separated from family and friends and thrust into a completely alien environment. 'It's going to be fine, Subaye,' he said kindly. 'You'll like it here after a while and, of course, I'll take you back home whenever you want to go.'

The girl looked back at him, her eyes penetrating. He held her stare although he felt uncomfortable. Smaller rushed on, 'Later we can go to Johannesburg and get you some decent clothes but, just for the moment, I'll get you a uniform from the supermarket down the road – and underwear. They have everything there.'

His mind raced on, trying to imagine how to outfit a young black girl with the basics, a girl who had nothing at all to wear except the tracksuit he had loaned her. 'Perhaps tomorrow we can go out and get clothes for you, but for the moment I'll quickly drive down to the supermarket and get you the essentials, they have pantihose, shoes, the lot. I know what we should do, we should have a cup of coffee and then both go, together. But we can't, Subaye,' he stumbled on. 'First I must organise overalls and things, you can't walk around here in that tracksuit.'

Smaller took the keys to the Escort from the board by the kitchen door. 'I'll be back in a few minutes Subaye, just you make yourself at home and have a look around the place.' He slipped out leaving the girl alone and ran to the garage. Retrieving his wallet from the VW, he started the XR3 and headed out of the driveway; the local Checkers store was only two blocks away. What the fuck am I getting myself into? he thought, and laughed aloud. He was still chuckling when he pulled into the carpark.

Smaller found a coloured assistant who was about the same build and size as Subaye. He drew her to one side and spoke to her in quiet confidential tones. 'Perhaps you can help me, Shereen,' he said, reading the name tag on her overall. 'I need advice on clothes for a new maid, she's about your size. She arrives tomorrow and is coming from my brother's farm in the Free State. You know what those farm girls are like.' The coloured girl nodded knowingly and shrugged her shoulders as if acknowledging a hopeless case. Smaller continued, 'I have to buy everything for her, my brother says her own stuff is so terrible that I wouldn't allow her inside my house wearing it. Can you imagine that!' Shereen clucked in sympathy and shook her head again.

With the invaluable help of Shereen, it took less than half an hour and Smaller had the basics of Subaye's emergency wardrobe. He bought two sets of maid's overalls, complete with cap and apron, one in blue and the other in pink. Next came shortie cotton nighties and bikini pants, then size thirty-four bra's that didn't look too bad. Shereen giggled when Smaller held these against her, trying to estimate the sizes, and the young Afrikaans floor manager arrived to politely ask what was going on. Smaller explained, and Shereen added her own comments in Afrikaans, whereupon the manager went away satisfied, if not a little bemused. Then Smaller bought sandals, hoping to hell that they'd fit; and pantihose, a couple of T-shirts and two pairs of cotton slacks in cream and navy. These had elasticated waists and were of the loose baggy style currently in vogue. 'They fit anyone from thirty-two to thirty-six,' Shereen said smilingly.

Later, he would give Subaye money to buy her own toiletries. But at least now she could walk around, without attracting attention, in a tracksuit obviously too large for her emblazoned with the words 'Windsurfers do it standing up.' Finally Smaller went to the food section and bought milk, bacon, eggs, bread, butter and some packs of meat and sausages. He had tea and coffee in the townhouse so they wouldn't starve. When he arrived at the check-out, Smaller discovered that he didn't have enough cash so he put the whole bill on his Master Charge card. It came to almost R120 but he didn't really mind; in fact he'd found the whole thing most enjoyable. Shereen checked off his items and he passed her five rand without anyone noticing. 'For your trouble,' whispered Smaller as he pushed his trolley out into the parking lot.

More pleasure was to come with Subaye's reaction. She was like a little girl, delighted with the things he had bought her. The slacks fitted perfectly, as did the T-shirts. Then she wanted to try on the underwear. He couldn't help staring at her body as she pulled off the tracksuit top and rolled down the pants. Even with the black eye and split lip, she somehow seemed more exciting standing here naked in his living room. Then he saw the open windows, not even protected by the flimsy net drapes. He spoke roughly. 'For God's sake Subaye, go upstairs to the spare room. There's a mirror there and you can try the stuff on in comfort.' He considered the possible setting of a precedent then thought, what the hell, and dismissed it. He added, 'You can have a bath too, the guest bathroom is right next to the spare room.'

Smaller packed the provisions he had bought into the fridge. He took out a beer which was warm because he'd left the fridge off whilst he'd been in the bushveld. He sipped the tepid liquid and looked at his watch. He should really phone Ashley to see what was happening at the magazine, but he could do it tomorrow. It had all been Ashley's idea anyway, the trip away from the concrete jungle to the great outdoors. It seemed as though he'd been away for ages and that something in his life had altered. Sure enough, he'd done the unthinkable, slept with a black girl. To compound it all he'd brought her back with him, back to his own home in the thick of white Johannesburg's elite townhouse area. He shook his head and grinned at himself in the little pub mirror over the sink. He really was a bloody lunatic, Ashley would die if he found out. But at this moment he, Smaller, couldn't care less. Half the white bastards in this town would love to have her, he knew that. The trouble was, they were all too bloody chicken.

Smaller sniffed himself under the arms. He too could do with a bath after the hassling morning and then the clearing out of Subaye's room. He listened carefully and could hear faint splashing sounds coming from upstairs; suddenly the thought of a shower seemed almost unbearably pleasant. He took a second slightly cooler beer out of the fridge and started up the stairs, heading for his bathroom located *en suite* to the main bedroom. On the landing he stopped and noted that the door to the other bathroom was half-open, fragrant steam eddying out into the passage.

He squashed his desire to go in and look at her, and touch her as he had only days ago in the Magaliesberg. Instead, he called out brusquely, oddly confused between lust and the annoying fact that Subaye was supposed to be his servant. 'Hurry up Subaye, we've got a lot to do.' He turned into his room slamming the door.

He stood under the shower for almost ten minutes running it hot and cold, then finally cold for as long as he could stand it. The needle jets stung his skin and he stood with his hands on the wall moving from side to side under the blast of water, the jets massaging his shoulders like probing fingers with blunt nails. The water seemed to blow away the woolly feeling in his head so that he was able to think more rationally. With the rationalisation came further doubts.

Should he get rid of Subaye now, tell her the whole thing was a mistake, a solution that just couldn't work? Smaller shook his head like a dog as he stepped out of the shower. He would leave it be for the time being. He towelled himself vigorously with a huge rough bath sheet and looked at himself in the mirror-wall of his bathroom. His skin glowed pinkly and his face and arms were tanned a light chestnut brown. The second beer stood half-finished on the vanity slab and he drained it in one gulp and smiled at his image wiping the froth off his moustache with the back of his hand. He certainly looked healthier, and without a doubt he felt it. He looked curiously into his own eyes, realising that he hadn't given a thought to Isobelle and Rebecca for over a week.

When he went down to the kitchen in fresh corduroys and an old denim shirt, Subaye was already busy at the stove stirring the contents of a small saucepan. Two pieces of golden brown bread stood up in the toaster and there was a pleasing aroma of freshly made coffee. Subaye smiled at him. 'Hello Master, I am making scrambled eggs for your lunch,' she said in a soft sing-song Tswana accent. 'There is coffee in the pot. If the Master will sit down in the dining room, Subaye will bring him lunch.'

Smaller grinned delightedly at this pantomime. Subaye wore the pink dress, complete with cap and frilly apron. She smelled fresh and clean. Already the left eye was losing its puffiness and her split lip didn't seem so swollen. Smaller sniffed the eggs when they arrived, they were soft and yellow, topped with freshly ground pepper and a touch of butter. He realised that he was remarkably hungry, having eaten nothing since supper with Bester last night. 'This is fantastic, Subaye,' he said and began to eat with relish.

That night Subaye slept on the floor in the servant's room. It was not too cold yet in the Transvaal and mid-winter was still almost two months away. Smaller gave her mattresses from his terrace loungers and the sleeping bag from the Kombi so she was quite warm on the cement floor. She lay on her back looking at the ceiling and thinking about Smaller in his bed just a few metres away in the townhouse. He was different now, back here in his own environment, with his own people. But she had expected that, had known that here in the big city she could not be as much a part of his life as she had for the few short days at Swartplaas. She thought about her mother and father and the mud-walled tin shack that had been her home since childhood.

She wondered what they thought, what they had heard about her and Martin Smaller. By now, with her missing, someone would have been bound to have told them of the rumour, the talk of her with the white man who had stayed in the little bus on *Baas* Bester's farm. Her mother would scoff at such news but she didn't think that her father really cared one way or the other, whilst her other friends, at *Baas* Hofmeyer's, would chatter about it for a few days and then forget all about her. Subaye closed her eyes but sleep wouldn't come. It was only last night that Temba had raped and beaten her, but already it seemed like a lifetime ago. Her eye still ached a little but she could half open it and old Sally had given her bicarbonate of soda to bathe it. There seemed to be unlimited supplies of hot water here in the city and Subaye had enjoyed a shower in the little bathroom off the laundry. It was the first time she had ever showered and the pressure of the little jets of warm water had been stimulating on her skin so that her nipples erected and her heartbeat quickened. Lying there in the quiet darkness she thought about her new life and the things she was learning.

She had sat with Sally talking for almost two hours after Martin had said he was going to bed. A young man had come by and stayed for a while drinking cane spirit out of a flat bottle which he kept inside his jacket. He hadn't offered any to Sally or Subaye but he had smiled at her often and talked in a confident way about the money he made and the car he was buying next month. He was Johannes, apparently a nephew of Sally's and Subaye

158

thought he was quite good looking, slighter in build than Temba but well dressed and athletic. When he left, Sally had winked at Subaye, inclining her head towards the door. 'He liked you, eh. That young Johannes, he's a one with the girls I hear. My sister says he's a clever one, got his matric in school and is earning four hundred rand a month in an office in town. A good boy I reckon even though he's a bit flashy, eh.'

Sally loved to chatter and seemed to have a wealth of information about Martin Smaller. Subaye recalled her words. '*Baas* Martin, he likes the girls too, eh. Yey, but they seem to like him that's for sure.' Subaye had nodded and smiled slightly, encouraging the older woman to continue with her gossip. She wanted to learn everything possible about Martin. Sally had continued in a conspiratorial tone. '*Baas* Martin, he had a very fast little car which cost nearly as much as one of these flats.' She paused for effect. 'Can you imagine a car like that, a little racer it was and those girls loved to go driving with him in it. Then he went and crashed it on the highway and that was nearly the end of him. I never saw the car again but *Baas* Martin was in the hospital for many days and the police were here after he came out.'

Shaking her head Sally had sipped milky tea from her battered enamel mug. Subaye, occasionally murmuring, had exhaled in amazement, prompting the fat Tswana woman to carry on. 'He had that girl Miss Caroline for quite a while. She was a pretty one alright with yellow hair and long legs but very thin, yey, but she was thin that one. But she loved the *Baas,* I used to clean his flat twice a week and on Monday mornings I'd find the ends of *dagga* cigarettes in the *Baas*'s bedroom after she'd been staying on the weekend. Yey, but they used to carry on something those two did,' Sally had continued importantly whilst Subaye sat entranced.

'Of course, *Baas* Martin used to drink a lot too, especially after Madam Isobelle and his little girl were killed overseas

159

in a plane that crashed. When he first came to stay here he was an unhappy man. He used to bring the little girl some weekends and once I saw the Madam, very pretty she was. But she used to shout at *Baas* Martin and the little girl would cry; divorced they were *Baas* Martin and Madam Isobelle.'

When Sally had got up to make more tea on the little paraffin stove, Subaye's mind had raced with fragmented thoughts. She had never even considered that Martin had been married, had enjoyed a family and a little daughter. She wondered why he and his wife had divorced; perhaps he would tell her one day. Divorce was not practised amongst Africans, at least not on the farms, it was unheard of there but she knew that it was quite normal for white people to break up and even get married again.

Subaye tried to picture the effects of an African divorce in a Swartplaas *kraal*. First, and most importantly, the unfortunate girl's father would have to give back the cattle and cash paid to him as *lobola* for his daughter. In return he would get back his daughter older and no longer virginal. It would then be impossible for such a girl to remarry because no self-respecting man would want a used woman. Subaye thought that should she ever have become married and then left her husband, her father would very likely have beaten her senseless. Of course, things were changing fast these days and the black man was undoubtedly becoming more like the white man, aping his customs and lusting after his money and material pleasures.

As old Sally had bustled about making the tea, Subaye experienced brief pangs of anguish. She thought of her family and Temba who had really seemed to love her. Again she fingered her bruised eye and ran her tongue over her fast-healing lower lip, remembering his vicious attack of last night which seemed now to be a lifetime away. She realised that he must have been crazed with jealousy to have beaten her and raped her like that, but couldn't imagine that he had enjoyed it because, although sometimes boastful, she had never known him to be violent.

With fresh mugs of tea, both women had eventually lapsed into silence in the warm smoky room. Subaye, sipping gingerly at the hot, sweet liquid, had considered her position. Martin had said he would pay her R150 a month and supply all her food. On top of that, he would give her an allowance for clothes and other things like perfume and lipstick. It would amount to more than twice as much as she had earned on the farm.

So far Martin had not been very affectionate towards her but Subaye was intelligent enough to realise yet again that it was not easy for him here, back in his home in white Johannesburg. For the moment she was happy to wait until he was ready for her and then she would go to him discreetly as she had on *Baas* Bester's farm; she would be there whenever he wanted her.

Turning over on her makeshift bed Subaye ran her hands over her body. She was clean and sweet smelling and the degradation and filth of the previous night was gone with the hot bath and recent shower. She felt drowsy and knew that sleep would come fast now. In the morning she would clean the townhouse so that it shone. Martin would not believe it when he came back from his work. She snuggled under the quilted sleeping bag which smelled wonderfully of him and settled her hand in the cleft of her thighs, tomorrow she would show him what a marvellous housekeeper she was. Old Sally was sweet to her and had said she would help. Subaye's features relaxed and she slept with a peaceful half-smile on her lips.

CHAPTER 9

Temba's poverty-stricken yet idyllic childhood had recently come back to him during his hours of sleep. When he awoke he would feel embarrassed to be dreaming about himself as a child, a bare-arsed bush African *piccanin,* often snot-nosed and sometimes with a belly slightly distended by mild malnutrition. It seemed that these visions had visited him regularly over the past week or so and, oddly, they occurred more often when he went to bed early and sober. Tonight it was happening again and the farm on which he lived was a nameless one, its features and geography vague yet somehow familiar. Wherever it was, he knew it well and could recognise its existence comfortably, somewhere back in his memory traces . . .

He plays in the endless dusty summer with boys like himself, most ragged and barefoot, filthy and always hungry. He wears only tattered navy cotton shorts and a T-shirt, once white and emblazoned with the red logo of 'OK Bazaars'. He rises at 6.30 each morning with the heat of the sun, then they gather, three or four of them, and dash off into the mealie fields to play until the hunger pangs drive them home around midday. The games are many and varied and the secret places seem only for them, like the bathing place at the river where they shrug off their rags and frolic in the water for hours with rusty cans and empty beer bottles that are too small to be refundable at the bottle store in

Magaliesberg. Sometimes a white boy joins them and so he has today. Temba looks with envy at young Anton in his washed-out khaki shorts and clean bright red T-shirt. On his feet are stout *veldskoens,* the suede desert boots favoured by the Afrikaans farmer and his clan for generations. They are worn without socks and can take any amount of battering, soaking and rock kicking so that their younger owners usually grow out of them before they fall apart. Anton is in his early teens, about the same age as Temba who is unsure of his exact date of birth. The boy's face and arms are burned to a light russet brown by the sun and his hair is dark blond, bleached into streaks, but always soft and silky looking. In contrast, Temba's is red with the dust of the *veld* and even when he ducks under the water in the *spruit* it never loses its tight curls and begrimed appearance. Today they go out as usual around seven in the morning, the three Africans and the blond white boy, only the latter sated with a breakfast of mealie porridge and bacon and eggs lying heavily yet comfortable in his stomach. He brings them a few scraps; cold buttered toast, spread with red jam and a stolen tin of corned beef from the larder. They scoop out the congealed meat with mealie stalks and spread it onto the toast and eat the lot, jam included, in a few giant bites. As usual Anton looks on in mild amazement. Although it is acknowledged between them that the white boy is the superior, the relationship they enjoy is one of mutual trust and admiration. Each one excels in his own right as a youthful example of his race, the blacks supple and agile in their nervous bright-eyed undernourishment and the white boy solid and strong, glowing with the pink and golden bloom of his people and their ancestors from half a world away. Temba leads the way, loping along through the *veld,* his feet flying over grass, rocks and low scrub heading for the *spruit* and their secret place under the huge old willows that line the bank. Here the little waterway makes a half circle around a rocky outcrop on the opposite bank and the current runs slowly, sometimes almost clear, and at other times red with the mud washed from the soft banks higher upstream where the farmers take their mealie furrows almost to the water's edge. The four boys stop, hardly even breathless, eyes shining and faces bright with the promise of a new day. As they steal nearer to the river they hear faint shouts and splashes, muffled by the curtain of willow branches yet clearly those of girls at play. Creeping closer they follow Temba who crouches now, screened from the bank, but only a few metres away from where two lithe young black girls frolic and splash in the shallow green water. At first Temba thinks of striding out of cover shouting, berating these females who are invading his all-male territory but something stops him. He can hear the soft breath of Anton at his ear and then the whispered words, 'Don't do anything. Let's watch.' Temba lies still, pressed to the cool moist earth, a strange butterfly sensation fluttering in the pit of his stomach. The others too are motionless and it seems that nothing exists in the tranquillity of this early summer morning, except the two graceful young girls now rinsing themselves, their bodies shining like oiled mahogany in the sunlight. Temba sees their budding breasts, firm and plumlike and tipped with dark nipples that stand erect from the slight chill of the water. Between their long legs are small triangles of closely curled black hair and when one of them walks up the bank and bends briefly to pick up a scrap of her clothing Temba glimpses a pink moistness between the tight buttocks that excites him greatly so that his adolescent groin hardens. He presses himself tighter against the soft ground and the blood pounds in his temples. Behind him he hears Anton's breathing become more ragged and then the young white boy rises and walks silently past Temba towards the two girls. Anton looks down and smiles briefly, his eyes alive with an odd light and his face slightly flushed. 'Stay here Temba, don't move, eh. I'm going to show you something.' He moves on and the girls look up to see him coming. Both stand and cover the space between their legs with their hands, looking at each other and then back to the white boy. They smile shyly and Temba hears a high trilling laugh, anxious and tremulous in the quiet morning. Then Anton beckons and they walk with him to the soft grass higher up the bank. It is only metres from where the three Africans lie. Anton takes off his shorts and brief white underpants and stands in his red T-shirt with his *umphambili* standing up, looking pink and almost angry. The girls giggle more confidently now. Then one of them puts both hands out and grasps Anton, pulling him gently towards her. Temba watched breathless and spellbound as the smaller of the two begins to rub Anton's thing, working it gently up and down; then they all sink down onto the grass and Anton lies on his back, stretching his legs out straight in front of him. The white boy begins to gasp and moan and then the girl stops and lies down beside him on her back; she opens her legs and Anton rolls on top of her. Temba has never seen the mating act between man and woman before. He has watched animals of course, the stringy, snapping village dogs often mount each other from behind, the dog pumping away at the bitch's rump for a few frantic minutes before quivering briefly and then climbing off. Now Anton is lying on top of the lissome young black girl whose legs are open wide, knees grasping his hips as he moves inside her. The second girl looks on, occasionally stroking Anton's bottom and rubbing herself briskly between the legs with the other hand. Temba has never seen anything so incredible. Finally the actions of the three figures, two brown and one pale gold, become more frenetic and Temba finds himself moving rhythmically with them, rubbing himself against the ground, his heart pounding and his mouth oddly wet with a thick metallic taste. After less than another minute Anton shudders and the girl below him grips him tightly with her knees while her head bends back and a low moan escapes her lips. In mounting excitement, Temba feels himself reaching a climax. It has happened many times before of course, but never without his touching himself. Now it seems to come without effort, a great bursting surge that seems to fill every vein in his body and finally explodes into his brain.

He awoke disgusted and sticky, lying on his stomach in his narrow iron-framed bed. His younger brother slept peacefully not even one metre away, and yet Temba still imagined that everybody in the little shack must have been aware of the contents of his dream, so palpably real were the sensations. Rising, chilled and confused, from his soiled bed, he stumbled to the zinc bath tub and made tentative efforts to wash himself with the cold, slightly brownish water from the rusted ten gallon drum in the yard. It was still dark and he knew that he could go back under his blankets to sleep for another hour before sunrise around 6.15 when he normally awoke.

But his digital watch seemed to state categorically that sleep would now be impossible. He stared at the face and ached for the figures in the right-hand column to reach sixty and change the hour, make it six o'clock when he could legitimately get up and start his day. His head still boiled with the images in his dream and he felt the unsated longing for Subaye which had filled his nights since she had disappeared. Today was Wednesday and on Saturday they would make the attack on the Bester farmstead. Temba couldn't wait, and as he considered the plans for that night the shame of his dream faded. The red digits on his watch face flickered to six o'clock but he failed to notice as he stared fixedly out of the glassless windows at the coming dawn.

Zak had planned the attack to perfection. He and Ruby had sat up late on Tuesday and Wednesday night going over the details until they both knew every move by heart. Ruby was an action man, all for storming the front *stoep* of the Bester farmstead, blowing the doors open and rushing the passage to the bedrooms then blasting the hell out of anything that moved. But Ruby was not too bright, Zak knew that and accepted it as a failing of the man who was his trusted follower. Ruby would die for the ANC without a second thought.

By nature, Zak was more careful. A thinker. More like the leopard than the rhino, he told himself as he lay in the silent darkness in his shack in Waltersville township. All the ANC money – just under R4,500 now, as quite a bit had been spent on preparing for Saturday's attack – was next to his skin in a light cotton money belt. His few other valuables were contained in a vinyl Adidas tog bag with a shoulder strap which lay on the old three-legged chair that served as his night table. Everything was ready. In a few hours it would be daylight and they would all meet at six here at the house. He would rest for most of the day and collect the weapons when it got dark. They were all safe and sound in the old schoolhouse.

Zak was intelligent enough to know that nothing ever went as planned, that there were always hidden pitfalls and hundred-to-one chances that could destroy the best operation. Because of this he had formulated his own escape route and did not plan to be around Waltersville any longer than midnight on Saturday. By midday Sunday, Zak reckoned that he'd be safely inside Botswana or Bophuthatswana at least. There were friends in both places and they were expecting him.

The cadre leader had no intention of taking any of his men with him, not even his lieutenant of the past few years, the faithful Ruby. It was important that he survive above all the rest because he was by far the most valuable and experienced man, was in fact one of the most senior ANC men within the borders of South Africa. He'd been here, in this backwater of the Magaliesberg, for over eighteen months, gradually building his reputation and attracting the odd recruit like young Temba. Ruby had been on his permanent payroll for almost five years and had come with him from Barberton in the eastern Transvaal, the little town close to the border with Swaziland where things were much hotter and the bloody Riot Police were always active with their roadblocks.

Of course, a plan had been worked out for the rest of the group, the other four who didn't realise that he wouldn't be with them. They would make a dash for Johannesburg and the sprawling black dormitory city of Soweto, there to be swallowed up amid the millions of black faces and looked after by comrades sympathetic to the cause. If nothing went wrong, Zak saw little reason why this route should not work. Ruby could not drive but Temba was more than capable and they had the vehicles they needed. In the final analysis however, each of them was expendable, including Ruby, who in fact could be dangerously stupid as a fugitive. A liability rather than an asset. During his first visit to Moçambique in 1977, Zak had been told that soldiers must be sacrificed if eventual victory was to be won. He had been given lengthy lectures on military history which had illustrated this maxim as a sad fact of warfare through the ages.

Zak lay in the warm mustiness of his blankets and listened to the faint roar of a truck on the Magaliesberg road almost a kilometre away. The South Africans too had died in quite a few wars. By nature they were a warlike lot, the white settlers of this country. First they had fought with the Zulu and the Matabele and then bitterly amongst themselves, the Dutch against the English, in the Boer Wars. Of course, the reason they fought each other was obvious to him. It was for the riches of this land which rightfully belonged to the black man. Xhosa, Tswana, Ndebele or Zulu, they would all share eventually in the great wealth of Azania. The ANC, with the help of the PAC, and the assistance of the comrades in Russia, Moçambique and Zimbabwe, would make it happen and in return, would rule.

Those who had fought early in the struggle would become a part of the new rule and amongst them would be faithful cadre leaders like himself. Zak stared up at the corrugated iron ceiling of his rented hut, eyes glistening in the first grey light of dawn. He hated the whites, loathed and detested them with a hatred that bordered on mania. It had started when he was a child in northern Natal, the traditional home of the Zulu and the place where his family had lived since the days of the great kings Chaka and Dingaan. Zak had attended the village school, one which served many *kraals* in the area, and from the beginning he had excelled in writing and mathematics. He had started school at age nine and had been a model pupil, intelligent and respectful to his teachers.

He recalled one memorable day when he was eleven. A group of friends had gone with him to the local supply store run by old Nandisa, the Indian trader who was mean and irritable and very dishonest. Zak and his young compatriots had collected some soft drink bottles from the roadside where holidaying white visitors from up-country would leave them after occasional picnics. In their ragged cast-off clothes, the little black boys would watch the white people with their big cars sitting on the grass, eating vast amounts of bread and meat off white tablecloths. They would drink beers and Coca Colas and laugh and joke about the 'little baboons' who watched them. Often they would chase Zak and his friends away.

Eventually they would go roaring off, leaving scraps of bread and uneaten fruit behind. The hungry black boys would rush forward, jostling and fighting for the morsels and the whites would laugh as they drove away and sometimes throw something out of the windows of their cars so that the *piccanins* would chase after them, ever hopeful of more.

Lying on his mattress, stomach full with last night's meal of steak and mealie porridge, Zak recalled the finding of those bottles and the meagre offerings which Nandisa would give them in return. He remembered the time in question as if it were yesterday because of something that happened first which to him was quite incredible.

There had been two young white boys with the family

who were picnicking beside the main road, the road which was a good two hours' trot from Zak's village. They had taken bread and meat from their parents and gone to sit a little way from the car where two of the big black and white crows, that all Africans hate, sat atop a telegraph pole.

Unbelievably, the boys had eaten little of their food and had begun to toss pieces to the crows, throwing them into the dirt beside the road. The ugly, beady-eyed birds wheeled down from their perch and snapped up the chunks of bread returning to safety to eat ravenously, fighting between themselves for each tiny morsel.

To Zak and his friends the feeding of these carrion-eating birds illustrated the stupidity of the whites more than anything else that had occurred previously in their young lives. Every Zulu child knew that crows were evil, that their presence always represented a bad omen, even death. To feed them was to encourage such happenings; it was unthinkable and totally ridiculous.

When the car had driven away, they had collected three bottles and Zak had thrown a pebble at the crows still settled on top of the telegraph pole. The stone had struck the cross piece and the two birds had squawked angrily and flapped away, shrieking their raucous displeasure. Zak and his friends began the long walk to Nandisa's, still chattering about the crazy white people.

They arrived at the dusty old warehouse which to them was a wonderland of smells and noise. There were always at least twenty people waiting to be served. Old Nandisa, assisted by his wife and sons, would snatch the bottles from them and grudgingly hand out a few sweets in return, usually one for each child and never more than two, however many bottles they brought. Zak had begun to realise that the old Indian was probably cheating them and, now that he could read, had observed that '5c return on bottle' was printed on each label. After waiting for twenty-five minutes the four boys stood solemnly at the counter with Zak at the head. Zak thrust the bottles forward and Nandisa snatched them away as usual, putting them in the wooden crate behind the counter ready for the twice weekly delivery and pick-up of empties. He counted out a few one cent chewing gums and handed six to Zak. 'There you are, you little black bugger. Here's your gum for your stolen bottles.' He grinned showing two gold teeth. 'I hope it chokes you,' he added mirthlessly.

Zak stood his ground and shook his woolly head. 'I don't want sweets,' he said loudly, his voice clear and penetrating. 'I want fifteen cents for the three bottles, please. Then I can choose my own sweets,' he added proudly. Nandisa stared down at the black child in shock and amusement but then the anger rose swiftly within him. He bent down so that his stale curry-smelling breath blasted into Zak's face.

'What have we here then? A little businessman, eh. You should take what I offer, you little thief. Do you think I don't know that the bottles weren't yours. You never bought them here, you cheeky little *kaffir*.' He snatched the small squares of bubble gum from the filthy counter and dropped them back into the paper sack behind the counter. 'You don't want my gift, eh. Well just get out of here. Go on, piss off you stinking little bastard and don't come back.'

Zak's eyes filled with tears and he shouted at the old Indian who had cheated him. 'I want my fifteen cents. It says on the label that the bottles pay five cents on return. You have to pay me, it doesn't matter who brings the bottles in.'

Nandisa leaned out over the counter and cuffed Zak around the ear so that he fell sprawling on the dirty floor. 'Get out of here,' shouted the enraged old Asian. 'Get out before I take my belt to you, you little monkey.'

The older blacks in the store laughed at the boy who had dared to argue with Nandisa the Indian, who was without doubt the most powerful man for many miles around and to whom they all owed differing amounts of money for food, clothing and the illegal beer he sold them on Fridays and Saturdays. They offered no support for the boy – to do so would be tantamount to cutting off all the luxuries Nandisa's store allowed them to enjoy. So they laughed loudly and added their own comments to those of Nandisa, siding with the strong against the weak.

Two days later Zak had taken his revenge. He had waited until everyone was asleep. His mother and father, cocooned in their tiny evil smelling bed which was partially screened off from the rest of the mud-walled shack, slept the sleep of exhaustion. At five in the morning they would both rise to walk the seventeen kilometres to the farm where they would cut sugar cane from dawn until dusk. They were lucky to have the work for these few short months every year because it paid very well; £12.10.0 per week for men and £10 for women, almost £100 a month combined or 'nearly as much as a white man' as Zak's father would say proudly.

None of his friends knew of Zak's plans for the midnight expedition. He hadn't told them because he knew that they would be too terrified to come anyway. They were even too frightened to walk in the *veld* at night. But Zak's inherent fear of the dark, and the spirits that he knew existed in the night-time bush, were suppressed by the hatred that boiled within him. He ran lightly, loping along under the light of a quarter moon, the matches rattling in the pocket of his ragged corduroy trousers.

When he reached Nandisa's he crouched, eyes straining for the movement of the Indian's dogs; one a half-breed German shepherd and the other a huge Rhodesian ridgeback. Silently he crept to the rear entrance of the long building where cardboard cartons and packing cases were stacked haphazardly outside the back door. Zak was unsure of his procedure from here on. He wanted to make a big fire, to burn down the sneering old thief's store, destroy this materialistic shrine at which every African for miles around worshipped.

He rummaged around in the dark and felt the pile of packing made from wood shavings. Now all he needed was some dry paper and he would have his blaze. Hands shaking with fear and excitement, he pulled out the box of matches and struck one, holding the flaring end to a screw of brown wrapping paper. The paper flamed encouragingly and Zak thrust it into the wood shavings which ignited with a faint roar so that he had to leap back nimbly from the heat. Within a minute the tinder dry tea chests were ablaze and flames were licking at the stout back door made from rough pine planks. Zak crouched in the shadows of the lean-to which was Nandisa's garage for his old Chevrolet. He watched the flames, hypnotised by the dancing orange and yellow light that he had created.

He never heard the ridgeback which came upon him silently and from nowhere. The dog stared at him, growling deep in its throat, its eyes glaring hideously red in the light from the fire. Zak backed away, crabbing desperately on hands and knees, never taking his eyes off the huge brindle-coloured hound. Then the dog pounced, knocking him onto his back in the dirt. Almost lazily, it gripped his shoulder between collarbone and bicep and began to growl and roar as it shook Zak like a rat.

More than twenty-five years later Zak could still feel the dog's fangs on his flesh and, even now, his hand strayed to the left shoulder where slight indentations in the skin surface could be felt as permanent evidence of the ridgeback's incisors. He shivered in his warm bed recalling the terror of the dog's attack and what had followed.

First the male African servants had come, rushing from their *khayas,* yelling and screaming to drive off the spirits which might be there in the dark of the yard. What else could have made the lion-dog go berserk in the dead of night? When they found out that it was merely the *piccanin* whom *Baas* Nandisa had thrown out of his store, they laughed their relief and struck casually at the writhing little body with their sticks and *kierries,* exciting the dog even more so that he worried away at Zak's shoulder, causing him to yell and wail in pain and terror.

Nandisa came out in his long grey nightshirt and the first thing he saw were the flames licking at the door of his trading store. He shrieked hysterically at his servants and buckets appeared, then a chain was formed and soon the blaze was reduced to a smouldering, steaming pile of debris. The odd steam-and-smoke blend of odours was to remain with Zak all his life and even now, when fires were doused with water, he recalled the pain and horror of that night quite clearly.

The sons of Nandisa had come and the two of them, together with the aid of the old man, had pulled Zak to his feet. The dog was driven off, still growling, and Zak could barely stand, so great was his pain from the mauling. They took him into the filthy kitchen and let him drop to the floor where they tied him with leather thonging to the leg of the huge blackwood table. Old Nandisa kicked him in the head and his sons followed suit, berating the cowering black child in Hindi. Eventually Zak passed out with severe shock and prolonged fright.

The policemen had come just after dawn, summoned from Ladysmith by Nandisa on his ancient wind-up telephone. One was old and fat and the other young and dark with a pimply face and the sallow olive skin of the Afrikaner. Nandisa gave them coffee and cake and packs of cigarettes, alternately grovelling and then ranting at them about the attempted arson; a premeditated plot aimed at the destruction of his precious store.

Nodding and winking to each other, the two policemen eventually pulled the cowering Zak from under the table where he had crawled in the chill hours before dawn. Nandisa was generous with them because they knew of his illegal liquor sales. They allowed him to continue this business with impunity on payment of £10 per week each. Good money indeed when a sergeant's wage was only £80 per month in those early post-war years.

As the grey light of dawn filled the shack, Zak shivered involuntarily even though he was still inside his blankets.

He recalled the terror that had gripped him as the younger policeman had dragged him across Nandisa's greasy kitchen floor. They had forced him to sit at the table and the older one, with the chevron stripes of a sergeant on his sleeve, had begun the inquisition.

'Now then, my little *skellem*,' he had said in a soft, almost kindly tone. 'What made you decide to try to burn down Mr Nandisa's store, eh? Who put you up to this my lad?' Encouraged by the pleasant-voiced old policeman, Zak had told again his tale of the bottles and the money that he should have rightfully received from Nandisa. The sergeant had nodded sympathetically and Zak had even smiled a little, noticing the enraged face of the old Indian who began to rant his protestations to the younger policeman.

Eventually the talking had finished and the sergeant seemed satisfied that the attempted arson had really been Zak's idea and his alone. He nodded to the constable who had watched the interrogation with bored yet oddly glittering eyes. A short conversation ensued in Afrikaans, a language Zak failed to understand other than a few odd words. Zak was then taken outside by the constable.

The morning had been clean and bright and the servants of Nandisa gathered to watch what would happen. Zak was led unprotestingly to the dark grey Commer police van. There he was turned around with his back to the vehicle and a pair of handcuffs appeared magically to fasten him to a grab bar, hands behind his back, secured close up to the cold steel sides. The constable stepped back and stared down at the small black boy, watching but doing nothing, allowing the fear to build, the fear that he wanted to see in the dark, well-formed face.

The nagging ache from the dog's jaws in his shoulders paled into insignificance when the real terror came so suddenly that Zak wet his pants, wriggling pathetically as the warm urine coursed uncontrollably down his leg. This was a signal for the policeman who casually drew his hardwood baton and swiped it backhand across Zak's face. The blow crushed the bones of the nose, cracked the left cheek-bone and broke five front teeth, the top two being shattered at gum level so that the nerves became exposed like tiny white worms from the bloodied stumps.

Remembering and sweating now on his mattress, Zak passed his tongue over the space where his top front teeth had been, clearly recalling the white-hot agony from the raw nerves which eclipsed even the mindless soaring ache of the broken bones. The beating had gone on and on, so that eventually he hung from the handcuffs with three fractured ribs, a cracked collarbone and a face so abused that it resembled a bloody, garish mask with features that were completely unrecognisable.

Barely conscious, his eyes closing rapidly from the blows with the baton, Zak had recognised Nandisa and his sons standing over him and beyond them a vague half circle of black faces. Nandisa was smiling and rubbing his hands together but his sons had hung back, seemingly appalled by the beating, as were the blacks who muttered quietly amongst themselves until the young constable turned towards them, his baton raised at shoulder height. Turning back to Zak, he had roughly unlocked the handcuffs and strolled back to Nandisa's house to report to his sergeant. The two policemen had left then and some women had brought water to rinse Zak's broken face. They talked to him quietly in Zulu and took him into a hut where he was laid on a pile of rags until they could send to his village for help.

It had taken almost six weeks for the wounds to heal but there was no doctor at hand to set the broken bones and even if there had been, Zak's family could not have afforded the treatment in a hospital. They had no way of getting him to Ladysmith, the small country town which they had never visited themselves. So the young body had healed itself, the bones setting themselves into positions dictated by healing muscles and scar tissue, the cheek remaining a little mis-shapen and the nose flattened somewhat to the right.

Zak's five front teeth were a total loss but, as the years progressed, his gums became so hard that he could bite into an apple and tear meat easily off the bone. His once handsome face continued to remind him of that beating at the hands of the young white policeman. As he grew through adolescence his hatred for these brutal men increased with the acceptance by his contemporaries of his toothless grinning mouth.

He continued to excel at schoolwork and then the chance had come for him to work for the municipality in Ladysmith and there he experienced his first impressions of the whites and their lifestyle in the sleepy little town. Zak's job as a messenger allowed him to take a driving test, first for a motor cycle and eventually, after almost five years in the job, for a motor car. He passed both tests easily and became a driver for the assistant town clerk who treated him like a pet dog, praising him and abusing him at will and occasionally cuffing the young black over the head. This happened especially on Friday afternoons when Zak picked him up after lunch at the Ladysmith Rotary Club.

During these years, between the ages of eighteen and twenty-three, Zak lived in a council sponsored tin hut in the Ladysmith black township. He shared these quarters with four other municipality employees and enjoyed a fairly easy life with unimagined luxuries compared with his meagre childhood in the cane fields. But although Zak had more money in his pocket than he would ever have thought possible in his twenty-fourth year, he was intelligent enough to realise that he, and others like him, were being used by the whites. He knew that the little acceptance he enjoyed was merely peripheral and that idle, corrupt men like his own boss really despised him. To them he was just another 'stupid *kaffir*'.

He began to see less and less of his parents who still toiled for half the year in the cane fields. They were very proud of him and boasted to friends and relations of his wonderful job in Ladysmith, 'the town', which, by 1973, they had still

177

never visited. Zak had come to realise that his mother and father were virtually illiterate bush Africans and with this realisation had come a lack of respect that increased with his own advancing knowledge.

In 1974, Zak met a young coloured man at a *shebeen* in the Ladysmith black township. The man was Jaap Kiddo, an acquaintance and devotee of James April. This young coloured member of the ANC had been jailed in May 1971 after a sensational trial. He was convicted on three counts of contravening the Terrorism Act and sentenced to fifteen years. Japie had related the story of James April to an admiring Zak and his fantastic tale was to inspire the young Zulu to join the ranks of those sworn to change the system of oppression in South Africa.

James had been a student in Cape Town in the early sixties. He had become obsessed with the plight of the coloured man in South Africa and, determined to try to make his mark against white supremacy, had taken 'the road north' to Zambia. From there he had gone on to Russia and East Germany where he was trained in guerilla tactics, weapons and explosive techniques. Back in Zambia in 1967, he took part in a raid into Rhodesia with a section of Joshua Nkomo's fledgling ZANU forces. Japie had related the story in detail, how James had fought a pitched battle with Rhodesian security forces near Wankie, the quiet little coal town adjacent to the vast national park in the north western corner of the country. The battle had been protracted and bloody and many of the comrades had been killed, but James claimed to have accounted for several of the white 'settler regime's' soldiers. When it was obvious that all was lost, he had escaped across the nearby border into Botswana.

There he was unfortunately captured and given a year's jail sentence for bringing arms and ammunition into Botswana. Eventually he was deported back to more friendly Zambia and there passage was arranged for him to London. The money was supplied by the ANC.

During this formative period in the Southern African political melting pot, James April was just what the ANC High Command in London were looking for. Here was an intelligent field operative with battle experience and an excellent knowledge of the terrain and its people. Plans were soon made to return James to South Africa and he successfully re-entered the country of his birth via Jan Smuts airport, Johannesburg, in December of 1970.

As Japie's story had developed, Zak became fired with a nationalistic fervour, a passion he had never before experienced, even in his vitriolic hate against white authority. Somehow he realised that an alliance with men such as James April had always been his fate in life and the bravery and ingenuity of the young coloured freedom fighter gripped his imagination to such an extent that his heart pounded and his mouth became drier as the saga unfolded.

Eyes blazing with enthusiasm, Jaap had told of the forged South African passport and identity card, both of East German origin, which had totally fooled the authorities in Johannesburg. James had stayed a few weeks in the city and then had moved on to Durban, the scene of his eventual capture. He had befriended some Indians; Jaap had spat and clenched his fists at the me...tion of this hated race. These so-called friends had informed on James so that, after only a matter of days, he was captured by an Indian South African police lieutenant and his ordeal with the Security Police began.

James' trial posed a number of problems for the authorities of law and order in South Africa. Most critical of these was whether other PAC and ANC operatives had been infiltrated into the country via the same lines of communication. James wasn't telling and although they had beaten him insensible on more than one occasion, he refused to give any information on ANC colleagues within the borders of South Africa. Jaap told Zak of his mentor's incredible bravery during the long and arduous trial. James had apparently spoken up, not berating his oppressors but rather advising them as a teacher would a child. 'You must realise,' he had said, 'that people will not tolerate apartheid indefinitely. We may have a tough time for the next few years, but I believe that in the end, we shall overcome.' Japie's eyes had misted as he spoke these words of destiny and Zak's throat had tightened as the blood pounded in his temples. Less than a week later he had been enrolled into the ranks of the ANC.

Zak left Ladysmith in March 1975, making for the northern Transvaal where he was to remain for a month in the border town of Messina. Beyond was Rhodesia and the ANC umbrella guerilla organisation under Bishop Abel Muzorewa, the controlling force behind the then fragmented terrorist armies opposing Prime Minister Ian Smith's white settler forces. In 1971 Muzorewa had led the ANC's opposition to the Anglo-Rhodesian settlement proposals and in 1978 was destined to become the first black prime minister of Rhodesia as leader of the United African National Council, his wing of the ANC, a regime which failed to stop the war and was itself doomed to failure.

Heady thoughts had filled Zak's mind as he travelled north, hitching a lift on a construction company's truck from Ladysmith to Johannesburg and then on to the border with a series of lifts and private African buses. At this time, the bush war in Rhodesia seemed to be heading for a stalemate which would eventually force the whites to give up that country to its rightful owners. Zak was to be smuggled into Rhodesia with forged documents and from there he would go on to Moçambique where the ZANLA comrades were readying themselves for the final onslaught on Smith's colonialists. He would work with them and perhaps share in their moments of glory, but more important, he would return to South Africa a trained and deadly soldier.

However, the days became weeks and finally months and Zak was still in Messina, vegetating in the sleepy little border town, trying to keep out of the way of South African security force personnel or South African police units heading for the Rhodesian border. The conventional police force too, was ever on the lookout for potential infiltrators, either into the Republic or from South Africa into hard-pressed Rhodesia, by then a country whose existence was almost completely dependent upon South African support.

Friends of Japie and the imprisoned James April had arranged work for Zak in a local petrol station and there he remained, filling up white Rhodesian and South African petrol tanks for almost six months. Finally, in September, his papers arrived and he crossed the border with a group of Shonas heading for Salisbury via Fort Victoria. The papers, which had been made in East Germany, sent by courier to London, then on to Johannesburg and finally to Messina, stood up to official scrutiny and in late 1975 Zak was transported to the garrison town of Umtali on Rhodesia's eastern border with Moçambique. From there he would slip across the border and his training would begin; it had taken almost nine months for him to reach this point.

Despite the endless delays and frustrations, Zak, then twenty-seven years old, was still determined to do his utmost to right the wrongs in South Africa. He had already experienced first-hand knowledge of the Rhodesian conflagration and Umtali was a town which bore graphic testimony to the success of the freedom fighters. White residents observed an unofficial curfew from around 5.30 p.m. until an hour after dawn because of after dark attacks and ambushes by the comrades. Zak noted this choking off of Rhodesia's lines of communication and liberty with approval and scented the smell of victory manifested in the obvious fear of the whites.

Even prior to 1965 and UDI, ZANU guerillas had been trained in many parts of the world. During the late sixties and early seventies most ZANU training, still under ANC control, was carried out at Itumbi and Mgagao in Tanzania. After Portugal lost Moçambique to FRELIMO in 1974, this country became the main ZANU/ZANLA training area and as such represented the closest threat to the Smith government in Salisbury. As a result, it became the main target of Rhodesia's varied security force attacks.

By the end of 1975, ZANLA, whose forces Zak was destined to join, had almost 6,000 guerillas and recruits undergoing training within Moçambique. Zak's willing indoctrination began with a series of lectures and it was some months before weapons training relieved the boredom of these endless lessons. Zak was told that the decisive factor in the struggle for Southern Africa was the people. ZANLA's doctrine was primarily Chinese theory coupled with the practical lessons learned by FRELIMO in their successful war with the Portuguese; the works of Chairman Mao thus became Zak's chief reading matter. He and a few other South African ANC recruits read the little red books in English, as did the other trainees. Regular tests were held and Zak excelled as he had at school; by mid 1976 he was a trainee section leader.

Zak's first real baptism of fire came in 1977. He and his section had operated successfully close to the border, laying mines and even strafing security force patrols; especially those of the BSAP Reserve, an ill-equipped and often rudimentarily trained unit unlike the elite Fire Force and Selous Scouts.

In March of that year Zak led his cadre, together with two others, on a mission to interrupt Rhodesia's vital flow of petrol from the southern railhead at Beit Bridge to depots in Salisbury. The bush war consumed this vital liquid in vast quantities and rationing had been in operation for some years. This fuel was Rhodesia's lifeblood and without it the war would come to a grinding halt. Zak had been chosen to attack a petrol convoy for two main reasons: the first was that he was a born leader and theoretically a well-trained freedom fighter and the second was that the South African ANC hierarchy in London demanded that he have first-hand experience of action. They wanted him to fire his weapon in close contact. Zak was aware of this rationale and relished the chance to show his mentors his real mettle.

Under cover of darkness, the sixteen blacks had laid out their firing lines and killing zones with great care. Soon after sunrise the action began. Zak used an RPG-7 rocket launcher to stop the leading Rhodesian KUDU mine-proofed personnel carrier and a decoy group of four men on the opposite side of the road began to fire on the burning vehicle with AK 47 and RPD machine-gun fire. Black and white police reservists spilled from this and a second vehicle and engaged the decoy party leaving their rear completely open to Zak and ten others lying just above them in the grey morning mists. Soon one tanker was ablaze and the others had reversed well out of range.

The Rhodesians held their ground and fought well although four of their number soon lay still and bloodied on the scarred and dirty tarmac. The survivors set up a mortar and shelled Zak's now consolidated position with some accuracy. Two of the comrades were killed, one blasted to pieces by a direct hit. Zak ordered a withdrawal and all three cadres disengaged in good order, making off through the shrouding mist evading a costly and fruitless pursuit operation mounted by a Police Anti-terrorist Unit section and even some limited air support.

Soaked with sweat and exhilarated beyond imagination, Zak had led his section home after splitting from the other two. Only one man had sustained a light flesh wound and the reception back at camp was ecstatic, the action retold again and again.

Shortly after this success Zak's home base was to be moved and his cadres – he then controlled two sections – were to be consolidated at New Chomwengi, an apparently impregnable hilltop base camp constructed and master-minded by East German advisors. Two days before Zak was due to move there in July 1977, a combined group of Rhodesian Light Infantry and Selous Scouts began a three-day attack on the ill-fated hill. With air support and ingenious use of their limited forces the Rhodesians, numbering only around two hundred men in total, completely routed the comrades leaving over three thousand dead in the trenches and on the slopes of the hill. This had been Zak's first lesson in the superiority of the white armed forces in Rhodesia and he knew that those in South Africa were vastly more advanced, if not in tenacity and training, in technology and weaponry. The New Chomwengi slaughter had been a great blow to ZANLA/ANC who were sure that victory was almost within their grasp. There were no questions asked when Zak informed his instructors and comrades that he was leaving Moçambique for South Africa and once again papers were prepared; this time a speedy false identity in the form of a South African reference/ID book which every African had to carry within that country.

Sad to leave Moçambique at the height of the struggle, yet feeling that his reprieve at Chomwengi was somehow an omen, Zak had travelled south to the border with Swaziland and slipped into that tiny kingdom in September 1977. By the end of that month he was in Barberton, safely ensconced in the black township and within a week he had a job driving a tourist bus for the Impala Hotel. It was in the Barberton black township that he met Ruby.

If Zachary Abel Mdhluli's development was a typical and logical progression from early abuse and violence by white authority to the ranks of the ANC and active service in the Rhodesian independence struggle, Ruben Nkhumische's was very different. Born in Johannesburg of reasonably wealthy black parents, Ruby had attended Alexandra primary school and proved from an early age that he was never going to be a scholar.

Ruby was short and powerful and, unlike his younger brother and older sister, he had no intention to progress in conventional academic terms. At the age of fourteen Ruby became a criminal when he and two friends beat up an old man returning to Alexandra township one Friday afternoon. The man was a lift operator in a downtown Johannesburg office block earning only ninety rands per month. This pay packet Ruby stole from him after kicking him several times in the head. The old man died of his injuries but Ruby escaped conviction because such matters were commonplace in Alexandra and Soweto every weekend. Black South African policemen made rudimentary enquiries and then dismissed the matter as they had countless others. Ruby, encouraged by his success, continued on his life of crime and brutality.

After robbing a small local supermarket, one of many owned by a consortium of Indians and coloureds, he ran into trouble. These tough traders had their own militia in the townships and their power was considerable. At the threat of his own health and that of his mother and father, a captured crony of Ruby's informed on him and the hunt was on for the seventeen-year-old thug who had dared to take on the supermarket syndicate.

Ruby fled to the eastern suburbs of Johannesburg, using money from the supermarket raid and R200 stolen from the old coffee tin in his mother's tiny kitchen. But the long arm of the syndicate caught up with him and he was chased further east to Bethal and then to the Eastern Transvaal town of Ermelo where he hid up in a dilapidated black hotel adjacent to the local township. They caught him there in a *shebeen* and beat him to the ground using socks filled with wet earth and rubber-covered lead pipes. Then they kicked him as he had the old man, but although they left him for dead, he was young and strong and so he survived. He had hidden some money in his girl's house in the township. She nursed him back to health, did fat Flora, and he stayed with her using her until all the money was finished. Then he beat her up one night, and stole the R70 she had been saving for their wedding.

Scarred and punch-drunk from the battering he'd received, Ruby travelled north, sleeping in the bush and occasionally in the *kraals* of friendly villagers. Wandering aimlessly in the summer of late 1977, he turned east again and reached Barberton, the sleepy Transvaal lowveld town which had seen great fame and fortune during the 1884 Gold Rush.

Ruby lived as a vagrant for two months, sleeping rough in the warm lowveld nights, owning only the tattered shirt and trousers he wore. Luck was on his side once again when he met a Swazi girl who worked as a maid in the Impala Hotel. She allowed him to sleep with her for two or three nights a week and he evaded the hotel security guard with ease and came to relish those nights in her warm bed, using her soft musky body as much as he wanted because too much was never enough for chubby sloe-eyed Evelyn. Eventually he was sleeping with her almost every night and one evening, in the smoky confines of her friend's room, he met Zak.

The big Zulu had a power and presence about him which captured Ruby from that first meeting and soon the two became firm friends. Zak found Ruby a job in the hotel as a kitchen boy, and Ruby's life became little short of idyllic with plenty to eat, Evey's bed every night and Zak as his friend and mentor. But this state of nirvana suddenly changed because Zak said he was going away to the Western Transvaal, to the Magaliesberg area of all places. Ruby couldn't understand the reasoning behind this move and pleaded with Zak to stay in the warm and comfortable nest that was Barberton, but Zak was adamant. 'I have to go Rube, it is not a matter of being able to choose.' Ruby's confusion increased so Zak had taken his arm and led him to a remote spot behind the hotel where the vehicles were parked and washed. 'I would like you to come with me Ruby because there are things that I would like to teach you and which I think you would learn fast. Don't worry about money, I have friends that supply me with everything I need. Come with me, Ruby, and you won't regret it,' Zak had said with great feeling.

They had left without saying anything to anyone, disappearing one night in March taking the little Volkswagen that Zak had bought a few months earlier. They had gone straight to Waltersville township near Boons where there was a house waiting for them with food, beer, women, everything arranged, so that they were even more comfortable than they had been in Barberton. Over the next few days, Zak had told Ruby about the ANC, swearing him to secrecy and instilling in his disciple the same burning fanaticism which had simmered within him during the months in Barberton.

He had done nothing in the lowveld, just watched and waited for instructions. These had come, as he knew they would, because he had written to the contact address Japie had given him in Ladysmith seemingly a lifetime ago. Zak maintained the same low profile in Waltersville for the first few months and then he began to assemble the rudiments of a cadre. His contact addresses changed over the years, his most recent being a box number in Johannesburg from where his requests seemed to be actioned with incredible speed.

All was now ready and within hours the strike would be made. Zak rose to urinate smiling to himself as he heard the rhythmic muffled creaks from Ruby's room, screened off like his with only a tattered curtain from the small living/dining area. His toothless smile widened. Ruby was taking his chances now. Although he may not realise it, that woman he had taken from the shebeen last night could well be his last on this Earth.

CHAPTER 10

Smaller was well back into the swing of things. Advertising revenue was improving and he had a new editor, a thirty-four-year-old female journalist who had worked on *House & Garden* in London and a society magazine in Los Angeles. Her name was Erica Waterhouse and she had recently married a South African and settled in Johannesburg. Ashley thought she was wonderful and Smaller had to admit that her pieces were good. At the moment, everything in the garden was more than satisfactory. In fact, Smaller considered it being close to lovely.

Since returning from the Magaliesberg his life really seemed to be going much better. He'd only been back a week but in those few short days the picture had become much rosier and he was rested and tanned and felt happier inside than he had since France. He'd been working better too, had even done a bit of writing; not just the Publisher's Message that he had previously found hard to manage.

Subaye was perhaps the cause of it. He had resisted her until Tuesday and then she had served him supper in the little dining area and he'd succumbed. Any man would have, he told himself afterwards. She had put fresh flowers on the table, the whole townhouse smelled fresh and clean. He'd come back from the office at around 6.30 and she'd had the ice, water and bottle of Ballantine's all ready and waiting on the sofa table together with the evening's *Star* which almost looked as though it had been ironed.

He'd thanked her, gone upstairs to change and then come down to his leather wing chair, newspaper and whisky. Subaye had been in the kitchen, softly humming and clattering dishes and pans in an oddly pleasing, muted fashion. Then she'd come out with a smile on her face to ask him to sit down at the little table where she'd set a place for one.

This was the first night that he'd told her he would be in for supper and it was obvious she'd gone to town to impress him. Even realising that, Smaller couldn't help but marvel at what she presented. It only served to reinforce his earlier impression of her intelligence and learning ability.

First there had been avocado pear, filled with tiny canned shrimps in a light sauce of oil, vinegar and chopped egg yolk; the bottle of Riesling was nicely chilled and the glass sparkled, it had been polished so well. Next came thinly sliced pork fillet with a *concasse* of onion and tomatoes served on a bed of fluffy rice. Smaller had gasped at this and eaten every morsel, while Subaye occasionally appeared in the kitchen doorway smiling shyly at his obvious pleasure. After the meal he had asked her to sit down at the table.

'How on earth did you do it Subaye, how did you learn to cook like that?' he had asked wonderingly.

Both her big black eyes had widened and then crinkled into a smile, the left was now almost back to normal. 'I've always known how to cook Martin, although not this type of food. My mother taught me when I was just a girl, how to make the most of meat and I read some of your cookery books in the kitchen. Sally showed me how to make the sauce for the avocado and the onion and tomatoes were simple enough because we eat that often on the farm with our meat and porridge. Did you really like it?'

Smaller had taken her hand, and that first touch had been enough because he saw her lower lip soften and tremble slightly. She'd brought coffee and a crème caramel that old Sally had bought from the corner supermarket. He'd followed this with another whisky which he sipped while he smoked a cigar. He then had a third refill and it was whilst he was finishing this last drink that Subaye appeared silently so that Smaller looked up startled from his newspaper.

'I've finished in the kitchen Martin and now I'm going for a shower.' she looked at him directly. 'There's some more recipe reading I'd like to do though. Perhaps you could leave the kitchen door open and I'll close it later when I leave.' Smaller had nodded, pretending ignorance of her intentions.

He'd gone up to bed around ten, feeling sleepy from the wine and whisky. But as he showered, his heart had pounded and the creeping warmth had begun in his lower stomach so that the hot water excited him, bringing him erect. He had got into bed and noted she had changed the sheets which felt crisp and clean, reminding him of his childhood and how he had always loved to fall asleep between fresh sheets. It had been after eleven when she had come, stealing up the stairs so that he failed to hear her as he dozed, heart pounding mildly, eyes closed. He smelled her before he heard her, a powdery perfumed woman smell mixed with the slight peppery skin odour of her race. The light was off and she had shed the cotton overall which all she wore and dived in beside him, a little breathless.

'Hello Martin,' she had said softly, and then he had turned and fallen on her, his lust for her body consuming them both alike in a wanton melting. Thrusting, writhing within her he boiled and spurted into her minutes before he wanted to, but she had been with him and she matched his shuddering, grinding spasms with her own. Afterwards she kissed him once on the lips and disappeared swiftly down the stairs without a sound. In the morning he was not sure if he hadn't dreamed the whole thing, but the smell of her in his bed shattered this waking illusion and then she was there with a mug of lemon tea, fresh and bright-eyed in her pink overall.

She smiled down at him as he lay, just awake. 'You look like a little boy, *Baas* Martin,' she'd said softly.

Smaller had tried to analyse what it was about Subaye that captivated him. It was Friday afternoon and he sat in his office after a pleasingly indulgent lunch with Ashley. The picture had continued to look rosier as the week progressed and, to celebrate advertising contracts to the value of over R20,000 by close of business on Thursday, Smaller and Ashley had gone off to lunch at the Sunnyside Park Hotel.

They had sat out on the terrace which was quite warm at midday in the bright early winter sun. Great plane trees formed an umbrella of russet orange and gold over the diners below. Occasionally a leaf would detach and spiral down onto the neatly barbered grass or stone-flagged terrace. They'd had pâté maison to start with and a bottle of Graves, then fresh-grilled crayfish from the Wild Coast. Smaller had splashed out and ordered a bottle of Laurent Perrier 1976. It had been a magic lunch; the moist and delicate crayfish and the peppery dryness of the champagne combined with the polite guffaws of wealthy men and the tinkling laughter of their women. Élegance and good food. Pleasure paid for and taken with relish by men that could afford it. Smaller had been happy to be one of this select band and his old confidence returned anew so that women stared at him with obvious appreciation and waiters hovered deferentially at his elbow.

Sitting quietly on his leather Chesterfield Smaller sipped his black coffee and considered Subaye and her effect on his life. It was ridiculous to suppose that she was influencing him really but his mood and demeanour had improved so much in the past week that he had to admit to some responsibility on her behalf. She had not come on Wednesday and he had found himself waiting for her last night and so, knowing and feeling his want, she had come. This time she had stayed until almost three in the morning, dozing with her soft springy head on his shoulder and he had lain awake, sated and calm, pondering on the incredible chemistry that existed between them.

Smaller lit a cigarette wondering where he was going with his life. It was odd that this black girl seemed to have engendered new meaning to his previously pointless existence. It had happened in two short weeks and he recognised the feeling from when he had first met Isobelle. Isobelle, his lovely radiant wife, who had now faded into a memory together with his beautiful little daughter. They had become misty images, like photographs of childhood acquaintances, long grown up and no longer recognisable.

He stubbed out the cigarette and looked at his watch. It was after 4.30 and most of Johannesburg was already well on the way home, or at the golf club, or still at lunch. That was the whites of course. The blacks would leave the city at around this time to jam themselves into buses and trains bound for the townships of Alexandra and Soweto. There they ran the gauntlet of the *tsotsi* gangs; young thugs who would lie in wait to rob and terrorise the returning workers who inevitably were paid on Fridays.

Those lucky enough, or strong enough, to resist this hazard would go out and drink later because it was Friday night and there was no more work until Monday. They would pack into the *shebeens*, ordinary houses where liquor was sold illegally and at considerable profit by the *shebeen* keepers. The police raided these drinking joints and people were arrested and heads broken with batons, but within a day or so a similar operation would open up maybe only half a block away.

Smaller considered the lot of the urban black, the city worker who lived in the vast and dirty townships which were only now being electrified in an agonisingly slow programme. It was true that South African blacks were the richest blacks in Africa, that migrant workers from neighbouring states clamoured to be chosen for the hellish life kilometres below the surface of the earth. Hundreds of thousands came every year to disappear into the great gasping, roaring maw of the gold mines where they would sweat and toil and occasionally die to quarry the great gold-bearing reef from which tiny particles of soft yellow metal were eked.

With the white man's meagre understanding of the African, Smaller still considered the South African black to be an odd specimen of humanity. In fact those varying and disparate tribes were often unfathomable, frequently mulishly stupid and not occasionally frighteningly violent. They quarrelled viciously amongst themselves and the faction fights on the mines were modern day re-enactions of the Zulu or Ndebele *Impis* going out to slaughter a few hundred Tswana or Sotho for sport. But the blacks relished their tribal traditions, feeding hungrily on the stories of their past and the great battles against each other and the white man. Despite westernisation and increasing wealth they still believed in spirits and the evil little man which they called *tokoloshe*.

Smaller recalled an incident with his very first maid in Johannesburg back in the late sixties. The girl was very intelligent and fluent in English. When they had kitted out her servant's room Isobelle had bought her a new iron divan bed. Smaller had looked in one morning at the clean and tidy little room to see the feet of the bed mounted on bricks so that the whole thing was waist-high above the ground. When he asked why this had been done the black girl told him quite seriously that it was because of the *tokoloshe*, the little man, who would come in the night and take you away if he could reach you.

Smaller smiled now in the calm quiet of his office, remembering the incident as though it were yesterday. The girl had looked at him, her big brown eyes wide with fear at even the mention of the dreaded little man and Smaller had smiled and asked her if she knew of anyone who had been 'taken'.

'No, *Baas,*' Pauline had said with very real gravity. 'But everyone knows that the *tokoloshe* is about at night and therefore we keep all our doors and windows tight shut – and anyway, our beds are too high for him to reach,' she had added triumphantly. Smaller had remembered the musty stench of countless servants' rooms in the years after and recalled that no black he had employed had ever left windows open at night. They really did believe in this little fearsome man, the childlike black people of this country. He had said to the girl, 'But Pauline, if the *tokoloshe* could take you, why could he not take me? The madam and I sleep on a very low bed, just above the ground and we have never been taken. Why is that do you think?'

Pauline had been unable to answer and looked wonderingly at Smaller as if he were slightly mad. It was as if she had never considered that white people slept within reach of the *tokoloshe*. Smaller had recounted the tale to Isobelle and they had laughed about it together. But now, after fifteen years in this southern part of Africa, he understood a little of the rationale of that young Tswana girl. She had been taught since childhood that the *tokoloshe* existed and therefore she believed that he did in the same way that a Christian believes in God; in the same way that a believer would make the sign of the cross to ward off evil.

Smaller was not in the least bit religious and held the theory that religion was just an advanced form of superstition. Didn't a dying man always say a prayer even if he'd never been inside a church in his life? The reason to Smaller was obvious. Although the man might have discounted religion all his life whilst he was young and healthy, when death stared him in the face in the shape of old age or severe mutilation due to accident or strife, he prayed. He prayed because since childhood he had been told that there really was a benevolent being, a kindly presence up there in the infinite blackness of the universe and, since he was dying, he may as well have a go because it might just be true.

Shaking off these morbid thoughts, Smaller shrugged into his jacket and left the deserted offices for the garage. As he went down in the lift he thought of the evening ahead.

He had nothing planned and had told Subaye to prepare dinner for him. A calming warmth enveloped him as he thought of her and he smiled to himself. He would have to ask her whether she believed in the *tokoloshe* If she did, she obviously knew that he didn't bother the white people because she'd spent more than an hour or two in his bed and that was nowhere near high enough.

It was 8.30 and they were all assembled in the shack that had been the home of Zak and Ruby for almost three years. Zak considered that the chances of his seeing it again after tonight were very remote. He had gone for the weapons after dusk and they now lay on the floor on a dusty canvas sheet. Temba's AK 47 was still hidden near his village but Zak had told him to leave it there. 'We have enough firepower for one farmer and his family, my boys. Temba can use my AK and I will use this little beauty.' Turning dramatically, he crouched to dig around under his bed and pulled out an ugly little sub-machine gun.

The weapon was a Schmeisser MP 40 of World War II vintage but it hadn't fired more than two magazines and was in mint condition. It had reached Zak via a tortuous route from Moçambique and had originally been intended for use by FRELIMO, one of a consignment of two hundred sent from Libya in 1973. The FRELIMO military favoured the use of Russian weaponry and were derisive of European cast-offs of 1940 vintage. They willingly shipped a dozen Schmeissers via Swaziland to ANC moles in South Africa and the weapons were carried across the border hidden in cars and trucks. Transported carefully, with trusted contacts who would only carry one weapon per vehicle, all the Schmeissers had reached South Africa undetected. Zak's had arrived partially disassembled in a brown paper covered cardboard box tightly packed with polystyrene. It hadn't rattled and he was amazed when he opened it to find a gun complete with two thirty-two-shot magazines.

Zak had never fired this weapon but he had tried the

Israeli Uzi which was not dissimilar to the MP 40. He knew that German weapons were first-class pieces of engineering and that this sub-machine gun had been carried by elite parabat units and had earned praise for its firepower and reliability in every major campaign that the Wehrmacht had embarked upon.

Ruby hefted the MP 40 and caressed it as a man would a woman's body. The other three looked at it wonderingly; at the collapsible stock and the long stick magazine which Zak had pushed into place in front of the forepiece. The whole gun was made of stamped steel, formed and welded into what Zak considered to be a beautifully functional shape. It was blued to a matt black finish, and loaded it weighed nine pounds. Zak took it back from Ruby and laid it on the floor with the four Kalashnikovs and pulled a canvas bag out from under the bed. His eyes bored into the four men. 'Now look at these very carefully' he said, 'one mistake with one of these things and you're dead.'

Inside the olive drab sack were five khaki-coloured canisters. Temba stared at them with fearful fascination, so menacing was their appearance. He knew them to be bombs and when Zak picked one up, holding it out to him by its handle, he shrank back, his eyes widening so that the whites showed clearly in the dark shiny mahogany face.

Zak smiled his toothless smile and put the grenade on the little pine table: 'Don't be afraid, Temba, they can't hurt you unless you pull the pin out and let go of the handle.' Still smiling Zak pulled out the pin and held out the canister at arm's length towards the four men. All but Ruby dived to the floor and Temba began a frantic backward scramble for the doorway but then Zak replaced the pin without releasing the handle and laughed out loud. Temba's face ran with sweat and his heart pounded uncontrollably. He realised that he had almost soiled himself and was so incensed that he jumped to his feet and grabbed a grenade from the four left in the bag. Aping Zak, he pulled out the pin and then held in the handle with only one hand; he

196

smiled mirthlessly and opposite him Ruby tensed while Zak's face paled to a dirty greyish brown hue.

Zak knew the failings of the Russian RTD fragmentation grenade. Like its predecessor, the F1, it had one design drawback that made it quite lethal in the hands of the uninitiated. The clasp handle flew off axially when the grenade was thrown, not radially as with the much safer British and US counterparts. This meant that if the hands were wet, as Temba's were now with the perspiration of fear, the pressure exerted could make the entire handle slip quite easily from under the fingers. Temba's grasp seemed firm but then he gestured with the ugly dun-coloured can, shaking it about in the faces of Zak and the now cowering Ruby. Zak knew that he was closer to death than at any other time in his life and he tried to summon every shred of self-control in order to try to save the critical situation. If Temba inadvertently released the handle, the four-to-five-second delay would not allow them all to get out of the shack. More important, even if two or three survived, the blast would bring the police down on Waltersville within fifteen minutes and their operation against the Bester farmstead would have to be aborted.

Zak spoke softly and quietly. 'Temba listen to me. You are now in great danger, as are we all. Please take great care and replace the pin, making sure that you hold the handle firmly all the time.' His eyes bored into those of the gesticulating Temba and it seemed as if they transmitted the awful danger in milliseconds because Temba's face paled instantly and his hand shook as he tried to replace the pin.

They all watched spellbound and then the pin went in with an audible snick. Zak let out a long shuddering sigh and took the grenade from Temba's hands; it was wet with perspiration and Zak's anger at this stupidity boiled up suddenly so that he smashed Temba backhanded across the mouth.

Ruby was all for beating the young black into insensibility but Zak realised that all of them had just experienced a

197

more than graphic lesson in how to handle the grenades. These five had been smuggled in from Lesotho and were of late fifties vintage. In fact, although the RTD was a World War II grenade, it had only recently been replaced in the USSR and many millions of this type were still in circulation. Zak had used them in Rhodesia and knew them to be very useful weapons with their six ounces of TNT and a very effective fragmentation sleeve inside the can.

It was almost 10.30 and time to go. Zak hefted the MP 40 and the others slung the AK 47s over their shoulders and Ruby grabbed the bag of grenades. The vehicles were right outside the door and they all climbed inside without speaking, Temba still grey and trembling slightly with reaction after his act of lunacy.

Zak had traded in the VW beetle for an Isuzu 1800 truck. The vehicle was painted a nondescript cream and was suitably battered and dented, very typical of farm vehicles in the area. But the engine was in excellent condition and the lightweight wagon had four-wheel-drive capability so that it could be driven hard and fast over dirt roads and rough terrain. Zak would drive the Isuzu and Ruby the old Peugeot 404 which Zak had bought for him to run around in during their tenure at Waltersville.

They left the township and Zak noted the familiar smell of smoke in the air. Most Africans cooked on makeshift wood-burning stoves and, as a result, the areas around their locations were denuded of trees. The evening was cloudless and still and a young moon gave little light as the two vehicles bounced and thumped along the dirt road that led to the tarmac. Zak turned the Isuzu left onto the main road from Magaliesberg to Derby and Koster, and within minutes they were through the little rail junction of Boons with its single store, post office and petrol station. Zak looked out into the faint silvery glow of the new moon and saw the oceans of mealie fields stunted and dried with the poor rains of the late summer. They stretched away on both sides of the road but this year there would be no rejoicing during the harvest in late June and July. Sometimes, when the crop had been good, the farmers would give great ox *braais* and beer drinks for their black workers. These were usually held on Friday night so that the weekend could be utilised to sleep off the terrible hangovers that resulted.

Zak glanced left at Temba who sat beside him moody and silent from the blow in the mouth. His lower lip was slightly puffed but it was his ego which was most damaged. Zak smiled and clapped Temba over the shoulders with his left hand. 'Cheer up boy, don't take it too hard that slap I gave you.' He paused and considered his words because he knew that the younger man needed to regain face. He continued in a softer voice. 'I understand that you were put down by my trick with the grenade, but that doesn't mean that you can pull the same stunt with a weapon you don't understand.'

Temba looked at Zak and the older man thought he resembled a wounded dog. Zak concentrated on the road and checked in his rearview mirror. Ruby was right there behind, barrelling along in the Peugeot. The big Zulu grinned mirthlessly into the blackness of the windshield and spoke his thoughts aloud for the benefit of Temba. 'Not much chance of a roadblock at this time of night, Temba. We'll be at the turn-off for Swartplaas in a couple of minutes.' Despite himself his heart thudded strongly in his chest. It had been the same when they crossed the border from Moçambique into Rhodesia back in '77. It was always the same before the action began, but once he was into it there was no problem.

Temba sat quietly although his heart too was beginning to beat faster. His mouth felt dry, despite the swollen lip, and he felt tiny rivulets of sweat trickling down his ribs under the loose navy-blue shirt he wore. Zak was dressed in dark denim jeans and a black shirt with a navy cotton windbreaker over it. Temba wore no jacket yet he felt hot and cold at the same time and the sweat beaded his forehead.

They turned off the tar road and the dirt road to Swart-plaas stretched ahead like a narrow cutting between the maize fields. Temba remembered his drive home that night with Subaye on this same farm track. He recalled how she had looked at him in the back of the old Ford Fairlane, how she had rolled down her pantihose and then finally taken him in her mouth. His mind filled with images of Subaye and, as they passed the point in the track where the small path led to her village, he stared out of the window of the truck trying to catch a glimpse of a known landmark in the blue blackness of the *veld*. Then they were past, had taken the left fork in the road and were bouncing on towards Bester's farm between Merindol and Swartplaas. Suddenly Temba thought of Benjie, his light-hearted little friend of many years. What was Benjie doing tonight, why had they lost touch with each other? Since Subaye had gone, his life had fallen apart and he'd been getting drunk and going late to work so that *Baas* Swanepoel had finally given him the sack a week ago. Now there was only Zak and Ruby and the ANC. There was no shortage of money, Zak paid for everything but he gave the orders too. Temba felt that he was bound to the big man, rather than the party. He was powerless under Zak's will, tonight had shown that. What else would tonight bring? he wondered distractedly and then his heart began to accelerate even more and a sharp pain flashed across his forehead. It was as though his brain couldn't cope with what had been happening in the past few weeks, and what was still to come tonight.

The old brown Peugeot 404 trundled along behind Zak's truck. Ruby didn't get too close because first of all he would be able to see nothing in the cloud of red dust raised by the bucking Isuzu, and secondly they should not appear to be driving in convoy. To be stopped in a roadblock, or even by a police car, would be fatal.

Smart sat silent beside him and William crouched in the back, like Ruby they were all fearful of what was to come when they reached Bester's farmstead. Ruby licked his dry lips and thought of the future, the time after tonight. Somehow it wouldn't seem to gel and the butterfly feeling surged in his stomach as he suddenly considered that there may be nothing after tonight. Smiling sickly he turned to Smart, an older and wiser man who had been an ANC member since the sixties.

'Tell me about the party, Smart, tell me about Mandela and Tambo.' Ruby knew the history by heart but he wanted to hear it again from Smart as Zak wasn't there beside him to reassure him, to tell him about the great martyrs, indoctrinating him gladly into the ANC way of thinking.

Smart's voice began to drone away in his subconscious but Ruby knew what he was saying, knew it all almost before the words came out. The ANC had been founded in 1912 by a brave group of Johannesburg blacks who were resolved to 'defend Africans against repression'. Initially the organisation wanted to effect change through peaceful reform rather than bloody revolution but progress was less than scant and, with the loss of the Smuts government to the Afrikaners in 1948, the writing was on the wall for black South Africans. It was shortly after, that the term *apartheid* was first used and then reviled by a world being swiftly purged of the old colonial ways. The ANC despaired of ever making headway and so they encouraged strikes and boycotts by blacks and demonstrations against discrimination. The most hated law had always been that all blacks within South Africa must carry pass books which would identify their 'homeland'. The appropriate stamp would allow them to work only in areas predetermined by the Department of Bantu Administration.

At Sharpeville, in 1960, police opened fire on a group of demonstrators killing sixty-nine, wounding over a hundred more. White South Africa reeled under the threat of urban revolt and the Johannesburg Stock Exchange plunged in the scramble to sell up and leave. At this time the ANC and its rival the PAC were proclaimed banned organisations and after a few years certain leaders were imprisoned under the

Terrorism Act. Most famous of these was Nelson Mandela, a charismatic lawyer, who still remains titular head of the ANC. Mandela was imprisoned on Robben Island in Table Bay and remains there to this day. Now, sixty-five years old and with failing health, Mandela has been replaced by Oliver Tambo who fled South Africa at the time of Mandela's arrest.

Under the direction of this mild-mannered former teacher and lawyer, the ANC has received a new lease of life since the fifteen years of chaos that followed Mandela's arrest in 1964. Tambo's base of operations is in Lusaka, Zambia, far enough away for South African raids to become international incidents. Ruby knew that the ANC now numbered over six thousand men and women and that many, like Zak, had been trained as freedom fighters. These people were billeted in camps within Moçambique, Tanzania and more recently Lesotho, previously the British Protectorate of Basutoland. There were comrades too, working with SWAPO in Angola, from where strikes were made against the South African forces that occupied Namibia. But the largest group of ANC members existed clandestinely within South Africa and were headed up by cadre leaders like Zak. Since 1981 almost one hundred acts of sabotage had been carried out against the white regime and communist weaponry from East Germany and Russia was finding its way into stockpiles via several devious routes.

Smart had stopped talking but Ruby's mind had continued with his review of the ANC's history so that now he felt confident and almost eager to get into action. He had never been in any military confrontation other than occasional brushes with the police, but Zak had assured him that, after the first few seconds, positive reaction to danger was virtually automatic. Like Temba, Smart and William, he had practised loading and unloading the AK 47 rifle until he could do it in the dark. He had squeezed the trigger on an empty chamber and knew how to sight and fire the weapon, how to change magazines swiftly and how to turn the action from semi-automatic to full automatic. The grenades had been quite another matter though. They had terrified him, especially when that fool, Temba, had pulled the pin. Somehow Ruby knew that he had been very close to death already tonight and the feeling would not leave him so that it dispelled his good mood of capable mastery. He watched the tail lights of the Isuzu shining dully through the orange haze of dust. Zak was slowing, they were close to the narrow dirt track that led to Bester's farm. Ruby knew that it was almost time now and his stomach revolted as adrenalin poured into his bloodstream. He looked at his watch. It was a few minutes before eleven.

Bester had enjoyed his evening with Loots and Marina in Klerksdorp. They'd talked about the old days and had more than a few *dops* and some bloody wonderful 1973 Pinotage with supper. He could have carried on all night, deeply into the old KWV brandy with Loots but Luna and the boys needed to get home. Hendrik, the ten year old, was always the first to go and he'd dropped off on the couch there in Loots' lounge; funny enough little Neels was still going strong when they left, and him only eight too.

Luna would always be a bit uppity when he and Loots talked about the old days when they were single. Loots was always winking and smiling, then Luna would get the hell in pretty damned quick. She and Marina went into the lounge to talk about kids and perfume and all the other bullshit women talk about. He and Loots had sat there at the table polishing off the brandy and smoking cigars.

They'd both done well enough, all things considered. Loots had a nice little house with a pool, a Mercedes in the garage and a Golf for Marina. Both cars had been insurance write-offs that Loots had rebuilt in his panel shop and now they both looked brand new. In the glow from the dashboard Bester smiled at his thoughts and his wife saw the expression and placed her hand on his knee. They were in the old BMW which Bester had to admit was getting a bit jaded. He considered an alternative. Surely old Loots would be able to fix him up with something nice.

It was almost 10.30 when they turned into the drive. Bester pulled up right outside the front door so that he could carry the boys in; both were now sound asleep. Luna took the key and went ahead to unlock the front door whilst Bester opened the BMW's rear door and looked down on his two sons. They slept peacefully on an old blanket head to toe, both sandwiched between the backrest of the big bench seat and the front seat backs which Bester and Luna had slid right back to keep them from rolling about. He lifted Hennie and felt the usual warmth welling up within him as he smelled the sweet child smell of his son. Quickly he carried the boy into his bedroom and slid him into his bunk fully dressed; Luna would come to undress them in a few minutes. Little Neels came next, curled up and sound asleep, sucking his thumb as usual. Bester grinned, that was a habit they'd have to get him out of. This boy was really just like his mother, blond, blue eyed and slender with slim wrists and ankles. Hendrik was more like him with darker blond hair and a sturdy, yet athletic frame. Neels would probably be the taller of the two but they were both fine boys and he loved them dearly.

Depositing his younger son in his bed, Bester went into the lounge to pour a last brandy. He reflected that life was not bad here in the Magaliesberg. They were far away from Johannesburg and all the noise, traffic and political nonsense. There'd been a car bomb in Bloemfontein that had made a hell of a mess but not killed anyone. Typical of the blacks that was. They couldn't get anything right, not even a bomb. The silly buggers had put the car under a garage forecourt which had a wall on two sides with a concrete slab above and this had absorbed most of the blast. The only person badly injured had been a black pump attendant.

Yes, it was peaceful here in the Magaliesberg. The blacks here knew their place. They were good chaps his boys and some of them had worked on the farm for years, for the old man before him. Bester locked the front door and checked the back door. All were locked securely as were the windows, all except the one in his bedroom, but that had burglar bars. He couldn't sleep without a window open, even in the winter. Luna said he was mad but there it was, he had to have fresh air. He finished his drink and switched off the lights in the lounge and hallway, then walked down the corridor to his bedroom, thinking of Luna and the big wide bed, the slim body with the firm breasts and soft buttocks. But by the time he had washed and brushed his teeth she was already asleep, knocked out by the unaccustomed amount of wine. He slipped in quietly beside her and switched off the light. Tomorrow was Sunday and they could sleep late once the boys went out to play. There would be plenty of time then.

Zak had driven past the target on no less than five occasions, spaced out over four weeks. He had even driven into the yard and asked for a fictitious labourer by name to be told rudely by the Boss Boy that there was no such person on *Baas* Bester's farm. The visit had given him a chance to work out the plan of attack. He knew that the living-room windows faced north onto the brushed dirt courtyard at the back of the farm. Chances were that the main bedroom windows also faced that way whilst the dining room looked onto the front of the property and the dirt road. The *stoep*, with its collection of garden chairs, was on the south side so it was likely that the dining room would be behind it, such was normally the plan with these farmhouses.

They had worked out the attack in Zak's house at Waltersville and he had gone over it more than a dozen times until each of the four others knew exactly what was to happen and in what order. As usual the problem would be the dogs. Bester had two and, like all farm dogs, they barked whenever any strange black came within one hundred metres of their home. In the satchel with the grenades there was a polythene bag which contained stewing steak liberally injected with cyanide. Zak hoped this might account for the dogs but he knew that it was quite possible the animals would ignore the meat if they had been well trained. Time would tell, it would only be a matter of minutes now. Then he would find out.

They parked both vehicles after turning them around, facing back towards the main road to Magaliesberg. Zak and Temba closed the doors of the Isuzu quietly and Ruby, Smart and William joined them silently, arriving suddenly like shadows in the gloom. That was one of the very positive points about being black, Zak thought as he looked at his men. Nobody could see you in the dark.

The narrow lane was silent and totally deserted. The Bester farm was at least two kilometres from any other inhabited buildings. They had left their transport parked, hard-up against the hedge of thorn bushes and creepers and now they crossed the track to fan out as planned, Zak and Temba together, Ruby, Smart and William in the other group. There were no lights on in the house but a *stoep* lamp flooded the yard at the rear and Zak knew that the dogs would be alert. He and Temba sprinted noiselessly down Bester's driveway and melted into the shadow of a giant plane tree some ten metres from the western corner of the house.

They waited for a couple of minutes while Zak unslung the MP 40 from his shoulder, making sure that the magazine was locked in place and cocking the gun, allowing the first 9 mm round to enter the chamber. He selected full automatic fire and folded out the steel butt, then he put the weapon on safety and checked Temba's Kalashnikov. Thirty seconds later a dog growled threateningly, then began barking loudly from the south eastern corner of the house where the other three were supposed to be. Zak cursed loudly and felt inside the canvas shoulder bag for a grenade; he had three and Ruby's group had the other two. Beside him Temba trembled with fear and anticipation of the action to come and Zak could clearly smell the rank odour that came off him. 'Come on boy, just follow me and take it easy.' The two ran across the yard towards the house just as a loud booming report sounded, oddly muffled, from the front of the farmstead.

Bester never knew how he managed to wake so quickly, especially considering the brandy and wine he'd consumed. He became fully conscious about a minute after Piet, the four-year-old ridgeback, growled just outside the window. Beside him, Luna slept soundly and he slid from the bed feeling the slight lightheadedness of being woken after only just falling asleep. Something seemed wrong. There was an almost tangible threat of great danger hanging over him and he went straight to the wardrobe to take the Smith and Wesson pump shotgun out. The box of SSG cartridges was there behind his neatly piled shirts on the middle shelf and he emptied it into both pockets of his towelling robe. The ridgeback started to bark now, deep genuine barking which left little doubt that something was amiss, then the alsatian started as well and Luna woke up suddenly, looking startled and a little frightened. Bester spoke urgently.

'Someone's out there darling. Get the kids and lock yourself in our bathroom, quickly'. Her mouth opened to reply but he was already gone, slipping down the passage towards the study next door. He whispered tensely over his shoulder, 'For God's sake, don't put any lights on.'

The shotgun was loaded but not cocked and Bester slid back the forepiece, pumping the first shell into the barrel. He crouched beside the window in the study, concealed by the heavy velvet curtains. There was hardly any moon and the dogs could just be seen advancing slowly across the front lawn, growling steadily now and moving close to the ground with menacing purposeful steps. Then Bester saw the slightest movement beside the big Bougainvillea bush and the glint of diffused moonlight on metal. He stepped back, aiming the shotgun through the window at the tiny point of light and pulled the trigger.

The glass blew out and the noise inside the small room was deafening. A great tongue of flame shot out of the end of the barrel. Bester was momentarily reminded of how they shot hares in the new mealies at night, going out with the Datsun truck and a handheld spotlight. The range was about fifteen metres and the charge of fourteen heavy lead balls hit Smart in the upper chest. The spread was around twenty-five centimetres at that distance and the black fell without a sound, his vital organs torn to pieces by the shot which knocked him over backwards into the purple blooms of the bush.

William screamed insanely and opened up in terror with his AK 47, aiming for the windows on the front of the house, but firing high and hitting the corrugated iron roof, which made a great deal of noise but did little damage. Bester ducked back from the shattered window and ran for the door, praying that his wife would keep her own and the boys' heads down. He crossed the corridor to the kitchen, pumped the action, and fired one shot at random out of the window in case there were any of the bastards at the back. The Smith and Wesson had four shots left in its tube magazine and Bester pushed a couple more into the loading aperture and raced back towards the main bedroom just as another burst of automatic fire began. Bullets blasted into the room and in the dim light he saw Luna and the children lying flat on the floor, the boys virtually covered by their mother's naked body. In that frantic half second Bester imagined what the *kaffirs* outside would do with her if they caught her alive and the rage that resulted gave him new strength and pushed the terror that was welling up inside him into the background.

'Stay exactly were you are!' he screamed and ran back down the passage and into the dining room. A movement on the *stoep* caught his eye but he was slow bringing the shotgun to bear and then flashes lit the room as a series of sharp, tugging jolts brushed at his left shoulder, spinning him backwards and mercifully away from the rest of the burst. 7.62 mm bullets ricocheted around the room, chipping plaster and wood from the walls and furniture and in pain and fear Bester stumbled and raged and fired the 12 bore wildly from the hip, pumping the action and pressing the trigger three times.

Ruby couldn't see anything because of the AK's muzzle flashes and then his right leg seemed to collapse without warning and he was lying on the cold slate of the *stoep*, the rifle flying away and a great dullness filling his brain. He rolled over and tried to sit up and then dreamily felt for the damage to his leg but there was only wetness there and he realised that his leg was gone, torn off well above the knee. He opened his mouth to scream but the vital blood was pumping fast from his femoral artery preventing his animal cry of terror and Ruby merely groaned once and then passed out. Within a minute he was dead.

Zak heard the blasts of sound from Bester's shotgun and had noted earlier the flash from the kitchen window. That shot didn't come anywhere near Temba and him but then there were three other reports in quick succession and Zak knew that things were going terribly wrong and thought that this bloody Boer, Bester, was not an easy man to take after all. He and Temba still crouched on the south-eastern corner of the single-storey house, waiting to see what would happen, Zak a little frightened yet totally rational and unwilling to take the slightest chance with his own very valuable skin. He crept to the kitchen window with Temba behind him and pulled the pin from a grenade, tossing it up through the broken glass. It landed with a metallic clonk and then came the roar of the explosion and, almost immediately, a high-pitched screaming from inside the house.

Zak grinned over his shoulder at Temba whose shirt was wet with sweat. 'Things should get better now, Temba. Follow me, we're going in through the kitchen door.' He gestured to the stable door which hung crazily off its hinges. 'But first let's give them another of these.' He tossed a second grenade through the shattered woodwork.

Luna lay terrified on top of her whimpering children. She had heard the bangs from Danie's shotgun and the hail of automatic fire and she was sure he must be dead. Those animals would come for her now and she was so frightened that she had urinated onto the bedroom carpet and could smell herself. She dismissed the self-loathing. It didn't really matter in the scheme of things. Summoning every shred of self-control she slithered over the floor to Danie's bedside table and opened the drawer. The heavy Star 9 mm pistol was there in its holster. She slid it out and checked the action. Danie had shown her how to use it and she had fired a couple of magazines into a target on the haystack. Her hand trembled but she pulled back the slide and made sure the safety catch was off. She gripped the pistol two-handed and went back to her sons who moaned softly like frightened puppies, holding each other tightly in terror. Then came the huge bang from the kitchen and plaster flakes fell from the ceiling all over Luna. Despite herself, she began to scream in mindless shrieks which were instantly echoed by the children.

Bester lay on the cold wood-block floor of the little hallway, just outside the dining room. The concussion of the grenade had deafened him temporarily but the single brick wall between corridor and kitchen had absorbed the blast and although it had cracked and loosened, it still held together. He could hear a terrible screaming coming from the bedroom but it was muted by his deafness. Then there was another clonk and a second enormous blast of sound which blew Bester back against the opposite wall of the corridor. The concussion deafened him anew but he could see that bricks had been blown out of the bottom of the common wall between kitchen and passage. Again he heard the screaming, and his shoulder was wet and it ached as though someone had punched it very hard. He rolled over onto his stomach and pushed the barrel of the Smith and Wesson towards the opening, one brick above the floor. He was sure they'd come in that way. There was a bit of light from the lamp in the yard; the stupid *kaffirs* should have put that out.

William had recovered from that first frantic burst and the gory death of Smart. One of the dogs had come at him and he'd shot it in the head from point-blank range and the other had run off in terror. He heard the first grenade and ran around the side of the house into the back yard. There were Zak and Temba, crouched in shadow below the kitchen window and his heart lifted with relief that they were still there and had not left him as he had suspected. He ran silently towards them and Zak turned, the MP 40 wheeling towards this new source of danger; then the barrel dropped and William exhaled a great sigh of relief. Zak gestured towards the kitchen door and William joined the two of them under the window. 'Smart is dead and I think that Ruby must have been shot, there was no sign of him after he ran onto the *stoep,* just that big shotgun blasting away and then nothing.' Zak grunted and lifted the MP 40. 'We're going to get the bastard. Come on, into the kitchen now, you two first. I'll be right behind you.'

If William questioned this order he gave no sign and leapt at the kitchen door, tearing it from its hinges, spraying the room with his AK. Bullets blasted plaster into dust and whanged off the kitchen appliances, then William was up the three steps and into the devastated room with Temba close behind him. Zak too went up the steps but waited on the threshold, instinct holding him back.

The blast of noise was huge in the little room and William fell screaming, one foot almost severed above the ankle and the other torn with shot. Temba fell back in horror, dimly seeing the stump gleaming black in the gloom. He cannoned into Zak in the doorway and the two men rolled down the steps into the dirt of the yard. Zak jumped to his feet and pulled Temba with him. 'That's it. That's enough now. We're going, William's had it.' He dragged the stunned Temba across the yard. 'You take the Peugeot, here are the spare keys. I'll go in the Isuzu. Don't follow me, you know what to do.'

Temba stumbled after the bulky figure of Zak who ran fast and easily down the driveway towards the road. He felt drained with reaction and couldn't seem to get his breath. The AK bounced against his hip and he wondered what to do with it. Zak seemed to read his mind. 'Throw the gun over the hedge and just drive slowly and carefully like I told you all when we made the plan. You remember, eh boy?'

Temba nodded and it seemed to come home to him now that he must get away, that the other three were dead or maimed. Screaming still came from the farmhouse but Temba couldn't tell who was making those awful bellowing noises of agony. He hoped it wasn't poor William.

Zak threw the Schmeisser into the thorn hedge and paused at the door of the truck. 'Best of luck Temba,' he grinned into the faint moonlight, but there was no flash of white in the toothless smile. 'It was just bad luck about that shotgun. We couldn't have reckoned on that, eh? But a good move for the party; these farmers will not feel quite so happy now, eh.' He gave a half-wave and climbed into the cab, starting the engine immediately. Temba stood helpless and open-mouthed as the Isuzu moved smoothly away in the direction of the main road.

Moving faster now that he was totally alone and vulnerable, he climbed into the Peugeot and, hands trembling, felt for the ignition. The old car started at the first turn and Temba pulled off, driving automatically. His mind filled with a maelstrom of conflicting thoughts. His shirt was still soaked with perspiration, so that he felt chilled and dull-witted with shock and reaction from the few mindless minutes at the farmstead. He came to a fork in the road and turned left towards Merindol, away from the main road,

bouncing along the dirt road, the headlights dim yellow a.
ineffectual so that he couldn't go very fast.

Bester crawled down the gloom of the corridor to his
bedroom, pushing the shotgun in front of him. He didn't
think it likely that there were any more of them but you
couldn't take chances with these fucking animals. There was
one screaming in the kitchen, screaming like a stuck pig.
His hearing was returning and the ringing in his ears was
lessening. He vaguely thought he heard a car start in the
lane outside and he knew that they must have gone His
heart lifted with relief. He pushed open the bedroom door
with the barrel of the shotgun and immediately there were
two sharp explosions, so close that they were like one long
blast of noise.

Unseen holes had appeared in the door about a metre
above his head and he shouted in fear. 'It's alright darling,
it's me, they've gone.' Unknowingly, and for no apparent
reason, he spoke in English but she heard him and gave a
great sobbing cry of relief. The door opened and she was
there and he felt for her. Then his head was in her naked
lap and her skin was strangely damp and he smelled an odd
animal smell. But it didn't matter because he lost
consciousness.

The Smits, on the neighbouring farm over two and a half
kilometres away, had heard the crump of the grenades and
the muted chatter of the AKs, muffled and deadened by
the shallow hills which separated the two properties. Old
Stevie Smit had come with his R1 rifle and his boss boy
and they'd found William half-dead with blood loss in the
kitchen. The *stoep* light was still on, high in the eaves of
the tin roof and it was with the aid of this limited light that
Bester had managed his shot at the black's legs; the shot
which had frightened the other two away. Smit called SAP
Magaliesberg on the Besters phone which, amazingly
enough, was still working and was told to sit tight and touch

213

othing. Smit discovered the Besters in their bedroom, the woman whimpering like a whipped dog and Bester still unconscious with shock and the damage to his shoulder and bicep from Ruby's AK burst. Ruby was dead on the *stoep* and Smart, with the two unused grenades, was still in the Bougainvillea bush, although they didn't find him until the morning. At a quarter past midnight a Riot Police major and half a dozen of his men arrived from Magaliesberg and a police medic examined Bester, advising that he be taken to hospital in Johannesburg as soon as possible. None of Bester's African workers had moved from their huts during the attack and the riot police interviewed them all individually and eventually satisfied themselves that this had not been an inside job.

The Sunday papers missed the drama but Monday's *Rand Daily Mail* and that evening's *Star* were full of the attack. 'Terrorists strike Magaliesberg farm' and 'Blood-bath at Swartplaas' were bold screaming headlines and SATV News visited the scene of the attack and showed graphic details of bullet-peppered walls and the half-demolished kitchen in their six o'clock news bulletin. Bester was closeted in Johannesburg's General Hospital, in a private room, and by Tuesday was well enough to answer reporters' questions. It was here that Smaller sought him on Tuesday evening, but only after a thorough security check was he allowed in.

Luna and the two boys were there too and it seemed that none was the worse for the terrible ordeal of Saturday night. Luna was a little pale but out of shock and the boys were enjoying the unusual amount of attention. Bester was strapped up and there were hollows under his eyes but the bullets had missed bone and he too seemed to have recovered pretty well. Smaller sat with him and opened the smuggled half bottle of Bell's. They drank from two water glasses. 'Christ Martin, I was only lucky to have woken up, man. Those fokkers had grenades and automatic weapons – AKs, the police say. They were the real thing man, ANC bastards. Imagine that in the Magaliesberg. Jesus, man but I only

214

moered them, eh. I guess I was lucky with the shotgun. My Dad bought that Smith and Wesson about a year before he died in 1968. What a bloody gun that is with that SSG in it, man. Christ, you could stop a bloody army with it.'

Bester had recounted the happenings of Saturday night many times to reporters and Riot Police, SAP detectives and Security Police investigators. The police had found the terrorist weapons and none had any doubt that the newly active ANC were responsible. Black townships from Waltersville, between Boons and Magaliesberg, to Alexandra and Soweto had been subjected to searches and road-blocks. The West Rand towns of Randfontein and Krugersdorp had also been included in the net but although quite a few weapons had been found, including one large cache in Alexandra north-west of Johannesburg, there was no link as yet with the Magaliesberg attack. So far, the three dead terrorists had not been identified; none had carried documents and no vehicle had been found.

The ANC strike made headlines world-wide and Oliver Tambo said in Nairobi, where he was addressing a meeting of the Organisation of African Unity. 'Now you will see that the time has come for military action. Never again are our people going to do all the bleeding. We have offered the other cheek enough times, now there is no cheek left to turn.'

Early on Wednesday, only four days after the attack on Bester's farm, twelve SAAF Impala jets laid waste to a suburb of Maputo, capital of Moçambique and acknowledged headquarters of ANC operations against South Africa. The South African government were incensed by this act of terrorism in the middle of the Transvaal heartland, a pointless and stupid act of course, but one calculated to instil fear into the very backbone of the Afrikaner nation; the *platteland* farmer. Revenge was sweet and some forty members of the ANC died in their suburban ghetto, together with twenty or so innocent civilians who, Pretoria alleged, were 'Unfortunate casualties of war'.

Danie and Luna Bester were to become mini heroes in the weeks to follow and their story was to be told in the leading weekly magazine that dealt in romance, drama and death. After ten days in hospital Danie returned home with his family to find their farmhouse had been repaired and refurbished by friends and neighbours so that virtually no evidence of the attack existed. Smaller had contributed much to this operation and *Lifestyle*'s decorating editor had used all her contacts to effect speedy and appealing renovations and repairs. If Luna Bester ever suspected the hand of Smaller in the revamping of her home, she never said so but she did write a letter thanking him for his kind wishes. Smaller kept it in the bottom drawer of his desk for months afterwards.

On that terrifying night, Temba drove like an automaton, seemingly following the lights of the old Peugeot until he recognised a landmark. Unknowingly he had driven close to Benjie's little village, a collection of seven corrugated iron and mud-brick shacks some eight kilometres west of Merindol. He parked the Peugeot and knocked tentatively on Benjie's window hoping that, as it was Saturday, his father would be dead to the world with mealie beer. Benjie's mother had died three years previously.

Temba was taken in and fed. He spent the night curled up with Benjie under two thin grey blankets but the chill of the early hours of the morning did not keep him awake. He slept the sleep of mental exhaustion until nine in the morning when his friend roused him with a cup of hot sweet tea. Temba drank this gratefully and told his tale to a wide-eyed Benjie. Predictably the stocky Ndebele decided what Temba must do to escape the police net which would even now be closing around him. 'They will check every village here in the Magaliesberg Temba. What did you do with the gun, did you wear gloves? I thought as much. You must go to Johannesburg. I have relatives in Tembisa who will look after you as long as they don't know why you are hiding up. I'll just tell them that you've been arrested for not having a pass and that you got away, we'll have to convince them that is the truth.'

Benjie went on asking questions until Temba was exhausted. 'It's not as bad as I thought, you must go home to get your driving licence and your passbook,' said Benjie. 'Then you can take the Peugeot, you say it belonged to Ruby and Zak bought it for him with proper papers and everything. They won't be looking for that car unless someone talked in Waltersville and I don't think they would, not yet anyway. So take the car and go to Tembisa, but you must cross the Magaliesberg road and go up to Rustenberg and from there on to the R27 to Pretoria.' Benjie smiled at his own intelligent suggestions. 'They won't expect anyone to come from that direction back towards Johannesburg, they'll think you've gone for the border, or at least for Bophuthatswana. But you must move at the right times. Stay here today and then sleep at home tonight, get going after lunch tomorrow. They'll have lifted most of the road-blocks around here by then and the ones into Tembisa and Soweto will be from this side, not from Pretoria.'

Benjie promised to telephone his uncle in Tembisa that evening, to leave a message there via the trading store as everyone did. He would have to hitchhike into the Magaliesberg – to the Portuguese café – to make the call, but he assured Temba he would do it. He gave Temba his uncle's address and ten rand that he had saved for the next week-end's drink up in the Waltersville *shebeens* and Temba, who would need every cent, took it with thanks. They checked the Peugeot: the fuel gauge showed the tank to be half full; the registration papers were in the glove box.

Temba left at dusk, driving over little-used farm tracks to his village. He drove without lights and saw no police cars. He crept into his mother's house just before eight. She didn't even ask him where he'd been.

Zak, using the four-wheel drive on the Isuzu, had gone fast

217

to within five kilometres of the Boons to the Magaliesberg tar road and then turned west on a farm track that was all but impassable for anything other than a four-wheel drive vehicle. The severe drought had caused huge potholes and foot-deep corrugations to form in the narrow track and the Isuzu bounced and leapt about on this brick hard surface. After almost an hour's driving Zak hit the main road again twenty kilometres to the west at the little town of Koster. He crossed straight over and then took to the farm tracks once more after only five kilometres. This time, travelling in a north-easterly direction, he eventually reached the major town of Rustenberg by one in the morning, turned west again and crossed the unmarked border into Bophuthatswana.

He travelled north on the R510 for a few kilometres before parking the Isuzu off the road under a copse of thorn trees. It was almost 2.30 and he jumped out of the cab and walked behind the truck to urinate. The night was cold and clear but Zak's heart beat steadily and his breathing was even. A few cars passed on the other side of the road, wealthy whites and a few Indians who had been to the pleasure palace called Sun City, close to Matrooster in the Pilansberg mountains. That was precisely where Zak was going and he opened the passenger door of the Isuzu's cab to release the bench seat, pulling it forward to open up the small luggage space behind.

He took out a light plastic suit bag which contained a lightweight white jacket and black slacks. In a side pocket was a black cotton shirt, socks and soft leather moccasins. Swiftly Zak crouched and took off his soiled clothes, transferring them to the suit bag. Dressed in his jacket and slacks, he finally took out the passbook and driver's licence which identified him as Josiah Leonard Ntembweni, a Zulu of Orlando, Soweto. The last thing he did was to peel the thin layers of cellulose plastic off his fingers and thumbs. It was a special preparation that he had sprayed on early that morning, a sort of plastic skin that was totally waterproof.

Like the false documents, it had come from East Germany. He ground the cellulose skin into the dirt and pushed the suit bag into the long grass under the thorn trees. Then he put on the horn-rim spectacles that were in the top pocket of the jacket. These had clear-glass lenses and they assisted with his rudimentary disguise. Zak put the Isuzu into gear and moved off north towards Sun City.

He had almost R400 in his wallet; the rest, over R3,000, was safe in a polythene packet underneath the spare wheel. It was well taped up and secured with the hub cap. He knew he would have need of it in the days ahead but, for now, he was a wealthy black gambler out to enjoy the multiracial delights of Sun City. The place was open all night, seven days a week and it was only forty kilometres away. In less than half an hour he'd be there. Zak hummed to himself and wished he had a radio, wished he could whistle and this thought made him remember the dental plate. He took it from the side pocket of his jacket and placed it in his mouth, pushing it around with his tongue and then pressing it snugly against the roof of his mouth with his thumb. He grinned at himself in the rearview mirror and caught a flash of white in the glow from the dashboard instruments. His disguise was now complete.

CHAPTER 11

Two weeks later Temba was still in Tembisa township, hating every minute of it and sleeping on a filthy mattress, wishing every night that he was back in the Magaliesberg. Benjie's uncle had been kind enough and had given this mysterious refugee from justice as much as available space and his limited budget allowed. But Temba had nobody to talk to, because they all left for work at the crack of dawn not returning until after six. In the evening it was a case of a scrappy meal and bed. There were five in the family already, besides coping with an extra mouth to feed and Temba felt the hardly disguised resentment of the nineteen-year-old twin brothers who were Benjie's cousins, Paul and Marcus. In the daytime he just sat around doing nothing. He hated the filthy, rambling township which was dusty and dry in the daytime and cold as hell at night when he would shiver on the rank-smelling mattress under a single thread-bare blanket. There was precious little water too and he was beginning to smell like a goat; he hadn't taken a bath since he arrived. The Peugeot still stood outside the shack and the twins looked at it enviously and had asked Temba if they could borrow it on two occasions. He'd refused of course. It seemed that the car had not yet been linked to the Magaliesberg attack because there had been police cars cruising around as usual and the old vehicle had been there for anyone to see if they'd been looking. Temba had read the newspaper reports on the deaths of William, Smart and

220

Ruby. The authorities had identified them all and were to be looking for another man who was thought to be highly motivated, suspected, ANC cadre leader. The man was presumed to be extremely dangerous. There had been no mention of anyone else and Temba had realised, with relief, that Bester had not seen how many pairs of legs were in the kitchen when he had fired the shotgun through the hole in the wall. Temba didn't know that Zak had, at that moment, been poised on the threshold and was not actually inside the little room. Only two pairs of legs had been seen by Bester.

One reason that the car couldn't be driven safely was because he'd changed the plates after leaving the Magaliesberg. It seemed like an age ago, that Sunday and he recalled the terror on waking, the desire just to burrow down in his bed and hope that they wouldn't come for him. But he'd got up, packed a few things and waited until around two before leaving. There had been two other sets of plates in the boot of the Peugeot but he'd driven to Johannesburg with the original ones on because they tied up with the registration papers. He'd sweated all the way, terrified in case they had somehow traced the car already, but again he hadn't seen any police and had made it to Tembisa by dusk on the roundabout route that Benjie had suggested. When they'd all been at work, he'd changed the plates on the Monday morning and nobody had noticed. He'd buried the old ones in the vast rubbish dump behind the little house and now it seemed that everything might be alright. He might even risk driving the Peugeot back on false plates. There were hundreds of old Peugeot 404s in the Transvaal and the risk of being stopped was minimal. But still he was terrified to take that chance, so he stayed on in Tembisa, hating it and being hated in return by the twins. He didn't know what else to do.

Another problem was that the money Zak had given each of them before the raid was fast disappearing. When he left his village he'd had almost R200, including the ten rand

Benjie. He'd been in Tembisa almost two weeks and
d given Benjie's uncle eighty rand for food and lodging
ut, more than anything, to keep him quiet. About thirty
had gone in the local *shebeen* and one night he'd met a
young coloured girl there and given her ten rand to do it
with him. She had smelled badly and he had only just
managed to finish it so that she had giggled at him afterwards
and called him a 'shy boy'. Somehow he now had only about
seventy-five rand left and there seemed no chance to earn
more. Things were piling up on him and he had no fixed
course of action to follow, nobody to advise him like Benjie
or Zak. His planned escape route had only been as far as
Soweto and he had tried four times to contact the man who
was supposed to look after him in the huge black township.
He'd left messages to phone him back, care of the trading
store, but he went there every day and there had been no
word. Perhaps the police had netted a number of ANC
people in their sweeps of the townships, or perhaps the man
thought it too dangerous to contact Temba. Perhaps there
had been no man there in the first place and Zak had been
lying to them all, using them as cannon fodder to make a
gesture for the party. There had been no further reports in
the newspapers, either white or black, and Temba knew
somehow that Zak had escaped completely. Like himself,
Zak hadn't fired a shot in anger and had thrown his gun
away. The other three were dead, because William too had
bled to death before the ambulance had reached him, so
there had been no one left to talk.

After his bad experience with the coloured prostitute,
Temba had begun to think more about Subaye. His days
were filled with longing for her and his desires vacillated
from mild emotional pangs to outright lust. He tried to
imagine where she was and who she was with, and his hatred
against the white man who had used her grew huge inside
him. During the long dusty days Temba dreamed of the
simplicity of his life back in the Magaliesberg, of the fine
job he had had with *Baas* Swanepoel and the fun he had

enjoyed with Benjie and Tom. More than anything he remembered the times with Subaye, almost three years of loving her and looking forward to seeing her two or three times a week.

Now there was nothing, just an empty life ahead with nowhere to go. He had a passbook which allowed him to work in the Western Transvaal area and he had stamps from *Baas* Swanepoel's farm. If they found him here the police would put him in jail and fine him up to R50 for being in an area he shouldn't be in. Furthermore, he could never work, was not allowed by law to even reside in this part of the country. Temba began to despair. He bought half bottles of cheap brandy for seven rand each in the *shebeen* and drank them alone in the long afternoons, but it didn't help really, it just made him forget for a little while. One night he decided to go out in the Peugeot but he got too drunk and Benjie's uncle slapped his face and made him drink water and go to bed. The anger at his helplessness continued to build.

Subaye's life was close to perfect. She had mastered the housekeeping of the little townhouse and it only took her until about eleven in the morning to finish everything. The kitchen had a new washing machine and spin-drier and she washed twice a week, using the afternoons of those days to iron Smaller's shirts and the casual slacks he wore at weekends. This meant that she had a great deal of time off and on most days she managed to read for at least three hours. Smaller brought her magazines from the office and newspapers arrived every morning and evening. Once a week she read *Time*. In less than no time she had improved her vocabulary impressively.

Late in the afternoon she would cook him supper, if he had told her he was coming home, which averaged out to about four nights a week. She loved to read recipe books and had finished the four he had in the kitchen although one was in French which she couldn't even start to follow.

The pictures were wonderful though and she longed to try out some of the recipes. Smaller was very receptive to her cooking and this encouraged her to try new things all the time. She had very few failures and had put pencilled ticks by the dishes which were his favourites. He trusted her implicitly with money and gave her R100 a week for housekeeping. She would keep a copy of the supermarket receipts and give him an account of everything she had spent at the end of each week. It never occurred to her to filch a few rand for herself because she thought of the money as hers and Martin's, not just his. She realised now that she loved him completely and that their life together was a magical event. It could not last and yet it must. In these few short weeks she had learned so much and it was all due to Martin. She couldn't go back to the Magaliesberg now, after living like this, experiencing all the new and incredible things here in Johannesburg.

Last Sunday they had gone out in the car, she sitting in the back and Smaller driving. Subaye had worn her maid's outfit as if she were being transported from one job to another, but Smaller had talked to her in words very different from those normally exchanged between employer and servant. He had taken her through Johannesburg and onto the motorway around the city. Finally they had driven into the Carlton Hotel underground car park and there, in the quiet deserted cavernous fourth parking level, she'd taken off her overall and he'd taken her to lunch in the coffee shop. The Carlton, part of the American based Westin Group, was designated an 'international hotel' and multiracial lunches and dinners were commonplace. Nevertheless, Subaye had felt incredibly excited. Marvelling at the huge hotel with its luxurious fittings she had eaten little and merely sipped at the glass of wine Smaller had poured for her. He had laughed and joked with her quietly and been courteous and kind, as he would be with a white girl. She had adored him so obviously that he had worried a bit about the other diners' response. But there were other blacks and coloureds there and the whole occasion had turned into a relaxed and memorable lunch. It was because of her, of course. Smaller had to admit that she captivated him more than ever. The way she absorbed knowledge was fantastic.

He'd taken her home to the townhouse at four o'clock and it had seemed unnecessary to insist that she put the overall back on. Old Sally had seen them going in and had smiled and chattered briefly to Subaye then Smaller had poured himself a brandy and they'd sat talking until it grew dark. It seemed quite natural to him that he should entertain this beautiful black girl in his own home. The fact that she was his servant, or housekeeper really, made little difference and in the quiet Sunday evening tranquillity of the townhouse the hours passed in intense discussion. She asked many questions and he tried his best to answer them all accurately and truthfully.

Finally, after he'd played all his favourite records and there had been more coffee and more brandy, he'd gone up to bed and she'd slipped out to her room, returning fifteen minutes later. She'd stayed with him all night and slipped away again around six in the morning leaving him asleep. A little later she'd come up with tea and scrambled eggs on toast, served on a tray so that he could breakfast in bed. He'd lain there, feeling wonderful though a bit guilty, reading the newspaper before getting up, showering, shaving and setting off to the office by 7.30. He'd whistled and hummed all day, causing both Natalie and Ashley to look at him in wonder. Natalie had said innocently, 'You must be in love Martin, what's her name?'

Old Sally knew about little Subaye and *Baas* Martin. She had suspected that there was something happening between them after she had seen Subaye slip into the kitchen after eleven o'clock at night on more than one occasion. What could she be doing in *Baas* Martin's house at that time of night? And the girl was always washing herself. She never stopped using the shower and she washed her hair just about every day. Sally thought it very strange, even unhealthy, to wash so much. She knew that the white people did it but then they smelled so bad that one could understand the necessity.

Sally talked with Subaye often. The girl was bright and pretty and her mind seemed never to rest so that she asked questions all the time. First she had asked just about *Baas* Martin but now she didn't ask about him any more. Now she asked about everything: Johannesburg, Soweto, what the *shebeens* were like in the townships, why the *tsotsi*'s were such bad people. The girl never stopped asking questions. Old Sally liked her though and because she liked her she feared for Subaye. Everyone knew that a white man could not be trusted, not even an Englishman like *Baas* Martin. It was therfore very dangerous for Subaye to lose her heart to *Baas* Martin; for lose her heart she most surely had, one only had to look at the girl when *Baas* Martin was around to see that.

Sally couldn't really understand it. White men were known to take young black girls in the old days but such things had not happened for years, in her experience, not since she had been a young one herself. She had come from Rustenberg, from a farm probably very similar to the one Subaye had been brought up on. There had been young white boys there in the thirties and in those days some of them had lain with black girls. It had never happened to her because she was always a bit on the fat side and they had seemed to prefer the slender girls. They had all played together on the farms as young teenagers, but then after the age of sixteen or seventeen things had somehow changed and the childlike rapport evaporated, to be replaced by a superior coolness shown to her people by their former playmates.

Sally wondered if she should talk to Subaye. The girl was clever and would obviously realise what the authorities would do if they discovered what was going on. But then when women, especially younger ones, were in love they never saw the holes that opened up in the ground before them. It was impossible to tell what *Baas* Martin felt. Of course he enjoyed the girl, men always enjoyed women, that was their way. Sally dimly recalled the lusts she had felt as a young girl but it was hard to visualise them, to feel them now. She was close to sixty and it had been more than seven years since she had lain with a man. Her husband was dead, killed in a mine disaster in 1972, and her four children were scattered around the Transvaal, the two girls married and the boys working the gold mines like their father.

Life was good enough for Sally. She cleaned and washed for old Mrs Goldberg who rarely shouted at her but often scolded her good-naturedly. Sally actually liked the old Jewish woman who was close to seventy but still quite active. Her children came to see her on Saturdays and every Friday her son would come to collect her for dinner at his house. Mrs Goldberg was good to Sally and gave her double wages at Christmas and plenty of old clothes. The two women actually liked each other and Sally had been with Mrs Goldberg since she first moved into the new townhouse six years back. Mrs Goldberg was Sally's Madam and was always addressed as Madam by Sally. Another thing was that she spoke Tswana quite well and sometimes she and Sally would have long conversations; the Madam had learned the language from her nannie when she was a young girl.

Captain Pieter Venter cursed and drank the lukewarm coffee that had sat untouched in his mug for more than five minutes. He had been so taken up with the report that had just come in from Johannesburg that he'd forgotten all about the bloody coffee. It tasted foul anyway, hot or cold, and he cursed again. This time the expletive was directed at Constable Bekker who was teaboy this week, the thick little bastard had no idea how to make anything. One thing was for sure, he wouldn't make higher than sergeant, even if he stayed in the bloody SAP all his life.

The trouble was that recently the sort of recruit they were enrolling into the police force was really up to shit. Some of them must have only just made standard eight, they were so dense. But in a way you could understand it. Who would want to join the SAP anyway? The pay was paltry, the hours were ridiculous and the fokking terries were getting cleverer all the time. What sort of a future could any young lad expect in the police force these days? A wanky, bloody wage and a good chance of getting his balls blown off. Venter sighed and began to read through the brief report again. There was still the best part of two days until his first Saturday off this month and it was already the 23rd.

After the attack on Danie Bester's farm, three weeks back, life at SAP Magaliesberg had become shitting well impossible. First the Riot Police major had taken over the station for almost a week, throwing up roadblocks everywhere with the help of a platoon or so from Johannesburg. That had lasted about two days until they realised that the birds had flown and someone must have guessed wrongly there anyway because Venter reckoned that no self-respecting terrorist would choose the obvious escape routes. They'd scrapped the local blocks after mid-morning on the Sunday and thinned them out, widening the circle almost to reach Krugersdorp in the east and bloody Bophuthatswana in the west. Venter reckoned that the terrie may have made it to the neighbouring state that night or holed up in a local *kraal,* may even still be holed up for that matter.

His job was regular police work and he'd established pretty quickly that the three dead *kaffirs* were locals. They'd had a real go in Waltersville, of course, and rounded up every petty criminal in the township. None had said a word, even when Sergeant Hendriks had whacked a few heads in the cells. It had been useless and they'd let the *kaffirs* go after a couple of days without discovering anything. They had then found the house in Waltersville where the big chief ANC *kaffir* had lived. Neighbours had been questioned but had all said they knew nothing, adopting that stupid dumb act all *kaffirs* do when they don't want to talk. Venter reckoned a good few of them must have known what was going on and one girl had said she'd seen the young one, Ruben Nkhumische, in the house with 'a big older man whose name was Zak'. That's all they had. There hadn't been a single paper in this Zak's home and what clothes were found could have been bought anywhere. All the cooking utensils, cups and glasses had been wiped clean of prints and although they'd turned the fokking place upside down there were no clues as to the identity of bloody Zak. He was a pro alright, that was for sure.

Nkhumische had been easy to trace. His parents were quite wealthy for *kaffirs*. They owned a small laundry business in Alexandra up in Jo'burg. They hadn't seen him for about three years but the local Bramley SAP had a file on him for petty theft and another for assault. Ruben had been a bad little bastard alright, but he wouldn't be making any more mischief because old Danie Bester had blown his leg clean off at the thigh with that SSG shot. Terrible stuff at close range that was. Ruben must have bled to death very quickly because the pool they'd found him in was a metre wide and as thick as your finger.

The report from Johannesburg stated that nothing of any note had been discovered about Ruben Nkhumische. Venter had hoped he might prove a live lead to the identity of Zak but the trail had died again, as it had with Smart Mdliniso and William Pelo. Smart was identified as a labourer from the Bosch's farm near Merindol and William had worked as a pump attendant at Boetie Smit's garage on the main road between Boons and Magaliesberg. Both had left their jobs some months before the attack on Bester and neither had any known relations, in this area at least. Venter knew that, in time, the laborious wheels of the West Rand Administration Board might come up with the name of a relative but it might take weeks and already the trail was cool. In any event, *kaffirs* often never saw their relations for years, if they even knew who they were. Venter shook his head in despair – how the hell was he supposed to trace this Zak? The man had no past or present. They would have to try Waltersville again, he'd go there himself and play it very cool. There was a man who used to inform for him who still lived in Waltersville. He was old and had been off the payroll for years but he was a real gannet for information, knew everything that went on in the township.

Venter made his decision. He would go to Waltersville that evening with one of his black constables. He knew old Desmond's last address and, very likely, he would still be there. The old bastard had nowhere else to go.

It took only twenty minutes to find Desmond. He had moved to his daughter's house, but it was only two streets away from where he used to live. Venter parked the unmarked police Cortina a couple of blocks away and Constable Theli went in to bring Desmond out. It was the right time to call, 7.30 in the evening when the blacks inevitably ate their main meal of the day. An added advantage was that it was cold, so none of them was out on the streets. Hopefully the neighbours wouldn't see Desmond talking with a white man, but it didn't really matter anyway.

Venter told Constable Theli to take a ride around the block, then the first thing he did was to put ten rand in Desmond's hand. The old black thanked him effusively and smiled as he recalled his last meeting with Venter. 'Ay, *Baas* Venter. It is long time since I see you, eh. What does the *Baas* want, what can Desmond do to help the *Baas*?'

Venter smiled back. 'It's about those *tsotsi's* that tried to shoot *Baas* Bester on his farm, Desmond. We can't find the man who lived there,' he gestured a few streets away. 'He was the big *Baas tsotsi,* that one, and his name is Zak. Do you know him, old friend?'

Desmond rolled his eyes and, although it was not warm in the car beads of sweat could just be seen on his forehead. 'Aiee, *Baas* Venter. That was a bad man, *Baas*. I know nothing of him my *Baas,* he was a very quiet man and told

230

nobody nothing.' Desmond lay back against the seat and his eyes glazed over whilst he stared ahead through the windscreen. Venter knew the signs.

'Desmond, you are an old man and this Zak cannot hurt you because he is far away now and all his friends are dead.' The old black man did not respond. Venter went on softly, 'I see that you live with your daughter now, old man. Do you have grandchildren?' Desmond nodded slightly. 'Ah, but that is a fine thing when a man can be with his grandchildren in his old age, how many does she have, two, three?' The old black mouthed the word two and Venter went on, encouraged.

'We want to find out about these men, Desmond. Especially we want to know about this Zak who you say was a bad man. We want to know how long he was here in Waltersville and who his friends were, who he had around to his house. I think that most of them are dead anyway, but maybe you could give us a name or two, maybe you could help.' He paused for effect. 'I know you haven't worked for me for a long time, Desmond, and prices have gone up a lot. We'd pay you well, you see. I'd give you a hundred rand, Desmond, think of that!'

The sweat sprang out clearly now on Desmond's brow and he turned to Venter. 'One hundred rand, *Baas*. Fifty pounds!' he said unbelievingly.

Venter smiled and nodded. 'I have it here, Desmond.' He gestured again to Theli as if to say: go once around the block again Constable, me and Desmond need to talk a bit. 'Now Desmond, tell me. You know me and this man –' he pointed at Theli '– can be trusted. He won't say a word to anyone because he's up for sergeant soon and he knows I don't like idle tongues.'

Old Desmond was convinced. He told of Ruby and William and of Smart and miraculously of another man, Temba Mthombeni, who had visited Zak once or twice. Venter marvelled at the old man's knowledge. He had guessed right – Desmond had nothing to do all day and

Waltersville was a small township by city standards. It was natural that he would find out all about Zak and his friends after the police had turned the house inside out. Information was second nature to the nosey old man. Venter thanked God for his own nose which had led him to the old informer. But Desmond knew nothing else about this Temba, or he wasn't telling. Venter gave him the R100 and dropped him back at his daughter's little house. All he'd needed was the name; he'd trace the *kaffir* somehow.

After a few days' thinking on the problem, Sally considered that she should have a talk with Subaye. The loving with *Baas* Martin could only end in pain and perhaps even imprisonment. As a woman of many years' experience, Sally thought it her duty to make Subaye see the error of her ways; she would talk to her about it this very afternoon, perhaps after lunch when the girl would be ironing in *Baas* Martin's kitchen.

Sally approached the subject with tact. Subaye hummed softly to herself as she worked on Smaller's shirts. Sally stood in the doorway, smiling benevolently at her young friend.

'Yey, but you are happy little sister,' said the older woman. 'Do you have a man who is bringing pleasure into your life? If so, who is it? I demand to know!'

Subaye smiled a sweet, slow smile but said nothing, so Sally went on briskly. 'Of course, you know that whilst this man may bring you pleasure, he will also bring pain. They always do, the bastards. It is their way to hurt women – in fact, I think it is part of their pleasure.' Nodding to herself Sally remained leaning on the door jamb, waiting for Subaye to make some comment, some word which would lead on to the next more gritty matter.

Subaye looked up from an immaculate shirt collar and began to fold the shirt lovingly. 'What are you trying to tell me, Mother?' she said quietly, using the politely familiar term for an older, wiser woman. She spoke with respect and Sally felt pleased at this, even though she was a little nonplussed by the directness of the reply.

'Only that all men are swines,' said Sally with relish. 'I can tell you that it doesn't matter, who or what they are.' She thought quickly and added, 'Not even the colour of their skin matters. I hear that the white people also treat their women badly.'

A sudden tension, a wariness, was evident in the little kitchen and Sally noted the warm, slightly perfumed smell of the spray-starch Subaye was using. The girl said nothing but her shoulders had hunched slightly and she seemed to be concentrating fixedly on the shirt she was ironing. Finally, after more than a minute, she raised her head, her huge brown eyes like great depthless pools. She looked straight at Sally and the old Tswana woman noted the fine features of the girl, as if for the first time. Subaye's chin lifted and her cheekbones seemed higher so that the soft velvet brown skin of her face was stretched tight. Her straight aquiline nose flared slightly at the nostrils and her eyes were wide and bright. The voice was proud and clear. 'You are talking obviously about myself and Martin Smaller, aren't you Sally,' she said in Tswana. 'Let me tell you, once only, that what I do with Martin is my business and mine alone. I don't expect you or anyone else to understand and I know that many people may think what we have together is wrong but remember, he is English, not South African.'

She paused taking a deep, slightly tremulous, breath. 'If we are to remain friends, I don't want you to speak of this again. It is my business and his, that's all I want to say.'

Old Sally opened her mouth to speak, then changed her mind and chose to remain silent. She turned on her heel and walked out of the little kitchen, humbled by the strikingly beautiful young girl and not quite knowing why. Shaking her head she went to her room to have a cup of tea and a smoke. The Madam would be wanting her afternoon tea soon but she had time for a quick one herself.

Over the one and a half metre high screen wall that

separated the rear of her townhouse from Smaller's, Mrs Goldberg stood transfixed. She had been watering her two begnonias that she hoped would one day grow up the back wall, over all the ugly pipes. Every word of the conversation between the two black women was imprinted on her mind and still she couldn't believe it. What to do? It was inconceivable that young Mr Smaller was sleeping with his maid, even though she was an exceptionally bright and pretty young girl. Mrs Goldberg trotted inside to the telephone. Cedric would know what to do – he was a good boy her eldest son, and a very good accountant too. She could safely leave the matter with him, but something would have to be done, surely. After all, Cedric had bought her the townhouse and it would be his one day when she was gone. One couldn't have such things happening in a neighbourhood like Sandton. The scandal would be too terrible and perhaps the property would lose value. Mrs Goldberg muttered to herself as she dialled her son's number; she would have to tell him to handle this carefully.

His mother's telephone call had completely disrupted Cedric Goldberg's afternoon. He had been right in the middle of a very complex liquidation, involving hundreds of thousands of rand of a major client's money, when his secretary had put the old lady through. 'It's your mother, Mr Goldberg, and she sounds very disturbed. I thought I'd better let her talk to you.'

The information had been nothing less than startling and Goldberg wondered quite how to handle it. First he had asked his mother if she was absolutely sure she had heard the facts correctly. Could she have heard it wrongly? Was there no way that the two blacks might have been joking between themselves? The old lady had been adamant and Cedric knew that she did speak Tswana fluently because she often started prattling away to strange blacks when he was with her and was forever trying to teach his kids Tswana words. He told her not to say anything to Sally or the younger girl, just sit tight and watch the situation.

'Don't worry, Ma, I'll deal with it,' he'd said convincingly. But could he? What should he do? First he'd have to confirm the facts beyond all doubt and then go to the police presumably. One couldn't allow that sort of thing to go on undetected in a prime white area such as Sandton. It may happen in Hillbrow and not even be frowned upon, but Sandton was a different case with townhouses now valued at anything up to a quarter of a million bucks each.

His mother's for instance, well it was his own really, was worth three times what he had paid for it in 1979. It had gone up by almost one hundred grand in the last eighteen months. Such was the Johannesburg property market and there was no way some silly Englishman who liked to screw *schwartze* was going to bugger up his little slice of it. Not that a scandal would do that really but it was not a nice thing for his mother to be exposed to, not living next door as she did.

He would have to find out if such happenings were really going on. That was not his line though, but he'd have to do it. Cedric envisaged himself in this unaccustomed cloak-and-dagger role and smiled at his image in the little framed mirror on his desk. His daughter, Debbie, had given it to him for Father's Day, 'so that you can see how nice you look, all day long, Dad,' she'd said in her breathy little voice and he'd grinned, but his wife had broken down laughing, great tears rolling down her cheeks, she'd laughed so much. Little Debbie had not found the matter funny but Sharon had gone on about it for days afterwards. Cedric didn't mind. He was no oil painting, that fact he knew, but he was doing alright and as long as you had the bucks you didn't have to look like frigging Paul Newman. He did alright. He never missed on trips to Durban and Cape Town and old Sharon never complained when he gave her a bit. In fact, she wanted it all the bloody time.

Cedric stood up to look at himself in the full-length mirror behind his closet door. He had put on a bit of weight. Perhaps he'd take up jogging again or go to a gym in the lunch hour. That was the trouble, it was those bloody business lunches that caused the rot to set in. His thoughts returned to the problem at hand. He'd have to go and check out the townhouse, wouldn't tell his mother or Sharon. Friday would be the best time, he'd go after supper, tell Sharon he had to visit a client. She never worried anyway as long as she had her videos to watch and the bloody Irish Mist liqueur she swigged by the gallon. He wondered obliquely whether his wife was becoming an alcoholic and then dismissed it instantly. Sharon went to gym every morning. Unlike him, she was in great shape. It was just that she loved Irish Mist and drank it like it was going out of fashion. Cedric returned to his desk and sat down. Tomorrow was Friday, he'd go over there at around ten and watch Smaller's townhouse. He'd check it out for himself.

The first thing Venter did on Friday morning was to check the station records for the name Temba Mthombeni. There it was in black and white. Only a few months back this Temba had been arrested in Magaliesberg for disturbing the peace and drinking liquor in a public place. With him had been two other offenders, arrested in the same place and at the same time; they were Thomas Ndhlovu and Benjamin Ndadza. All three had given the same address – c/o Swanepoel, Doornspruit Farm, Swartplaas. Venter smiled to himself and rubbed his hands together in the age-old gesture of self-congratulation. It was too easy, he had the hottest lead possible and he'd done it all on his own.

Venter took the station's Dodge catcher van and a dog with its African handler. Sergeant Hendriks and Constable Theli went with him; four of them and the dog. Venter reckoned that was more than enough for three bush *kaffirs*. They arrived at Swanepoel's farm just after nine in the morning and went directly to the large farmhouse. Gelda Swanepoel opened the door and looked only a little surprised to see Venter and Hendriks. The blacks waited in the van.

'Well, hello and good morning, Captain Venter,' she said brightly. 'Looking for those *bliksem* terries that shot up poor Danie Bester, eh. Well, I can tell you that none of my husband's boys would do such a thing. They are a good lot on this farm and we treat them well.' She stepped aside, gesturing them into the warmth of the hallway.

Venter smiled and removed his cap, as did Hendriks. 'Thank you my dear *Mevrou* Swanepoel,' he said in Afrikaans.

They sat in the huge lounge with its Louis XIV reproduction chairs and Chinese silk carpet. Swanepoel was doing alright, that was no maybe. These bloody farmers made a fortune, born with a silver spoon in the mouth they were. The Swanepoels had owned Doornspruit for three generations. Venter looked around as Mrs Swanepoel went off to organise tea and he compared the luxurious room with his own bungalow in Magaliesberg. He grimaced at Hendriks who was also suitably impressed.

'It's alright for some, eh, Jannie?' he said to the sergeant. Hendriks smiled and was about to reply when Mrs Swanepoel returned followed by two servants with tea and a tray of rusks and biscuits. Both policemen smiled winningly at the middle-aged farmer's wife and Venter took out his cigarettes. 'Do you mind if I smoke, *Mevrou?*' he said politely.

Swanepoel would return for his tea at ten o'clock. Until then Venter and his sergeant spent a pleasant hour chatting with his wife. She had shown them her new kitchen which had come from a specialist decorating outlet in Johannesburg and Hendriks had been open-mouthed in his admiration. Venter too was impressed and could barely quell his envy. He could imagine how his Marie-Louise would react to a set-up like that.

The farmer was surprised at the policemen's interest in Temba, Thomas and Benjie. He sipped his tea and smiled ruefully. 'Well, man, Captain Venter. Those are good boys, never had any trouble with any of them and they've all been here about three years. Temba the longest. A good lad he was and a hard worker, but he started buggering about a bit a few months back and so I had to let him go three or four weeks ago. I asked Tom and Benjie where he'd gone but they didn't know, or weren't telling me. That's the thing with *kaffirs,* you never can trust them or even rely on them.' He looked up at Venter who was leaning forward attentively.

'You say that Temba has gone, Mr Swanepoel?' he said urgently and Swanepoel reacted to the tone of voice.

'Yes, Captain. I told you, I fired him about a month ago and that was the last time I saw him. Why, what has the *skellem* done?'

Venter wondered how much to tell Swanepoel. 'We think he may have known the man who was responsible for the attack on Bester's farm. He has been identified as visiting at that man's house in the township. Obviously we'd like to talk to him, but now the bird has flown, so to speak.' He smiled briefly. 'Perhaps you could organise for us to talk to Tom or Benjie. Were they good friends of Temba's?'

Swanepoel confirmed that Temba and Benjie had been almost inseparable and offered to take the policemen down to the bottom pasture where Benjie and Tom were working. They set off in the van, the V8 thundering along the dry farm track watched by dozens of blacks who were working in the fields along the route. Swanepoel finally called a halt and a boss boy ran towards the van after a few moments' hesitation, not recognising his master in the hated police vehicle.

'Go and call Benjie and Tom to me, Alfred. Quick now, this *Baas* wants to talk to them.' Swanepoel offered a cigarette, turning to Venter. 'I suppose you'll have to take them to the station, Captain?' he asked conversationally.

Venter simply nodded and drew smoke into his lungs. He looked up at the deep blue of the clear winter sky and felt the sun just beginning to warm the air after the dawn frost.

What it must be like to own all this land, he thought, and then Tom and Benjie were there and his daydream was broken.

After a few minutes of initial questioning it was obvious to Venter that Tom knew very little about Temba's movements since he had left his job. Benjie too protested any knowledge of his friend's whereabouts but Venter could see that he was hiding something, recognising a certain cunning in this small, stocky black who was over-polite. If such a thing were possible when a *kaffir* talked to a policeman.

Venter decided to take him back to Magaliesberg and give him the treatment. Hendriks was a past master at it and he, Venter, could play the good guy to Hendriks' bad guy. They'd get information. He was bloody sure that this little bugger knew something. He looked at Tom who held his gaze without flinching. 'You can go Thomas,' he said quietly.

Nothing was said to Benjie who stood looking down at the ground in silence. Then Venter spoke harshly. 'Sergeant Hendriks, put this man in the van, I want to take him in for questioning.' Benjie looked up and Venter saw the fear in his eyes as Hendriks and Theli grabbed him. Theli secured the handcuffs and Benji was shoved in the back of the Dodge.

Venter smiled at the farmer. 'Sorry for the inconvenience, *Meneer* Swanepoel,' he said politely. 'But I think that man knows something – in fact I'm absolutely sure he does.'

Swanepoel nodded agreement. 'I think you're right, Captain. It just shows you, eh.' He shook his head in wonderment. 'You can never tell with a *kaffir,* eh. Who would have thought it of Temba or Benjie? You never can tell with the buggers.'

They booked Benjamin Ndadza under the Terrorism Act. 'Suspicion of consorting with a known terrorist' was the way Venter phrased it in the operations book. Hendriks took Benjie out into the cells at the back until Venter was ready for him. Let him stew a while, thought Venter, then we'll get to him after lunch.

Benjie sat in the same cold dingy cell that he had shared with Tom and Temba some month earlier. He wondered what had happened to Temba, whether he was still in Tembisa with Uncle Phineas. Benjie knew that he was in serious trouble. Hendriks frightened him but it was the older man, the Captain, who really brought the sweat springing out on his forehead. Even now, in this cold bare cell, he was sweating. He would never tell them about Temba, of course. They could do what the hell they liked but he wouldn't tell. Temba was his blood brother and, in any case, he, Benjie, basically agreed with ANC policy even though he wasn't a member, wasn't involved himself. Then he heard the noise of heavy boots on the concrete courtyard outside his cell and the fear rose up inside him. The bastards were coming for him. What would they do to him? How would they try to get the information out of him?

Captain Venter was very pleased with himself. The security police and the riot boys had all had a go at finding this missing terrorist and now he, an ordinary copper, was on the right track. He could smell success just around the corner but he wouldn't call up the SPs in Jo'burg just yet. He wanted to present them with a cut-and-dried case, solid leads that they could follow up with their computers and complicated undercover network.

Hendriks brought Ndadza into the bare little room where Venter sat at a bare pine table. The room was located under the station, like a cellar really. It was designed as a storeroom and had been one before Venter took over as station commander in 1977. Since then, he and Hendriks had rarely used it, but it was ideal for the purposes of interrogation, almost soundproof when the door was closed. Hendriks closed it behind him now and shoved Ndadza across to the single chair which faced Venter's across the desk.

'Sit down *kaffir*,' he said roughly. Benjie sat, his hands securely handcuffed behind his back.

Venter began in a soft almost kindly tone. 'Alright Benjie, we know that you are a pal of Temba's, eh.' Benjie said nothing. 'Now what we want to know is, when did you last see him Benjie, and more important, where is he now?'

Benjie remained mute and Hendriks moved to Venter's side at the desk. 'Let me make him tell us, Captain,' he said harshly. 'I can get him to tell us, sir.'

Venter smiled up at his sergeant. The trick was centuries old but it usually worked. He saw the black's eyes flicking between the two of them, there was intelligence there. Was it possible that the *kaffir* was onto their pantomime. He decided to find out. He gave a half nod and Hendriks moved fast. His fist slammed into Benjie's face knocking him backwards off the chair, breaking his nose and bursting his bottom lip. Benjie could not get up on his own, neither could he wipe his bleeding mouth or feel the damage to his numb, throbbing nose. Hendriks pulled him up by the collar of his work overalls and slammed him back into the chair. 'Tell us Benjie,' said Venter quietly, 'tell us what you know and there won't be any more of this treatment.'

Benjie's head was spinning and little red lights moved slowly across his vision. Blood dripped from his nose and lip onto the collar of his overalls and he could feel a front tooth wobbling as he passed his tongue over it. Strangely there was not much pain and he supposed that he was shocked, perhaps stunned. He heard the voice of the policeman and shook his head automatically. Hendriks moved in again.

It took the best part of an hour before Venter had all the information he wanted. Zak's second name was Mhluli and, as Desmond had said, he had been active in Waltersville for around three years. Ruben Nkhumische had lived with him and Temba had become involved with the two of them about four months ago. Benjie had stopped there and Hendriks had to put severe pressure on him to get the final piece of information. The black had resisted incredibly and then had just suddenly given up telling Venter the name of his uncle in Tembisa. Temba Mthombeni was there, staying with Benjie's relations. It was an amazing breakthrough and Venter would relish the telling of it to his colleagues in Johannesburg. Benjie had also confessed that Temba had been a fifth man in the raid on the Bester farmhouse but he had no idea where Zak might be and, instinctively, Venter believed him.

By the time Hendriks had finished with him, the black was barely conscious and had lost three front teeth. Two fingers were broken but the doctor could set those again easily enough. The van would run him through to the African hospital at Krugersdorp and they'd put him in a private room under guard. The story would be that he was the victim of a hit-and-run accident but the doctors there knew the score anyway. Benjie would soon be fit to stand trial for 'consorting with known terrorists and aiding and abetting the same'. He would go down for three years or so at least. They didn't take kindly to this sort of thing in Pretoria.

Friday afternoon had been like any other for Temba. The endless days since he'd arrived in Tembisa were all the same. At around four o'clock, he decided he couldn't stand it any longer. He'd already had almost a half bottle of Limosin brandy, diluted slightly with Coca Cola, and was feeling the effects as he lay in the weak afternoon sun, lounging against the dusty side of the Peugeot. The keys were in his pocket and he had started the car that morning, just to see whether the battery was still charged. The engine had fired on the first turn of the key and Temba had lingered there, aching to leave this filthy dust bowl of a place. But he had remained, succumbing to the fear within him, as had happened on similar afternoons in the last twelve days.

Now, fortified by the liquor, he climbed once again into the Peugeot. He started the car, turned it around and then

parked it by the front door of the mean little house t.
was actually smaller than his mother's back in the Magalie.
berg. He ran inside and grabbed his plastic hold-all,
desperate to leave, now that he had made up his mind. He
didn't know where he was going but it didn't matter; he
would head for Hillbrow, the vast sprawling flatland north
of Johannesburg and try the telephone number again in
Soweto. At least in Hillbrow he could park the Peugeot and
disappear into the Friday-night crowds to find a telephone.
Instinctively he knew that he was doing the right thing. He
was hastened by a sense of impending doom which rose
suddenly within him; a force that was driving him away
from Tembisa which seemed to be somehow at the centre
of his terror.

The brandy had made him a little dazed. He shook his
head and drank water from the dirty little sink in the tiny
kitchen. After two glasses he felt better, then he was running
for the car, slinging the hold-all onto the back seat.

It was around six o'clock and Tembisa township was filling
up for the night with old cars and trucks bringing home the
black workers who finished early on Fridays. Many others
were on foot. Old women wearily carried huge newspaper
wrapped parcels and cardboard boxes on their heads.
Younger girls hurried home whilst it was still light; before
the *tsotsis* would come looking for an easy mark to mug and
possibly rape. Temba was driving in the right direction and
within twenty minutes he was on the M1 highway heading
south towards Johannesburg. He was unsure how to find
the way to Hillbrow and felt totally alien in this huge city.
But Zak had mentioned Hillbrow as a good place in which
to lose oneself, in the event that the roads into the African
townships should be blocked by police.

Temba drove the Peugeot at a steady eighty kilometres
an hour, keeping well on the left, allowing faster traffic to
pass him. He had his headlights on but the yellow sodium
lamps on the highway gave excellent illumination and he
watched for an overhead sign reading 'Hillbrow'.

After fifteen minutes he had passed the Braamfontein off-ramp and could see the famed Hillbrow tower over on his left. His heart sank when he realised that he had missed Hillbrow and had no idea how to get back. The motorway stretched ahead, heavy with traffic, much of it black. Temba followed a battered Datsun pick-up which had three Africans in the back and another two, besides the driver, sandwiched in the cab. The truck turned into the right lane following the signs which said M1 south and Soweto. Temba relaxed and was content to idle along with the stream. There was still almost half a tank of petrol in the car and he had about sixty rand in his pocket. He would take his chances in Soweto and find a café, or store, and call up the contact Zak had given him. His fear began to ebb away and his confidence returned. He could find something to eat and drink in Soweto, perhaps even a bed. He patted the breast pocket of his cotton zipper jacket; the money was still there. Things could be worse, thought Temba. Anything was better than another night in Tembisa and it was nearly three weeks now since the Magaliesberg raid.

Temba considered his chances. He was sure that nobody could tie him into the raid and he hadn't killed anyone anyway, hadn't fired his gun even. Here he was, driving an old Peugeot which had false plates, and he wondered where Zak had found them, whether they were off a stolen vehicle. Perhaps it was just as dangerous to be driving with these plates as the original ones which could be linked to the raid. But strangely, Temba felt little fear now. It was as if leaving Tembisa had improved his chances immeasurably. He had a very strong hunch that he was making the right move. One thing was definite, he had had it with the ANC; there was no way he was going to get involved in that sort of danger again. He'd try to sit it out for a while in Soweto and then make it back to Magaliesberg. By then everything would have blown over and *Baas* Swanepoel might even give him his old job back. He shivered in the dark interior of the car as he thought of the horrific night just three weeks ago. William and Smart were dead and Ruby too. What of bloody Zak? He had made his break and disappeared. Temba had more than a suspicion that he'd had it all nicely worked out the whole time.

Eventually the Datsun pick-up he was following headed into Soweto and Temba could see the vast smoke haze just visible against the red dusk sky. There were literally thousands of people milling about, obliging him to drive very slowly – only about thirty – to avoid hitting those that just wandered into the road without regard to traffic. He carried on, driving aimlessly into the huge black township which was, in reality, a city within a city. He had no idea of its size and the vastness and the numbers of people disconcerted him. He passed a station where a train was disgorging thousands more blacks like himself but they were strained and hurrying people who ran from the station under loads of varying sizes. Flashily dressed young men stood idly by, watching like birds of prey, looking for the old or the weak whom they could terrorise and rob without risk.

The traffic became lighter as Temba left the vicinity of the station and then he spotted a store on the left and pulled into the packed forecourt. He climbed out, locked the Peugeot and, going into the crowded, noisy interior, he looked around for a pay phone. There was one in the corner but two people were waiting to use it whilst a third gripped the receiver, completely involved in an animated conversation. Temba bought a pack of cigarettes and settled down to wait, fascinated by the activity, the Friday night bustle of Soweto. He looked out through the window at the Peugeot, he was safe now, deep inside this huge township, a place where even the white police didn't come very often. This was a refuge for blacks and he felt at home in the smell, noise and frenetic activity, even though it was all a bit hard to handle, the very size and the countless numbers of people.

Cedric parked the Mercedes well down the road, about two

blocks from the townhouse where Smaller and his mother lived adjacent to each other. He had dressed for the occasion in black corduroys and a black polo-neck sweater. Over these he had his black leather jacket and wore driving gloves and soft leather moccasins. He felt like a TV hero and admitted to himself that he quite enjoyed his role. Sharon had noted his odd garb and commented in her usual sarcastic manner. 'Well, Cedric. You must be going to a gay bar dressed like that dear.' She'd become convulsed with giggles, adding, 'Just don't bring anything nasty home with you, my boy.' Cedric had failed to reply and let himself out soundlessly; the martyred husband having to do his duty for family and society at large.

Now he lurked in the shadowed rear entrance of his mother's house, head close to the low dividing wall between the two townhouses. The light was still on on the ground floor of the neighbouring property and Cedric could see a glow from his mother's bedroom some four metres above his head. He had observed that Smaller's garage door was closed and thought this a good sign, reckoning that Smaller was at home.

It was almost eleven o'clock and Cedric had been at his station for forty minutes when a door closed softly in the servant's quarters across the yard. A slim, dark figure in a maid's overall flitted across to the back of Smaller's townhouse and Cedric heard the scrabble of a key and then the kitchen door opened and closed. The light stayed on downstairs and Cedric listened for voices but could hear only an occasional low murmur, then there was the sound of soft music and he distinctly heard the clink of a bottle. It was cold now, bitter in fact, and Cedric recalled that morning's weather report which had forecast temperatures below freezing in the early hours of Saturday morning.

Cedric had been born in Durban and lived the first fourteen years of his life in its moderate coastal climate. His blood had never become used to the highveld winters and he wished now that he had worn his heavy sheepskin coat.

Somehow it hadn't seemed dashing enough for tonight's operation. Then Cedric forgot the cold because the downstairs lights went out next door and the upstairs ones went on. He waited, heart beating hard, noting the bathroom light going on next to the main bedroom. Ten minutes later all the lights went out and Cedric waited, his instinct telling him that his mother had been absolutely right. After a further thirty minutes he was shivering, his feet were frozen and his face chilled with the severe drop in temperature. But now he was positive and would have to act on this knowledge. The black girl hadn't come out.

Feet numb and hands almost as cold, Cedric jogged silently back to his parked car. He started the engine and sat there waiting for the heater to thaw him out. His mind raced with possibilities but there was only one way he could safely use the information he had gathered. He made a quiet U-turn in the road and headed home. It was almost 12.15 and Sharon would be in bed. He would go into his study and make the call.

By the time he had parked the Mercedes and entered the house, Cedric's heart was pounding again and he was sweating slightly. He went into the study and opened his liquor cabinet. He found the telephone directory in his desk drawer and looked up the number of Sandton police. He pressed the digits on his telephone and poured himself two fingers of brandy into a water glass. The telephone rang for ages, then a bored voice answered, 'SAP Sandton, Constable Nel, can I help?' The words were repeated swiftly in Afrikaans. Cedric paused, took a swig of brandy and then whispered conspiratorially into the telephone.

'Constable, I think you should know that the Immorality Act is being contravened at this very moment in Sandton.' Cedric paused and heard Nel's intake of breath, then the policeman's voice came back, no longer bored. 'Can you give me any other details, sir?'

Cedric gave Smaller's address and the location of the townhouse in the block. He further informed the constable that the offending couple were in the main bedroom upstairs 'in the act' so to speak. Nel asked for Cedric's name and address but Cedric put the instrument down without answering. He sat back in his chair and wiped his sweaty forehead. That would settle Mr Smaller's game.

Cedric drained the brandy and turned out the desk light. He walked down the soft carpeted passage to his bedroom feeling the underfloor heating warming his feet, even through the soles of his moccasins. Sharon was in bed naked, her head a dark mass on the pillow. Beside her on the night table was a liqueur glass with a trace of brownish liquid in it and, as Cedric watched, she turned in her sleep and muttered something. She was stoned again, he thought moodily and then she sat up in bed and looked at him.

'Come to bed, darling. I've been waiting for you for ages.' Cedric looked at his slim and beautiful wife with her year-round tan from the health-club solarium. He thought of Smaller with the black girl. Oddly the visions excited him and then Sharon's next words made him hurry to brush his teeth and undress. 'I want you inside me, Cedric,' she said softly.

Subaye lay still beside him. They had made love for almost an hour and it had been better than anything Smaller ever remembered. They had achieved a oneness, a melding into one another, which had been almost miraculous. Smaller's heart thudded in his chest and he felt masterful and sated. It was a wonderfully primitive feeling.

The room was pleasantly warm; he could just hear the soft whir of the fan heater and pop music played very softly from his clock radio on the bedside table. He smelled the perfumed, pepperyness of Subaye and felt the warmth of her buttock which was half-turned towards him. She slept like a child, one arm flung out and partially covering her face. He touched her firm thigh which lay along his and she murmured immediately, responding by pressing slightly closer to him. Her whole body was like chocolate brown velvet, the skin incredibly smooth. Smaller marvelled at her as he did every time they made love. She was feline, feminine and wanton, but now he felt tender towards her. Earlier he had enjoyed her, even used her, and she had loved all of it.

The bed was soft and cosy and it smelled of them, of her powdery perfume and that clean metallic odour of sex. He loved the taste of her and began to want her again as he thought of the soft folds of her body, the warm wetness that was right there for him. But he did not wake her.

Then he stiffened, hearing a tiny alien sound in the absolute silence of the house; and a second muffled click. He tried to analyse the fear which flickered like a small, yet bright, flame in his psyche and he knew instinctively that something was very wrong. Carefully throwing back the covers on his side of the big bed, he rose and took his towelling robe from where he had dropped it on the floor an hour earlier. He walked silently to the landing and peered down the short flight of stairs, still feeling the disturbing hunch that all was not right in his world. The front door knob turned as he watched it and he heard slight movement and the snick of the lock. Two large white policemen walked into the tiny hall and looked up the stairs, directly at him.

Smaller began to protest, his voice outraged, but already he knew that it would be useless. A feeling of helplessness and dread washed over him and then he saw the camera raised towards him and the flash blinded him as it discharged. A great weariness drained his strength and he knew that he was in terrible trouble, that his whole life was now on a knife's edge and that nothing could ever be quite the same for him again in South Africa. This burden was almost impossible to handle and he sank down on the landing allowing the policemen to pass by him as they headed for the main bedroom. Subaye's short scream of terror was echoed by the soft pop of the flash gun and then she started to cry. The policemen chattered excitedly in Afrikaans. The nightmare had just begun.

Temba had found a *shebeen*. He had tried his contact number several times from various trading stores but there had been no answer and now he sat in the dim smoky front room of the *shebeen* thinking of his next move. The brandy and Coca Cola was sweet and heavy on his palate and he realised that he had eaten nothing since breakfast which seemed days away. Funnily enough, he didn't feel hungry and the sugar in the cola was maintaining his strength. He'd had five or six drinks but he felt fine, never better in fact. There was a short girl in a red polo-neck sweater and blue jeans who kept looking at him and Temba knew that now was the time to find a billet for the night. It was already 11.30 and he had no idea of where he was going to sleep.

The girl's name was Miriam and she responded encouragingly when he bought her a gin and orange. Temba was painfully aware of his dwindling wad of cash and yet, buoyed up by the alcohol he had been drinking for most of the day, he felt confident that something would turn up to improve his position. The girl smelled of cheap perfume and a musky smell emanated from her jersey which was skin tight like the denims it was tucked into. Under the sweater Temba could see large soft breasts and he wanted this plump friendly girl who had a pleasant round face and flashing white teeth. Her lips were painted red and when she looked at him she parted them slightly and her eyes dropped once or twice to the area below his belt. Temba knew then that he could have her and realised that he hadn't been with a woman since he'd taken Subaye on the hillside back on Bester's farm; not counting the prostitute in Tembisa and even that was an age ago. The lust built in him so that he pulled the girl to him confidently. She giggled but did not try to free herself from the circle of his arm and he pressed himself against her thigh so that she felt him hot and hard and wanting her.

But Miriam told him that he couldn't stay with her because she lived with her uncle who would kill her if she took a man to her bed. Temba pleaded and begged, swearing love at first sight, and eventually she mellowed and said that they would have to be very quiet and could only go at around two o'clock because her uncle was a truck driver and left early on Saturday mornings to take his rig down to Durban. This meant a further two hours of drinking and Temba didn't think his pocket or his head could take it.

He smiled winningly. 'Alright Miriam, we will go later but first I must eat. Can you take me somewhere to get some hot food?' The girl seemed disappointed at the prospect of no more gin but she agreed and, weaving a little, Temba led her outside to the car.

She seemed impressed by the old Peugeot and Temba put the heater on. They drove only a short distance and found a late night café which served him a plate of stew and mealie porridge. He was so hungry that he had a second helping and then he felt sleepy and Miriam started to look restless. She drank endless Coca Colas and Temba had tea. He looked at the dial of his watch and saw that it was only 12.15. Somehow he had to stay awake and get to this girl's bed.

At 1.30 they left the café and drove through mazelike streets for about twenty minutes before Miriam asked him to pull into the side of the rough unlit, unpaved road. There were endless little houses made from rough concrete blocks. They had corrugated iron roofs and few showed any lights or sign of life. Miriam asked him to go on slowly and then she relaxed when she saw that her uncle's car was gone, he had already left for the depot and his long night drive to Durban.

Her tiny room was at the back of the house and there was only her aunt and a young cousin to contend with; both were asleep. Miriam took off her clothes in the chilly air of the thinly walled house and scrambled into her narrow bed. Temba followed rapidly. She was hot and excited and he pulled her to him. Immediately her hand went to his groin. He entered her quickly and it was over very fast because he was in desperate need of release and yet he could sense

251

her disappointment. After only ten minutes he began again, working himself to a controlled pitch and driving the girl to two orgasms before she reached a third with him shuddering and clenching his body on top of her.

They fell asleep in a tangle of limbs and Temba's last thought was of Subaye. How different she was to Miriam who was more like a farm girl than a city dweller. It was as though their roles were reversed; Subaye was neat and clean, almost sophisticated and undoubtedly intelligent. This one was just a silly, chubby girl looking for a good time and a man to give her pleasure. Well, he had done that alright, and he felt just a slight tenderness towards her because without her he'd be sleeping in the back of the Peugeot, cold and shivering because there would be frost tonight – he could smell it in the air.

Pieter Venter had reported his findings to SAP Bramley just before 4.30 on the last Friday in June. It was a bitterly cold day and after Hendriks had seen Benjamin Ndadza carted off to the van, en route to hospital, the two men had shared a bottle of brandy back in Venter's office. Venter had cause to celebrate.

'Sure, Ewart,' he said exultantly, 'that little *kaffir* was a hard nut to crack, eh. But I had a feeling man, I felt that the bugger knew something as soon as I set eyes on him.'

The big sergeant nodded and drank deeply from his tumbler of neat spirit. 'You're so right, Captain, he did look like he was into the whole thing. *Meneer* Swanepoel said that he and this Temba were best buddies, eh. It just shows you that these ANC terries are running about everywhere. Hell man, but we're going to have our work cut out with the buggers, eh Captain.'

The two men sat and finished over two-thirds of the bottle. Outside it was almost dark and Venter thought of getting home, enjoying a good hot meal and watching television with Marie-Lou. Hendriks was silent, smoking and swigging his brandy. He was a simple man, the sergeant,

like an older version of young Constable Bekker. He'd ar.
come to the end of the line pretty soon and in about ter.
years he'd retire with a police pension. Venter couldn't see
old Ewart getting much further up the ladder of success in
the SAP. Sure, there were too few young blokes coming
into the force these days, but the ones that did were bloody
clever, straight out of the police college at Heidelberg and
all set to take the world by storm. They were the new breed
of career cop in South Africa and even he, Venter, would
eventually be outpaced by their kind. Well, this business of
Temba Mthombeni was a feather in his cap, that was no
maybe. By now the Bramley chaps would probably be
putting him in the cells. They'd be very careful not to hurt
him too much because the security police would want to get
as much out of him as possible.

The telephone on Venter's desk rang shrilly, shattering
the tranquil dusky atmosphere of the small office. Venter
listened for a few minutes and swore silently. He put the
receiver down and turned to Hendriks who looked up
vacantly. 'The bugger's gone, Ewart. Can you believe it?
The black bugger has pushed off in some old Peugeot and
they've no clue at all which way he went. Bloody Benjie's
folks had no idea who he was and, as far as they knew, he
had no plans to leave. Must have smelled a rat, eh.' He
shook his head again draining his brandy in one gulp. 'Well,
that's screwed up my Saturday. The security police are
coming down tomorrow to interview me. They want to know
everything possible about Mthombeni. Think they can find
him in one of the townships in Jo'burg?' He answered his
own question with an expletive and Hendriks nodded in
sympathy. Venter stood up abruptly. 'They've more chance
of falling pregnant,' he said softly and walked out of the
office.

They took Smaller and Subaye to SAP Sandton. It was a
new station, modern and brightly lit. Smaller flinched under
the fluorescent lights. The charge office sergeant and two

ung constables smiled at his discomfort and, as Subaye was led off to the cells, they commented in Afrikaans and laughed coarsely. Smaller hated them and wanted to wipe the smiles off their faces. Instead he sat mutely in the charge office whilst they telephoned John Vorster Square in Johannesburg. Subaye hadn't said a word to him in the police car, she'd just sat there looking blankly out of the window and he hadn't tried to talk to her either. Both of them were shattered and overcome by the enormity of the discovery.

On arrival Smaller had asked the desk sergeant whether he could call his lawyer. 'All in good time, *Meneer,*' the man had said knowingly. Smaller felt the hopelessness well up in him again. He stared without seeing at a poster on the wall which illustrated various communist made firearms. My God, he thought bleakly, I could do with a drink.

It was well after midnight when they let him call Frank Liebenberg. The lawyer had been unbelieving at first and then coldly practical. 'Don't say anything Martin. Even if they try to threaten you. They'll take you to John Vorster Square and I'll be there by the time you arrive. They'll keep the girl there at Sandton so don't worry about her.' He paused and said quietly, 'You realise that this is going to get into the papers, don't you.' Smaller said nothing and Liebenberg rang off.

Saturday was a nightmare. They let him go at four in the morning on R2,000 bail which Liebenberg arranged through Norman Ashley and the bookkeeper at *Lifestyle. The Star* called the townhouse at midday and Smaller refused to talk to them. Ashley and Liebenberg were there and a general sense of gloom pervaded the atmosphere. Smaller sat with his head in his hands drinking black coffee and Ashley stood in the corner, not trusting himself to speak, feeling only that he had unknowingly engineered this whole catastrophic series of events because he'd insisted that Martin go off into the hills to get away from it all.

Liebenberg was businesslike although it was pretty obvious he had little sympathy with Smaller on this occasion. 'You know, of course Martin, that they can throw you out of the country for this.' He sipped coffee Ashley had made and continued, his voice quiet and serious with the enormity of the problem at hand. 'It may not come to that, however, but I'm just telling you what could happen. You are something of a public figure so they may decide to make quite a lot of this whole matter. Now, I know this is not going to be pleasant, but I want you to tell us everything that happened out there in the hills. Don't leave out a thing because there may be a lot of material we can use in your defence.' He reached into his briefcase and took out a compact four-track tape recorder which he placed on the coffee table as if it were Dresden china. 'Now, let's go Martin. Let me have it all.'

The retelling of events in the Magaliesberg somehow cheapened the whole *affaire* and Smaller felt the weight of the stony looks that the two men gave him. How could he explain the earthy magic of Subaye, the smell of her and the feeling of her wonderful brown body, firm and at the same time velvety smooth; unlike any white woman he had ever known?

Liebenberg pressed him for details of the attack on Subaye, the rape and beating she had succumbed to. He was trying for mitigating circumstances, attempting to build a case around his client's humanitarian regard for another human being. However, this regard did not explain the suspected copulation in the townhouse, the terrible social stigma of sexual activity between black and white.

Smaller felt drained by eleven in the morning. At the same time he felt a burning, raging helplessness which eventually caused him to leap up from his slumped position on the sofa. 'I've had it Frank, be honest for God's sake. There's no chance I'm going to get off with this one, is there. Is there!' he shouted. Liebenberg remained staring at the tape recorder towards which he slowly reached out a hand. The attorney switched off the little machine and leaned back against the cushions.

'I'll be honest with you, Martin. There is little chance of you getting off, as you put it, but I'm trying to justify your actions somehow. I want to plead emotional disturbance, temporary estrangement from society, anything which might help.' He paused looking at Smaller with narrowed eyes. 'I'm trying to assist you as much as possible Martin, really I am.'

Smaller stared at his smooth-talking, clever lawyer who always looked like a fashion plate, even now after being up since four in the morning. He noticed Ashley, sitting rumpled and silent in the corner and felt a sudden pity for the big hard-working man who loved *Lifestyle* much more than he did. This would quite possibly finish the magazine, or make it, depending upon how one looked at it. Suddenly, he had an idea and his eyes lit up with excitement.

'This is what we are going to do. Listen Frank, and you too Norman. We're going to fight this thing through *Lifestyle.*' The two men looked at him blankly. 'Don't you see?' continued Smaller in an animated voice. 'I'm not going to deny that I fell for this black girl. I'm going to admit it, tell the reasons why. We're going to get into that jail and photograph her, in fact –' he looked at Liebenberg intently '– you, Frank are going to apply to get her out on bail and you're going to do it now, today, even though it's Saturday. I want an urgent application in whatever court deals with this sort of thing and I want it within two hours.'

Ashley began to look interested and Liebenberg stood up briskly. 'I think you're crazy but there might just be a way out in that direction.' He stroked his nose in a characteristic gesture. 'It will probably finish you socially, Martin, but there might be an approach. I'll go home and change,' he said and left quickly.

Smaller looked at Ashley and grinned. 'So much for a few days in the country, eh Norman.' Both men laughed nervously.

Saturday evening's *Star* carried a short piece in its stop-press column which was headed 'Leading society publisher caught in Sandton townhouse with black lover.' It went on, 'Martin Smaller, controversial publisher of *Lifestyle* magazine was arrested by police in the early hours of the morning. He was found in bed in his luxury Sandton townhouse in Catherine Street with Subaye Matsamela, a Tswana, lately of Swartplaas in the Magaliesberg foothills. Both refused to talk to our reporters.'

Liebenberg managed to obtain Subaye's release on a second amount of R2,000 bail and Ashley picked her up and returned her to her room at the townhouse after lunch on Saturday. Smaller was in bed asleep when they arrived and Ashley wondered abstractedly how anyone could manage to sleep at a time like this.

At four o'clock, reporters and photographers from the *Sunday Times* and the *Sunday Express* were pounding on the door and Ashley woke Smaller who grinned wolfishly and told him to let them in. A makeshift press conference was held in the lounge with Smaller in his towelling bathrobe. Liebenberg was back from SAP Sandton in appropriately immaculate weekend casuals and only Ashley seemed disconcerted by ensuing events. Smaller orchestrated the whole proceedings with a mastery which left courtroom wizard Liebenberg almost speechless. Finally Subaye was produced, simply dressed in blue jeans and a white T-shirt, the very clothes in which Smaller had first met her. The couple sat together on the couch but did not embrace; flashguns popped and motor-drives whirred. The press were having a field day.

Subaye was amazed at her release from jail. She had been sure that all was lost when the heavy barred door slammed and the policewoman's footsteps retreated in the bare concrete passageway. She had lain down on the narrow cot and dozed fitfully, frightened and exhausted by the terrible turn of events but yet not blaming Martin. She thought only of the ruination that this would bring him, recalling the things she had read about blacks and whites being caught together. Then Mr Ashley and another man had come and, miraculously, they'd let her out and brought her back home to the townhouse. She smiled at Smaller adoringly and the shutters clicked anew. It was obvious to anyone that she was in love with him and the journalists looked on astounded while their photographers performed feverishly. Chasing six o'clock deadlines, the press finally left and hurtled off in a procession of cars for the city. What a story this was going to make – that was the sole thought in every mind.

Temba left Miriam's bed at 8.30 on Saturday morning. He wasn't gone for long however, because she told him that it didn't really matter if her aunt and cousin saw him in her bed; apparently they didn't mind. It was only her uncle who went mad if she brought a man home and he was off out of town until Sunday night. Temba wondered at the rationale behind this statement and thought that perhaps there might be something between the girl and her uncle. He'd heard about places like Soweto. Everything and anything went on if you believed the rumours. As far as Miriam was concerned, he didn't care one way or the other. She provided a comfortable bed for the night and was an enthusiastic partner. She'd already hinted that he could stay tonight as well. Temba finished urinating in the little corrugated iron shack behind the house. The place stank like a fish market and he could clearly smell the girl on himself. They weren't too clean here in Soweto and he thought of his mother's little house and the big water tank in the yard in which they all washed, every day, winter or summer. The water was changed twice a week but it never really got dirty and his mother had that good red coal-tar soap that made you feel so clean after you used it.

Temba zipped up his jeans and headed back to Miriam's bed. All things considered, he had done reasonably well and he felt quite sprightly even after all the brandy and

258

coke he had drunk. Later they'd go out in the car to get something to eat and now he'd go back to bed and sleep. It was chilly in the morning air but the day was fresh and clear. He opened the door to the girl's room silently and looked down at her huddled under the thin blankets. He took off his jeans and shorts and immediately erected again, his bladder now free from pressure. Things could be worse, thought Temba as he climbed into bed and pressed himself against Miriam's soft, warm body.

They woke at eleven and both made rudimentary efforts at washing in the tiny kitchen. The water was freezing cold but Temba was used to that. He found a bar of the red soap which at least made him feel clean. He changed his T-shirt from the bag in the car and then they went out to the nearest café for a breakfast of mealie porridge and tea. Temba counted his money to find that he had only R42 left, meaning he had somehow spent nearly twenty the night before. This figure seemed incredible and he wondered if Miriam's aunt or her child could have stolen some from him whilst he slept. He discounted this possibility. There had been no sign of either of them that morning and Temba thought that perhaps they were a figment of Miriam's imagination. She probably lived with some man who wasn't even her uncle, in fact he might even be her husband. Temba hadn't looked around the house to see whether there were any other bedrooms, it wasn't his business, but he suspected that there must be. Poor man, whoever he was, whether husband or lover. He was off driving his truck to Durban whilst he, Temba, enjoyed his woman.

That afternoon they went to watch a football match at Orlando stadium. Temba paid the one rand entrance fee for both of them. Then the evening stretched ahead and Miriam clamoured to go to the *shebeen* again. Temba resisted but then capitulated, knowing that he needed her bed again that night. He was another fifteen rand lighter when they finally got to sleep after one o'clock on Sunday morning.

Posters headlining the Smaller affair were used as point-of-sale display teasers throughout Johannesburg and its widespread suburbs from 10.30 on Saturday evening. Both Sunday papers' editions had run tens of thousands of extra copies in anticipation of a high sale and by eleven on Sunday morning most outlets were sold out. If Smaller had been partially famous as publisher of *Lifestyle,* he was now infamous as a man who had consorted sexually with his black servant. This contravention of the Immorality Act, No. 23 of 1957 meant that Smaller had become a criminal. In terms of the Act, whites and non-whites who have, or attempt to have, sexual intercourse are liable to up to seven years' imprisonment.

Smaller's telephone was disconnected at his own request and the post office gave him a new unlisted number after Liebenberg had made representation to them on Monday. But the instrument had rung virtually without stopping for the whole of Sunday morning and he left it off the hook from midday onwards. Callers had various messages: many obscene, others rabidly racist, some congratulatory. Natalie came to the townhouse without being asked and handled many of those in the morning but by twelve o'clock she was jaded and edgy from the continual abuse interspersed with the odd kind wishes from liberals and coloured or black callers.

Smaller too became fractious as the day progressed. He had not seen Subaye who remained in her room under the care and protection of old Sally who had unwittingly caused the whole fracas. Black newsmen from the *Sowetan, Drum, Bona* and *Pace* magazines had tried to interview Subaye but Liebenberg had sworn her to silence, allowing only one or two photographs. The canny attorney had a few ideas which would improve his client's chances and he had arranged a second press conference for Monday afternoon. Black journalists would of course be allowed to attend and the police had been notified and would be on hand to protect the accused. even though they were out on bail.

Temba bought the Soweto edition of the *Sunday Times* in the general store next to the café where they again went for breakfast. Subaye's picture leapt out at him from the front cover and he saw the white man, Smaller, beside her. She was dressed in a white T-shirt and blue jeans but it was the expression on her face which captivated Temba and made the bitter gall of an acute anger rise in his throat. Miriam looked at him strangely as he studied the newspaper, silently reading it over again, staring closely at the small printed words in English which he spoke well enough but had some difficulty in reading.

Temba folded the paper carefully, putting it under his arm. He returned to the counter and bought an *A to Z of Johannesburg,* then he walked quickly out to the Peugeot, Miriam trailing behind and having to trot to keep up. He jumped into the car and she tried to follow but he ignored her completely accelerating away from the parking area, barrelling onto the dirt road beyond. The girl looked after him open-mouthed and then began to cry. Somehow she knew that she would never see him again.

The old car seemed to drive itself and Temba moved hands and feet without thought, his mind filled with the image of Subaye's face and what he had learned from the newspaper. His hands clenched the steering wheel so hard that the knuckles stood out white against dark brown skin and his mouth was set in a closed line. His eyes bored ahead through the cracked and dusty windscreen but they failed to register what they saw so that he drove straight over an intersection being narrowly missed by a battered Ford taxi. The blaring of horns seemed to wake Temba from his trancelike state and he turned left into the next side street pulling the Peugeot into the side of the road. He sat quietly, trying to rationalise with himself, wondering what he should do, what he could do to take revenge on the white man who had stolen Subaye from him and consequently caused him to virtually destroy his life.

It all became clear to Temba now. It was not Subaye who

had left him, it was the white man who had lured her away with promises of riches and a new life in Johannesburg. Now it was obvious that this paradise was not to be and the whole thing had backfired horribly. Subaye was a branded woman, a harlot in the eyes of the whole country, both black and white. The realisation of this brought moisture to Temba's eyes so that he sat silently in the old car still staring unseeingly out of the windscreen his face wet with sadness and anger.

He'd thought of her, even when he had been with fat Miriam. Somehow he had believed that he could make it back to the Swartplaas, that Subaye would be there again in her village. The ANC business and the attack on Bester's farm all seemed like a frightening dream that had never really happened, and buried in his subconscious had been the soothing thought that, when he returned home, everything would be the same as always. They would all be there; Benjie and Tom and most of all Subaye. His Subaye who had been promised to him.

Now he knew that this was not to be. Subaye would never be his, even now they were probably looking for him. There had been nothing more in the papers about the search for Zak; Zak who had thrown away his gun and run. Temba thought suddenly of the AK 47 rifle he had carried and the fingerprints which would be on it. But he had never been fingerprinted so there was no link there. Then he remembered the time he had been arrested with Benjie after the Saturday morning beer drink in Magaliesberg. They had taken his thumb and forefinger prints and they'd have them on record at the police station. It all really depended on whether they had discovered that a fifth man had been on the raid.

Perhaps the police had talked with Benjie or interviewed *Baas* Swanepoel. But why should they unless they were suspicious? Perhaps someone had informed them that he had gone to Zak's house in the township, had been seen there on quite a few occasions. Temba's tortured brain boiled with possibilities but deep inside some instinct hinted that he was a wanted man. They were after him, those bloody white bastard policemen who never gave up until they found you. Perhaps they were even looking for this car, right now in the streets of Johannesburg. Even in the townships.

Captain Venter had made the link between the prints on the AK and his suspect. Temba Mthombeni was now positively identified as the fifth man on the Bester farm raid. On Saturday afternoon Venter had heard from Bramley SAP. They had nothing new on Mthombeni's whereabouts but the riot police and the CID were combing Alexandra, Tembisa and Soweto for any sign of the old white Peugeot 404. By Saturday evening they had nothing to report but Venter did give his home telephone number in Magaliesberg village to his opposite number at Bramley. He had a feeling that nothing was going to break on Sunday anyway.

Monday's *Rand Daily Mail* had a follow-up story on Martin Smaller and Subaye Matsamela, but it didn't really say anything that hadn't already been said. *Lifestyle's* Johannesburg office was plagued by early phone calls but Natalie reported that they were lessening by mid-morning. Smaller was at his desk in a sombre navy suit with white shirt, and Norman Ashley was dressed likewise. Both were ready for the press conference at the townhouse that afternoon. They were lunching with Liebenberg to discuss strategy for the initial hearing which would be on Wednesday at the magistrates courts in Johannesburg, the case having been passed to the central police station at John Vorster Square.

Liebenberg had done his homework and had discovered that any such case as this was referred to the Attorney General after initial hearing – often, in fact, before. With the complaint having been made by a neighbour, the police had been duty-bound to investigate but even though Smaller and the black girl had been found in a very compromising position, Liebenberg thought his chances were far better than he had at first imagined. It seemed that the authorities, ever conscious of world abhorrence of the domestic policies of South Africa, were now taking it very easy on such cases as this. The attorney welcomed this attitude and hoped it would benefit his client and all concerned in the case.

On Sunday night Temba slept, cold and hungry, in the back of the Peugeot. He had very little money left now and would need petrol to return to the Magaliesberg. But first he was going to try to find Subaye, try to talk some sense into her head and persuade her to come with him. Temba knew that it was a dangerous thing he was contemplating and felt instinctively that some sort of confrontation was in the offing. His queasy gut told him they would be looking hard for him and that he would have little time once he was out of Soweto.

He drifted just under the full surface of wakefulness, tossing on the hard cracked plastic leatherette of the rear seat, dreaming wildly and starting awake from time to time as cars passed close by to him. He recalled the winters of his childhood and the few ragged clothes and bare feet that had been covered only from the age of fourteen. On those winter mornings they would go searching for guinea fowl, setting snares to trap the big strong birds which would make a nice dinner for four people if they were boiled slowly in the pot with potatoes, onions and tomatoes. Even in his sleep Temba's mouth salivated at the thought of the *tarantaal* stews his mother used to make.

One night they had set their snares and gone back just after dawn to check them. It was simple really. All you had to do was bore a tiny hole in a mealie seed and thread it with a thin fishing line which was strong and not very expensive at the store in Magaliesberg. Some of his friends would cut the top of little straight pins and push these through the mealie so that when the poor *tarantaal* swallowed them he would become paralysed with fright when they stuck in his

264

throat. Often he would just stand still and could be picked up and tossed in a sack but the trouble was that a jackal or *meerkat* might find him before you did. Temba had preferred the fishing-line method which was almost like real fishing. Often the heavy bird would fly off after swallowing the mealie seed and the line would pull tight and break his neck. Sometimes you found him swinging from a branch of a tree, stone dead and still warm.

He had enjoyed his childhood in the veld and life had been quite good until very recently when the trouble had started between himself and Subaye. *Baas* Swanepoel had been quite upset when he fired him but Temba hadn't cared then because he had been full to bursting with the ANC propaganda and he had even thought that Swanepoel's farm might be the next on the list. At that time Temba had hated *Baas* Swanepoel even though the *Baas* had never done anything to engender such emotions. In fact, the farmer had been a fair man and had treated his workers well, feeding them good meat and porridge and giving them each an extra week's wages at Christmas. Temba writhed in half-sleep and whimpered like a sick dog as he considered the pleasant life he had lost. Subaye was the root of the problem and if he had her back everything would be fine. The ghost of a smile crossed his features and his body relaxed. He slept more easily.

Summer and winter alike, Soweto awakes in the dark. Black workers commute daily to the white city of Johannesburg by various methods but most use public transport which means trains or the privately owned Putco bus service. Families awaken to a chilly dawn during the four-month winter season on the Highveld and most wash in cold water. A few can boil water for washing on wood-burning stoves. Breakfast is usually rudimentary, some maize porridge and tea, then perhaps a couple of slices of bread. The journey to work begins at any time between six and seven when commuters wrap themselves in ancient, seldom used, coats on extra cold mornings.

Building workers will wear two shirts and three sweaters, taking them off one by one during the morning until lunchtime when temperatures can soar to twenty degrees Celsius; akin to an early summer day in Europe. In the winter, the Highveld is crystal clear and fresh, the air winelike and invigorating due to the altitude which is almost two thousand metres above sea level. Most black workers are not really disenchanted with their lot and happily pack the trains and buses en route to Johannesburg business district and various other industrial or commercial centres.

Unfortunately, the transport facilities are not sufficient for the ever-increasing numbers of black commuters and when accidents happen there are often many fatalities. Trains leave stations with blacks hanging out of doorways, pushed outwards by the masses inside who are jostling for more comfortable positions in the packed, stifling carriages. Sometimes people are simply wiped off the sides of the trains, smeared along bridge buttresses and tunnel walls or ejected from the carriages, like corks from frozen wine bottles, to fall under the train into oblivion.

More fortunate blacks travel by car, often in a pool system or in overcrowded and illegal taxis which are usually minibuses or panel vans. It was a fleet of such vehicles roaring and clanging past the old Peugeot, that woke Temba on the last Monday in July. He twisted upright in the cramped space of the back seat and winced at the unaccustomed stiffness in his legs. His hunger pangs had depreciated a little and his mind came slowly awake as he reconsidered his position. He had to get to Subaye, but it was still dark, the light of a new day was just smudging the eastern horizon with pale coral. Temba knew that the glow of dawn would follow swiftly and he got out of the car stretching in the chill half dark. This was his usual time to get up but he felt little rested after the uncomfortable night in the car. He would have to find something to eat before he went into Johannesburg and he checked the few crumpled notes in his pants' pocket. He returned to the car starting the engine and sat there in the early dawn, waiting for the heater to warm him. Steam billowed into the air behind the Peugeot and slowly warm air filtered into the car. Temba shoved the gear lever into first and headed back to the café where he had read the news about Subaye. Today he would see her. Today he would have her back.

Venter was in his office by eight o'clock and sat at his desk, hands clasped around a mug of tea. It was freezing cold and the ancient two-bar electric fire gave out about as much heat as a fag end in the dark. Venter had already telephoned Bramley but there was no news of the fugitive, Mthombeni.

The Sunday papers lay on his desk and he read through the articles about Smaller and the *kaffir* girl who came from a farm just down the road here in the Magaliesberg. Venter failed to understand just how any European, like this *rooinek* Smaller, who had plenty of money and a good position in society, would want to mix himself up with a black girl. Of course, the man was an *Engelsman* and they were a liberal lot over there, even with Margaret Thatcher back in the driving seat again. Venter mused on the problem of miscegenation. It seemed that the government of old P. W. Botha was actually turning a blind eye to this sort of thing these days. They hated any sort of exposure of racial prejudice which might damage South Africa's already very dented image overseas.

In that regard, the Englishman had been clever. Very clever in fact, to call a press conference virtually. Because of all the fuss and bother, the authorities would very likely make a test case out of this whole unsavoury matter and if this man Smaller got off, it would set a precedent for future assignations across the colour line. There was talk of the government scrapping racial segregation completely as far as sexual matters were concerned. Venter couldn't see this happening himself, however. Hell, how things had changed since he was a youngster. In those days the *kaffir* knew his place and stayed in it or he had his arse kicked. Now, everyone was talking about a new liberal attitude towards the blacks, about 'an understanding with our black neighbours' and 'a constellation of Southern African States'.

It was the fucking ANC bastards that were causing all the grief, of course. They were trying to force the issue just when the government were prepared to give more to the blacks than ever before imaginable. That was the trouble with the *kaffirs* though – you gave them an inch and they wanted an arm and a leg.

Foreign journalists were already comparing South Africa to Israel. One thing was for sure, Pretoria had identified the ANC as its enemy and the army were very much opposed to an ANC presence in neighbouring states like Lesotho and Moçambique. Venter had read recently that a lot of the new ANC men were young radicals who had fled South Africa at the time of the Soweto Riots in 1976. The piece in the SAP magazine had said that these men were replacing the old guard like Mandela and Oliver Tambo and that they were committed to all-out war against the Republic. Venter sipped his coffee as he pondered the future. It didn't look too bloody bright when you thought about it.

Zak was back in South Africa after an uneventful and reasonably pleasant sojourn in the neighbouring and newly independent black state of Bophuthatswana. He had made it across the unmarked border before the road-blocks had been erected on the road to Sun City and now the whole thing had quietened down nicely after a very satisfactory response publicity-wise. It was a pity about the boys; Smart, William and especially poor old Ruby, who had been like a faithful dog these past three years.

Five days ago, a man had come to see Zak in his little cabana at Sun City and told him that it was time for yet another blow at the hated white regime. He had given Zak a further R3,000 and another set of papers which he could use on his trip to Johannesburg, although with any luck it was unlikely that he would even be stopped. The papers identified him as a local farmer in Bophuthatswana; Samuel Jiyane of Mbatha. New white number plates with black lettering showed the Isuzu to be registered in Bophuthatswana and registration papers were provided to prove it.

On Sunday, Zak had driven quietly to Johannesburg, puttering through Magaliesberg and, before that, close by the township at Boons where he had lived for the last three years. The little village was deserted and Zak passed within one hundred metres of Captain Venter's bungalow and stopped at the café in the centre of town to test his disguise.

He had bleached his hair at the temples to a snowy white and wore metal-framed spectacles with clear glass lenses. He wore his dental plate and had become used to having front teeth like everybody else, although the fit wasn't too good because they had been made by post, so to speak, from photographs and gum impressions he had made himself. Nobody recognised him in the Portuguese café and he paid for his Coca Cola and toasted sandwich and left. He was dressed in worn, yet clean, corduroy trousers, a denim work shirt and an old tweed jacket and there were a couple of sacks of grain in the rear of the Isuzu. If such a phenomenon were possible, Zak looked like an African version of a gentleman farmer.

Zak drove into Alexandra township at four o'clock on Sunday afternoon and went directly to the safe house that the ANC contact in Bophuthatswana had told him of. He used a map of the township and had no trouble in finding the little house which was one of many in a dusty refuse-strewn street. Children played in the dirt and lean-looking curs scrabbled in the rubbish dumps which existed behind every couple of shacks. The township was very still in the late winter afternoon and a pall of smoke from woodburning stoves hung at around two hundred feet in the air, causing the indigo blue of the sky to turn an incredible burgundy. Alexandra was in a slight valley and the layer of purple smoke covered the township like a flat umbrella. It looked beautiful but it was actually a man-made phenomenon; the pollution of clear, pure air by thousands of cooking fires. Zak grimaced and despaired at the lot of his people who were confined in these black ghettos.

Two hours later he was fed and given brandy to drink with a few cigarettes. He sat with the two young men who were his contacts, black ANC moles in a rich and fertile white meadow. They had the explosives; twenty-five sticks of dynamite stolen from a mine at Western Deep outside Johannesburg and a couple of kilos of P4 *plastique* with detonators and timers. The whole lot would fit nicely into a suitcase or similar container. Zak had the plan outlined to him now and he knew how he was going to get the package to its destination. There was little risk but much to gain.

Temba had found a nondescript beige cap and some goggle sunglasses deep in the glove compartment of the Peugeot; these had presumably belonged to Ruby. He put them on outside the café and got into the car, turning it slowly around in the forecourt, somehow loathe to set out on the journey to Johannesburg. He had delayed his departure until mid-morning and was even now hanging around, mentally trying to find excuses to linger a bit longer.

It was close to 11.30 when he finally left Soweto, turning left onto the old Golden Highway towards Johannesburg. Within fifteen minutes he was on the M1 motorway which circled the city heading north towards Pretoria. He knew where Sandton was because he had studied the A – Z map of the area which lay open on the seat beside him and he drew deeply on an unaccustomed cigarette as he peered ahead through the dark and dirty lenses of the sunglasses. The Peugeot's tank was almost empty, the needle flickering above the reserve level and he prayed that the gauge was accurate, that he wouldn't run out of petrol on the motorway and be towed off by traffic police who would want to see his passbook. Somehow he knew that they must all be looking for him by now.

He reached the Sandton exit ramp without incident and turned off to the left, heading into the heart of white Johannesburg's most elite suburb, Sandton. This enlarged and ever-growing municipal area was once a tiny village north of the city where early settlers would go for Sunday picnics and shooting parties in the veld. Decentralisation has manifested itself in Johannesburg with a flight of whites from the city centre which is all but black as far as retail trading is concerned. Although the stock exchange and the business district of Braamfontein is still very much downtown, the whites who work in the city commute north, and to a lesser extent west, on a daily basis. Here are all-white residential areas with massive shopping centre complexes housing cinemas and provided with vast parking lots. Although Johannesburg boasts one of the most temperate climates in the world, very similar to that of Southern California, it has no open shopping malls and promenades like those in Europe.

White South Africans have become very troglodytic and prefer to bury themselves in huge underground shopping centres which are air conditioned, humidified, piped with music and so totally aesthetic that they border on being clinical. There are no such structures anywhere else in the world in terms of sophistication and finish and the sad fact is that this is possibly because massive closed areas are more susceptible to urban terrorism than open spaces. This fact seems to have escaped shopping centre developers in South Africa whose security is often so lax as to be pathetic and such centres are likely to become terrorist targets of the future.

Temba thought little of this as he passed the monumental Sandton City complex and made his way towards Catherine Street. His T-shirt was wet under the arms and he smelled rankly because he hadn't washed properly for four days and it was hot in the midday sun. He had no clear-cut plan but would just wait for an opportunity. Maybe tonight when it was dark the chance would come to get to Subaye and take her away. He would buy petrol later on.

Zak drove a yellow Toyota panel van with the legend 'Renown Ham, Polony and cooked meats' written on the side in red. He wore a white Renown dust coat and a white hat with the company logo printed above the peak. The coat, hat and van had all come from an ANC sympathiser who was second in command in the despatch department of this large cold meat concern. He had delivered the van to a vacant lot in Doornfontein and Zak had parked the Isuzu there and found the keys to the Renown van under the driver's seat where the mole had said they would be. The mole would report the van as being stolen in about two hours' time and it would be found on the vacant lot where Zak would return it. By then Zak would be halfway back to Bophuthatswana and nobody would be any the wiser.

Following the detailed map he had been given, Zak carefully circled the Carlton Centre in downtown Johannesburg and noted the goods entrance to the hotel which appeared to be a ramp going down into the bowels of the earth. He couldn't help but marvel at the size of the massive hotel and nearby office block, all built with white money earned from black labours in the gold mines, diamond mines and coal mines of this mineral-rich land of Azania. He took one more turn around the block and then headed down the ramp marked 'Goods deliveries only'. At the bottom was a pointer sign saying 'Hotel parking' and Zak turned the Renown van in that direction and backed it in next to the off-loading platform which was in fact the basement level of the hotel. There were several other light- delivery vehicles there and although his heart pounded and his shirt was wet under the cotton dustcoat, he was not really afraid.

He climbed out of the van and walked casually to the back to open the doors. Inside were about a dozen large yellow polythene baskets containing cold meats, hams and sausages, and Zak pushed and pulled them about sliding one out from the centre. This contained cold meat like the rest but these were carefully arranged on top of a cardboard suitcase. The suitcase was covered by a red and white checkered cloth, and the three dozen smoked pork fillets on top and jammed in around it were part of a regular daily delivery to the Carlton Hotel. The despatch man at Renown had said there would be no problem, that all Zak had to do was to carry the load to security and they would give him a temporary ID sticker, then he'd be into the basement of the hotel without a problem.

Zak's heart thudded harder and sweat trickled down the sides of his chest as he lifted the heavy basket onto his shoulder and walked idly towards the black security man who sat at a table with a roll of red ID stickers in front of him. The man was old and grey with a walrus moustache which must have taken him years to grow. He was self-important and so Zak was deferential and polite. If the man noticed that he was not the usual Renown delivery man, he made no comment. The sticker was slapped on his chest and he was in; a map of the hotel was in the top pocket of his dustcoat. It was almost 12.30.

Once inside the hotel Zak walked swiftly down the corridor until he turned to the left and was out of sight of the security guard. He passed the butchery, the bakery and the liquor store and reached the bank of six huge lifts that gave access to the upper floors. He put the basket down and pressed the UP button, taking out the map from his top pocket whilst waiting for a lift. He was heading for the lobby level but would not be going out into the foyer area. His target was to get as close as possible to Charlie's Bar, a popular and usually crowded lunchtime rendezvous for local office personnel and hotel guests alike. There was a kitchen directly behind Charlie's and this was where Zak intended to dump the basket of pork fillets. He had a delivery slip for one of the chefs to sign and would choose a black one if he could; hopefully the basket would remain ntouched during the lunchtime rush hour. Zak only needed ten more minutes at the outside. The charge of dynamite, supplemented with *plastique,* was set to explode at 1.10 p.m. when the little restaurant should be at maximum capacity. The area was small and the charge big enough to cause massive carnage if he could get it up against the rear wall of the bar. There was a quiet ping as the lift came down and Zak hefted the basket again and walked into the huge steel box. It was almost 12.40.

Seven minutes later Zak was in the tiny lobby outside the rear of Charlie's Bar, again waiting for the lift. He had wandered into the side entrance to the kitchen and the place was like a madhouse with chefs, waiters and assistants charging all over the place, shouting to each other in a barely controlled frenzy. From the bar outside came the muted burble of many voices and the clink of glasses. Zak had handed his slip to a black chef and, as expected, the man had scribbled on it hurriedly and pointed to a counter which was conveniently on the wall which formed the back of the bar. Zak tore off the blue copy and left it in the basket on top of the pork fillets and headed for the lifts. It had all been so easy.

It was just after one o'clock when Anton, the Austrian *maître d'hôtel,* lost his temper over an order he had given to one of the black trainee chefs. In characteristic fashion he threw the tuna fish and avocado salad he had been handed at the young black who ducked so that the plate smashed against the rear wall of the bar showering Zak's basket of pork fillets with a sloppy mash of avocado pear and fish. '*Gott im himmel,*' screamed Anton, 'how many times must I speak? How must I work with idiots? I have told you we must have dishes that are presented properly. Have I not given you instructions, even pictures so that you can follow?' He glowered at the quivering black. 'Now do it right or I kill you!' he screamed and marched out of the kitchen to the amusement of all but the luckless trainee.

A young black kitchen maid made the discovery some

five minutes later. She began wiping the mess off th
fillets and then found the suitcase underneath the cloth
called the head chef who in turn called security and wit.
two minutes the suitcase was whisked out of the kitchen
carried by Roger Harrison, a young white security officer
who had sweated right through his uniform within the first
thirty seconds of the discovery.

Harrison ran down the dingy staircase to the basement
not knowing quite what he should do with the suitcase but
wanting to get it away from any public area. Once in the
corridor outside the patisserie he used a butcher's knife to
prise the lid off and almost fainted when he saw the
contents. There were wires and long thin pencil-like things
sticking out of a putty-like substance under which there was
dynamite. He had seen enough movies to recognise that
stuff.

He shouted for everyone to get back and the few chefs
and black workers who had gathered ran off down the
corridors. Upstairs, the police anti-terrorist squad had been
called and the bomb disposal experts were already on their
way from John Vorster Square which was only a few blocks
away. Guests would have been cleared from Charlie's and
the lobby. In any case there were two floors and almost a
metre of concrete between them and the basement.

Roger Harrison put his hand out and gingerly touched a
wire wondering whether the device was booby-trapped. He
pulled at the wire gently but nothing seemed to happen. He
sat back considering what to do, hands sweaty and blood
pounding in his temples. The best thing would be to leave
it to the experts – what did he know about bombs other
than a very rudimentary lecture a couple of months back
when he joined Carlton Security. The cops would be on
their way now anyway and they would know what to do.
Roger stood up and looked at his watch, noting it was 1.11
seconds. It was the last thing he ever did.

Zak was already three blocks away when the explosion

...he tarmac shudder under the wheels of the panel ...He smiled to himself in the rearview mirror, imagining ...chaos and the broken bodies in the little bar. That would ...ach the white elitist bastards a lesson.

In fact Roger Harrison was the only casualty in the bomb blast, although a few people were hurt by flying glass on the ground floor and first floor of the hotel. Kitchen staff and others in the basement suffered concussion from the explosion but apart from a few nosebleeds were none the worse for wear. By 1.20 the police had an all points call out for a large black man in a Renown Toyota cold-meat van, but Zak was unaware of this, presuming that anyone who could have identified him with the explosion would be killed or maimed in the ruins of the kitchen behind Charlie's Bar.

The Toyota trundled slowly down Marshall Street and Zak took the ramp up onto the M1. He had learned his escape route by heart and would take the Harrow Road exit ramp, driving down into the narrow streets of Doornfontein and the vacant lot where his Isuzu was parked. He drove sedately along the motorway keeping well to the left and then suddenly there were two traffic policemen driving alongside him in a big Ford Granada. One was pointing an automatic pistol at him out of the side window. Zak's heart missed several beats and his mouth went dry with terror. How could they have found out? How did they know so quickly? The only thing that was possible was that somebody must have discovered the bomb and that it hadn't gone off in the kitchen.

Zak spat out of the open side window and accelerated, swerving the Toyota panel van at the Granada, rage driving the fear from him even though he knew that his action was useless. They were onto the Harrow Road off-ramp now and the big Ford held back before drawing alongside once more. Traffic Officer Martinus Kloppers fired his Walther P 38 through the open side window whilst his partner tried to keep out of the way of the weaving Toyota. The 9 mm bullet caught Zak below his right cheekbone and smashed

up through the roof of his mouth and out via his left te
The force of the bullet made him swerve to the left and
Toyota smashed through the Armco barrier and hung pois
on the edge of the overpass before crashing through and
falling five metres onto a vacant lot below. A cream Isuzu
wagon was parked only a few metres from the point of
impact.

Temba drove into Catherine Street and parked well down
the road from the townhouse. It was obvious which was
Smaller's property because there were lots of cars outside
and people milling around the forecourt. Temba switched
off the ignition and sat in the car, his mouth dry with
tension. He tried to work out what to do next.

If he was to get inside, it might be best to go with those
people. Some of them were black and he could maybe pass
as one of them even though he had no camera or tape
recorder, not even a notebook. Still wearing the black sunglasses and the cap he climbed out of the Peugeot but didn't
lock it. He walked back the fifty metres to the townhouse
and saw a black photographer fiddling with his cameras.
The man looked up as he approached and smiled at Temba.

'Hi man, you going in there too, eh? What paper you
with, man?' Temba thought desperately and then hit on an
answer. 'I'm from the country, friend. From the *Magaliesberg Advertiser,* it's a weekly. You know that the girl comes
from near Magaliesberg, that's where the white man met
her.' He tried to think what to say next and, aping the
photographer's hip language went on. 'Hey man, I got no
pass to get in here, just driven right through this morning.
You reckon I might have trouble getting in, eh?'

The photographer stuck out his hand. 'No problem,
brother, you just stick with me. They all know me 'cos I'm
one of the top men on the *Sowetan.* Name's Stanley, and
yours?'

Talking with Stanley helped Temba to relax and when a
large well dressed white man walked up to the chattering

277

of journalists he almost felt like one of them. The
man was forceful yet courteous. 'Good afternoon, ladies
d gentlemen. My name's Norman Ashley and I'm with
ifestyle magazine. Mr Smaller has asked me to tell you
that the press conference will commence at two o'clock.'
He looked down at his wrist. 'That is in precisely ten
minutes. We have arranged refreshments for you and if you
follow me you can enjoy some tea and cake on the patio.'
He looked up at the deep blue sky and smiled. 'After all,
it is a rather beautiful day, isn't it?'

Still very hungry, Temba gorged himself on biscuits, cake
and hot sweet tea. There were two white policemen hanging
about on the little terrace of the townhouse and Temba
kept well out of their way; it had been a wonder that nobody
had asked for his credentials so far. He kept well to the
rear of the group but the adrenalin sang in his veins when
Smaller suddenly arrived at two o'clock with Subaye behind
him. Immediately the journalists began to ask questions and
flashguns popped. Subaye looked at him but her gaze passed
over his face without recognition and Temba was thankful
for Ruby's sunglasses and cap. He was sweating freely inside
the beige zipper jacket and the grubby white T-shirt clung
to his ribs while his heartbeat seemed loud enough for
anyone to hear. But then Subaye turned to Smaller and the
look in her eyes held so much love that Temba's control
snapped.

He sprang forward bowling over Stanley who crouched
at his feet, taking a film out of his camera. Temba reached
the coffee table and snatched up the carving knife which lay
beside the remnants of a Swiss roll. He lurched over to
Subaye, grabbing her, holding her close against him, then
slithering around behind her to hold the knife at her throat.
He spoke to her in Tswana and her eyes rolled back in her
head as she recognised his voice. 'Do not move Subaye or
I may kill you right here. I have come to take you away from
this place, from the disgrace this white man has brought you.
I am taking you back home, back to where you belong in

the Magaliesberg. But first we have to get out of her[...] am going to hold you hostage. Remember, you are [...] ticket to freedom so do as I say.'

Subaye was terrified by the madness in Temba's voice and she did exactly as told. He smelled of sweat and a rank, unwashed odour that she recalled as a part of her past, the time in her life she was trying to forget. Martin had gone white and Mr Ashley had moved in on Temba's flank to try to prevent them from backing out of the sliding door to the patio. Out of the corner of her eye she saw that the two policemen had drawn their guns and were holding them two-handed, pointing at her and Temba. Two of the white women journalists were screaming quietly to themselves, a sort of high keening sound like that of a wounded dog and some of the other people were lying face down on the tiled floor of the patio. Temba continued moving backwards slowly, and still the knife was pressed hard into her throat. She felt it, cold and terribly alien against her skin, and knew that he would cut her with it if he was prevented from taking her away.

Ashley knew that they had to break the black's concentration so that the police could get in a shot from behind or so that he, Ashley, could try to disarm him. He sidled closer. Having guessed his intention, the two policemen also moved sideways out of Temba's line of sight. The black had to try to watch almost twenty people at once and his eyes flickered from side to side, but never behind him.

Committing himself in a sudden rush, Ashley ran in on Temba's right rear and grabbed the knife hand at elbow and forearm in the classic policeman's hold.

Temba reacted instinctively. Dropping to one knee, he rolled forward over Subaye, taking Ashley with him and breaking his hold. Before anyone could move he had righted himself on top of Ashley and sat astride him, holding the knife high.

Subaye and the journalists were in too close proximity for the police to try a shot and Norman Ashley screamed

279

...ly as the knife descended. He held out his hands to ...o protect himself but Temba hacked down through them ...d buried the blade in the big white man's chest, stabbing ...nce, twice and three times, all the time screaming and roaring in a raging, demented voice, 'White bastard, white bastard'.

The whole sequence of events had happened in less than a minute and Smaller looked on appalled at the mutilation of his friend, powerless to help him. In desperation the two young constables opened up with their 9 mm automatics and three shots were fired swiftly, then two more. The second bullet took Temba in the chest, blasting him off Ashley's bloodsoaked body but one of the others passed through Subaye's neck as she sat, winded, trying to rise after falling under the two men. The slim black girl collapsed without a word and Smaller ran forward, oblivious of the bullets.

Subaye's jugular vein had been torn by the steel-jacketed slug travelling at around 1,500 feet per second and blood pumped from her neck in little spurts which ran slick and red onto the cream tiles. Smaller tried to stop the bleeding, holding his fingers to the exit wound but it was useless and the girl died in his arms, never once opening her eyes after the bullet struck her.

Before the enormity of this could completely overwhelm him he moved over to Ashley whose eyes were open, though he was grievously injured. Blood bubbled in his open mouth which indicated a pierced lung. As Smaller was bending over him Liebenberg arrived and immediately went inside to call an ambulance.

Temba lay where he had fallen and one policeman stood over him whilst the other went to his car to radio in a report on the drama. The photographers had recovered sufficiently to begin taking pictures and the journalists gabbled amongst themselves in the fashion that people who have been close to death are inclined to do. They told and retold the series of

events to each other in loud, high voices and Smaller, s.
ened by them, walked slowly inside to sit down on t.
sofa, head in hands, once again despairing at the death and
destruction he had unwittingly engineered.

The coldness of the tiles penetrated Temba's jacket and T-
shirt which were wet with sweat and blood. But now there
was a strange heat in his chest as if a great warm hand was
grasping him, squeezing him so tightly that it was difficult
to breath. He could just move his head and he turned
sideways and saw Subaye lying close to him in a pool of
blood. Her eyes were closed and he knew that she was dead,
killed by a shot meant for him, but it didn't seem to mean
much now.

His brain seemed to function with an acuteness and clarity
that he had never experienced before and he saw everything
around him with a hard-edged brightness that obviously
meant there was little wrong with him. Voices washed over
him and he could see the black shoes and blue trouser legs
of the policeman who stood nearby. The white man was
speaking in Afrikaans but Temba could understand little of
what was said and it didn't seem important anyway. He felt
warmer now and there seemed to be little feeling in his legs
but he was in no great discomfort and he knew they'd have
to take him to hospital to fix him up. After all, what had
he done other than threaten a servant girl with a knife? If
they didn't identify him with the Bester farm attack, he'd
probably be out within a few weeks. Where there is life
there is hope, thought Temba and smiled to himself. It was
all so simple really, there was nothing to worry about. He
closed his eyes so that he could rest before the ambulance
arrived and as he did so the life left his body with a last
tremulous sigh.

The young SAP constable looked down at the dead black
man dispassionately. The *kaffir* had soiled himself in death
and the smell of him hung thick and pungent in the mild
sheltered air of the patio. They would have to find out who

bugger was. Obviously he must have known *Meneer* ~naller's black girl and wanted her for himself. The constable had to admit she was very nice-looking for a native, that was no maybe. But he couldn't imagine her with the white man, or even with himself for that matter. Although there was a lot of talk about dropping the colour bar, the constable couldn't see it happening in his lifetime. As for these two, they were just dead *kaffirs* now, like any others. The morgue in Johannesburg was full of them and in the big fridge he'd seen unclaimed bodies piled on the shelves; most with fearful mutilations. The morgue people kept them for a few months and then they all went into the oven and that was the end of them. Here today gone tomorrow.

The policeman grimaced when he considered the enquiry that would follow this bloody drama. He and Stefan had been forced to fire. What were they supposed to do, stand by and watch a bloody mad *tsotsi* stabbing a white man? They would be blamed of course, the police always were, but thank God their colonel was a fair man who always stood up for his men. Even so, it wasn't going to be any fun at all, this bloody lot.

Old Desmond was brought from Boons to identify the shattered mask that was all that remained of Zak's face. Venter accompanied him and was satisfied that this had been the cadre leader, Zachary Abel Mhluli. Desmond also seemed to recognise Temba Mthombeni who lay beside Mhluli on the shelf in the morgue, looking relaxed and almost at peace with himself; Venter guessed correctly that he hadn't died in any great pain. In contrast, Mhluli's face was hard to look at, even though the morticians had tried to put it back into some semblance of normality.

The bullet had caused great bruising, besides the displacement and destruction of bone and tissue, and the skull had been crushed in the fall through the barrier on the overpass. Venter stared down at the awful head and felt little. The black had been a terrorist, sworn to wreak death and destruction in South Africa and it was a miracle that his bomb in the Carlton Hotel hadn't killed and maimed dozens of innocents.

Now it was all neatly sorted out. They had found the old Peugeot used by Temba Mthombeni and originally owned by Ruben Nkhumische who had no doubt bought it with ANC funds. They had also arrested the mole at the Renown factory in Doornfontein and had taken in Benjamin Ndadza's relations in Tembisa for questioning. It seemed as though all the loose ends had been tied up, in this case anyhow, and Venter was pleased. Next week they'd go through Waltersville with a fine-toothed comb and he was sure they'd find more weapons and explosives, perhaps even a few more ANC moles. Now that Mhluli was dead, a lot of the others would lose heart and give themselves up as state witnesses in return for light sentences and sometimes an outright pardon. It always happened with the blacks, they had no stomach for a real confrontation and couldn't handle being alone without at least a figurehead, if not a leader to look up to.

Of course, this didn't mean that the ANC wouldn't start operations somewhere else tomorrow. Venter knew there were thousands of the buggers within South Africa's borders and it wouldn't be long before they'd start having successes. The government's policy was to hammer their bases in the neighbouring states and it seemed like the old Republic was in for a vicious war, a battle of attrition, on both sides. It wasn't going to get any easier; again Venter had no doubt of that.

Smaller felt he had to leave the townhouse, had to sell it. The place held so many awful memories for him and he had begun to drink again. At first half a bottle of whisky a night but, lately, almost a full bottle. Ashley was in the Sandton Clinic in intensive care but he would pull through. The first twenty-four hours, up until Tuesday lunchtime, had been

283

critical but now he was out of danger and lying back against a pile of pillows full of drips and drainage tubes. Two thoracic surgeons had worked on the damaged lungs, spleen and trachea, and they had wired up one severed rib, chopped up badly by Temba's crazed stabs with the carving knife.

Smaller had met Ashley's wife, Margaret, at the hospital and tried to talk to her but the ashen-faced woman had cut him dead after one brief sentence.

'I've had it with you, Martin, and if I can persuade Norman to leave you, I will do so. This is the last straw and it's all your fault as usual. I don't ever want to see or speak to you again.'

Without Ashley, Smaller couldn't see himself keeping *Lifestyle* going on a profitable basis. The future looked very bleak and he felt that his chances in Johannesburg had been severely weakened by recent events. He set up a meeting with Liebenberg and considered his options. They both discussed the matter further with Ashley and the decision to sell was made.

A large publishing group with a growing stable of magazines and some newspaper connections had been after *Lifestyle* for some years. Smaller had always refused to sell because the magazine was his way of life, in fact he lived out of it and it had become a very valuable tool for his own particular lifestyle. His cars, entertaining, travel expenses and hotels were all paid for by *Lifestyle* and it was difficult to compute the magazine's real worth to a sole owner such as himself. Once absorbed into a publishing group, these benefits could not accrue to any one person and therefore that particular value would not be as forthcoming. Smaller talked over the matter with Liebenberg and tentative telephone calls were made. He felt as if he were selling a part of himself but there was little option because his heart wasn't in it any more, wasn't into anything for that matter.

The preliminary hearing under the Immorality Act had been postponed indefinitely after the death of Subaye. Liebenberg reckoned that nothing would come of it now. By week's end a figure had been decided upon for *Lifestyle* and Smaller was offered R100,000 in cash and R125,000 in shares; he was also offered a service contract to run the magazine for one year but turned this down. He had no real idea of what he was going to do or where he would go and vaguely considered Australia and the United States.

But first he would get away from it all and follow the sun to the Indian Ocean. One of Natalie's last tasks was to research vacation possibilities for her soon-to-be ex-boss.

Ten days later, Smaller sat comfortably on genuine hide sipping a glass of Veuve Cliquot champagne. Over 40,000 feet below him the eastern coastline of Africa unfolded like a roughly spread green and brown shroud thrown over a puddle of aquamarine water. Even at this height, white wave flecks could be seen in the Indian Ocean which lapped passively against the shores of Mozambique. At Beira, the Gates Learjet made a seventy degree turn to the west and headed out over the vast expanse of water, its sophisticated inboard computer locked on the tiny island of Mayotte in the Comores Archipelago.

The flight was already ninety minutes long and there was about as long still to go. Smaller felt jaded and yet resigned to his new life which was completely directionless at this point. He was still numbed by the tragic happenings at the Sandton townhouse and had made arrangements to sell it, completely furnished if possible. The sale of *Lifestyle* had been approved and the deal was done, the cheque for R100,000 safely on deposit in the bank at fifteen per cent interest. Interpub SA, the purchasers, had taken over the *Lifestyle* offices and their contents, having paid an additional R35,000 for Smaller's not insubstantial décor and appointments. Smaller had given R20,000 of this to Ashley, who still languished in the clinic.

He now had no job, no future and had spent R2,000 for eight days on a yacht in the Comores, a place where he could perhaps sit, think and consider his next move. After all he was free and reasonably wealthy and he had no commitments to anyone, not even to himself. Unsummoned, an image of Subaye arose in his mind.

GLOSSARY

baas	boss or master
bakkie	light truck
bedonnered	enraged or angry
bliksem(se)	swear word, literal meaning thundered, meaning rascally, as with *donderse*
boontjie sop	bean soup
braai	roast
braaivleis	barbecue
bushveld	indigenous bushland
dagga	marijuana
donderse	swear word, literal meaning: thundered
dop	drink
dorp	village
Engelsman	Englishman
Here	exclamation meaning God or Jesus (pronounced yerrer)
Impi	Zulu or Matabele raiding party
jou skellems	you rascals
kaffir	derived from the Arabic *kaffre* meaning unbeliever or heathen
kerrie	knobkerrie, club
khaya	African hut, shack or group of living units
kombi	panel van
kraal	enclosed area or small village
lobola	bride price
meerkat	vole-like bush animal

meisie	girl
meneer	sir, Mr
mevrou	married woman, Mrs
moer(se)	Swear word meaning hit (also used as an exclamation of quantity)
oom	uncle
piccanin	toddler
platteland	flat farming area of the Transvaal
riempie	raw hide webbing for seats
rooinek	red neck, derogatory term for an Englishman from the Boer War days
shebeen	illegal drinking area
skaap	sheep
spruit	stream
stoep	veranda
tarantaal	guinea fowl
tokoloshe	legendary leprechaun-like little man
tsotsi	young black or coloured thug
umphambili	male organ
veld	field
veldskoens	veld shoes (desert boots)
verligte	enlightened or liberal
voetsak	swear word meaning get lost
volk	folk